S0-BYG-759

The Girls Saga

Kenni York

www.urbanbooks.net

Urban Books, LLC
300 Farmingdale Road, NY-Route 109
Farmingdale, NY 11735

The Girls Saga Copyright © 2017 Kenni York

All rights reserved. No part of this book may be reproduced in any form or by any means without prior consent of the Publisher, except brief quotes used in reviews.

ISBN 13: 978-1-62286-784-4
ISBN 10: 1-62286-784-X

First Trade Paperback Printing January 2017
Printed in the United States of America

10 9 8 7 6 5 4 3 2 1

This is a work of fiction. Any references or similarities to actual events, real people, living or dead, or to real locales are intended to give the novel a sense of reality. Any similarity in other names, characters, places, and incidents is entirely coincidental.

Distributed by Kensington Publishing Corp.
Submit Orders to:
Customer Service
400 Hahn Road
Westminster, MD 21157-4627
Phone: 1-800-733-3000
Fax: 1-800-659-2436

Chapter 1

Miranda

"This marriage is a sham," Alex told her friends, her voice too loud to be considered a whisper, though she made every attempt to speak softly.

The woman sitting in front of Alex turned slightly, taking note of the person who had just made this rude comment.

Ever the polite, nice-nasty princess, Alex simply smiled and reiterated her belief. "This is a joke."

The girls were situated in the second row of only five at an outdoor wedding venue. They were surrounded by beautiful, fragrant roses and white satin-covered folding chairs filled with family members, and the sun was preparing to set behind them. Opinionated Alex was seated between demure Jada and outspoken Stephanie. Jada nudged Alex's left arm in an attempt to shut her up just as Stephanie sucked her teeth and nudged Alex's right arm in agreement.

"You're right," Stephanie announced. "That Negro don't make enough money for her. Soon as she finds somebody else with fatter pockets and a bigger dick, she'll be ghost."

Alex and Stephanie chuckled at their not-so-private joke, and Jada tried hard not to laugh.

"You two are incorrigible," Jada stated, shaking her head and staring straight ahead.

Miranda, their other partner in crime, sat silently, looking toward the altar as one of her best friends was staring into the eyes of a chocolate teddy bear and pledging her life to him forever. Miranda Wilson-Cox was jealous. She envied Candace for having so quickly put together such an intimate and beautiful wedding. Perhaps too quickly, which was why she and the other girls weren't part of the bridal party. There was no bridal party—just the bride and the groom. The wedding had been thrown together so fast that the loving couple had barely had time to pick out apparel and get fitted. There had been no time to assemble a bridal party.

The rose garden venue was the perfect choice for the springtime, outdoor wedding and was one of just a few available on such short notice. Candace's wedding colors of white and silver were a beautiful contrast to the white and pink roses that adorned the area. And Candace was gorgeous in her A-line gown with the plunging neckline and back. A very sexy selection, one that Miranda was sure Candace's parents were not too fond of.

As they sat among Candace and Quincy's handful of friends and family, Alex, Stephanie, Jada, and Miranda watched as the couple commence their oneness with the ceremonial kiss. After the couple strolled down the aisle as husband and wife, the crowd dispersed and headed toward the banquet hall nearby for the reception. The girls sauntered over to a nearby gazebo, their designated meeting place, where they would catch up with Candace once she was done with taking pictures. As they chatted about the beauty of the gardens and the simplicity and elegance of the wedding, Miranda's phone began to chime the familiar Nokia ring. Miranda rejected the call and checked the time.

"Who keeps blowing you up, girl?" Alex asked.

Miranda stuffed her cell phone into her purse, trying to appear nonchalant. "Norris," she answered. "Trying to check up on me."

Alex cocked her head to the side. "You not gon' call him back?"

Miranda pursed her lips and shook her head.

"Well, shit. Tell him to stop calling," Jada said, gazing over toward the ceremony area, where Candace and Quincy were posing for their wedding photos. "If he wanted to talk to you so bad, he shoulda come with you."

"Girl, you know men don't like going to weddings," Stephanie interjected.

"He'll be okay," Miranda replied, silently planning to make a break for home as soon as Candace was done with her pictures. Norris had called her four times since she left home for the wedding. He'd been adamant about not wanting to accompany her. However, he'd been just as adamant about her returning home in time for him to meet up with his boys to play poker. Not wanting to risk pissing him off, Miranda thought it best to just wrap up her time with the girls and head home immediately.

As if sensing Miranda's thoughts, across the garden Candace kissed Quincy on his lips before quickly sashaying her short brown frame toward her awaiting friends as the photographers moved their equipment to the banquet hall. She approached the gazebo, and instantly the girlfriends found themselves huddled together in a heartfelt embrace. Candace reveled in the spotlight, loving the attention.

"I did it, y'all," she boasted, kicking off her diamond-studded stiletto heels. "I finally did it."

"Finally?" Alex questioned. "Are you kidding me? You've known this man for all of two months, and you've married him. 'I did it quickly,' is what you should be saying."

"Shut up." Candace giggled. "Don't hate." She flashed them her modest 1.3 carat wedding band, smiling proudly.

Miranda forced a smile, fighting back the green monster in her that was reminding her that she no longer possessed a wedding band.

"So when are we getting drunk?" Stephanie was glad to be free of her five year old son and mother. Her mom had readily agreed to babysit knowing that Stephanie wouldn't be on a date with the child's father whom she despised.

"The real party goes down after my parents and our older family members leave," Candace assured them. "They won't be around long."

The Nokia tune sounded again. All eyes went to Miranda as she fumbled to silence the small phone. "Sorry," she offered.

"I know you do not have your cell on at my wedding, girlie." Candace pouted. "Today is all about me. Tell that Negro you'll see him later."

The girls laughed, and Miranda shyly shook her head as she began to say her good-byes.

"Do you have to leave now?" Jada asked suspiciously.

"Yeah. Norris needs the car," she explained.

As the others began to protest, Candace stood firm, supporting Miranda.

"It's all right," Candace said. "Hubby comes first."

Alex rolled her eyes, already not feeling Candace's fake happily married attitude.

"I'm just glad all my girls could be here with me. Y'all do understand why I didn't have you as bridesmaids, right?"

Alex, Stephanie, Miranda, and Jada all nodded and waved off Candace's apology.

"We just wanted to keep it simple," Candace stated.

"It's all right, girl," Jada replied. "We understand."

"I love y'all!"

The group embraced again, giggling at each other and feeling blissful in each other's company. A moment later the others regretfully wished Miranda a safe ride home and then parted ways with the short, light-skinned woman.

Miranda trotted to her Nissan Maxima and began the journey home to her awaiting husband. She dreaded going home to him, never knowing what type of mood he would be in when she arrived. They had been married for a year now, yet Miranda felt like she didn't really know Norris at all. Perhaps they hadn't known each other well enough when they wedded. Miranda had been so swept up in the courting process that she had been blind to Norris's shortcomings.

Fresh out of high school, Miranda had decided to visit her brother Malachi, who was in the Navy and was stationed in Virginia. During her summer vacation there, she'd met Norris on the naval base. He'd approached her, all mannish, telling her how fine she was and filling her head up. Having lived a somewhat sheltered life, despite growing up in the city of Atlanta with her parents, Miranda wasn't used to such advances. She had rarely dated in high school and had never been in a serious relationship. She had never even come close to any type of physical encounter. She'd been surprised at herself when she allowed Norris to kiss her on the very first day that they met and then to take her virginity that very same night. At the time she'd thought it was romantic. He had taken her on a tour of the city and then back to his place, where they drank Belvedere mixed with cranberry juice. He proceeded to seduce her with his probing fingers and talented tongue. Never mind that she didn't even know his last name on that first night, she was sexually free and decidedly in love.

Nose wide open and heart filled with a schoolgirl notion of love, Miranda moved to Virginia soon after attaching herself to Norris. She would cook and clean his off-base apartment during the day and allow him to ravish her body ruthlessly at night. It felt liberating to be away from her parents and to do whatever pleased her, or mostly whatever pleased Norris. It didn't take long for her to convince Norris that they should get married. He never proposed to her directly. He simply shrugged and agreed when she approached him with the idea.

Their big day was the polar opposite of Candace's ceremony. There were no fragrant roses, no lavish gown, no smiling friends and family to wish them well, and no lively reception to celebrate their union. The couple elected to exchange vows at their county courthouse, in the small, impersonal space of a judge's chamber. It was a hasty decision, and so they had not even purchased rings. Miranda was simply excited about the addition of the title Mrs. to her name. The honeymoon period was short-lived, and just several weeks following their commitment, Miranda began to see Norris in a different light.

He was a difficult man, manic at best. When he was happy, times were good. He'd joke around, make her laugh, and make love to her. When he was down, he made sure Miranda was down as well. He belittled her around company, ignored her when she tried to communicate, and was unpleasantly rough when he decided to have sex with her. There were even times when he would leave and not return home for days. Miranda never complained about this to her friends back home or her parents, because she never wanted to hear them say that she should never have married so young.

It was Norris's antics that forced the couple to relocate to Atlanta. Shortly before he was due to ship out on tour, Norris found himself in a dangerous bar fight. Drunk, high, and belligerent, he'd pulled a knife on a senior officer, a move that ultimately led to him being dishonorably discharged from the U.S. Navy. Disheartened and desperate, Miranda had pleaded with her parents to allow her and her husband to stay with them until the couple was able to get back on their feet.

In Virginia, Miranda hadn't worked. In Atlanta, she knew that it would take two incomes for them to repair their lives and become self-sufficient. But instead of them both obtaining employment, Miranda ended up working two jobs while Norris sat home drinking, smoking, and hanging out with his buddies. It was not exactly the life she had imagined for herself. Once they were finally in a place of their own, Miranda got up the nerve to complain about his lack of ambition and their dire need for money. Norris reacted by scolding her. He accused her of doubting him as a man and being an unsupportive wife. When he was really mad, he would throw things around or hit the furniture or walls with his fist. Not wanting to feel the impact of his ferociousness, Miranda would never continue on with the argument, electing instead to walk away and leave him to deal with his own raging emotions.

No one really liked Norris. Not her parents, not her friends. But despite their blatant disapproval of the man, he was still her husband. Miranda always tried to focus on the good in their relationship. She'd felt a small ray of hope when Norris finally found employment at a body shop. Not only had they been able to move into their own apartment, but now they were also able to purchase a Maxima. For that, Miranda was grateful. Riding MARTA for two hours just to get somewhere that was only fifteen minutes away was not fun. Sure they shared the car, which was purchased in her name, but it was better than relying on public transit.

However, with more money in his possession, Norris developed a new bad habit, gambling. He was an avid poker player and would bet on a sports game in a minute. He lost more than he won, but that was not enough to discourage him. Rather than complain, Miranda tried to overlook this additional shortcoming. And she kept a private bank account, into which her paychecks were direct deposited, in order to ensure that Norris didn't smoke or gamble away their rent money.

Pulling into her usual spot in front of their Shoals Crossing apartment building, Miranda sighed. She wished she was back in the beautiful atmosphere of the rose garden with her girls instead of in the stifling environment of her unhappy home. Not looking forward to seeing Norris, who was sure to be in a foul mood, Miranda dragged herself up the stairs to her second-floor apartment. As she walked through the door, she could smell the aroma of marijuana lingering in the air. She'd asked him a million times not to smoke in the house, as if he ever listened.

"'Bout time." She heard his voice boom from the back of the apartment.

Placing her keys on the coffee table, Miranda plopped down on the ash-gray couch and watched as Norris emerged from the bedroom. She took in his appearance: sagging jeans, like he was a high school kid, black tee with matching plain black baseball cap, and the requisite black Air Force Ones. He was short for a man—five feet, seven inches—and thin. His dark skin was a perfect contrast to her lighter skin. It was his beautiful white teeth that made the man's face light up. But tonight he wasn't smiling.

"What took yo' ass so long?" he snapped, grabbing up the car keys. "Told you I had somewhere to go."

"That's why I'm back, Norris," she responded, leaning back and shutting her eyes, willing him to just leave.

"Yo' girl all good and married?"

Miranda nodded.

She heard him walk into the kitchen. The sound of the cabinet door opening and closing resounded throughout the otherwise quiet house. Norris poured himself a drink of something and then threw his cup carelessly into the sink.

"Still don't know who the hell would marry her gold-digging ass. She looks like an ant."

Miranda peeked with one eye open, catching only his back as he moved to exit the apartment. She was astonished by his gall. If only he knew the names the girls used to describe him. Miranda smirked to herself and glanced over at the clock on the VCR. Seven p.m. In fifteen more hours she would have to rise to get ready for her part-time job at Rainbow clothing store. She worked only every other weekend and had been reluctant to give up this Saturday for the wedding. Realizing that Norris hadn't told her when he'd be back, Miranda hopped off the couch and ran to the door. As she swung it open, the house phone began to ring.

Leaning over the railing, she called down to her husband in the parking lot. "Norris! Norris, when will you be back?" She watched as he slammed the car door shut and revved the engine. "Norris!"

Unfazed, Norris backed out of the parking spot and tore through the maze of the complex to hit the street.

Miranda sucked her teeth and scurried back into her home. The phone was still ringing. Absentminded, she answered without checking the caller ID.

"Hello?"

Instantly the line went dead. Stunned, Miranda plopped down on the couch again and pressed the END button on the cordless. As an afterthought, she clicked the CALLER ID button to see who the rude caller was. The number was foreign to her. The name on the screen was Tamara Williams. *What the fuck?* An uneasy feeling crept into her heart. Something didn't feel right.

Chapter 2

Stephanie

Stephanie entered her mother's home and was greeted by Ms. Johnson, who was peddling breathlessly on the exercise bike she kept in the living room, in front of the television. Stephanie kicked her shoes off and walked past her mom and into the kitchen.

"How was the wedding?" Ms. Johnson asked as she peddled away.

"It was nice," she offered in response.

Stephanie didn't want to hear her mom rant and rave about how accomplished Candace or any of her girlfriends were. Ms. Johnson had been so elated to hear that Candace was marrying someone and not just sleeping with him or shacking up. She constantly reminded Stephanie of how disappointed she was in her for being an unwed mother. Stephanie had never heard the end of it after she confessed to her mother that she was pregnant during her very first and only semester at Morris Brown.

Even though the incident was nearly four years in the past, Stephanie remembered it as if it were just yesterday. Ms. Johnson had informed her that she had ruined her life and had asked her if it was her desire to be a welfare mother. Stephanie had been forced to quit college in November of 2001, after she found out that she was expecting. Her mother had made it perfectly clear that the baby would be Stephanie's responsibility and that she was not about to support her and her unborn child. With no other alternative, Stephanie had to get a job. Luckily, she had an aunt who managed to pull some strings and got her hired as a librarian assistant at a DeKalb County library. The pay was decent, and the hours were good.

To her surprise, and much to her benefit, Stephanie's mother never kicked her out of the house. But she was adamant that the young woman would pull her own weight.

Ms. Johnson got over the fact that her only child had gotten pregnant at a young age and at the start of her collegiate career. In fact, when Damien was born, she was right beside Stephanie, ever the proud grandmother. What really infuriated Ms. Johnson was Stephanie's relationship with Damien's father. Corey Polk was every mother's nightmare. He was five years older than Stephanie and was a thug, in Ms. Johnson's opinion. Corey lived in their neighborhood and was known as one of the neighborhood hustlers. Four years ago he would have been found on any corner near or around Line Street in Decatur. Like all the other misguided brothers of his generation, he made his money in the streets.

It was Corey's persistence that had drawn Stephanie to him. She'd seen him around the way for years, and he had frequently made advances toward her. No matter how many times she'd said no, he'd never backed down. Sure, she'd dated some guys, and she'd even had sex with a few before Corey.

But there was something about this man that made her throw all caution aside. She loved him for reasons even she couldn't understand. She knew he was the neighborhood weed man. But she also knew that no one else had ever made her feel beautiful and wanted the way he did. Stephanie couldn't understand how someone she loved so much could hurt her so badly. When she had told Corey she was pregnant, his initial reaction was typical.

"That can't be my kid," he'd told her. "How I know you ain't been fucking around?"

She'd gone to his mother's house, where he was living at the time. She thought telling him face-to-face would be kinder than telling him over the phone. They were alone in his room. She was greasing his scalp, with him sitting between her legs. When she mentioned that she was pregnant, he quickly jumped up from the floor and glared down at her small frame. An argument erupted, and they called each other all types

Check Out Receipt

Spauldings Branch
301-817-3750
www.pgcmls.info

Saturday, October 7, 2017 12:45:32 PM
95382

Item: 31268121347468
Title: The girls saga
Material: Book
Due: 10/28/2017

Total items: 1

You just saved $14.95 by using your library. You have saved $122.86 this past year and $122.86 since you began using the library!

Retain receipt to confirm your item due dates.

Thank You For Visiting
Prince George's County Memorial Library System
http://www.pgcmls.info

"Enrich, Engage, Educate."

946

Check Out Receipt

Spauldings Branch
301-817-3750
www.pgcmls.info

Saturday, October 7, 2017 12:45:32 PM
95362

Item: 31268121347468
Title: The girls saga
Material: Book
Due: 10/28/2017

Total items: 1

You just saved $14.95 by using your library. You
 have saved $122.86 this past year and $122.86 s
ince you began using the library!

Retain receipts to confirm your item due dates.

Thank You For Visiting
Prince George's County Memorial Library System
http://www.pgcmls.info

"Enrich, Engage, Educate"

946

of four-letter words. Ultimately, he told her to leave. They didn't speak for several weeks. During that time, Ms. Johnson never missed an opportunity to say, "I told you so." Unable to deal with the silence or Corey's absence in her life, Stephanie ventured over to his mother's house one day after work. It was then that she learned that he was no longer living there. Feeling hopeless with regards to a reconciliation, Stephanie simply left a message with his mom for him to call her.

Two more weeks passed, and he finally called from an unknown number. He spoke to her as if nothing had happened, as if they'd just spoken the day before. When she told him that she had to quit school and didn't know if she'd be able to return, he seemed disinterested. He was too excited about his own news, which was that he had gotten his own place over in Midtown. It was a one-bedroom luxury apartment in a Gables community. Stephanie didn't ask him how he was able to afford such lavish accommodations. She was simply hurt that he did not ask her to move in with him.

Still, they rekindled their relationship. He succumbed and gave her his new cell number. Every so often, he stopped by her house to hang out. Ms. Johnson was never pleased by his visits, so Stephanie began to visit Corey at his place after work most evenings during the week. On the weekends she would spend the night.

"That boy is never going to marry you," her mother warned her one Sunday night, when she strolled in late from a weekend visit. By this time her belly was swollen, and she was beginning to tire from the weight of the pregnancy. She ignored her mother's comment, feeling that things between her and Corey were going great.

Secretly, she prayed that he would hurry up and ask her to move in so that she could escape her mother's disapproving glares and hurtful comments. Stephanie reasoned that he just didn't want them to be crammed into the one-bedroom unit and that he was waiting until he could afford a bigger place. But just when she was feeling good about their relationship, Corey withdrew again. He would go days, sometimes weeks, without calling. He cut their visits down to the point where she rarely got to see him, let alone have sex with him. He advised her never to just show up to his place without his permission, and she respected that.

Stephanie realized that any other chick would have just left him alone, but she just couldn't bring herself to give up on him. Not even when he missed the birth of their son, not even when he failed to put in an appearance at the hospital when she experienced complications following Damien's birth, and not even when he neglected to pitch in with caring for the infant. Corey came around when he was ready, never mind what Stephanie or Damien needed. He often told her that he loved her, and she wanted more than anything to believe him. Their relationship continued on in this same manner. She never really knew when she would see him or hear from him, but she was always pathetically eager to receive him when she did.

As of today, two days had passed since his last call. He'd told her that he wanted to go to the movies tonight, after she returned from Candace's wedding, and that he would call her back to confirm. Stephanie poured herself a glass of juice and wondered if she should change into something cute or into her pajamas. Walking back into the living room, she saw her mother abandon the exercise bike, mopping her face.

"Was it pretty?" her mother asked, panting.

Stephanie didn't want to talk about the wedding. She shrugged her mother off and headed toward her room. "It was all right."

"Mmm-hmm," Ms. Johnson responded. "And don't be going back there, messing with that child. He's already had his bath and is sleeping like a log."

Stephanie tiptoed into her bedroom and quickly shut her door behind her in an attempt to ward off any further conversation with her mother. Damien lay sprawled across her queen-size bed, arms and legs everywhere. In his SpongeBob pajamas, he was precious. Stephanie eased onto the bed, struggled to straighten his body, and then covered him with his favorite Elmo blanket. She kissed his forehead, and the child didn't budge. She marveled over how much he favored Corey, with his fair brown skin and somewhat slanted eyes.

Damien was a beautiful child, and Stephanie couldn't imagine what her life would be like without him.

The phone rang, interrupting her thoughts. She grabbed it quickly, not wanting her mom to complain about the late-night call. Besides, she was sure it was Corey calling to see if she wanted to catch the last show of the night at the AMC.

"Hello," she answered, putting on her sexy voice to entice him to take part in the event that he was calling to cancel.

"This is the Fulton County Police Department with a collect call from—"

"Corey." Stephanie's heart plummeted.

"Will you accept the charges?"

"Yes," she answered without thinking. "Hello?"

"What's up, baby?"

She hated how he was acting like there was nothing unusual about this situation. "You tell me," she countered.

"I got a problem. . . ."

"Clearly."

"Look, I need you to come get me. You got some money?"

"Not much . . . How much are we talking?"

"Two hundred."

Stephanie looked over at her sleeping son and caressed his head. "I don't have that, Corey," she said softly. "Don't you have it somewhere?"

"Yeah, but that ain't helping me, 'cause you can't get to it," he replied with attitude. "Look, get up what you can. I'll get it back to you ASAP."

He wasn't asking; he was ordering her. And Stephanie knew she would do whatever he said. Getting up to change into some jeans, she sighed.

"Okay. I'll be down there."

"Don't take forever, man," he complained. "Okay?"

"Okay. But what happened, Corey?"

"It ain't nothing."

"It ain't nothing?" Her voice was a little muffled as she switched the phone to her other ear in order to slip off the dress she'd worn to the wedding. This trip to the county jail warranted jeans and a T-shirt versus her semiformal look.

"Just come on."

He disconnected the line, and Stephanie simply pressed
FLASH and dialed the first number that came to mind.
"Hello?"
"Hey, girl. It's Steph. I need a favor."

Chapter 3

Candace

A relaxing vacation on a beautiful beach on a tropical island with fruity drinks and half-naked waiters attending to her every need would have been nice. Instead, it was business as usual as Candace sat at her desk in the downtown Decatur law firm. Would these phones ever stop ringing? Everyone was surprised that she was returning to work after just having gotten married this past Saturday. Ideally, a honeymoon would have been nice. Realistically, she knew that she had to show up to work, because the bills weren't going to pay themselves, and since she'd already used her vacation time earlier in the year to cope with family issues, there was no paid vacation time in sight for her.

Lost in her thoughts, Candace ignored the ringing phone. As she stared into space, she thought of the splendor of her wedding ceremony and reception. She was sure that her girls had been envious of her on Saturday. She was finally married, and she had done it in style while on a budget. Her parents, on the other hand, were probably still livid with her for running off with Quincy in the first place. At least we got married, she thought. They had to give her some credit for that.

Candace's relationship with her parents was strained at best. Just a couple of years ago, she'd been living in their house and struggling to abide by their rules. Mr. and Mrs. Lewis were strict parents. They were also very disciplined Jehovah's Witnesses. They expected their children to walk in the same faith as they did and to practice Jehovah's teachings and commandments in all aspects of their lives. Additionally, Mr. Walter Lewis, a high school assistant principal, was big on education. His hope for his girls was that they would excel academically throughout high school and then strive to graduate magna cum laude from college.

While growing up, Candace could never meet their expectations. By her senior year of high school, she simply stopped trying. She stopped studying constantly, causing her grade point average to slide downward. To her, a C was just fine, since she was never able to surpass a B+ when she did try harder. Feeling like she was missing out on fun, Candace started hanging out more with her girlfriends. At times she would sneak out to meet a guy for a date. Her parents were against dating, even when she was eighteen. They claimed that they wanted her and her younger sister, Amelia, to stay focused on what was most important. Candace loved her parents, but when she was in high school, she felt as if she had outgrown their old-school frame of mind.

She met Quincy just one year after graduation. At the time she'd been working as a part-time receptionist at the law firm for half a year. The pay was decent enough to cover her personal needs and her car note, but unfortunately, she was still living with her parents and their strict rules. Quincy Lawson was a simple mail clerk at a federal building in downtown Atlanta. Candace met him at a convenience store near his job when she was out with her girlfriends one Saturday. She accepted his number only because she didn't know if she'd need him one day, be it to cover a meal or foot the bill for a shopping expenditure or two. It was superficial, but she took note of his clean black 2003 Impala. Candace assumed that the man had money. Physically, she was not completely attracted to him. He was a little thick for her taste, but he could definitely dress. At twenty-five, Quincy also owned his own home. Candace was impressed by this.

For several months she dated Quincy, sneaking out and lying to her parents about where she was going. Eventually, they caught on and decided to teach her a lesson. She'd gone over to Quincy's one night, just to hang out. Of course, they had sex and Candace accidently fell asleep afterward. When she finally awoke, it was two in the morning. She shook Quincy awake, and he took her home, where she discovered that the door was locked. She had a key, but it didn't seem to work. Candace was confused. She walked around to the back of the house and tapped on Amelia's window, but to no avail. It was her mother, Barbara Lewis, who finally opened the front door. Candace simply lowered her head and attempted to pass over the threshold to her home. She was surprised when her mother blocked her way and shook her head.

"No," she said. "No floozies live here. Only floozies and whores stay out until the early hours of the morning. You want to be out in the streets, you can stay out in the streets."

Mrs. Lewis then shut the door in her eldest daughter's face. Candace was stunned, but her first reaction was to call Quincy, who eagerly returned to get her. Candace knew her mom would eventually let up and allow her back home. However, she didn't want to go back. She also knew that they would only become more infuriated with her if she simply moved in with Quincy without being married. It went against their beliefs, both religious and personal. So she devised a plan. Quincy wanted her to live with him, but she told him that she would stay only until she could get her own place, unless he married her. Once the seed was planted in his head, Quincy was on board with the idea.

It was the perfect plan to Candace. Quincy already had a home and money. She figured that all she would have to do was cover her own car note with her income, and she could splurge on herself with the rest. The added bonus was that her relationship with her parents would be repaired once she told them that she was getting married. She thought they would be proud of her for doing the right, wholesome thing. Sure, they'd paid for the wedding, but the relationship between Candace and her parents still needed work. *In time,* she thought to herself.

The intercom was buzzing, and Mr. Japlan was calling her, interrupting her thoughts.

"Candace, the phone lines were all lit up. What's going on out there?"

Snapping back to reality and thinking quickly on her feet, Candace put on her polite, professional voice. "Sorry, Bob. I was with the deliveryman. That package you were expecting has arrived."

She glanced down at the box behind her desk. UPS had delivered it an hour ago, but he didn't know that. At the time she'd been too busy to advise him that it was there. Looking up, she saw a familiar face wave to her through the firm's glass entrance door. She smiled, reached for her purse, and buzzed Bob back. "Going to lunch," she informed him.

"Enjoy."

Candace picked up her office phone and pressed a series of buttons to forward all calls to voice mail during her lunch break. Slipping back into her tan stilettos, she sashayed out of the office suite and to the elevators. She knew that her friend wouldn't be waiting there. It was customary for them to meet across the street, at one of the local eateries. Today it would be Crescent Moon. Feeling confident and sexy, Candace descended in the elevator, then walked quickly across the street and down the walk before sauntering into the already crowded restaurant. Without breaking her stride, Candace made a right and headed over to their usual corner booth. There she was greeted by her tall ebony companion.

Khalil stood to hug her, briefly brushing his lips past her cheek. He waited until she was seated, then slid back into the booth, across from her. "Good afternoon, you beautiful goddess," he said seductively.

Candace blushed. "Hey, yourself."

"I took the liberty of ordering for you. Hope you don't mind."

She did. "No. Thanks."

She stared at the man across from her, taking in his long, neatly kept dreads, his beautiful dark skin, and his nicely trimmed mustache and goatee. Her eyes met his hazel ones, and it was clear to her that he was wearing contacts. He smiled at her, bringing attention to the fine wrinkles that kissed the corners of his eyes. Khalil Bradley was nearly twice her age. At nineteen—she'd be twenty in two more months—Candace was surprised at herself for being a woman of interest to this older gentleman. Khalil was forty-three and had three children, one of whom was two years older than Candace. He didn't seem to mind her age, for it was he who had pursued her.

Candace met Khalil in passing two short months ago, around the time when she'd been put out of her parents' place. He worked for the firm across the hall from hers, and they had shared an elevator up to their floor one morning. By the time the doors opened on the fifth floor, they had arranged to meet for lunch. Ever since that day, lunch had been on Khalil. She had been honest, telling him about Quincy and their abrupt engagement. He'd been honest, telling her about Sheila, the woman he was living with currently. Neither had cared when they skipped food one day, devouring each other instead on their lunch break. The sex was good, but it had happened only once. Candace didn't expect a repeat performance.

"So you did it, huh?" He nodded toward her left hand.

She looked down at her wedding ring and quickly removed her hand from the table. "Yeah," she said. "I did."

"So how do you feel?"

"No different right now, I suppose. Why do you ask that?"

Their waitress brought over two glasses of iced tea and advised them that their orders would be up shortly.

Khalil sipped through his straw and shook his head. "I don't know why you married that man in the first place."

"Why not?"

"Why so?"

She sucked her teeth. "This is juvenile."

He chuckled. "Says the woman who married some out-of-touch dude just to escape her parents."

She was offended. "I resent that."

"Why? It's the truth. When you talk about him, I don't get the impression that you are in love with him. It was a calculated move of survival for you. Either marry dumb ass or go back to living with Mommy and Daddy."

"Don't call him dumb ass."

Khalil laughed again. "That's right, gorgeous. Defend your husband. But I'd like to point out that you didn't disagree with what I said."

Their food arrived, and Candace concentrated on dowsing her fries with ketchup. Khalil had this "I'm always right" attitude, which she couldn't quite get with. But she never complained. After all, he wasn't her man. They were just friends.

Khalil took the ketchup bottle from her and covered his home-style meat loaf with it. Taking a bite of it, he nodded his head, moaned, and then pointed his fork at the red lump.

"Mmm. That's it right there. That's good stuff."

Candace giggled. "Okay . . ."

"Can you cook?"

She sucked her teeth. "Yeah. I can cook," she said. "I got skills."

"Uh-huh. I'm a real man. I likes to eat me some good ole-fashioned home cooking."

She cut her club sandwich into fourths and smirked at him. "Well, you better tell Sheila to get on it."

"Ha-ha," he said between chews. "Sheila can't boil water."

"Better get her some lessons, then."

"That's like teaching a blind man to read."

"Ah! But blind people *do* read," Candace retorted. "In braille."

"Touché. But there's only one method of cooking, and that's simply to get in the kitchen and do it."

Candace bit into her sandwich and immediately regretted letting Khalil choose her meal. The sandwich was dry. She needed more mayo. Not wanting to complain, she continued to chew, all the while willing the waitress to return. They sat in silence for a moment, each eating and entertaining their own thoughts. By the way Khalil kept looking at her cleavage, which was nicely accented by her V-necked shirt, Candace knew that he was having erotic thoughts. She smiled at him and licked her lips seductively. He winked at her between bites of mashed potatoes.

She wondered why he hadn't made any advances toward her since their one encounter. Not that she was disappointed. She simply wondered what his thoughts on the matter were. They'd never really discussed the little tryst, and at times she asked herself if maybe she just didn't do it for him.

"You look like you're deep in thought about something," he commented. "Care to share?"

She picked at a fry and instantly felt shy. She didn't want to say what she had been thinking, especially if he hadn't been pleased by their lovemaking. "Not really thinkin' 'bout anything worth mentioning," she answered, not looking at his face.

"You're lying," he said bluntly. "Come on. Be real with me. We can talk about anything."

She looked at him as he gave her his serious look. Candace was turned on by the way he focused on her so intently. He was nothing if not attentive. "Well . . ." She hesitated, wondering how real she should keep it. "I was just thinking about that time."

"What time?"

He was actually playing dumb with her. *What is he? Like, sixteen?* she thought. *He's gonna make me spell it out for him?*

As if hearing her thoughts, he stated, "Just say it, Candace. Say what you're thinking. Don't beat around the bush. Straightforwardness is sexy."

She hated the way he spoke to her like she was a naive idiot.

"I was thinking about when we slept together," she said, staring square into his eyes without blinking.

"Oh?" He picked up his glass and took a long slurp through the straw. "What about it?"

She felt deflated. His nonchalant response was all the assurance she needed to know that he definitely had not been feeling her. It didn't matter; she was married now, anyway. It wasn't as if she was losing anything.

She shrugged. "I was just remembering it. Nothing in particular about it . . . just the fact that it happened."

He nodded. "It pops up in my mind like that sometimes too. . . ."

"Does it?" She tried to sound disinterested as she polished off the last of her fries.

"Yes. Particularly the image of you moaning in my ear with your eyes shut tightly and your fingers caressing my dreads . . . very sensual image. No memory could be sweeter, so I figured I'd hold on to it, versus trying to recapture the moment . . . especially since you are a married woman now."

Khalil drained his iced tea and placed his glass on the table. Taking his napkin from his lap, he thoroughly wiped his hands and mouth before smiling at her devilishly. "What man wouldn't remember experiencing the essence that is you, pretty lady?"

Candace was stunned. Her assumption had been wrong. Obviously, he had enjoyed their episode. Listening to him speak was almost like reading erotica. He knew exactly the right words to say to excite her. She looked down at her half-eaten sandwich and immediately forgave him for ordering her a crappy lunch. Any man who could be so smooth and have so much game could order her whatever he liked. Feeling sexy and desirable, Candace lightly touched Khalil's hand and smiled. This man was definitely good for her ego.

WITHDRAWN

The Girls Saga

WITHDRAWN

Chapter 4

Jada

"No, she didn't."

"Yes, the hell she did!" Jada shouted into her cell phone. Holding the cell with her left hand, she guided her little Ford Focus with her right, trying to focus on the highway signs, so as not to miss her exit, while filling Candace in on the shenanigans that had ensued on the night of her wedding.

It had been a long, tedious day at the office, and the last thing she wanted to be doing was traveling on 285 South at six thirty on a Monday evening. But here she was, heading to I-75 to rescue the damsel in distress.

Somehow in her circle of friends, Jada had become the rescuer, the one everyone turned to. Maybe it made sense. After all, she was the most reliable one in the group. Jada Presley was twenty-two and was an administrative assistant for an adoption agency. A few short months ago she'd worked with Candace at the small downtown Decatur law firm. Having recently graduated from Agnes Scott College, Jada was working toward building up her career as a social service worker. Her girls had always envied her for being so driven and goal-oriented. Once Jada decided to do something, she carried it out 100 percent. Her personal life was no different. As a junior in college, Jada had met and fallen in love with the man she knew she'd spend her life with. Jordan Presley was a communications major when the two met. Now he excelled at his work and was becoming a popular DJ on one of the hottest radio stations in Atlanta.

"In the middle of the night, she called, asking me for money to bail that asshole out of jail."

"That's some bullshit," Candace remarked in her ear. "For real? So did you give it to her?"

Jada sucked her teeth, exiting onto Tara Boulevard in the midst of the wind down of rush-hour traffic. "Are you kidding me? I told her that I didn't have the cash, 'cause I don't."

"So what did she do?"

"Hell if I know," Jada answered. "But I'll tell you this. I'm tired of her asking me for money to help that boy out."

Jada made a right into the Value City parking lot and scanned the crowd for her stranded friend. Thinking about Stephanie's antics was upsetting her, and she already wasn't happy about riding around Riverdale in search of her other troubled girl.

"Well, she knew to call you," Candace said. "'Cause had she called me, I would've had to tell her what's up."

"She wouldn't have called you on your wedding night," Jada replied. "She said they were supposed to hook up after the wedding. He had her waiting by the phone, only to call her from jail, demanding bail money. Asshole."

"I'm just saying."

Jada shook her head. "Yeah." *You probably would have given it to her*, she thought.

Jada's eyes fell on the tall, dark chick posted at the entrance to Value City. She had her cell phone to her ear, lip gloss shining, sporting sparkly hip huggers and a colorful shirt depicting a woman with a large Afro accented with rhinestones. She looked like a model. The problem was that she behaved like one too.

"Let me call you back, girl," Jada said to Candace, then ended the call and leaned over to unlock the passenger door. Glancing at the clock, she noticed that it was now fifteen minutes to seven. Jordan was expecting her home no later than seven thirty for their usual quiet Monday night wind down, but here she was, playing the heroine. The pretty girl slid into the seat, clicked her phone shut, and closed the door.

"Thank you, friend," Alex said in her sugary sweet, innocent little girl voice.

Jada pulled off and headed toward home. "Thank you nothing," she responded. "You wanna tell me how your ass ended up stuck out here?"

Alex took a deep breath and stared out the window. "That lame dude left me."

"Who?"

"Ronnie."

"Where do you know him from?"

"The club. He said he was gon' take me to dinner, and then he brings me to some bootleg Chinese food place," Alex said. "I assumed we'd go to Outback or Red Lobster, somewhere like that. Then the punk was late picking me up, talking 'bout he was at the studio with his boys."

"Okay, so how did you end up here?" Jada interjected.

"He got mad 'cause I was complaining about him being cheap, so he said that I was a spoiled little princess and that I should find my ass a way home. So I got out of the car and he left."

Jada laughed so hard, tears welled up in her eyes. The thought that some dude had called Alex on her attitude was hilarious. Yes, it was messed up that he would leave her in an unfamiliar place, but Jada was sure that this would be a lesson learned. She loved her girl, but ole boy was right. Alex was a spoiled little princess. She often complained about not being able to find a nice, decent guy. The reality was that Alex's attitude was often the cause of all her boyfriends' mistreatment of her.

"Don't laugh at me!" Alex squeaked, making a pouty face.

Jada laughed harder. "Did you give him that same look as he pulled off?"

"Okay. You got jokes."

Recovering from her hysteria, Jada shook her head and adopted a more solemn look. "Why are you out with no money?" she asked her friend. "I'm assuming you don't have any money, or else you would've caught a cab home."

Alex fidgeted with her little pink cell phone, avoiding eye contact with Jada. "I'm broke right now. That's why I agreed to go out to eat with that fool. I was hungry."

"You wouldn't be broke if you got a job," Jada advised.

"I'm trying, 'cause I know Mommy and Daddy aren't gonna pay my bills forever."

Mommy and Daddy? Jada drove in silence, thinking to herself how privileged her friend really was. As long as she'd known the girl, Alex had never worked. Her parents basically took care of all her financial needs, from her rent to her personal expenses. Jada was not jealous of the girl, but it irked her that she had had to work hard throughout college while Alex had partied hard. Kudos to the Masons for being able to afford to support their only child; however, now that school was over, Jada felt that by still fronting the bill, Alex's parents were hurting Alex more than helping. Alex had no sense of responsibility or independence. Her being stranded in Riverdale after going out with a dude she barely knew only confirmed this.

Jada was officially annoyed. When would her girls ever learn? She was tired of being the one everybody turned to for help. It was exhausting. And now, because she was rescuing Alex, she would be late getting home and late starting dinner. Jordan hated eating after eight. He would understand, but personally she just wanted to be home with her husband. The thought of Jordan made a smile creep upon her lips.

Alex noticed immediately. "What are you thinking about?"

Jada shook her head. "Nothing."

The rest of their ride back to Decatur was quiet. When Jada dropped Alex off at the front gate of her apartment complex, the two said a cordial good-bye, and then Jada sped off. Jordan hadn't called to check on her, and she had not called to check in. She wondered if he was even home yet.

She arrived home in record time, letting herself into their beautiful apartment with a great feeling of relief. Relief was replaced with surprise as she kicked her heels off and noticed the flicker of light cascading on the wall of their dining room. Quickly she entered and saw the candles and roses adorning their cherry oak dining table. Two place settings had been arranged. Her right brow rose in anticipation as the aroma from the kitchen filled her nose. After soaking in the ambience of the dining room for a moment longer, Jada turned and entered the kitchen, just in time to see Jordan pop open a bottle of wine.

"Welcome home, beautiful," he said without looking up.

He poured her a glass of Riesling and walked over to her, then placed the glass in her hand and a long, lingering kiss on her lips. He pulled away and watched as she sipped the chilled wine.

"To what do I owe this pleasure?" she asked, savoring the wine.

He chuckled. "What? A man can't pamper his woman?"

"Trust me, I am not complaining."

Jordan walked away to grab two awaiting plates from the counter. He walked past her and into the dining room. She trailed behind him.

"Sorry for being so late," she said sweetly. "It smells so good in here. What's for dinner?"

"Cube steaks, creamed potatoes, and sweet peas." He sat the plates down, turned to his wife, and took her glass and placed it on the table.

Jada smiled and allowed herself to be pulled into his embrace. She inhaled the wonderful scent that was him, a mixture of Right Guard deodorant, Curve for men, and sweat. She felt the tension in her body ease up as he massaged her back.

Jordan kissed her forehead. "I love you, woman."

Jada sighed. It felt good to be with a man who she knew would never leave her stranded.

Chapter 5

Alex

Alexandria Mason was exhausted. Upon entering her apartment, she discarded her cute maroon sandals by the front door and trotted over to the couch. Kacey, her roommate, would be furious with her for leaving the shoes in the middle of the floor like that. But Alex didn't care. She was tired, hot, and humiliated. Throwing her head back against the couch, she sucked her teeth. The nerve of that punk for leaving her! *Why is it so hard to find a good man?*

Alex knew she was smart and beautiful. Perhaps this intimidated the brothers. Ever since she moved to Atlanta for school, it had seemed as if all the jerks flocked to her. She had not experienced one serious relationship. Being single was starting to suck. All her girls were getting married, leaving her alone and making her feel pathetic and lonely. Sure, she was young and should be simply enjoying life, but life seemed empty when she came home to a quiet apartment with no one there to care for her.

Alex laughed aloud at her thoughts. *Even Candace's vain ass has a husband!* She was happy for her girl, despite her belief that the union was destined to be broken. But at least the girl had someone to spend her nights with. Alex reached for her remote and tuned into her usual prime-time shows. *I have only Kim, Nikki, and the professor to chill with,* she thought as the theme music to her favorite show, *The Parkers,* started. At the first commercial, she sauntered to the kitchen and peered into the refrigerator. There was nothing aside from some orange juice, a container of old Chinese takeout that Kacey had had three days ago, and some cheese. She contemplated making a grilled cheese sandwich, but that idea was canceled when she realized that they were out of bread.

Feeling that she was about to have a serious breakdown, Alex pulled her cell out of its holster and dialed her favorite number.

"What's up, pimpin'?"

She was used to this greeting.

"Hey, friend," she replied, putting on her innocent voice.

Laughter filled her ear.

"What's wrong with you, girl?"

Alex hopped up on the kitchen counter and swung her legs back and forth. "I'm hungry."

"Thought you had a date with your new boo."

"Yeah, well, he's a punk, and I'm hungry. So—"

"Say no more." His keys jingled through the receiver. "Chicken or beef?"

"Beef," she answered.

"A'ight. Be there in twenty."

"'Kay."

Alex flipped the phone closed and jumped down from the counter. Ignoring the laughter from the living room television, she headed to her bedroom and quickly changed into purple lounging pants and a lavender tank top. Brushing her wrapped hair into a ponytail, she toyed with the idea of applying her MAC Lustreglass gloss to her full lips. She quickly abandoned the idea, thinking it unnecessary to go an extra mile to be cute for her homeboy. Twenty minutes later there was a tap at the front door, and Alex went to greet her friend.

Standing outside her door was Clayton Paul, her oldest and best friend. She and Clayton, better known as Clay to others and Precious to Alex, had gone to high school together in Beaumont, Texas. When Alex decided to go to Agnes Scott, Clay decided upon Morehouse. They figured at least they would have each other in Atlanta. Clay was a thin, average-looking guy. He was no athlete or stud, but there was a certain cuteness to him, which never left him without a date. His sense of fashion was unique—preppy-boy style, if you will. Only Clay could wear a soft pink polo and not emit a gay vibe. Alex liked that about him. Clay dared to be different and didn't care what anyone thought about him.

Alex stepped to the side and allowed him to enter her apartment. He carried a Wendy's bag, along with what Alex knew was a chocolate Frosty for her. Alex loved chocolate, and Clay, being the ever attentive, good friend that he was, knew exactly what she liked. The two set up their meal on the floor, resting their backs against the front of the couch. Delighted and relieved, Alex bit into her Jr. Bacon Cheeseburger.

"Mmm."

Clay laughed at her, shoving fries into his own mouth. His eyes crinkled up when he laughed, giving him an almost Asian look. Alex had noticed it many times, not realizing how cute it was until now.

"What are you laughing at?" she asked him.

"You."

"You think I'm a joke?" she retorted playfully.

Clay shook his head solemnly. "Never that, pretty lady."

Alex ignored the compliment, savoring her Frosty. "No date tonight, playboy?" she asked between slurps.

Clay shrugged. "Naw."

Alex clutched her chest with her right hand. "What?" she asked in mock disbelief. "You with no date? The world must be coming to an end."

Clay gave a half smile and shook his head, not really amused by Alex's humor. He reached for a fry, and Alex quickly took it from him.

"What's up with that?" she asked, popping the fry into her mouth.

Clay looked at her and was hesitant to speak. It was as if he was lost in his stare. Alex raised her right eyebrow, and as if snapping back to reality, Clay quickly looked away.

"Nothing," he finally replied, reaching for another fry. "Just tired of hanging out with all these apple-head-ass chicks. It's just not what's up for me anymore."

Alex nodded knowingly. Using her straw, she stirred up her rapidly melting Frosty while listening to her friend speak the words that mirrored her own emotions.

"I just wanna go out with one girl," Clay said. "I just want one girl with some business about herself that likes me for me, just the way I am. I want someone that I can chill with, someone I can joke with, someone that's hella fine, 'cause she just has mad confidence like that, someone I can spoil. . . ."

Alex giggled. "And I want to be all that to someone who is worth my time and won't treat me like shit."

Clay looked up at his homegirl. Alex missed the hopeful glint in his eyes.

"Yeah." Clay leaned his head back on the couch. "Guess we're both looking for the same thing, huh?"

Alex discarded her burger wrapper and sat her half-finished Frosty on the coffee table. As she'd often done before, Alex leaned over and rested her head on Clay's lap.

Instinctively, he began to caress her hair, removing her ponytail holder.

Alex closed her eyes, allowing herself to be comforted by her friend's gentle strokes. "Are we ever gonna find it, Precious?" she asked softly.

Clay lightly touched her face. "Yeah, Alex. I think we will."

Chapter 6

Stephanie

A week had passed since Stephanie had bailed Corey out of jail. It had not been easy to get the money together. She'd had no luck with Jada, so she'd asked the old man up the street for a loan. Mr. Carter had a thing for her, always had. Stephanie knew that he would be more than willing to loan her the money. The issue was how the man would want to be repaid. Stephanie's plan was to get the money back quickly from Corey so that she could return it to Carter with no problems. The flaw in her plan was that Corey was pulling one of his disappearing acts. She hadn't heard from him, and he was not answering or returning any of her calls.

It hurt her feelings that he would show such disregard for her after she had helped him out. The night of the incident, he hadn't even bothered to fill her in on what had happened. Once he was released, he'd simply told her to go home. Without so much as a thank-you, a kiss, or a hug, he'd just turned and walked away. Stephanie hadn't known where he was going on foot, and she'd wondered how he would get home. But, like the obedient girlfriend that she was, she got into her Nissan Sentra and drove home.

Now, completely pissed that the whole weekend had come and gone without a peep from him, Stephanie was determined to have it out with Corey. It was Monday afternoon, and she was tired from working. However, as soon as six o'clock hit, Stephanie hopped into her car and headed straight to Corey's Midtown apartment. She hated that he lived in a gated community. But not even that obstacle was going to stop her: she tailed a resident and got inside the iron gates. Driving through the maze of the complex, Stephanie started to become apprehensive about her decision to just show up.

What if there's a girl in there? How will I react? Parking in front of his building, she shrugged off her misgivings and decided that whatever happened was going to happen. She was determined to confront the bastard.

She noticed his car parked in its usual spot and was confident that the jerk was home. Slowly ascending the stairs, she pulled out her cell and dialed Corey's number. As she reached the top floor, she also reached his voice mail. Disgusted and further infuriated, Stephanie walked up to his door and began to bang loudly. For several minutes she stood there, knocking and banging like a madwoman possessed. Her inhibitions began to leave her, and she found herself shouting obscenities at the heavy door.

"Open the damn door, you fuckin' bastard! I know you're fuckin' in there, you ass!"

When she was in mid-knock, the door flew open, and Stephanie barely had time to blink before she was grabbed, pulled inside, and tossed to the floor. Corey was on top of her, pinning her to the floor, a look of hot fury upon his face.

"Are you fuckin' crazy?" he asked repeatedly. "Are you fuckin' crazy, girl? Are you stupid? What the fuck is wrong with you?"

Stephanie was scared speechless. She was not sure what his intentions were and feared that he was about to brutally kick her ass.

Corey shook her. "How many times have I told your ass not to just show up at my spot? You think I'm fuckin' playin' with you, girl? You think this shit is a fuckin' joke?" He glared down at her small, tensed-up body and shook his head. Finally, he released his grip and climbed off of her. He turned away, heading for his kitchen. "Stupid ass," he muttered.

Stephanie rose from the floor and watched him retreat. Anger replaced fear, and she followed him into the kitchen. Coming up behind him, she tried to push the man up against the refrigerator. "Fuck you, Corey," she spat out.

Corey quickly spun around and grabbed her left arm. "What the fuck is wrong with you, girl? You don't put yo' hands on me."

Stephanie shook her arm free from his hold. "Don't put yo' damn hands on me, then."

Corey shook his head and turned back toward the fridge. He opened it and reached inside for a beer. "You need to take yo' crazy ass somewhere wit' all dat shit, Steph." He turned back to face her as he popped off the beer cap. "You out here making a fool of yo'self. What the fuck's wrong with you, man?"

Stephanie's eyes widened. She put her hands on her hips and glared back at Corey. "What the fuck's wrong with me? What the fuck's wrong with *you*? You're the fuckin' trifling one. Ignoring my calls. Haven't called me or come to see your son. Didn't even bother to say thank you for bailing yo' sorry ass out of jail."

"So what? You doing all this shit for me to say thank you? You trippin'." Corey tried to step away, but Stephanie moved in front of him. "Stop playing, man," he warned her. "Take yo' ass home."

Stephanie stepped up to him and poked him in the chest, realizing for the first time that he was shirtless. "I didn't come for a thank-you. I came to see why you acting like you don't care about me and Damien. But, yeah, a thank-you *would* be nice."

"I don't need this shit, Steph." Corey slapped her hand away, spilling a little of his Heineken. "I ain't down with all this drama and shit."

"You cause the drama!" Stephanie shouted, trying again to push him. "This is all you, Corey."

They struggled for a minute, Stephanie trying to punch at Corey and Corey pushing her away. Tired of the commotion, Corey sat his beer on the counter beside them, picked the petite woman up, carried her to his leather sofa, and threw her down. Stephanie was breathless as he towered over her, pulling her arms over her head and pinning them down.

"You want me to say thank you?" he asked. "You want me to thank yo' ass? Well, here you go. Here goes your fuckin' thank-you."

He leaned down and began to suck on her neck. Stephanie was powerless underneath him and struggled without success to move. Moving away from her neck, Corey tried to kiss her.

Still infuriated, she turned her head to the right while trying to move her legs. "Get the fuck off of me!" she ordered.

Corey ignored her and turned her face toward his with his right hand. His left hand still held both of her small wrists above her head. "This is what you came for, right? Over here, all heated up and shit. Ain't this what you came for?"

He crushed his lips against hers and forced his tongue into her mouth. She tried once more to free herself but was disappointed in her own lack of control as she felt herself succumb to the effect he was having on her body. Corey could feel her relax and begin to thrust her tongue against his. At that point he released her arms and began groping her breasts through her shirt. Becoming more and more turned on, Stephanie could feel the moisture seeping between her legs. Sensing her growing arousal, Corey unzipped her slacks and disposed of them and her bikini briefs. Stephanie's heart rate increased as Corey entered her with two fingers, then three. The slight penetration teased her, driving her into a sexual fit. Spreading her legs for him, Stephanie began to rotate her hips to better feel the pleasure of his fingers.

"*Mmm.* This is what you came for, huh?" he whispered, watching as she moved her hips around and around to match his probing.

She felt helpless against his advances and did not protest as he entered her bare and began to thrust ferociously. His grunts filled her ear as he moved in and out of her. Stephanie tried to caress his head, but he shook her hand away. She tried to grab his face and engage him in a kiss, but Corey turned his head to the side, avoiding the romantic exchange. His pumping became fiercer, and Stephanie's arousal began to diminish. Arms lying flat by her sides, she found herself staring at the ceiling, waiting for the encounter to be over. She didn't have the nerve to tell him to stop. She didn't want to start another argument just as they were making up. Oblivious to her growing dryness, Corey mannishly pushed her legs over to the left, forcing her to turn around. She obeyed.

"Lift your ass up more," he ordered her, pushing her torso into the sticky wetness on the sofa. He reentered her in the doggy-style position. Stephanie buried her face in the sofa pillow, willing herself not to cry. His roughness was beginning to hurt, but Corey seemed more turned on by her discomfort. As he slapped her ass and squeezed her butt cheeks, Stephanie grimaced, trying to remain silent. They'd never had rough sex like this, and she wasn't sure what it meant.

Corey tried to spread her cheeks wider and pushed her legs open more, causing her left leg to dangle off the sofa. He pushed himself deeper inside, grabbing her hips as he climaxed inside of her. Stephanie was gripping the arm of the sofa and biting her lower lip. As Corey came, she breathed an inaudible sigh of relief. Without hesitation, he quickly jumped up and headed to his bathroom.

As she lay there, Stephanie heard the water running in the shower. Sitting up, she looked around for her clothes, thinking it best for her to just dress and leave. In mid-thought she decided that it was unfair for Corey to be the only satisfied one. With renewed confidence, she strolled into the bathroom and pulled back the shower curtain.

Corey was stunned by her presence and gave her a questioning look. "What's up?" he asked. "What you doing?"

"I can't join you?" Stephanie placed one foot in the tub.

Corey held his soapy hand out in protest. "Naw. Hold up. I'm almost done. Plus, I gotta bounce real quick. I got business to take care of. A'ight? Just give me a minute."

Feeling rejected, Stephanie just nodded and retreated from the bathroom. The whole visit had not gone according to plan, and she was disappointed in herself. She quickly dressed and grabbed her purse, but she was not out the door before Corey entered the living room, wrapped in a towel.

"Hey, man, you can wash up if you want to, but I'm leaving in, like, ten minutes," he announced.

Stephanie walked past him to the door, half expecting him to stop her, half knowing that he wouldn't.

"You out?" he asked her.

She turned to look at the man whom she undoubtedly loved but hated. "Yeah. Why? You wanna kiss me good-bye?"

He surprised her by walking over to her. However, he simply pecked her forehead and patted her ass. "I'll call you." He opened the door to usher her out.

"Yeah. Sure."

Stephanie exited the apartment, descended the stairs, and walked back to her little Sentra, mission unaccomplished.

Chapter 7

Miranda

It was eleven o'clock at night, and he still wasn't home. Miranda glanced up again at the clock on the VCR. It wasn't unlike him not to call, but it had been an annoying habit as of late. For the past two weeks Norris had been coming and going with no regard for her. Ever since the infamous hang up after Candace's wedding, he'd been behaving more and more suspiciously. Her eyes were getting heavy and she was growing impatient as she watched *The Golden Girls* on Lifetime. Miranda had half a mind to go out and search for the car. The thought was a desperate one, but she was becoming increasingly angry as she wondered where the hell her husband was. With working two jobs, Miranda rarely had time alone with Norris. *The nerve of him not to be home to spend quality time,* she seethed.

Just as she was about to give up for the night and silence Rose in the middle of a St. Olaf anecdote, Miranda heard the lock turn on the front door. In strolled Norris, as if it were five in the afternoon. Tossing his red and white A's cap onto the coffee table, he nearly walked right past her, but she stopped him. Miranda was astonished by his gall.

"So you just ain't gon' say nothing?" she questioned him.

Norris walked into their bedroom. Not backing down and ready to confront his late-night creeping, Miranda followed behind him. He emitted his usual marijuana scent, but tonight Miranda's nose was picking up a hint of something else.

"Where have you been, Norris?" Miranda stood in the bedroom doorway, with her hands on her hips.

Norris unbuttoned his jersey and then began to remove the rest of his clothes. His back was turned to his hot-tempered wife. She was not appreciative of his silence. As he shrugged off the jersey, Miranda quickly stepped forward and snatched it.

"What the fuck!" Norris shouted, turning to face Miranda. "Man, stop playing." Norris reached for the jersey, but Miranda turned and took a quick sniff of the material. The scent of Victoria's Secret Pear Glacé fragrance was unmistakable. She allowed Norris to snatch the jersey from her hands as she looked at him, anger reflecting in her glare.

"Look at me," she demanded.

He ignored the command, tossing the shirt into the nearby clothes hamper. He busied himself with removing the rest of his clothing, as if Miranda was not even in the room.

"Look at me!" she screamed at him.

He looked over at her as he stood in his boxers, ready to head to the shower. "For what?" His voice was laced with attitude.

Miranda stepped up to him, fists clenched, as if she was going to hit the man. She fought back tears and looked into the eyes of the man she'd tried so hard to be good to. "I have been a good wife to you, and this is the best you can do for me?"

"What are you talking about? Ain't nobody done shit to you."

"Norris! You're cheating on me! You think I'm too stupid to notice that something's going on?"

He sucked his teeth. "Whatever." Norris pushed past her and walked into their bathroom. He turned on the water in the shower, then turned to open the linen closet, situated behind the bathroom door.

Miranda approached the bathroom, pushed the door, and held it ajar, hampering Norris's access to the linen closet.

"Man, watch out," he told her.

"I work two jobs to support us, Norris. I begged my parents to let us live with them when you fucked up and got discharged."

"Get out of my way, Miranda," he said, his tone warning.

"I stuck by you when you didn't have shit. I should've left your sorry ass. But I stayed with you, and this . . . this is how you repay me?"

"I'm not gon' to tell yo' ass to move no more." He balled up his fists in anger.

"How you gonna have the nerve to be cheating on me? Who in the hell is even messing with your sorry ass? All you do is smoke all day, and you barely keeping ya' li'l piece of a job."

Without warning or hesitation, Norris opened his right palm and slapped Miranda with such force that she tumbled backward. Capitalizing on her moment of vulnerability, Norris shoved her over and over again, until she fell to the floor. "You wanna talk shit?" He kicked the woman's legs with his bare foot. "Go 'head. Talk shit now. Go 'head."

Miranda's cries for help resounded throughout the otherwise silent apartment. She pleaded with him for some mercy, swatting at his leg and trying to get him to stop kicking her. She turned her body away from him, curling up against the wall. There she found no solace. Norris turned his concentration from her legs to her side, giving her two swift kicks in her rib cage. As she winced from the contact, Miranda felt one of her contact lenses slip. Doubled over in pain from Norris's blows, she frantically tried to find it.

Realizing what she was doing, Norris quickly surveyed the floor. They spotted the errant contact lens at the same time. Norris was quicker, stomping the tiny lens with his right foot while pushing her away with his left hand.

"Get the fuck up!" he ordered, laughing at her helplessness. "Let me see you get up now."

"Stop," she pleaded desperately. "Please leave me alone."

"Naw. You wanted a confrontation, right? Walking up on me like you're ready to go at it. Come on. Get up." He reached down and pulled her up by her arms.

Miranda struggled with him, trying with all her might to shake herself loose from his grip, despite the searing pain in her side.

"You wanna hit me?" With his right hand he gripped her throat as he pinned her up against the wall. "I don't hear you talking no more. You ain't saying shit."

Tears streamed from Miranda's eyes as she tried to pry Norris's fingers from her neck. Her vision was slightly skewed, but she could see that he was looking at her with the most devious smirk. Miranda was scared for her life.

Norris tightened his grip and gritted his teeth. "Shut the fuck up. Stop whimpering," he ordered.

She closed her eyes in prayer, hoping that he would not kill her.

"Understand this. If you ever call me sorry again, if you ever step to me like you want to scrap again, I will fuckin' kill you. You understand?"

Miranda was quiet, her eyes still shut, her breath escaping her. Norris shoved her forehead, causing Miranda's head to bang against the wall.

"Answer me, damn it. Do you fuckin' understand?"

Miranda's eyes blinked rapidly as she struggled to give him a slight nod. He stared at her briefly and then released his hold on her. Unsure of her next move, Miranda stood awkwardly in the hall, waiting to see what Norris would do. Her husband simply shook his head at her.

"I don't want to go through this shit again," he told her.

She just stood there, trying to regulate her breathing. Norris turned away and went back into the bathroom, slamming the door behind him. Miranda could feel herself beginning to hyperventilate. Staggering into the bedroom, she felt immense pain in her side. Her senses were leaving her as she began to panic all over again. Standing at the dresser, she absentmindedly picked up her hairbrush and frantically brushed at her mane, her sobs coming more quickly and loudly. She caught her reflection in the mirror and dropped the brush to the floor in mid-stroke. Her eyes were swollen with tears, her bottom lip was busted and bleeding, and bruises were becoming discernible beneath her right eye and on her neck. She barely recognized herself.

Afraid of the image staring back at her, Miranda turned from the mirror, turned off the light, and crawled into her bed. Common sense told her to pack a bag and get out. Fear of others ridiculing her, along with a fear of failure and pure shock, kept her from moving. She balled herself up in one corner of the bed, hysteria overcoming her. Lost in her struggle for breath and her inability to block the memory of Norris's blows, she slowly slipped into unconsciousness, until she was enveloped in peaceful darkness.

Chapter 8

Candace

What is he doing here? she asked herself. Candace had just made it home from a long, exhausting day. Her plan had been to come home, throw some chicken wings in the oven, pour herself a glass of Hpnotiq, and enjoy a hot bubble bath in peace while Quincy was still heading home. Her dream had deflated when she pulled into the driveway and found his car sitting there. He never beat her home. She was genuinely surprised and equally suspicious. As she carried her purse and lunch bag toward the door to the kitchen, she reached out to touch Quincy's car. It was cool to the touch.

Inside a shirtless Quincy was chilling, his feet up as he watched *106 & Park* with a goblet full of the Hpnotiq she'd been craving all day.

"What's up?" she asked him. She sat her bags down on the table in the breakfast nook in the kitchen and then walked into the living room.

Quincy simply nodded his head in acknowledgment and took a hearty gulp of the Hpnotiq.

Candace sat next to him on the couch, waiting for some form of explanation for his unexpected presence. Seeing that none was forthcoming, she kicked off her pumps and shrugged her shoulders. "I'm guessing that you don't want to tell me why you're home so early."

Quincy sucked his teeth. "I gotta give you a reason for me being in my own house?"

Candace rolled her eyes and ran her fingers through her wrapped hair. "I'm just wondering because you never get home before me. Is everything okay?"

Quincy nodded.

"How long have you been home?"

"Dang, man. Why you asking all these questions?"

She sucked her teeth. "I'm just making conversation."

Quincy changed the channel to *SportsCenter* and took another swig of the blue liquor. "I don't feel like conversating."

Candace rose from the couch and eyeballed Quincy. "*Conversate* isn't a word."

"Whatever."

"Yeah. Whatever." Candace turned and climbed the steps to their bedroom. She wasn't surprised to see Quincy's clothes strewn all over their bed once she entered the room. Reluctantly, she began to rummage through the clothes, sorting the laundry. Quincy never put his things away, no matter how many times she complained about his sloppiness. He was also notorious for leaving money and paper, usually receipts, in his pants pockets. Candace had banned him from doing the laundry because he never checked his pockets.

Tired and not wanting to pick up after her grown husband, Candace grabbed Quincy's work pants and hurriedly inspected the pockets. Her search yielded two dollars in change, a five-dollar bill, and a folded-up sheet of paper. After tossing the pants into the clothes hamper, she stuck the money in her own sock drawer and moved toward the trash can to discard the folded piece of paper. Mindlessly she unfolded it, just to ascertain that it wasn't anything of importance. The big, bold print at the top of the page made her gasp. Instantly she realized why Quincy was laid out in their living room, as if on vacation. Quickly, she left the bedroom, descended the stairs, approached her husband, and snatched the remote from his hand.

"Hey, man! What the fuck?" he protested as she snapped off the television.

She threw the remote down on the coffee table and glared at the big man. "Yeah, what the fuck?" she repeated, waving the paper in his face. "What the fuck is this?"

Quincy squinted to see what she was waving around. He snatched the paper from her, took a quick glance at it, and then threw it on the couch, beside him. "You going through my stuff now?" Was he really trying to change the subject?

"Nobody's going through your stinking stuff. I was sorting the laundry and—" She caught herself. "No, hell no. Don't flip this. What the fuck is up, Q?"

He shrugged.

She shoved him. "What the fuck? You're not going to say anything?"

"Don't touch me like that, man," he replied.

"You owe me an explanation. This is serious, Quincy."

"It ain't nothing."

"*It ain't nothing*? It's a separation notice, dude. That's a whole lot of something. You want to tell me what happened and how we're going to manage these bills without your income?"

"Man, that ole trick-ass supervisor never liked me. He been trying to get me fired for the longest."

"Uh-huh."

Quincy reached for the remote, and Candace quickly knocked it off the coffee table. He looked at her and rolled his eyes. "Don't worry about it, a'ight?"

"Don't worry about it?" Candace couldn't believe her ears.

"Yeah, man. I got an interview somewhere else tomorrow. It'll be all right."

She stared at him in total disbelief. Why wouldn't he tell her something as important as this? His unemployment could be a major setback for them, and he was acting as if nothing had happened. The sight of his chunky, chocolate body clad in nothing but his boxers, some sweatpants, and dingy socks was making her sick. There was nothing worse than a broke slob to her. Annoyed with his presence and nonchalant attitude, Candace hurriedly stepped into her shoes, retrieved her purse and keys, and headed for the door.

"Where you going?" Quincy had the nerve to ask her.

"None of ya'," she replied, slamming the kitchen door behind her.

Hopping into her car, she realized that she truly had no destination in mind. All she knew was that she had to get away from Quincy immediately. After backing out of the garage, she took her cell out of her purse, scrolled through to the first name that came to mind, and placed a call. He answered on the third ring.

"Pleasant surprise," he greeted her.

Candace drove down the street and zipped through a four-way stop without stopping, her mind set on hastily getting away. "Can you meet me somewhere?"

Khalil caught the urgency in her tone. "Something wrong, beautiful?"

"I just need to talk."

"Hmm. Have you had dinner?"

"No," she answered, making a quick right onto Stone Mountain–Lithonia Road, clueless as to where she was headed.

"Come to my house. I'm making jambalaya. You like spicy food?"

Candace thought for a second. "Where's Sheila?"

"Out of town for a week. You coming over or what?"

She was hesitant, but she needed somewhere to seek solace and was not yet ready to inform any of her girls of Quincy's recent antics. "Yeah," she said. "I'm coming. Give me directions."

Twenty-five minutes later she found herself parked outside of a ranch-style home off of Columbia Drive. Taking a deep breath, Candace silently prayed that this man's woman would not return home early to find her in her house. A confrontation did not sound appealing to her at this time. Reaching the front door, she rang the bell and patiently waited to be let in.

Khalil opened the door, looking sexier than ever. His long, gorgeous locks hung loosely. He wore a cream-colored lounging suit, the top completely unbuttoned, exposing his firm and nicely sculpted chest and abs. In his left hand he held a glass of white wine. He stepped back, opening the door wider to allow her to enter. Once she crossed the threshold, he closed the door and promptly handed her the glass.

"For you," he stated.

She took the glass, and before she could say thank you, he leaned in and kissed her so softly and quickly that a second later she barely remembered if it had happened or not.

He ushered her into the living room, where he had Sade playing softly and candles burning on the mantel. "Sit down," he ordered.

She did as instructed, allowing herself to melt into the velvety plushness of the cream-colored couch. Khalil pushed an ottoman over to her, and she instinctively lifted her legs to rest her feet upon it.

"Let me check on the food, and I'll be right back," he informed her.

Candace simply nodded and savored her wine. Looking around the room, she took in the ambience. Many African replicas and statues adorned the end tables and the base of the fireplace. Pictures of smiling children filled several shelves of the entertainment center. Candace noticed that there were no pictures of Khalil and Sheila together. The room smelled of fresh jasmine. On the coffee table a stick of incense burned from its respective stand.

The wine was starting to take effect, as Candace felt herself beginning to mellow out. She let the sound of Sade's sultry voice, the light fragrance of the incense, and the hint of spices wafting in the air from the kitchen take her away from her earlier emotions.

Khalil sauntered back into the room, carrying a bottle of Riesling. He topped off her glass and sat the bottle on the coffee table. He joined her on the couch, and looking into her eyes, he began to stroke her soft hair. His fingers combed through her relaxed tresses, massaging her scalp and giving her comfort.

"What's going on, pretty lady?" he asked in a delicate whisper.

Candace closed her eyes, not wanting to remember Quincy's situation. "Quincy lost his job. His dumb ass wasn't even going to tell me."

"So how did you find out?"

"I found his separation notice when I was sorting through his laundry."

"Hmm."

They sat in silence, Candace's eyes still closed and her eyebrows knit up in concern and Khalil continuously stroking her mane.

"Turn around," he ordered her a few minutes later.

Candace opened her eyes and turned her back to him. Khalil placed both hands firmly on her shoulders and began to give her a massage. She was sure that he could feel the tension in her neck. His firm probes of her skin helped her to relax. She lifted her glass to her lips and swallowed its sweetness.

"I don't know what we're going to do about these bills now, especially the mortgage," she said.

Khalil kissed her neck gently. "Don't worry about it tonight. He's your man. It's his job to provide for you, no matter what. Let him figure out how to fix his own mess." He kissed her neck again and then kissed the other side. "Don't worry about it tonight," he repeated. "Tonight just relax and let me pamper you."

She felt his tongue trace the ridges of her right ear. The sensation sent a tingle down her spine.

He commenced delicately sucking on her earlobe and then massaging her back. Perhaps sensing that she'd reached a pivotal point of relaxation, Khalil took her wineglass from her, sat it on the coffee table, and turned her toward him. Before she could speak or protest, his lips conquered hers in a kiss that began gently and ended up wild with passion. She didn't stop him. Instead, she gave in to the pleasure of his tongue. Her hands grabbed at his dreads as she eagerly received and matched each thrust of his tongue. She felt his hand slip under her blouse and cup her right breast. She moaned, wanting to encourage him to dispose of her top and her bra.

Without warning he withdrew from her, and Candace struggled to catch her breath, wondering what was going on. Slowly, he rose and reached over to lift up her black skirt. Underneath, he edged her thong downward, his eyes focused on hers seductively. She lifted her hips slightly to aid him. Still looking into her eyes, he kneeled down in front of her and grabbed her legs with his big, strong hands. Softly he trailed kisses down her right leg until he reached her foot. Once there, he slipped off her pump and took her pedicured toes into his moist mouth. Candace could barely contain herself. He sucked until her head fell back onto the couch and she released a pleasurable sigh. He repeated the routine with her left leg, giving it and her toes the same great pleasure and attention. Candace could feel herself dripping onto his couch.

As if becoming aware of her raging pheromones and the moisture seeping from her kitty, Khalil spread her legs, draping them over his muscular shoulders. With his tongue, he expertly traced the walls of her labia minora, flicking up and down, up and down. He licked around her pleasure point, driving her insane and forcing her to grab on to his glistening locks. He hardened his tongue and drove it inside of her, an act she'd never before experienced. He darted his tongue in and out as her hips rose from the couch, her pelvis moving in a circular motion.

She heard him moan from giving her pleasure. This increased her wetness.

Khalil withdrew his tongue and flicked it across her clit rapidly. The sensation was sending her into sheer ecstasy. Picking up on her increased excitement, Khalil took her clit into his mouth and sucked with such might and intent, showing Candace no mercy.

She pleaded with him to wait, to slow down, to stop. She was overcome by the intense sensation, but he forced her to handle it. He wanted her to relinquish all control. Making his intent clear, Khalil inserted two fingers into her slippery entrance and instantly found her G-spot, as if he had a long-term familiarity with her body.

She lost control, her body bucking ferociously against his fingers, which were nestled deep inside of her, and his lips, which held her clit hostage. His speed increased to match her passion-driven fervor. Within seconds Candace felt herself reach the point of no return, experiencing a G-spot orgasm more powerful than any clitoral orgasm she'd ever had. As her cum slid out of her, Khalil's tongue moved to catch and savor it. He licked her until she was dry and her body ceased its convulsions.

She was spent. Khalil lowered her weakening legs, leaned up to kiss her gently on the forehead, then rose from the floor. He left her without a word, and Candace curled up on the couch. He was gone long enough for her to drift off into an ecstasy-induced sleep. She was startled awake by him lifting her from the couch.

He carried her down the hall to the master bedroom and then into the adjoining bathroom. A lavender-scented bubble bath awaited her. Candles lined the four steps to the exquisite garden tub. He put her down and slowly unbuttoned her blouse. Candace remained speechless as he removed the top and unhooked her bra. As the material slipped down her arms and fell to the floor, he caressed each breast softly. He helped her out of her skirt and ushered her toward the tub. Once she was settled, he turned on the spa jets to increase her pleasure.

"Relax," he told her, placing tiny kisses upon her face. "Tonight is all about you. We'll have dinner after your bath." He left the room to retrieve her wineglass and the bottle of Riesling. Upon returning, he promptly topped off her wine once more, and then he left her to enjoy her solitude.

Candace relished the moment, enjoying the delight of being pampered by such a sexy and enticing man. Remembering the way he took her with his mouth made her hot all over again. Penetration was needed. She drained her glass and quickly bathed in the heavenly lavender water. After exiting the tub and drying off with a nearby towel, she found one of Khalil's white T-shirts lying across the chaise longue in his bedroom. With nothing else to put on, Candace pulled the shirt over her head and got a whiff of Khalil's unique scent. It made her smile.

She momentarily forgot that this was another woman's home and man as she comfortably maneuvered her way through the house and to the kitchen.

Khalil was just lighting a candle on the table. He smiled at her as she entered the room and sat at the table. "Refreshed?" he asked, dimming the overhead light.

"Mmm-hmm. And relaxed."

Khalil sat a bowl of steaming hot jambalaya before her. The spices accosted her nose immediately. Beside the bowl stood another glass of wine. Picking up her spoon, Candace sampled the well-seasoned blend of rice, cheese, peppers, sausage, and shrimp. The hint of Cajun flavoring pleased her taste buds, providing just enough spice without going overboard.

"Mmm." She was delighted. *A man who knows how to please in many ways,* she thought.

Khalil lifted his glass to her in a mock toast. "I take that to mean you like it."

"It's so good," Candace answered between bites. "You have a little bit of skills, I see."

Khalil laughed. "You haven't seen anything yet."

He winked at her seductively, and Candace could feel her temperature rising. This man evoked such erotic thoughts and emotions within her that Candace was not sure she would make it through the meal. But make it she did. After they emptied their bowls, Khalil cleared the table, retrieved a new bottle of Riesling, and reached for Candace's hand. Obliged to follow, she placed her hand in his and allowed him to lead her back to his bedroom.

The second they crossed the threshold, Khalil sat the wine on the floor near the foot of the bed and embraced Candace from behind. He kissed her neck on both sides and slid his large hands up and down her body. He followed the curves of her hips, then cupped her ass as he licked and nibbled on her earlobe. Candace felt her legs grow weak with desire. Sliding his left hand up the T-shirt that she'd thrown on, Khalil grabbed her left breast and squeezed it gently while firmly pushing her back with his right hand, forcing her to bend over the foot of the bed.

Candace leaned over more and waited only seconds as he discarded his lounging pants. Her breath escaped her as he slowly entered her from behind. The thickness of him filled her walls completely, and Candace's wetness became intensified. He slid his hands over her ass, spreading the cheeks apart in order to plunge deeper inside of her. She could hear him grunting with each forceful, pleasurable thrust. Sensing that she could no longer stay on her feet, Khalil guided her onto the bed and turned her over. He lifted the T-shirt over her head and took each of her breasts in his hands as he effortlessly slid back into her.

Candace wrapped her legs around his perfectly toned waist. His girth was incredible. She'd never had anyone who was so well endowed. Each thrust caught her by surprise. Wanting to dive deeper, Khalil spread her legs apart and pounded into the depths of her warmth.

"Damn, you feel so good, baby," he said in a raspy, seductive voice, causing Candace to moan. "You're so wet."

His speed increased, and Candace reached out to touch his long, thin locks. She fingered them and then ran her hand over his cheeks, his nose, and his lips. He took her fingers into his mouth and sucked them gently as he lifted her right leg over his shoulder.

"Yes," she cried out as he rhythmically stroked her insides with his manhood. The bed squeaked and rocked in unison to the sounds of their lovemaking. Khalil's eyes were closed as he pumped in and out of her. Candace tried to keep her focus on the look of satisfaction that showed on Khalil's face, but her own pleasure caused her lids to flutter as she continuously cried out. "Yes, yes, yes."

Releasing her leg and leaning into her, Khalil expertly suckled her right breast while pivoting in a circular motion inside of her. Candace wrapped her arms around him, and Khalil reciprocated. They clung to each other's misted body and created a rhythm all their own. They kissed with a hunger that could not be satisfied.

Khalil was the first to approach release. "Come with me, baby," he urged, trying to postpone his pleasure for the sake of hers. He sucked on her bottom lip. Her moans filled his ear. "Come with me," he whispered.

Before either of them could utter another exclamation of ecstasy, Khalil reached orgasm, causing him to pump into her ferociously once more. The intensity of the friction his movement created brought Candace right over the edge behind him. In the aftermath of their climax, the couple lay stuck to one another, still tight in their embrace, waiting for their breathing to become regulated.

Khalil kissed her forehead, then the bridge of her nose, before pulling himself from their embrace. With no energy to spare, Candace simply rolled over and curled up into a ball. Khalil cuddled up behind her. Together they fell into a comfortable sleep, the kind that only good sex could create.

Chapter 9

Jada

The grills were fired up. Balloons had been blown up and adorned all the walls. The coolers were loaded with ice-cold sodas and beer galore. DJ Johnny Dynamite was getting the growing crowd crunk as he played the popular hits of the season. The party was definitely on. It was Jordan's birthday, and Jada had gone all out to make it a memorable celebration.

To accommodate the large guest list and have room for the DJ, Jada's brother, Antwan, had been kind enough to offer the use of his four-bedroom home in Lithonia. Jada had spent half of the previous night and all morning cooking the side dishes for the party. There were meatballs, macaroni and cheese, potato salad, spinach dip, baked beans, and collard greens. All prepared by Jada herself. She was thankful that Twan and Jordan's brother, Sean, had volunteered to cook the meat. Ribs, chicken thighs and wings, hot dogs, hamburgers, and sausages filled the grills. The aroma of barbecue lingered in the air, tantalizing everybody's taste buds.

Jada was in the kitchen, stirring up a fresh pitcher of lemonade, when Jordan approached her from behind, wrapped his arms around her, and kissed her on her right cheek. She smiled and swatted his head with a nearby dish towel.

"Thank you for my party, baby," he said to her, stealing another kiss.

"Yeah, yeah." She playfully wiggled free from his embrace. "Go play with your company."

Jordan swatted her on the ass and sauntered out of the kitchen. As he exited, Miranda and Alex entered.

"Hey, friend," Alex shrilled.

Jada smiled. "Y'all having fun?"

"You got enough people up in here?" Miranda asked, glancing out the patio door and eyeing the backyard.

DJ Dynamite was bumping OutKast's "Hey Ya!" and Alex was moving her body to the beat.

Jada surveyed the backyard and the living room area. She laughed aloud. "Shit. It *is* a lot of people."

Miranda opened a nearby cooler and retrieved a Zima.

"Where's Norris?" Jada asked her, putting the lemonade in the refrigerator.

Miranda shrugged and put the bottle up to her lips. "Don't know."

"You don't know," Alex repeated. "How do you not know where your husband is?"

Miranda gulped the alcohol, draining the bottle, and rolled her eyes at the tall, dark beauty. "He's my husband, not my child. It's not my place to keep up with him. You would know that if you had a husband."

"Whoa," Jada piped in, walking over to the two women, prepared to run interference.

"Dang, girl," Alex said, seemingly unfazed. "I was just asking."

Miranda discarded her empty bottle and reached into the cooler for another. Without a word she opened the beverage and left the kitchen. Alex and Jada watched her retreat, then looked at each other and shrugged.

"She's acting weird," Alex stated. "Maybe she's on her period."

Jada proceeded to wipe down the counter with a dish towel. She shook her head in response to Alex's assumption. "Nah. She's obviously pissed the hell off with Norris, and you struck a nerve."

Alex shrugged. "So that ain't my fault. She shouldn't take it out on me."

"Now, you know she didn't mean nothing by that. She's just venting . . . acting out. You know?"

"Uh-huh," Alex muttered. "Well, I hope that Stephanie doesn't act out on her."

"What?" Jada looked up and followed Alex's focused stare into the living room. In a corner by themselves, Corey was whispering something into Miranda's ear as she blushed and continued to nurse her malt beverage. Jada bit her bottom lip lightly, and her left eyebrow rose. *What the hell?* she thought.

"What do you think he's saying to her?" Alex asked.

Jada threw the dish towel down on the counter and grabbed a fuzzy navel out of the cooler. "Don't know." She hurried out of the kitchen, with Alex quick on her heels. "But I'm 'bout to put a stop to it real quick."

Jada approached the couple, who were oblivious to the fact that she was heading their way. Corey was sucking on a piece of ice, and Miranda was watching him intently.

"I'm dead serious," Corey stated, slurping at the ice in his mouth.

"What's up, y'all?" Jada said, interrupting their private moment. Her eyes searched Miranda's face for some clue as to what the hell was going on.

Miranda refused to give her eye contact.

"Sup, J?" Corey replied nonchalantly. "Crunk party. Jordan enjoying his birthday?"

Jada gave him a heartless half smile. "Of course. Corey, can you do me a favor and take this drink out to Steph?" She handed him the bottle before he had time to protest. "Thanks."

Corey lifted his head up and looked at her, understanding that he was being dismissed. He looked over at the shorter girl. "A'ight, then, Miranda," he stated before leaving the group.

Miranda stepped forward to follow him. "I think I'ma get another drink myself."

"Naw, I think you've had enough drinks," Jada replied, lightly grabbing her friend's arm.

The women were silent as Corey walked out of earshot. Alex stood beside Jada, observing the scene with her arms crossed, shaking her head accusingly.

"What's wrong with y'all?" Miranda looked down at Jada's hand, which was still resting on her forearm.

Jada quickly removed it and eyed her friend. "It looked like Corey was over here macking you," Jada accused.

"And you looked like you were enjoying being macked," Alex added. She had to throw her two cents in.

Miranda sucked her teeth and rolled her eyes at her girls. "Puh-lease! He was over here ragging on Norris. Trust me, there was nothing going on over here. Ain't nobody trying to get at Stephanie's li'l dope boy."

The girls turned to watch Corey and Stephanie's interaction as they stood outside. His arm was around her, and she was beaming up at him like he was a prince.

Jada shook her head. "I don't like him," she stated. "I don't like him at all."

"Well, Stephanie is obviously crazy in love with him, so he must be doing something right," Alex mused.

Jada crossed her arms and shook her head. "Uh-huh. He's full of shit. Something ain't right."

Miranda remained silent, not voicing any opinion on the matter. Alex simply shrugged.

Jada had an uneasy feeling in her stomach, something that told her that the presence of Corey in their lives could mean trouble for the girls. *Could it be his street hustle?* Jada thought. They all knew that Corey was the neighborhood dope man. The girls didn't condone Corey's hustle, and many times they had warned Stephanie against having a relationship with him. But once Steph became pregnant with Damien, all their warnings flew out the window. Steph was too far gone with her emotions and her obsession with the minor-league thug. No one wanted to waste their breath. Jada frequently prayed that her friend would find a better man, someone worthy of her time and love.

"Stop it." Jordan was behind Jada, tweaking her butt. She turned around to face him with a questioning look. She couldn't feign innocence with Jordan. She knew from his expression that he'd seen her surveying the interaction between Steph and Corey with her usual look of disdain.

"It's a party," Jordan reminded her. "Have fun."

Jada kissed him dead on the lips and plucked at this wide nose. "Happy birthday, baby."

Jordan grinned. "Thanks to you, it is."

Chapter 10

Miranda

The Nokia ring tone sounded. Miranda scrambled to find her cell, which was nestled under the bedcovers. After finding it near the pillows, she gazed at the name and number on the caller ID and raised an eyebrow. She quickly glanced at the clock. One thirty in the morning. Was he serious? She pressed the green TALK button.

"Hello?"

"What's up? You still want to fall through?"

"It's late—"

"I told you it would be," he said, cutting her off. "I can get at you some other time. I know you don't want ya' man to be tripping."

Miranda sucked her teeth and climbed out of bed, ready to throw on some decent clothes. "Norris isn't home, so don't be worrying about him."

"Yeah, so call me when you're in your ride and I'll give you directions."

"Okay."

"And, Miranda, don't be telling everything you know to ya' girls and shit. Some shit you keep to yourself."

"Do you think I'm stupid or something?" She grabbed a nearby pair of jeans.

"Just saying, boo."

"Uh-huh. I'll call you back in ten minutes."

"Bet."

The call was disconnected. As she quickly dressed, Miranda tried not to think of the potential damage she was about to cause herself. She desperately needed something to help her escape mentally and emotionally from Norris and the hurt he inflicted upon her. Thinking about it, she chuckled at the irony. How funny it was that the very thing that had started all their troubles was the one outlet Miranda had decided to turn to as a way of avoiding their issues.

Chapter 11

Alex

Things were starting to look up. Alex had secured a sales position at a downtown Decatur boutique and was awaiting the start of classes at American InterContinental University, where she would be taking up fashion design. Being on the track to her dream career, she was feeling pretty good. It also helped that she'd met a pretty decent guy. Mario Johnson was a twenty-six-year old admissions representative at Georgia Piedmont Technical College. When she first met him, he was an admissions rep for AIU. Mario had his own apartment in Clarkston, drove a clean cream-colored PT Cruiser, and was as fine as they come.

Alex had been drawn to his sense of style. Mario was *GQ* all the way. When they met, he was wearing a blue button-down dress shirt with a white collar and white cuffs, blue slacks, and blue Stacy Adams dress shoes. His hair was cut low, with waves so neat and well groomed that Alex couldn't imagine him any other way. His face was devoid of any facial hair, and his chocolate complexion itself turned her on. The man was very well put together and always smelled so manly with his mixture of Sean John cologne and Right Guard deodorant.

Mario had enrolled Alex at AIU. Shortly thereafter, he quit AIU and took his current position at Georgia Piedmont Tech. It had surprised her to hear from him after he quit AIU. She was flattered that he had been so attracted to her that he had made it a point to take down her number before leaving the college. For their first date, he took her to the movies and dinner. Not once during the course of the evening did he try to so much as kiss her. At first she wasn't sure if he was really interested in her, but those misgivings quickly vanished once they had a second, a third, and a fourth date.

Tonight would be date five. Alex wanted to do something special for Mario given how sweet he had been to her in the past few weeks. With Kacey spending the weekend with her boyfriend, Alex had the apartment to herself. She planned to have a simple, candle-lit dinner alone with Mario. Never mind the fact that Alex couldn't cook. This obstacle was easily overcome by purchasing takeout from the neighborhood soul food restaurant, This Is It.

Ever the good friend, Clay willingly drove her to the restaurant and back home. Then he hung around as Alex cleaned her bedroom and prepared for her date.

"You expecting to get laid?" he asked as he tossed a pink teddy bear into the air repetitively while sitting on her bed.

Alex was stunned by his inquiry and threw him a quizzical look as she tied a scarf around her roller-filled head.

Clay caught her look and laughed. "I'm just saying. You cleaning up your room like you're expecting someone to see it. You never clean it when I come over."

"Shut up," Alex retorted.

"It's true."

"So. You ain't nobody. Plus, you already know how junky I can get, so why I gotta try to impress you?"

Alex missed the hurt expression that crossed his face, then quickly vanished. He threw the teddy bear at her, hitting the back of her head.

"Hey!" Alex was caught off guard.

"So the answer to my original question is yes," he said, leaning back against Alex's headboard.

"I didn't say that."

"Yeah. Okay."

Alex walked over to her friend and poked his nose. "Why do you care so much, anyway?"

Clay smiled at her. "I don't."

Alex rolled her eyes and retrieved some underwear from her dresser drawer. "Why are you still here?"

"You want me to leave?" he asked, sitting up.

"If you're going to be rude, meanie."

Clay laughed at her and leaned back once more. "That wasn't mean, crybaby. If you fuck him, you fuck him."

"Ugh! Is that all you're thinking about?"

"That's all he's going to be thinking about. Trust me."

Alex headed toward the door, shaking her head. "It's so not going down."

She went into the bathroom and turned on the shower. Only pushing the bathroom door up slightly, she took off her clothes and stepped into the warmth of the water. Her nostrils filled with the scent of grapefruit as she began to lather herself with Dove body wash. *Clay is tripping,* Alex thought to herself. So far Mario had been a perfect gentleman, and she had no reason to expect him to behave any differently tonight. Sure, she was creating a very intimate mood. Sure, she was planning on wearing a very revealing slip dress. Sure, she secretly wished he would hold her tighter and longer whenever he hugged her. But all of that was irrelevant. *Right?*

Alex closed her eyes and let the water cascade down her back. Her sexual experiences were very limited, and she was a little nervous about the prospect of going there with Mario. Mainly, she feared disappointing him. As fine as he was, Alex knew that he must be getting offers from women left and right. How could she compare to the older, more experienced women he'd sexed?

"You gonna stay in here forever?"

Alex blinked profusely and turned her head to the sound of his voice. Stunned, she stuck her head out of the shower curtain. Clay sat smiling back at her, perched atop the toilet seat, his figure enveloped by the steam from the shower.

"That's a little rude, you know," she told him, ducking back into the shower.

"You left the door open. Sheesh. What? Are you afraid I'll see your goodies?"

Alex snickered behind the shower curtain.

"Anyway, I'm about to bounce," Clay informed her. "I'll let you get ready for ole boy."

Alex quickly rinsed off, turned off the water, and reached for her towel, which she thought she'd hung over the shower rod. She sucked her teeth and looked up to see Clay's hand holding the pink terry-cloth towel. She grabbed it, wrapped it around her body, and pulled back the shower curtain.

There he stood, Clayton Paul, her longtime friend turned hottie, staring her dead in the eyes at such a vulnerable moment.

"Thank you," she said softly, barely able to utter the words.

Alex was unsure of what she was feeling. Why did looking at Clay give her stomach butterflies? He just stood there, almost as if he was expecting her to do or say something, and when the expected failed to occur, he lowered his eyes and stepped backward.

"I'll get at you tomorrow," he said as she stepped out of the tub.

Alex nodded. "Okay, friend. Thanks for coming over."

"Yep."

He quickly turned from her and left the bathroom. Alex listened as he made his way through the apartment and let himself out the front door. She hadn't realized that she'd been holding her breath. The awkwardness of the moment lingered with her. She was unsure of what the encounter meant. Perhaps Clay had wanted to tell her something but just couldn't find the words. That would explain his stares and his lost expression. Hurriedly, Alex focused on getting herself dressed and ready for her night with Mario.

Chapter 12

Candace

For the next few weeks, Candace and Khalil's relationship was hot and heavy. At any and every opportune moment the two of them were together. Candace never questioned Khalil as to where Sheila was, and Khalil never expressed an interest in Quincy's existence. Khalil sent her flowers at work for no apparent reason, continued to buy her lunch on a daily basis, and escorted her to various upscale restaurants in Midtown on the weekends. He made her feel so happy and special that Candace almost lost track of the fact that she was only borrowing this man and his affection.

She was becoming so involved that she barely had time to chill with the girls. Her absence had obviously been noticed, given the many messages and texts she'd received recently. So when Stephanie asked her to go to lunch one Saturday, she felt obligated to attend. It wouldn't do any good to piss off the girls any more than she already had.

The duo met at the O'Charley's on Northlake Parkway. Stephanie had requested Chili's, but Candace was not in the mood for baby back ribs. Settled in a corner booth and munching on spinach dip, Candace was trying to focus on their cordial conversation. In the back of her mind she was really awaiting the text she knew would soon come. She had told Khalil to get at her during the early afternoon so they could hook up for a movie. She was anxious to see him again, especially after the way he'd put it on her the night before.

"There's something I have to tell you," Stephanie was saying.

Candace shook her head free of her sensual memories and focused on her friend. "Huh?"

"There's something I gotta tell you. And I haven't told Jada or Alex, because both of them would just be disappointed."

"What's wrong?" Candace became concerned. Stephanie's eyes were starting to well up, and Candace began to assume the worst. She reached out and touched Stephanie's hand softly. "What is it, Steph? Whatever it is, we can work through it together."

"I'm pregnant," Stephanie whispered. "I'm pregnant again."

"By Corey?"

Stephanie shot Candace a hurt look. "Of course by Corey. What the hell kind of question is that?"

"I was just asking. So how far along are you?"

"Six weeks. Six fuckin' weeks."

"Does he know?"

Stephanie shook her head and looked away. "He's barely helping with Damien. What's he going to say or do if I tell him I'm expecting another kid? You're the first person I've told."

Candace picked up a chip and nibbled at it in contemplation. "Why do you think that Jada and Alex would be disappointed?"

"You know them. Alex is the last adult virgin, and Jada is just Ms. Goody-Goody. They wouldn't understand."

"Shit happens," Candace stated bluntly. "And while I don't necessarily condone your relationship with Corey's ass, either, I don't think you should feel like any of us would shun you for this." Candace leaned forward and touched Stephanie's hand once more. "We love you, girlie, and the girls will always have your back."

Stephanie gave her a weak smile and nodded. "I know. I just needed an empathetic ear right now. I know I can count on all my girls."

They shared a smile and focused their attention on the entrées being placed before them. Neither spoke for several moments, each caught up in her own thoughts and her meal. Stephanie was busy wondering how she was going to tell her mother she was knocked up again. Candace was becoming irritated because her phone had yet to vibrate.

"So what are you going to do?" Candace asked, breaking the silence.

Stephanie shrugged. "I'm going to leave my mom's house, for one thing. She loves Damien, but she was not pleased with me when I first told her about him."

"Can you afford your own place?"

"Maybe somewhere, but nowhere decent, you know what I mean?"

Candace nodded.

"I'll figure something out," Stephanie said with feigned confidence.

"That which doesn't kill us makes us stronger," Candace offered.

Stephanie simply nodded and polished off her pasta. Candace silently said a quick prayer for her girl and was guiltily thankful that she wasn't in Steph's shoes. It had never been a goal of Candace's to have children. She didn't feel like she possessed any maternal instincts. She saw her life filled with traveling, a glamorous legal career, and shopping. Crying babies, soiled diapers, and childhood illnesses just didn't fit into her plan.

After lunch the girls hugged, said their good-byes, and rode off in their respective cars. As Candace headed toward 285, she pulled out her cell and dialed a familiar number. She was surprised when her call was sent straight to voice mail. Too pissed to leave a message, she simply clicked the phone shut and drove home to her husband.

Quincy was sitting on the couch, in his favorite spot, with his cordless PlayStation controller, playing *Madden,* when she walked in. Her eyes fell upon the dishes resting in the sink as she walked through the kitchen and into the living room. It was so typical of him to ignore the necessary housework and sit around playing all afternoon. Candace held her tongue, though, not wanting to spark an argument. She was grateful that he'd finally gotten a new job. His position with UPS didn't pay as much as his BellSouth gig, but income was income.

"What's up?" he asked her as she sat beside him on the couch.

"Nothing."

"Where you been?"

"Since when have you taken an interest in where I go and what I do?"

Quincy shot her a look and sucked his teeth.

Candace sat silently for a moment, watching the football game on the screen. "I had lunch with Stephanie," she finally said.

"You didn't invite me."

"Didn't know you wanted to go."

Quincy playfully pushed her leg, and Candace giggled. He paused the game and put his arm around her. Licking her left ear, he whispered to her, "I'm gon' tell you where I wanna go."

Candace raised an eyebrow. "Where's that?"

"Trapeze."

Candace crinkled her nose and cocked her head to the side, trying to understand where the conversation was going. She had heard of the popular adult club but knew of no one who had actually gone. She looked at her husband askance.

"Don't be looking like you not interested," he teased her. "You know you wanna go."

"Why you want to go there?" she questioned.

"To spice shit up," he said earnestly. "Ain't nothing wrong with that, is there?"

Candace considered it. She'd be lying if she said she wasn't at least curious as to what went on in the private club. Since the loss of his BellSouth job, there had been a lack of romance and affection between herself and Quincy. She looked at her husband. He was no Khalil, and there was little sexual attraction there. Deep down, Candace wanted to make her marriage work, if for no other reason than to save face with her parents. Perhaps this adventure would add a little spice to their relationship.

"Man, imagine all the buck naked chicks walking around that place," Quincy thought aloud, throwing his head back on the couch in bewilderment. He nudged her. "You might see something you like."

Candace rolled her eyes and dismissed the idea. Quincy's real intentions were becoming evident to her. "Ain't nobody trying to have no threesome," she said, shooting down his hopes and dreams.

Quincy laughed and grabbed her playfully, trying to nibble on the side of her neck. He knew that was her spot. "Aww, come on. Don't act like that. It ain't about that."

Candace tried to free herself from his embrace, but Quincy's hold was firm. She maneuvered her neck, trying to avoid contact with his tongue. She was in no mood for his sexual advances. "Stop, Q." She elbowed him in his gut. "Quit it."

Quincy started tickling her and didn't let up until she erupted in fits of laughter. Trying to squirm away from him, Candace ended up falling to the floor. Quincy towered over her, tickling away and showing no mercy.

"Okay," she said breathlessly, relenting. "Okay. We can go."

Quincy ceased his torture and smiled wickedly at his wife. "When?"

Candace sat upright on the floor and struggled to even out her breathing. "Let's look it up online first to see how much it costs to get in."

Quincy jumped up from the floor and moved toward the stairs.

"Where you going?" she called after him.

"To check it out now."

Candace rose from the floor and followed her eager spouse up the stairs and to their guest room, where the computer was set up. Quincy was already clicking on the big *E*.

"Damn, you act like you want to go right this minute," Candace stated, sitting on the bed next to the desk.

Quincy winked at her. "No time like the present."

Candace sucked her teeth as she watched Quincy do a Yahoo search for the club. Finding it listed, Quincy clicked on the link and bypassed the intro page. Taking a look at the admission prices, Quincy sucked in his breath.

"What?" Candace asked, leaning in closer to take a look at the screen.

"Damn! This shit costs a grip for a dude," Quincy stated. "Couples and single men cost the most. Single chicks have it made."

Quincy was shaking his head, and Candace understood his meaning. Their finances were tight these days due to their recent setback. Lavish spending was not feasible, and judging by Quincy's face and the price list waving on the screen to them, Candace knew that they would not be making a trip to Trapeze anytime soon.

Candace stood up and placed her arms around Quincy's neck. "Well, we can do something else," she said sweetly.

"What's that?"

"We can join a Web site and meet other couples that might wanna hook up or something."

Quincy turned around and looked at his wife. "A swinger's Web site?"

Candace smiled devilishly. "It's like bringing Trapeze to us."

Quincy began clicking the keyboard once more. "You ain't said nothing but a word, boo. Nothing but a word."

Chapter 13

Stephanie

She wasn't sure what she was going to say. She hadn't even alerted him that anything was going on when she called to say that she was coming over. Grateful that he hadn't acted like an ass when she called, Stephanie was feeling a little confident that there wouldn't be a big scene between the two of them. Taking a deep breath, Stephanie took the familiar path to Corey's apartment and raised her fist to knock on the door. She paused with her fist in the air, opened her palm, and rested it against the heavy door. Her left hand grabbed at her stomach as a wave of nausea hit her. Or was it her nerves? Or perhaps it was both.

What am I doing? she asked herself. *What the hell am I doing having another baby with a man that acts like he can't even stand me half of the time?* She contemplated turning around and going home. But determined to stand her ground and not be a punk, she raised her hand again and knocked on her boyfriend's door. She knocked twice before Corey answered.

"What up?" he greeted her after opening the door, and then he quickly walked toward the kitchen.

Stephanie entered the living room and closed the door behind her. She started to follow him into the kitchen, but something began to nag at her senses. Stephanie just wasn't sure what it was. Looking around, surveying the room for any sign that something was amiss, Stephanie sat down on the comfortable couch.

Corey entered the room, drinking a Heineken, and sat next to her. "What up?" he repeated.

Stephanie looked up at her longtime boyfriend and reached up to hug him. Corey put one arm around her and gave her a half hug in return. As she snuggled up to him, Stephanie's senses were heightened. She pulled her head back slightly, making her nose even with his neck. *Uh-huh,* she thought to herself, recognizing a familiar scent lingering on him that was certainly not masculine.

Stephanie pulled away from him and leaned back against the couch. "What you been up to?"

Corey shrugged. "Nada. Handling business. Making some money. What's good?"

"I'm pregnant." She just blurted it out in an effort to get it over with. She stared at her hands, waiting for the vulgarities to pour from Corey's mouth.

Instead, all she got was laughter. Corey was cracking up, as if she'd told a world-class joke. "Stop playing," he managed to say.

"I'm not playing," she said curtly. "And I wish you'd stop laughing at me."

Corey looked over at her and searched her face for the truth. "Oh, shit. For real?" Stephanie wasn't sure if that was a smile she saw forming at the corner of his lips.

"For real." She stared at him. "What you thinking?"

Corey sat his beer on the carpet and rubbed his hands together. "Shit! I hope it's a girl this time."

Stephanie leaned toward him and rubbed his head. "You're not mad?"

He considered her question before pulling her toward him and giving her a bear hug. "Naw, I ain't mad. Shit, it takes two, and I'm a man. Plus, I needa start taking better care of my shorty and my girl. I'm on top of my game deez days, baby, so money ain't shit."

Stephanie knew better than to inquire about Corey's "game." Instead, she decided to push further to see if today was really her lucky day. "I haven't told my mom yet. You know she's going to be pissed. I think she's gon' put us out."

Corey sighed. Stephanie felt his body tense up as her unasked question sank into his mind.

"Tell you what," he said, kissing her forehead. "Let's try to do this family thing. You and D can move in here, and we'll see 'bout getting a bigger place before the baby's born."

Stephanie pulled away from him and stared at the dark brother in disbelief. She had waited a long time for Corey to invite her to move in, and the day had finally come. Ecstatic about this pending change in their relationship, Stephanie consciously decided to overlook her suspicion regarding Corey's activities prior to her arrival and that hint of perfume resting on his neck. Now that they would be living together, Stephanie would no longer have to worry about Corey and his little indiscretions. In her mind, they were one step closer to getting married and being a real family.

"You sure about this?" She needed reassurance.

"Yeah, Ma. I'm sure."

Stephanie crawled up on top of him and began to kiss his lips, cheeks, nose, and forehead. Corey's hands found their way underneath her shirt.

"Thank you, baby. Thank you." She kissed his left ear as he began to ease her jeans down.

"You wanna thank me?" he asked.

"Mmm-hmm."

He released himself from his joggers, exposing his erection. "Go 'head and thank me, then."

Stephanie wasn't really in the mood for sexual activity. But feeling it was best to play it cool and keep him happy, she raised her hips to guide him into her, all the while trying not to think about where his dick had been before she arrived.

Chapter 14

Miranda

Norris strolled into the bedroom, apparently oblivious to the stench in the room. Miranda ignored his presence, lying peacefully on their bed, reading the new *Star* magazine. Her husband sat on the edge of the bed and looked at her as if he was waiting for her to acknowledge him. Miranda said nothing. As she turned a page of her magazine, Norris reached over and grabbed the periodical from her.

"What the fuck?" she questioned, finally addressing the man.

"Yeah, what the fuck?" he repeated after her. "You act like you ain't even noticed me sitting here."

Not interested in his fake need for attention, Miranda reached for her magazine. Norris snatched it back out of her reach. "What do you want me to say, Norris? Welcome home, sweetie? I missed you? You want me to lie to you?"

Norris threw the magazine at her, and it hit her in the face. She grabbed it and tried to focus her attention back on the story about Britney Spears.

"Any other nigga goes home to his wife, he gets a fuckin' hug and kiss and some dinner," Norris spat out. "I don't get shit from you."

"You don't give shit, either," Miranda muttered, not realizing that she'd vocalized the thought.

"What did you say?" Norris crawled up on the bed, snatched the magazine away once more, and held Miranda's neck against the headboard with one hand. "What the fuck did you say?"

Miranda shook her head, her eyes staring blankly at Norris. She was a little numb given the pressure he was applying to her neck and simply sat there staring at him as his rage grew.

"Is it too much to ask for my *wife* to cook dinner for a change? To be affectionate?"

He shook her a little, yet Miranda still failed to respond to his ranting. For a second, they sat staring into each other's eyes, each trying to figure out what the other was thinking. Bored with her unresponsiveness, Norris released his grip and walked out of the room.

Miranda felt her neck and shook her head from side to side. She was so over him bullying her. Determined to talk to him in a civilized manner, Miranda rose from the bed and followed Norris into the kitchen.

He was reaching for a can of salmon in the pantry when she entered. Thinking it would be a sign of peace, she retrieved an egg, an onion, and a bell pepper from the refrigerator. As she placed the items on the counter, Norris lightly shoved her out of the way.

"I don't need your help," he told her. "A nigga nearly gotta beg you to fix him some food. I don't need that shit. I can take care of myself. I don't need your sorry ass."

"My sorry ass? Are you kidding me, Norris? I have always taken care of you and our home. How you gonna act like that's not true?"

"It hasn't been true lately, has it?" He used the electric can opener to open the salmon.

Miranda let the hum of the machine calm her down. The noise gave her a chance to think of what she would say next. The objective was not to argue or fight. To achieve this, she had to set the tone, rather than setting Norris off. She watched Norris pour the fish mush into a bowl. Grabbing a knife from the nearby cutting block and the cutting board, Miranda set up an area to dice the onion.

"I just want to help, Norris," she said, chopping the vegetable into tiny pieces. "I'm sorry. I didn't mean to upset you. I just want to help you with dinner and try to see what we can do to make things better."

Norris chuckled. "You just want to help Norris, huh?"

Miranda ignored his sarcasm and kept on chopping and talking. "Things aren't right between us, Norris. . . . Anybody can see that. We got married for a reason, and I think that if we really tried to make it work . . . it could."

Norris loudly slammed a pot down onto the stove top, the water in it sloshing over the sides.

Miranda jumped a little but did not look up at her husband. Still chopping, she continued on with her speech. "I think you love me, Norris, and I love you, you know. . . . We just need to . . . I don't know. Maybe we can go to counseling or something to—"

"Shut up!" Norris demanded, cutting her off. "What the fuck is wrong with you? Have you been watching *Oprah* or something?"

Miranda shook her head and reached for the bell pepper. "I'm just trying to preserve our marriage. That's all."

Norris poured white rice into the boiling pot, his eyes glued to his frantically chopping wife. "Preserve our marriage, huh? What do you think is wrong with us, M? Let me guess. You think I'm a bad husband."

"I didn't say that," she protested. "It's not just you. It's me too."

"Damn right it's you too," he agreed, walking up closely behind her. "It's you that always looks at me like I'm a fuckin' failure every time I have a setback. It's you that thinks you're better than me, with your two fuckin' jobs, like I can't manage to take care of my family."

Miranda stopped cutting. "Nobody called you a failure. I have only tried to be a good wife . . . to be helpful."

"You are helpful in making a nigga feel like he ain't shit," he whispered into her ear. "You think I don't know that you talk shit about me to your phony-ass girls and to your parents? Your parents don't even respect me as a man, because of *you* and your bright idea for us to move in with them like some li'l-ass kids."

Knife firmly in hand and tired of listening to her husband talk down to her like she was the root of all their problems, Miranda spun around quickly, aiming at his dick. "I am so fuckin' tired of you talking to me like I ain't shit," she told him.

Norris began backing away from her, but Miranda steadily approached him, the sharp knife dangerously close to his member.

"Put that fuckin' shit down, man. . . . Stop playing," Norris said weakly.

"Fuck you, Norris." She backed him up against the counter. "Fuck you, fuck you, fuck you. I am so tired of the way you walk around here acting like you are the only one suffering. You think I *wanted* to live with my parents? *Hell no!* But I swallowed my own pride and asked them for the favor for *us!* For us, Norris. Just till we could do better."

"I didn't ask you to do that shit."

"You didn't have to! You see, that's the kind of shit you do when you love someone . . . when you're committed to your relationship. You do whatever you gotta do to keep that shit intact, and that's what I did, or at least that's what I was trying to do."

"So what you trying to prove now by holding a fuckin' knife to my balls?"

Miranda stared at him in disbelief, shocked that he had the audacity to still be talking shit to her as she stood before him, threatening his manhood. They stood silently, squaring off and willing the other to say something.

"I've been a good wife to you, Norris," Miranda stated. "I've been faithful, supportive, and caring. I am not your enemy, Norris. I'm your partner, your wife. I'm your fuckin' wife!"

Norris blinked at her and said nothing.

Miranda lifted the knife to his neck, and she saw him flinch slightly. It felt good to be in control for a change. Pressing the knife lightly against his skin, she stared directly into his eyes. "I've been a good wife, Norris," she said slowly for effect. "But if you ever put your hands on me again, I swear that I will fuckin' kill you. I will slice your shit from here to there"—she dragged the knife across his neck—"should you ever, ever, ever put your fuckin' hands on me again. Do you understand?"

Norris gave her a sinister half smile. "Fuck you, bitch." He quickly shoved her backward.

Then he tried to rush her and extract the knife from her hand, but Miranda's movements were so frantic and swift that he was unsuccessful. In their struggle, Miranda managed to slice her husband across his left cheek. Surprised at the sting of the cut, Norris reached up to touch his face. Blood dripped from his fingers.

Miranda watched his movements, shocked at herself for
having actually wounded him. The anger in his eyes told her
that she had better do something quickly. Turning to run
from the room, Miranda was not quick enough. Norris was
fast on her heels, pulling her left leg and causing her to hit
the floor. She lost her grip on the knife, and Norris kicked
it away before she could reach for it. He turned her over,
and Miranda struggled to free herself from his grasp. She
was unsuccessful. He pulled her glasses off her face, and she
began to protest. Ignoring her, Norris threw the glasses to the
floor and stepped on them.

"Nooo . . . Norris, no!" She could barely see without the
glasses.

"You cut me!" he spat at her. "You fuckin' cut me!"

He kicked her swiftly in her right side once, twice, three
times. Miranda whimpered. Her hands flailed this way and
that as she tried to grab his leg to get him to stop. But he
wouldn't.

Norris kept kicking and kicking in the same tender spot
over and over. Miranda kept trying to scramble away from
his blows and raise herself from the floor. Each time, Norris
simply knocked her right back down.

"Stupid bitch," he yelled at her. "Trying to preserve our
marriage? Preserve this shit!" Norris kicked her extremely
hard so that his final blow would have a lasting effect.

Miranda screamed out in pain. Not only was her side
aching from the abuse, but horrid cramps were beginning to
overcome her abdomen. She was doubled over in pain. She
held her left hand up in surrender, pleading with Norris to
leave her alone.

"I hope you lay there and bleed to death." He touched his
face again and was completely astonished by the fact that she
had actually cut him.

Bleed to death. Miranda concentrated on his last words.
Was she bleeding? She was unaware if she was. Only the
cramping and aching in her side could she focus on. Through
her blurred vision she watched the figure of Norris exit the
kitchen. She could hear him let himself out of the apartment.
Sore, bruised, and in excruciating pain, she struggled to

lean over to feel around underneath her. Sure enough, her lounging pants were damp. Apparently, she was bleeding. As the realization hit her, so did a forceful tear through her abdomen, down to her lower stomach. Then Miranda experienced a pulling feeling in her lower abdomen.

"Ahhh," she screamed out, overcome by the pain. "Help me! Please. Somebody . . ."

She laid her head back on the linoleum floor, feeling defeated. No one was going to hear her. Norris had literally left her there to bleed to death. Just as she was beginning to lose consciousness, Miranda heard a voice.

"Hello? Ma'am?"

Was she hallucinating? The unfamiliar voice was that of a female. *Where's it coming from?* she wondered. Miranda continued to lie on the floor, cradling her bruised side and trying not to pass out before she could see who it was that was calling out to her.

"Hello? Oh my God!" A woman was beside her, touching her face and sounding completely taken aback. "Why did you let him do this to you?" she was asking. "Oh my God. Howard! Howard!"

The woman was calling out to an accomplice. Miranda couldn't make out who they were as they stood over her and called 911. The woman asked her a series of questions, which she couldn't answer, because she was gradually fading away. Just as sirens could be heard in the distance, Miranda heard the woman speak to her male partner.

"What kind of man does shit like this?"

That was the last thing she heard before slipping into the darkness.

Chapter 15

Jada

Jada stood there in a state of shock. She knew that things weren't good between them, but she had no idea that things were this bad. The room was cold and sterile, and the many machines were steadily beeping and clicking. Miranda was lying still on the bed, cords hanging from her all over. They'd just wheeled her in from surgery, where they'd repaired the broken ribs that her husband had caused her. Miranda was still asleep from the anesthesia.

Watching the frail woman, all bandaged up and laid out, Jada had to fight back her tears. Why the hell did you stay with him? Jada wondered of her friend. Anyone would be a fool to believe that this was the first time Norris had abused her. Jada was just grateful that he hadn't succeeded in killing her. Her thoughts were interrupted by the creak of the door. A tall, slender woman and a muscular man whom she'd never met entered the room.

"Hi," the woman said softly. "I'm Tasha, and this is my boyfriend, Howard. We're her neighbors."

Jada sighed and reached out to shake the pretty woman's hand. The man also held his out, and Jada obligingly shook it too.

"I'm Jada, one of her best friends," Jada said. "She has me listed as her emergency contact on something in her purse."

"It's good to know that she has some friends that love her," Tasha said solemnly. "Because her husband obviously doesn't."

"Tasha," Howard said, a note of warning in his voice.

"I'm just saying."

"It's okay," Jada offered. "You can be candid with me. The girls knew that she was having marital problems, but this . . ." Jada trailed off and looked at her battered friend. It was all so unbelievable. "This was totally unexpected."

Tasha and Howard shared a look, which Jada didn't miss. Howard grabbed Tasha's hand as she looked Jada squarely in the eyes.

"Or perhaps not?" Jada said, more as a question than a statement.

Tasha cleared her throat. "Look, Jada, since you are one of her best friends, I want to encourage you to, um . . . well, encourage her to leave that asshole. This isn't their first altercation. We hear them arguing all the time—"

"Everybody argues," Jada interjected.

"Yeah, but everybody doesn't get their ass kicked on a regular basis. There's arguing, and then there's abuse. And your girl is constantly being abused."

"If you thought he was hurting her, why didn't you ever call the police?"

"We like to mind our own business," Howard answered.

"Mind your own business?" Jada was becoming upset with the couple. "You don't think that if you'd done something before, maybe all of this could have been avoided?"

"With all due respect, ma'am, this incident isn't because of our negligence," Howard replied. "Remember that your girl decided to stick around and put up with this shit. At any time she could've said enough was enough, but she didn't."

"We went over to her place this time because we could hear her calling for help," Tasha stated. "I was scared that he'd nearly killed her this time. I guess I was right."

Jada nodded her head, coming to terms with reality. They were right. It wasn't their fault that Miranda was in this predicament. But Jada still wished that the good neighbors had had the sense to call the police during prior incidents. Maybe Norris could have been arrested, and Miranda wouldn't be lying in this hospital, all broken up.

"Thank you," Jada said softly. "Thank you for helping her."

Tasha nodded. "I just hope that she is smart enough to go ahead and leave him. She was bleeding so profusely, I was afraid that she really would die."

Jada took a deep breath, tears trailing from her eyes, despite her fight to hold them in. "He caused her to have a miscarriage. Apparently, she was six weeks pregnant."

Tasha gasped and quickly moved to hug Jada. The two embraced in silence before Tasha pulled away and extended her apologies for Miranda's loss. Shortly after, the couple left Jada to cry over Miranda in private. Sitting in the chair next to her friend's bed, she said a silent prayer for the girl, mirroring the hopes of Tasha. She prayed that Miranda would have the presence of mind to leave Norris's trifling ass.

Chapter 16

Alex

The relationship was going smoothly. Alex and Mario were getting closer and enjoying each other's company more frequently. Unfortunately, Alex hadn't gotten up the nerve to seal the deal. But she was glad to see that he was still interested in her, nonetheless. Mario would call several times a day just to say hi and send text messages to let her know that he was thinking about her. Alex had never felt more special. Between school, work, and her budding relationship, Alex's time was consumed. She hadn't spent much time lately hanging out with the girls or chilling with Clay. Clay was beginning to notice her absence.

Just as Alex was on her way home from school, Clay called her cell with attitude lacing his voice.

"Oh, shit! She's alive," he commented when she answered the phone.

Alex looked both ways before she walked across East College Avenue, sucked her teeth, and rolled her eyes. "Whatever. What's up?"

"What's up is that I haven't heard from you in a minute. Ya' boy got you going like that?"

"Don't be jealous," Alex joked.

Clay didn't respond.

"What are you doing?" Alex asked him.

"Getting dressed."

"Where you going?"

"To the movies."

Alex smiled. "Want me to come with?"

Clay laughed, amused that she had invited herself along. "Not unless you mind being the oddball."

"What's that 'posed to mean?"

"I have a date."

Alex made a right into her apartment complex, then walked along the sidewalk to her apartment. She was surprised to hear that Clay had plans. "Who you going out with?"

"Nobody you know. But, hey, I just wanted to try and get at you, since you don't know how to return calls."

"'Kay. You can come over when you get done with your date if you want to. I'll be here."

Clay made a funny sound before responding. "Yeah, I'll keep that in mind. Lata."

The call was disconnected. Alex let herself into her apartment, threw her book bag on the floor, and slammed the door behind her. Mario was hanging out with his boys for the night, and Alex wasn't sure what was up with her girls. Her Friday night was starting to look a little bit bleak.

Alex sauntered into the kitchen and surveyed the contents of the refrigerator. Settling on leftover spaghetti, she fixed herself a plate, placed it in the microwave, and went off to her room to get comfortable. As she sat on the bed to remove her shoes, she pulled out her cell and dialed a familiar number. There were three rings before she answered.

"What's up, stranger?" Jada's voice boomed.

Alex removed her jeans and smiled. "Hey, girl. What's poppin'?"

"Nothing, honey child. I'm waiting on Jordan."

"Y'all going out?" Alex asked with a twinge of disappointment in her voice.

"Nope. We're gonna make it a Blockbuster night. I'm tired, girl. It's been a long week."

"Oh yeah?"

"What you doing at home? I'm surprised you don't have a date."

Alex pulled on a pair of shorts from a nearby drawer and lay back on her bed, missing the ding of the microwave. "Mario's having boys' night. Kacey ain't here—"

"Kacey ain't ever there. You sure you even have a room-mate?"

Alex laughed. "I'm sure she's paying her half of the rent. But, girl, get this. . . . Clay has a date."

"Your boy? What? Is that unusual?"

Alex turned over on her side and considered Jada's questions. "No . . . I mean . . . I'm just used to being able to hang out with him when I want to."

Jada sucked her teeth. "That sounds a li'l bit selfish, girl."

"Nuh-uh. I'm a princess and—"

"Oh, girl, please. I gotta go, with all that princess shit. Look, all us girls needa get together real soon. So much has been going on. I'll organize something. 'Kay?"

Alex sat up on the bed, ready to end the call. "All right. Bye, girl."

Clicking the phone shut, Alex got up and headed to the kitchen. She removed her plate from the microwave, checked the temperature of the food, and decided it was fine for her. As she sat at the kitchen counter and ate, she thought about Clay. She wondered what movie he'd gone to see and what the chick whom he was with was like. Alex mulled over Jada's statement that she was selfish for wanting Clay at her disposal.

That's just the nature of our relationship, she thought, reasoning with herself. *Clay is always there when I need him.* Having resolved that in her mind, she polished off her dinner and returned to her bedroom. Settling into bed, she turned on her television, prepared to watch TV Land reruns until she fell asleep. In the back of her mind, she was sure that Clay would show up later that night.

At some point, she drifted off. She was startled awake by the ringing of her phone. Regaining consciousness, she fumbled around in the bedcovers, looking for the hot pink phone. Not wanting to miss the call, she hurriedly flipped the phone open and gave a sheepish hello.

"You sleeping?" It was Clay.

Alex rubbed her eyes and yawned. "I was. What's up?"

"I'm down the street. Thought I'd see if you were still up. I got Krispy Kremes."

Alex smiled. "Come on, boy."

Within minutes, Clay was sauntering through her front door with the doughnut box in tow. He sat the box on the kitchen counter and flipped open the top. "Whatever you want, I got it."

Alex peeked into the box and did a giddy schoolgirl dance as she reached for a cream-filled doughnut. "Mmm. This is so good. You are the best."

Clay smiled. "I know."

He walked into the living room, kicked off his shoes, and plopped down on the sofa, getting comfortable. Alex stretched out over the armchair and devoured her doughnut.

"How'd your little date go?"

Clay threw his head back on a throw pillow and smiled. "It was good. I think she's digging me."

"It must not have been too good, 'cause you're over here now."

"Trust me," he said with a confidence that would have seemed arrogant to anyone else. "If I wanted to stay over, I could have."

"Uh-huh," Alex teased him. "So why didn't you, then?"

Clay looked over at the ebony beauty. "Because I respect her, and I want to see where this is going to go."

Sensing that Clay was serious about this, Alex looked at her friend intently. She wasn't sure what to say next. Clay had such an earnest look on his face.

"You're serious about her?" Alex asked him.

Clay shrugged. "I mean, it could get there. I don't wanna ruin it before I get the chance to see. I wanna be like you."

Alex raised her eyebrow. "Like me?"

"Yeah. Booed up."

Alex cut her eyes at him. "Whatever."

"So where's your boy? Why weren't you with him tonight?"

Alex sat up straight in the chair and wiped her hands against each other, ridding them of the sugary crumbs of the doughnut. "He had boys' night with his friends." She shrugged noncommittally. "I'll probably see him some time tomorrow."

"So did you?"

"Did I what?"

Clay gave her the evil eye. "Don't act. Did you give him some ass or what?"

Alex's eyes grew big. She was shocked by Clay's bluntness. She pouted her lips and crossed her arms, giving him a hurt expression. "You don't have to say it like that."

"Like what? It is what it is."

She sucked her teeth. "Well, it *isn't* anything, then."

"So you didn't do it?"

Alex shook her head. "No. I don't know. . . . I just couldn't."

Clay made a noise that sounded like a sigh to Alex. She didn't give him eye contact and hoped that he wouldn't press the issue further.

"Good. You should wait. Get to know him a little better and see where his head's at. See if he can put up with you for longer than three months."

"So what? You're playing my daddy now?"

Clay cocked his head to the side. "You'd like that, huh? Calling me Daddy?"

Alex reached over and slapped Clay's leg playfully. "Shut up! Ain't nobody calling you Daddy . . . unless you get your little girlfriend pregnant."

Clay grabbed Alex's hand and pulled her over to the sofa. He began to tickle her mercilessly, and Alex broke into a fit of hysterical laughter.

"You jealous of my li'l girlfriend or something?" he asked her. "You don't like me going out with someone that isn't you?"

He stopped tickling her and just sat staring at her face, as if he was waiting for an answer. Alex tried to compose herself, as the question he had asked finally sank into her head. She coughed away her laughter and sat upright on the sofa.

"You're crazy," she said, trying to play it off.

"Am I?"

When Alex didn't respond, Clay cleared his throat and moved to the edge of the sofa. "Look, I think there's something that needs to be said," he stated. "For a long time I've felt like we've skirted around this issue, but I can't do that anymore."

Alex took a deep breath and leaned back against the sofa cushion, giving Clay her full attention.

"We're best friends," he began. "We've been friends for a long time. I know everything about you, and you know everything about me. And, uh . . . I think friendship is a very solid foundation. I don't know what you've been feeling over the years. But I know what I've been feeling, and . . . well, I think it's either now or never—"

Ring. Ring. Ring. Alex's cell interrupted Clay's speech. Alex reached to grab it and held a finger up to Clay, indicating that he should give her just a moment.

"Hey, Mario. Nothing. Now? Um, okay. Yeah. That's fine. I'm here."

She ended the call and looked up at Clay. "Um, I'm sorry."

Clay reached for his shoes. "I guess it's never."

Alex was speechless. She watched as Clay put his shoes on and cleaned up their mess from the doughnuts. When he was ready to leave, she walked him over to the door.

"Clay, don't be mad. We can talk later."

He kissed her on the forehead. "It's cool. I think that was a sign for me to keep my thoughts to myself. It's all good."

Before she could respond, he opened the door to leave. He started to pull the door closed behind him, then stopped and looked back at her. "By the way, you know this is a booty call for him, right? It's late. You don't really think he's coming over here for some conversation after drinking all night, do you?"

With that, he closed the door, leaving Alex with her thoughts.

Chapter 17

Miranda

Miranda was dressed and sitting on the hospital bed when Jada walked into the room. Her body looked frail as she sat slumped over. She jutted her chin out and slowly rose from the bed.

"Thanks for the ride," she said to Jada.

"No problem," Jada responded lightly. "Where am I taking you?"

"Home."

"No."

Miranda stood at the side of the bed, staring at the plastic hospital bag containing her belongings. She sighed. "Don't do this, Jada. Please."

"You don't do this, Miranda. You cannot go back to that man. You can't go back to that house."

"It's where I live."

"Can't you go stay with your parents?"

"No. I don't want them to know."

Jada walked over to Miranda and gingerly cupped her face, bringing them eye to eye.

"You cannot go back to that man, Miranda. You just cannot. You're lucky it was only a couple of ribs this time, girl. But next time, next time that man *will* kill you."

Miranda shook her head. "No, he won't. He's probably gone for good. I'm not worried about him, and I'm not letting him run me away from the home I pay for."

Miranda moved away from Jada, grabbed her bag, and headed for the door. "And please don't say anything to the other girls about this. That's if you haven't already."

"Miranda," Jada called out to her friend's retreating figure.

Miranda turned around and looked at her.

"You don't want anyone to know what's up with you, you keep letting this dude pound on you, and you expect me to take you back to him? I'm not doing it, girl. I don't want any part of this."

Jada moved to exit the room, but Miranda grabbed her arm before she could walk past her. "You're really not going to take me home? You told me you'd give me a lift."

"That was before I knew your intention was to go back to him. If you want me to take you there just to get your stuff, that's cool. Otherwise, you're on your own, boo."

There was a brief silence. Miranda looked at Jada in disbelief, and Jada returned the stare with a challenging expression of her own.

"That's what I thought." Jada shook her head. "I'm not going to sit around and watch that man kill you, girl. I'm going to be praying for you."

Jada brushed past her friend and left the hospital room. Miranda stood in the doorway and watched as Jada walked down the hall and disappeared around the corner. Seconds passed before Miranda realized that she was not coming back. Dropping her bag onto the hospital bed, Miranda walked over to the phone and called a cab.

The apartment was still and quiet as she entered. Dropping her bag by the door, Miranda eased into her home and slowly walked through the space she shared with her husband. In her bedroom an uneasy feeling came over her. Something wasn't right. Looking around her room, she searched for the source of her discomfort. She found it lying on the floor on her side of the bed. A cheap pair of gold heels that weren't hers stood upright, as if their owner had just stepped out of them. Miranda kicked the shoes. Sighing, she went into her bathroom and gasped when she turned on the light and saw that someone had totally redecorated.

"What the hell!" The words barely had time to escape her lips before she heard the lock turn on the front door. Bracing herself and totally prepared to have it out with Norris, she quickly headed to the living room. He was startled to see her walk in, but not more than the chick by his side.

"Excuse you?" the woman blurted out. "Who the hell gave you permission to be coming all up and through here?"

"Tammy, I got this," Norris interjected, holding his hand up at the younger woman. He approached Miranda with his head tilted back and his nose flaring. "What's good, Miranda? What are you doing here?"

"What am I *doing* here? This is my home. The real question is, what is that bitch doing in my house, Norris?"

"Uh-uh, no, this trick ain't calling me no bitch." Tammy stepped up beside Norris. "I got your bitch, bitch. Don't be coming at me all sideways just 'cause you can't handle yours, boo. 'Cause trust, I'm handling him very well."

Miranda bit her lip, rolled her eyes at Tammy, and addressed Norris. "Get this woman out of my house or—"

"Or what?" Norris challenged.

"Oh, you've forgotten? My name is on this lease, not yours. Technically, you're both trespassing."

"I ain't got time for this shit, Miranda. I didn't even expect your ass to come back."

"Why? You thought you killed me? I'm your wife, Norris. Your *wife!* You didn't so much as check to see if I was okay. You just try to move some li'l girl into my home like you're just going to forget that I exist? Who does that?"

"Shut that whiny-ass shit up," Tammy complained. "Sorry ass."

Fed up, Miranda ran off to the bathroom, where she ripped down towels and knickknacks. Norris and Tammy continued to stand in the living room, arguing.

"I said let me handle this, a'ight?" Norris insisted.

Tammy pointed toward the bathroom. "Hell, she's the one starting with me—"

"Fuck you!" Miranda screamed as she reentered the living room and threw the bathroom items at the two of them. "Fuck you, fuck this bitch, and fuck this situation. Take y'all's pathetic asses the hell on out of my house before I call the police."

She ran back into the bedroom and snatched up the stripper shoes by her bed. Back in the living room, she tossed the left shoe, barely missing Norris's head. "You want to lay up with trash, do it! But you will not do it in my house. I'm not fuckin' scared of you anymore! Get out!" She tossed the right shoe, which connected with Tammy's face, the heel grazing her cheek and leaving a bloody scratch.

"Bitch!" Tammy exclaimed.

"You're lucky that I haven't kicked your ass, bitch. But you have all of ten seconds before that changes."

Norris ushered Tammy toward the door. "Fuck you, Miranda. I'm done with your ass. I wish I'd never married your ass."

The couple exited the apartment, and Miranda quickly ran to the door to fasten the night latch. She touched her side gingerly, becoming aware of the immense pain she was feeling. She picked up her bag and fumbled for her phone. Finding it, she scrolled through the phone book and dialed the desired number.

"Hey. Can you come, though? I can't make it over there. . . . No, he's not here. He's not coming back, so don't worry about that. . . . Okay, that's fine. Thanks." Disconnecting the call, she sank onto her couch, willing the pain in her side and in her heart to go away.

Chapter 18

Candace

Dressed in a short, thin black dress, Candace walked slowly through the crowd, holding on to a cheesing Quincy. Couples were dancing, drinking, and laughing the same as they would at any normal club. The only difference was that some people were naked and others were practically making out right there in the open.

Quincy led her over to the bar. "If you grip my hand any tighter, you're going to pull it off, woman," he complained as he signaled the bartender. He ordered a martini for her and a Long Island Iced Tea for himself as his eyes took in the sight of beautiful and not so beautiful bodies. "So, you see anybody you like?"

Candace was annoyed by the question. "Like who? Dang, you're ready to jump somebody's bones already? What's wrong with just observing?"

Quincy sucked his teeth. "We coulda *observed* a flick at home if it's like that."

"Shut up. Don't start with me, please."

The bartender placed their orders on the counter, and Quincy turned his attention to his drink as Candace continued to stare in awe at all the freeness. She would have never noticed the woman next to her if she hadn't lightly touched her arm. Candace jumped and stared at the slender, light-skinned woman with curly hair.

"I'm sorry." The woman smiled at her. "I didn't mean to startle you. You just look so tense."

"Oh yeah . . . it's our first time here." She motioned to Quincy. "This is my husband, Quincy, and I'm Candace."

Quincy said a quick hello. The pretty lady merely nodded at him.

"I'm Lydia. Listen, I'm a licensed massage therapist. I'd love to give you a full body massage. You really do seem to have a lot of built-up tension."

Candace was at a loss for words as she toyed with the stem of her glass. "Well, I—"

Quincy cut in. "Can we make it a massage for two?"

Lydia gave a polite smile and reached inside her clutch bag. She handed Candace a business card. "I'm sorry. I didn't intend the offer to be a come-on."

A man approached Lydia, and Candace threw a dirty look at Quincy.

"Babes, I want you to meet someone," the man said to Lydia, reaching for her hand.

Lydia smiled at Candace. "This is my husband, Michael."

Michael nodded.

"Nothing wrong with a foursome," Quincy blurted.

Candace elbowed her husband. "Excuse him."

"It's all right, dear," Lydia said lightly. "Try to relax. Both of you. You'll find what you're looking for. Consider the massage, okay?"

"Okay. Thank you," Candace replied.

"Enjoy your evening," Michael said politely before ushering his wife away.

Candace put the card in her bag and looked at Quincy in disgust as he ordered another drink. "Unbelievable," she muttered.

"What?" Quincy was oblivious to his embarrassing behavior.

"You have no class, dear."

"You married me, so I must have something."

"Grow up."

"What's your problem? I thought we came here to have fun. Why you acting like a crab?"

Candace sighed. "You know what? This was a mistake. We should have never come here."

"So what you saying?"

"I'm saying that I want to go home. Now!"

"All the money we paid to get up in here and now you want to go?" he asked a little loudly.

"Shhh. You're embarrassing me. Please, let's just go."

Quincy sucked his teeth and downed his glass. Reaching into his pocket, he grabbed the keys and threw them at her. "Fine, designated driver. Be a punk. Let's go."

She snatched the keys up and walked off. "Whatever."

Candace took a deep breath as she checked her reflection in the rearview mirror. Satisfied with her appearance, she exited her car and slowly strolled up the walk to the all-brick mini-mansion. Anxiety filled her with each step she took past the beautifully arranged flowers decorating the lawn. It was apparent that these people had money. Before she could reach out for the doorbell, the door flew open.

"Hey, Ms. Ma'am," Lydia greeted her. "Come on in."

Candace smiled and walked into the foyer. The scent of lavender quickly filled her nose. She took note of the crystal chandelier overhead and the black art adorning the walls. Lydia led her to a room just past the formal living room. She looked very comfortable in her blue sarong tied tightly at the top of her bosom.

"You look so tense," Lydia commented. "You must have a lot going on in your life. Either that or you're nervous about being here. Which is it? You're safe here. I won't bite." Lydia chuckled, and Candace cracked a smile.

"No, I just have a lot going on and a lot on my mind."

"Well, you definitely need to relax, and that's what I'm here for. A massage could really do you some good." Lydia gestured toward the middle of the room, at her massage table and display of oils. "This is the sanctuary of peace. Get completely undressed and cover yourself with the sheet that's on the table. "

Candace was a little hesitant. "Is your husband here?"

"No. He's playing golf. But relax, hon. This is my business. He has respect enough not to barge in on a session. Get undressed. I'm going to bring you a glass of wine. Back in ten minutes."

Lydia left her alone and pulled the door closed behind her. Candace took a look around and shrugged. Quickly, she disrobed and placed her clothes on a nearby chair. When she was done, she wrapped the soft white sheet around her curvy body.

"What am I tripping about?" she asked out loud as she tried to relax.

There was a tap on the door; then Lydia poked her head inside. "You ready?"

Candace smiled. "Yes."

Lydia entered and kicked the door shut behind her. In her hands she carried a bottle of wine and two glasses.

Candace watched as she poured the drinks. "What is that?"

"Moscato. You've never had it before?"

Candace shook her head no, and Lydia handed her a glass. "Tell me what you think."

Candace took a sip of the drink and raised an eyebrow. "Mmm. It's sweet and smooth. I likes."

The ladies giggled. Lydia took a swig from her own glass. "That's why I like it, girl. Sweet and smooth, just like me."

They shared another laugh and finished off their drinks.

"How long have you been doing this?" Candace asked.

"Just a couple of years now. I was in real estate—well, Michael and I both did real estate— but after a while I decided that I wanted to do something different. So I went to school, got licensed, and here I am."

"That's cool."

"What do you do?"

"I'm a legal assistant, but I'm trying to figure out what my passion is."

Lydia sat her glass down and turned on some soft jazz music. "Believe me, once you figure it out, you'll feel so good inside. At peace with yourself kinda." Lydia took Candace's glass and sat it down. "Okay, dear. Lie on your tummy for me."

Candace got into position, closed her eyes, and let the music lure her into relaxation. Lydia lit a few candles and sorted through some oils. Finally, Candace felt her soft hands firmly gripping her shoulders as she began to work her magic.

"Wow," Candace murmured.

"Just relax, girl," Lydia instructed. "You are so tense in this area."

She continued to knead for a while, engrossed in her craft. Candace became increasingly relaxed. The probing and rubbing carried her into a state of peace she had never experienced.

"So how often do you and Michael go to the club?" Candace asked as Lydia moved down her back with deep compressions.

"Every once in a while. Just something to do to spice things up a little bit every now and then. You plan on going back?"

"Probably not."

"It's not for everyone. That's for sure."

"Have you guys ever met someone? You know—"

"Have we ever had a ménage à trois? We did once. We've never actually had sex at the club. I have . . . well . . ."

"What?"

"I've had, like, foreplay at the club. Even some personal, private encounters."

"You mean without Michael? Does he know?"

"Of course he knows." She moved down to Candace's lower back. "They were with other women."

There was silence as Lydia continued to massage deeply the small of Candace's back. Each woman considered her own private thoughts. Lydia moved down Candace's legs, and shivers rose up Candace's spine. As she worked Candace's entire body, time seemed to fly by. Before Candace knew it, the session was over, the music was still going, and she was completely relaxed.

"Okay, girl. You're done," Lydia informed her.

Candace sat up slowly, pulled the sheet around her, and stretched. "Wow. That was so amazing. Thank you."

Lydia refilled Candace's wineglass and handed it to her before refilling her own. "Not a problem. You just make sure that you tell a friend. Gotta make that money."

They clinked their glasses in agreement.

"How much do I owe you?" Candace asked.

"This session is free. Hopefully, you'll be back." Lydia sat her glass down, then approached Candace. She placed her hands in the crook of Candace's neck. "This is your problem area. It's where all your tension goes, girl. We may want to continuously work out this area."

Lydia's scent was so sweet and inviting. Perhaps it was the alcohol or the serenity of the room that prompted Candace to reach out and touch Lydia's curly mane. "Your hair is so beautiful."

Lydia smiled. "Thank you." Her hands lingered on Candace's shoulders. She began to caress her skin. "Your skin is so soft. Smooth like a baby's."

Before Candace could find the words to respond, Lydia ran her hands gently up and down her arms. Looking into her eyes, as if for a hint of permission, Lydia took Candace's glass and sat it down. Candace sat still on the massage table, not sure what to do next or what would happen next. Lydia slowly pulled the sheet from Candace's body. Candace did not protest. She sat still as Lydia massaged her breasts gently with both hands. Watching Candace's response, she massaged a little more intensely as a soft moan escaped Candace's lips. Lydia smiled sinfully and took Candace's right breast in her mouth. Her tongue was so warm on Candace's skin. She flicked her nipple playfully over and over until Candace reached for her head, signaling for more pressure. Lydia licked circles around her areola before taking the whole breast in her mouth once more, sucking with a hungry passion.

Candace could feel the pressure building between her legs, and the moisture began to seep involuntarily. Lydia must have sensed it, because she moved her hand slowly up Candace's thighs, one then the other, teasing her. Candace spread her legs a little to encourage her to enter. Slowly, Lydia's index finger toyed with her clit. Candace moaned impatiently, her heat rising by the second. She began to gyrate against Lydia's flickers while stroking the woman's mass of curls. Without warning, Lydia stopped and looked up at her. Candace's breathing was heavy, and she didn't realize that her eyes had been shut until she opened them to look back at Lydia.

"There's no going back," Lydia said softly. "Do you want this?"

"Yes," Candace answered, nearly inaudibly.

Lydia kept her eyes on Candace as she slowly inserted her finger into Candace's hot and throbbing pussy. She stroked in and out, slowly at first and then more forcefully with two fingers as Candace began to thrust back.

"Ooh, shit!" Candace exclaimed as she grabbed her own breasts and began to squeeze.

Candace's juices flowed down Lydia's hand as she pounded her with her fingers. To intensify the sensation, she lowered her head and took Candace's clit into her mouth. Perfectly in sync, she sucked her relentlessly and fingered her deeper and rougher. Candace spread her legs wider, giving complete access to her womanhood.

"Cum for me," Lydia encouraged seductively. "I want to taste you. Cum for me."

Candace bucked ferociously against her hot tongue and probing fingers. It felt so good that she wanted to feel Lydia deeper inside of her. Lifting her hips a little, she lost control and climaxed in shudders against Lydia's face. Spent from the experience, Candace fell over on the massage table. Lydia stood up and ran her fingers across her stomach.

"It's not nap time yet," she told her.

Candace sat up, unsure of what to do or say at that moment. She didn't have to say anything. Lydia slowly untied her sarong and let it fall to the floor, exposing her beautiful, fit body. She reached out and grabbed Candace's hand and guided it across her silky skin. Candace didn't need much direction after that.

She found pleasure in toying with her breast, just as Lydia had done to her. Surprised by her second wind, as well as her moxie, Candace slid from the table and kneeled down to bury her face in Lydia's womanhood. Lydia slightly raised her leg and leaned on the massage table, getting into the groove of the moment. Candace sucked and licked with a vigor and passion she didn't know she had. When she began to feel as if she couldn't breathe, she came up for air and inserted her perfectly manicured fingers inside Lydia's gush.

Lydia moved with her but soon hungered for a different sensation. She reached down and caressed her clit with a sensual back-and-forth motion. The harder she rubbed, the louder her moans got. The louder her moans, the wetter she became. The wetter she got, the harder Candace dove her fingers into her insides. In moments, Lydia was bucking madly on Candace's fingers, assaulting her clit passionately until her climatic wave had passed.

Candace was turned on by the feeling of Lydia's pussy muscles contracting around her fingers. She slowly withdrew her hand, lay down on the plush carpet, and opened her legs wide. Watching Lydia, she began to play with herself just as Lydia had. Lydia joined her on the floor, licking around her lips as Candace pleasured herself. She caressed Candace's breast, becoming aroused once more herself. Candace reached over to feel Lydia's wetness.

An idea occurred to Lydia. She mounted Candace backward and initiated a sixty-nine. They sucked, licked, and probed, daring the other to cum first. Lydia lost, her pleasure juice dripping down onto Candace's face. Seconds later, Candace finished with a startling shudder. It was by far the strongest orgasm she'd ever achieved. The two collapsed against one another, too tired and worn out for words. Surprised at herself, Candace merely turned over and let the sound of smooth jazz lure her into a lust-induced slumber.

Chapter 19

Alex

"Ah-choo. Ah-choo."

"I think your germs are creeping through the phone."

Alex blew her nose and coughed. "Shut up, you turd."

"Whatever. You want me to bring you over some soup? Some medicine? Some disinfectant spray?"

Alex started to laugh, then choked on mucus. "You suck. Don't bring me nothing."

Clay laughed. "I was just joking, crybaby."

"Ha-ha. Anyway . . . ugh." She sneezed again. "Mario is coming over in a minute."

"Oh yeah? Your knight in shining armor, huh?"

"Why does it seem like you don't like him, when you've never even met him? Why you hating?"

Clay chuckled. "Yeah, right. I'm the last to be hating. Game recognize game."

"You ain't got no game."

"Let you tell it."

"I gotta go and get ready for Mario."

"What you getting ready for exactly? Isn't he coming over to nurse you back to good health? What? You still gon' primp ya' self so you can give that lame some ass, even though you're burning up with a fever?"

"Clay, shut up. You don't know what you're talking about."

"We'll see. Hope you feel better, pitiful princess."

"Bye, Clay."

"Later."

The sound of the doorbell scared her out of her sleep. Alex looked at the clock. It was just past eleven. She struggled out of bed and then out to the living room to open the door.

"Seriously? Eleven?"

Mario raised an eyebrow and gave her a shrug. "I got caught up. My bad. You gon' let me in?"

Alex moved to the side, and he entered with a grocery bag. He took the bag to the kitchen, and Alex followed him.

"You could have called."

"I could have not come at all. Would you have preferred that?"

Alex looked hurt. She pulled a piece of tissue from the pocket of her robe and blew her nose, trying to ward off her tears. "I'm sick, Mario. If you were going to be nasty to me, you could have stayed home or wherever you were. For real."

Mario sighed, walked over to her, and gave her a hug. "Sorry, baby. I'm just tired. I came to see about you, okay? Let's just chill. I brought you some soup."

Alex buried her face in his shirt. With her cold, her senses were a bit altered, but Alex could have sworn that she smelled the faint scent of Victoria's Secret Pure Seduction. *What the hell?* she thought as she moved away from his embrace. "I don't want any soup. I just want to go back to bed."

"Okay, but you have to drink this first." Mario went back to the grocery bag and pulled out a fifth of E&J.

"Ew, no. You know I don't drink," Alex protested.

"It'll make you feel better. I promise."

Alex watched as he took a cup from the cabinet, pulled out a Theraflu box, and began to mix his medicinal concoction. Once it was mixed, he placed the cup in the microwave and heated it for one minute. With a huge smile, as if he'd really done something great, he retrieved the cup from the one minute warm-up in the microwave and handed it to Alex. The smell of the liquor opened up her nose.

"This smells." She screwed up her nose.

"Drink it. Trust me. You are going to feel so much better."

Alex took a sip and frowned in disgust. "Mario, I can't drink this."

"Don't be a punk." He retrieved a glass and poured himself a shot of the E&J, never once turning to face her as she stood there, cringing at the smell of her drink.

"But, baby—"

"If you're going to whine and moan, I can always leave." He downed his liquor, then poured another shot. "I'm trying to help you. Just drink the stuff and get in the bed. Why do you have to make such a big deal about it?"

Alex pouted, opened her mouth to speak, then closed her mouth. She was too sick to argue. Taking a deep breath, she sat down at the kitchen table and nursed her drink.

"You sure you don't want the soup?" he asked her.

"I'm sure."

Mario busied himself with putting away the groceries he'd brought and straightening up the kitchen.

"So what were you doing tonight?" Alex took a hearty gulp of her drink as she studied his facial expressions and movements.

"Hanging."

Alex sighed, feeling that the conversation was going nowhere. She inhaled, then knocked back the remainder of her drink. Plopping the cup down on the table, she stood up and looked over at Mario, who was now on his third drink. "I'm going to get in my bed. Are you staying?"

"You want me to stay?"

"Mario, I wanted you to be here all evening. Ugh. Never mind." She moved to walk away and felt herself sway.

"Whoa." Mario was by her side. "You better be careful. That E&J is the truth. Come on. Let's go watch a movie."

He led her to her bedroom and helped her into bed. She lay there, watching him as he popped in a DVD, turned off the lights, kicked off his shoes, and crawled onto the bed beside her.

"You okay?" he asked.

She shrugged. "I'm floating, and I feel all warm inside."

He got under the covers and hugged her. "That's the point. To get you all warm and make you sweat it out."

The opening credits for the movie began to play, and Alex was lured into a cinema-, virus-, and alcohol-induced sleep. At some point she felt herself slipping in and out of consciousness as warm kisses covered her face and neck. Mario's hand was caressing the inside of her thighs, tickling her awake. Alex wasn't sure if she was dreaming or not. Her

answer came when she felt a very real finger probing inside
her vaginal walls.

"Mario," she whispered. Her mouth felt like cotton. She
opened her eyes to the darkness and reached for his hand.

He shook her off and planted a loud, wet kiss over her ear.
His breath was hot on her skin as he whispered in her ear, "I
love you, Alexandria."

Confused and sedated, Alex tried to sit up, but Mario's body
was already towering over her. He lifted her nightgown and
moved his kisses to her abdomen while easing her legs apart.

"I can't. I can't." Alex grabbed his shoulders in protest.

He rose up to mount her and kissed her lips to silence her.
Her moans of pain were lost in the murmur of his kisses.
When the sensation felt unbearable, she grabbed his arms,
shaking her head. "I can't. . . . It h-hurts. . . . I c-can't."

"Yes, you can," he said, encouraging her, still penetrating.
"Yes, you can. You can. I got you. Come on, baby."

He continued to thrust until her lining gave way to his
advances and let him in. Alex lay beneath him, eyes shut,
tightly holding on to his arms as he moved in and out of her.
She didn't return his thrusts or his kisses. She had no energy
to participate or protest further. Her thoughts got lost in the
sound of his body meshing with hers and the fever that was
overcoming her. She was not sure when he stopped or how
it ended. Hours later, in the stillness of the night, she turned
over to find him hanging off the opposite side of her bed. Her
womanhood was sore, and her nightgown was drenched with
sweat.

Quietly, she slid from the bed and pulled a clean nightgown
from her dresser. In the bathroom, she turned on the light to
find that the moisture on her gown was not just sweat, but
blood as well. "Great," she muttered, getting a washcloth to
clean herself up. Once cleaned and changed, she pulled down
a towel and returned to bed. She laid the towel down on her
side and lay on top of it.

Sighing, she looked over at the snoring figure of Mario. A
beeping sound was coming from his side of the bed, but Mario
did not move. Alex reached over him slowly and picked his
cell phone up off the floor. The phone beeped again, indi-

cating that he had a text. The screen read Erica. Lying back against her pillows, Alex debated whether or not to read the text. Before long, the phone beeped again. She looked over at Mario. He was still sound asleep.

She pressed VIEW on the phone. Are you coming back over tonight? She clicked back to the previous message. I'm ready for round three. She clicked to the first message. You missing me yet? Disgusted and disappointed, she threw the phone onto the bed and turned her back to Mario. The tears were uncontrollable, and her sobs were loud.

Mario never budged.

Chapter 20

The Girls

Jada sat the pizza boxes on the coffee table, next to the paper plates. Stephanie, now three months pregnant, sat on the sofa, directly in front of the boxes, with her plate in hand. Sitting next to her, Alex gave her a sideways glance.

"Is it like that?" Alex asked her.

"Girl, I stay hungry." Stephanie flipped open the top of the meat lover's pizza and grabbed a slice. She bit into the slice, and cheese dripped down her chin. "Mmm." She taunted Alex by chewing slowly and savoring the taste. "Divine."

Alex threw a napkin at her. "You're a pig."

It was officially girls' night at Candace's house. The group hadn't been together since Candace's wedding. As Alex and Stephanie began to feast on the pizza, Candace entered the room with a piping hot bowl of the dip she made for every occasion.

"Watch out, ladies," she instructed as she sat the bowl on the table, beside the pizza. "This is very hot."

Jada opened the bag of tortilla chips and scooped up some of the cheesy concoction with a chip. She took a bite and smiled. "Just right, girl."

Candace plopped down onto the nearby armchair with a bottle of Smirnoff in hand. "You know how I do."

Jada laughed. "I know that you usually don't, so it's amazing when you actually do."

The others laughed.

"Whatever," Candace protested. "I can cook, girl. Everyone loves my food."

"Uh-huh. I hope you cook Quincy something other than cheese dip," Stephanie interjected.

"He's the main one who loves my culinary skills. Why you think he married me?"

Alex laughed. "That's a good question. Why *did* he marry you?"

Candace reached for a slice of pizza and rolled her eyes at Alex. "Ha-ha."

"Honestly, he doesn't even seem like your type."

"Alex," Jada said, intervening.

"What? I'm just saying. We've known you for a long time, girl, and he just don't seem like your kinda guy."

"Please get off it." Candace was tired of defending her marriage. "We're married. We're in love. End of discussion. God, if I didn't know any better, I'd say that you were jealous."

"That must be your alcohol talking," Alex snapped.

"Ladies, really," Jada said, jumping in. "We're supposed to be having fun."

"And we are," Candace retorted, rising from her chair. "I just don't get why some people can't be happy for me and leave it at that. I'm going to make some margaritas."

Candace left the room, and Jada stared at Alex, who was munching nonchalantly on chips and dip. She caught Jada's glare and shrugged.

"What?"

"Don't what me. That was mean, girl."

"I was just being honest. I wasn't trying to hurt her little feelings or anything. But come on. You know good and well this marriage is ridiculous."

"Who are we to judge?" Jada asked.

"We're her friends."

"If the woman says she's happy, then believe her and shut the hell up about it."

"If she's happy, why did she get all pissed by what I said?"

Jada sighed. "Steph, can I get a little help here?"

Stephanie chugged her soda and shook her head. "Nuh-uh, girl. I'm with Alex on this. Seeing Candace and Quincy together does not make me think that they are in love."

"And what are you comparing them to? You and ya' baby's daddy?" Jada asked.

Stephanie sucked her teeth. "Well, we can't all be perfect like you and Jordan, can we?"

The doorbell sounded just then, and in walked Miranda before anyone could move to answer the door.

"Hey, chicks," she said, greeting the group, unusually upbeat. She went around the room and hugged the others just as Candace entered with a pitcher of margaritas.

"Well, look who decided to finally show up," Candace commented.

Miranda hugged her. "I love you too, bitch."

"Yeah, yeah, yeah."

Miranda made herself comfortable on the floor by the sofa and reached for a slice of pizza. "So what have I missed?"

Candace poured her a glass of the margarita mix and handed it to her before returning to her chair. "Just Alex trying to persuade me to get divorced."

"Stop exaggerating," Alex said.

"Ignore them," Jada advised, then changed the subject. "How are you doing?"

Miranda covered her mouth with a napkin. "I'm good."

The other girls simply looked at her sympathetically, waiting for her to say more. Miranda began to feel uncomfortable from their stares. She sighed and looked at her friends sternly.

"Stop it, guys. I'm fine. Really."

"We're girls, right?" Candace asked her as she sipped her drink.

Miranda nodded.

"Well, why didn't you call us? Any of us? Why didn't you tell us what was going on with you? That you were in trouble?"

"Because I didn't want you looking at me the way you are now . . . feeling sorry for me."

"Why did you stay?" Stephanie asked. "I mean, I'm assuming this wasn't the first time. So why would you stay with a man that hits you?"

"Why do you stay with Corey?"

"Corey doesn't hit me," Stephanie returned.

"No, but he blows you off. He treats you like a toy. Takes you out when he wants to play with you, then abandons you when he's bored with you."

Stephanie frowned. "Wait a minute now. That's not fair, Miranda. We're concerned about you. Where do you get off attacking me and being all judgmental?"

"I'm sorry, but it's the truth." Miranda stared down at her napkin. "Maybe we all just have some fucked-up relationships."

The girls sat in silence, munching and considering their own thoughts.

Alex broke the silence a few minutes later. "Mario is cheating on me."

A series of aws filled the room as the others tried to console her.

"How do you know?" Stephanie asked.

"I saw messages in his phone one night, after he came to my place smelling like a girl. And ever since then I've barely heard from him or seen him."

"I'm sorry, girl," Jada offered. "I know you really liked him."

"Maybe it's for the best," Candace said.

"What?" Alex questioned. "What is this? Payback?"

"No, I'm not studying you like that, girl. I'm just saying that perhaps that's not who Jehovah intended for you to be with."

Alex considered it. "I guess not."

Candace threw a pillow at her friend. "You are sooo slow."

"What?" Alex looked perplexed.

"Clay, that's what," Candace replied.

"What about him?"

"She's asking what's up with him," Stephanie answered. "Why aren't you hooking up with his fine ass?"

Alex helped herself to some more dip. "Y'all are crazy. Clay and I are just friends. That's it."

Jada's attention wandered off to Miranda, who was sitting quietly on the floor, nursing her drink. She looked so frail and simply different. Before she could say anything, Jada was pulled into the current conversation by Stephanie.

"Jada, please tell Ms. Princess over here that she needs to stop messing with these crazy dudes and get with that fine-ass Clay."

Jada shrugged. "Um, I don't know. Has he ever said anything to you? Given you a sign that he's interested?"

"I don't know," Alex answered, unsure.

"Yeah, right." Stephanie couldn't believe that Alex could be so blind. "All I know is that if I had a fine-ass friend like Clay always hanging around, Corey would sho' 'nough beat my ass, thinking we were messing around."

The girls started to laugh, then realized what had just been said. The laughter ceased as all eyes went over to Miranda. Sensing their stares, Miranda looked up and once again felt uncomfortable.

"Oh, damn. I'm sorry, girl." Stephanie bit her bottom lip.

"Sorry for what?" Miranda asked.

"I didn't mean to make light of . . . I mean, I was just kidding."

"It's okay. I'm not offended. I'm more offended that y'all keep treating me like I'm broken or something."

Candace sat her cup down, rose from her seat, and kneeled beside Miranda. "You had a broken rib, girl. You *were* broken. And we are concerned about you."

"Don't be. It's over now."

"Is it? Have you filed for divorce? Have you pressed charges against his sorry ass?' Candace quizzed.

Miranda shook her head no.

Stephanie leaned forward, and her brow crinkled with concern. "Please don't tell me that you are still holed up over at the apartment with his trifling ass."

Miranda shook her head again. "He moved in with some chick."

Candace plopped down on the floor beside Miranda and shook her head. "You're a stronger person than I could ever be, girl. I would have whupped his ass."

Miranda shrugged. "I'm dealing with it. I've been going to my battered wives meeting and—"

Jada cut her off. "Battered wives meeting? Do you hear yourself? That doesn't even sound right. You are twenty-two years old, and you're sitting up in some group for battered women? What the hell?"

"You need to file those papers, girl," Stephanie added. "Get rid of that man for good. What are you waiting on?"

"Divorces cost money," Miranda stated.

Candace patted her on the leg. "The attorney I work for handles divorces. I got you."

Alex sat her plate on the table and moaned a little. "What is wrong with all of us?" She rose from her seat. "We sound like a pitiful Lifetime movie. Excuse me." Alex hurried from the living room and headed in the direction of the bathroom.

Jada chuckled a little. "Alex is right. We have got to get it together, ladies."

"*We?*" Candace remarked. "What kind of problems do you have little, Ms. Perfect Princess?"

"Don't start with me, Candace. Everybody has issues," Jada replied.

"Uh-huh. So I'm asking you, what are your issues? I never hear you utter a word about your relationship. Nada. So either you're holding on to the secret of how to make shit work or you're holding out on us."

Jada rolled her eyes and took a sip of her drink. "I just don't have *these* types of issues."

"That's some sidity shit to say," Candace told her.

"But it's some real shit."

Candace abruptly left the room, and the others looked at Jada in awe. Jada shrugged her shoulders and grabbed a slice of pizza.

"What was that about?" Stephanie asked Jada.

"Hell if I know. As often as I go to bat for her, I don't know why she felt the need to come at me like that."

"It's funny," Miranda said softly. She stared at the carpet, and tears rolled down her cheeks as she spoke. "It's funny how you want something so badly. Then when you get it, you realize it ain't what you really wanted at all. But instead of admitting that you made a mistake, you just stick it out. You try to mask it, but in the process every bit of who you are gets destroyed—the way you think, your outlook on life, your relationships with others in your life. You start lashing out at others or at yourself."

Taking a deep breath, Miranda looked up at her two friends, who were too stunned to respond to her unexpected revelation. Jada sat down her pizza and moved to the floor beside her, wrapping her arms around the frail frame of her body. Stephanie moved beside Miranda as well and grabbed her hand.

"It's funny," Miranda whispered between sobs. "It's funny how we get to this place and don't even know how we got here . . . all because we want to be loved."

"Love doesn't hurt, though, Miranda," Jada said softly. "Not like he's hurt you. That's not love."

Miranda looked into Jada's eyes innocently. "Sometimes, we take what we can get, even if it is a lie."

In the bathroom Alex leaned over the toilet, gripping the seat with her left hand, her eyes shut tightly. She tried to take a deep breath before her body convulsed once more, involuntarily freeing her of her lunch. With her right hand she held her stomach, trying to will it to settle down. In moments it was over. She flushed the toilet and rested her head against the cold porcelain. Her face was wet with tears and sweat. "Get it together," she ordered her body. "Get it together."

She rose from the floor, went to the sink, and splashed water on her face. Catching a glimpse of herself in the mirror, she almost didn't recognize the woman looking back at her. How long could she ignore the weakness of her stomach, the violent hurls, or the fatigue that was evident in her eyes? No one else noticed, but she did. No one else knew, and she wasn't ready to be certain. Quickly, she patted her face dry, washed her hands, and left the bathroom before anyone decided to come looking for her.

Candace was in the kitchen, preparing another batch of margaritas. She found herself literally throwing the ingredients into the blender and ferociously pressing the BLEND button. She wasn't sure if she was frustrated with the others for pulling her card regarding her marriage or with herself for being jealous of Jada. Sure, they were girls, but it was hard to follow in someone else's shadow. Everything seemed to come with such ease for Jada. Why couldn't her marriage be like Jada's?

Her phone buzzed, interrupting her thoughts. She pulled it out of her pocket and looked to see who the text was from. It was Khalil. A smile crossed her lips. She read the text. Want to see you tonight. She quickly texted back. Call you when I'm done with the girls.

Alex sauntered into the kitchen and poured herself a cup of cranberry juice. She looked at Candace as she put her phone back in her pocket. "Look, I wasn't trying to be rude or to piss you off in there."

Candace shrugged. "I know. And between you and me, I know my marriage isn't perfect, but it's mine."

Alex leaned over the counter and smiled slyly at her friend. "Do you really love him? I mean really?"

Candace bopped her on the nose. "He's my husband. Of course I love him."

Alex turned up her lips and cocked her head to the side. "I guess." She couldn't help but giggle.

Candace poured herself a drink and laughed. "I guess too."

Chapter 21

Candace

Candace agreed to meet Khalil at a coffee shop on his side of town. When she entered, he was sitting at a cozy table tucked away in a corner of the coffee shop. She glided over to him, and his eyes danced as he watched her approach. He gave her that sexy, killer smile of his, and she could feel her panties moisten at the thought of where his lips had once been. He stood up to greet her with a soft kiss on her right cheek and a firm hug as he lightly and quickly grazed her ass. She sat in the vacant seat across from him.

"How are you?" he asked, sipping from his latte.

"I'm good. Thanks. How are you, dear?"

"Doing much better, now that you're here. I've missed you."

She blushed. "Have you? You haven't called."

"I've been busy. You know how it is." Her eyebrow rose. He reached over and grabbed her hand. "You look very beautiful today. Can I get you anything?"

She shook her head. "No, thank you. So tell me, what have you been so busy doing?"

Khalil leaned back and took another swig of his drink. "Dealing with this crazy woman and her nonsense."

"Oh? What's up with Sheila?"

"This nut had the audacity to give me an ultimatum. She wants to get married. Talking about she's tired of shacking up and wants me to make a commitment to her."

"So why won't you? Marriage can be a beautiful thing."

"Could be, but I've been married before, and it wasn't beautiful. Marriage doesn't fix a situation that's already jacked up. It just complicates things. I don't want to mess up my life or hers any more than I have to by promising her forever and then failing her when it ultimately doesn't work out. That's just foolish."

"Do you love her?"

He chuckled. "I stopped loving her a long time ago. It's just a relationship of convenience now."

"Then why won't you break up with her? Move on and find someone you actually love?"

"Because you're married."

Candace was shocked by his insinuation. "Is that right?"

"And love is overrated."

"Is it? You don't believe you can be in love with someone, Khalil?"

"I don't know. All I know is that I am definitely not marrying Sheila. I'm not doing that again."

"What made her bring up marriage?"

He stared down into his cup, as if debating whether or not he was going to answer her. He toyed with the rim of the cup before answering, "She's pregnant."

There was silence. Candace didn't know what to say to him. "Are you happy?" It was the only thing she could get her lips to say, although she had many other questions in her mind.

"What am I going to do with another kid? She knows I don't want any children."

"Well, you impregnated her."

"Mistake . . . I'm tired of arguing with her, damn sure ain't about to marry her, and then she up and tells me she's knocked up."

"Wow." Candace was relieved that she wasn't the woman carrying this man's baby.

"Enough about my problems, though. What's up with you?"

She smiled slyly. "Nothing much. Trying some new things."

"Like what?"

"Trying to spice up our love life. Let's see. We've been to a swingers club. Um, I've been done by a girl, and I—"

"Hold up. You turning lesbian on me?"

Candace was slightly offended. "A little experimentation doesn't make me a lesbian."

"Really? Let a man do another man, and he would quickly be labeled a fag."

"Okay, don't act like the thought of me with another woman doesn't get you all hard and horny."

He laughed. "It doesn't. It makes me think that you need a real man dicking you down so that you don't feel the need to chase after another woman's pussy."

"Fuck you, Khalil." Angrily, she grabbed her purse. "What happened to 'we can talk about anything'?"

"Nothing happened to it. We're talking, but I'm not going to mask my opinions just to make you happy, young lady. I'm being real with you."

"Hmm." She looked at her watch. "Well, as much as I'd like to stay here and get berated by you, I really gotta go. My husband's expecting me. Tell Sheila I said hello."

She rose from the table and started to walk away.

Khalil shook his headd and motioned to her empty chair. "Stop acting childish and sit down. Come on. You know you want to stay."

She gave a fake smile. "Some other time."

Candace quickly left the coffee shop and was pissed with herself for even showing up. Khalil had some nerve to be talking down to her when he wasn't even man enough to tell his live-in girlfriend that he no longer wanted her. She trotted off to her car and hurried home to the other trifling man in her life.

Chapter 22

Stephanie

Two months after their last girls' night, Stephanie finally moved in with Corey. To accommodate their growing family, he had secured them a two-bedroom apartment in the same gated community. Already five months pregnant, Stephanie was tired from the hustle and bustle of getting everything moved in. Her mom had been reluctant to accept the fact that she was moving in with her baby's daddy.

"I don't know what you see in that thug," Ms. Johnson had told her. "He's nothing but trouble. Your nose is too wide open for you to see it."

She hadn't wanted to argue. She'd just gone along, packing her boxes and ignoring her mother's negativity, not heeding the warning she was being given. But her silence hadn't deterred her mother from elaborating.

"It's not a stable environment for Damien. Let something happen, DFCS will sho' 'nough come and snatch that child clean away from you. You'd be better off to leave that child right here with me. You want to mess your life up, fine. But you shouldn't be taking that child into that house of ill-repute."

That was where Stephanie had drawn the line. Damien was her son, not her mother's. "Corey is his dad. A child should be with both their parents. Anywhere I go, my child goes."

"And what are you going to do the next time his *daddy* gets arrested? What you gonna do if he gets arrested while Damien is with him?"

"Why can't you be happy for me? This is my family. Don't worry about us."

That had ended the conversation. Ms. Johnson was out of words and fight. She'd simply turned and left the room, leaving Stephanie with her own thoughts as she continued packing.

Now she was sitting in the living room of the place she proudly called home as Damien napped in his new bedroom. Corey wasn't home. He'd told her that he had a run to make. Looking around at the unopened boxes, Stephanie rubbed her stomach and smiled to herself. *Finally,* she thought. *All that's left is to get married.* She was sure it would come. Moving in together was a big step on Corey's part. Marriage was seemingly inevitable.

Wanting to be the best wifey possible, Stephanie pushed herself up from the couch and wobbled into the kitchen. Already the weight of her baby bump was affecting her movement. As she rummaged through the refrigerator, the house phone began to ring. She had never answered Corey's phone before, but since she now lived with him, it only felt natural that she would.

She grabbed it on the third ring. "Hello?"

"Who is this?" a female voice demanded.

"Who were you calling?"

"Where's Corey?"

"He's not in. May I ask who's calling?"

The line went dead. She held the cordless phone in her hand, staring into space as the dial tone returned to the line and the phone began to buzz. She clicked off the phone and quickly pressed the button to view the caller ID. The screen read **Private Number**. Her intuition told her that something wasn't right, but her heart didn't want to listen to any hints of doubt. She returned the phone to its cradle and continued with preparing the family's lunch.

Lunchtime came and went, but still no Corey. Dinnertime came and went, yet there was still no word from him. She'd called his cell phone twice, and each time she was sent straight to voice mail. This was their official first night at home together, and he had the audacity not to come home. To keep from worrying or crying, Stephanie occupied herself with caring for Damien. Together they played with his train set and had dinner before she assisted him with his bubble bath. Then they lay together reading his favorite Thomas the

Tank Engine book for the umpteenth time. By now, Damien knew the plot by heart. As he told the story to her, Stephanie felt herself falling asleep. Damien noticed it too.

"Wake up, Mommy," he told her in his precious voice.

"I'm not 'sleep," she lied, forcing a smile. "I'm listening."

"Nuh-uh. Mommy, when's Daddy coming home?"

Stephanie sat up and put her arm around her toddler. "I don't know, baby. Daddy had to work."

"Where does Daddy work?"

"He works with people." She didn't know how to explain to her son that his father was the neighborhood dope man. *You spend your whole life teaching your kids to just say no,* she thought. *How do you then tell your children that their father is the man they're supposed to be saying no to?*

Damien rested his head on her chest. "When are we going back to Grandma's house?"

"We're not going to live there anymore," she told him. "We'll only go to visit."

They both heard the front door close and keys hit the table.

"Daddy, Daddy!" Damien exclaimed, hopping from the bed and peeling through the apartment to the living room. He ran right into Corey's open arms, and Corey lifted him up into the air and spun him around, making the child giggle with delight. Stephanie entered the room and was instantly pleased at the sight of her son and his father. It was a touching moment.

"What's up, big man?" Corey asked him playfully. "What you doing up? It's late."

"I was waiting on you." Damien poked his dad in the chest.

Corey sat the young boy down and patted him on the head. "Well, I'm here now. Go on and get in your bed."

Damien wrapped his arms around Corey's leg and squeezed. "Mommy made dinner, and you didn't come home to eat it. Mommy was looking sad, Daddy. I think she wanted you to come home. I wanted you to come home too."

Corey pulled the little boy away from him and patted his head once more. "Okay, son. Go on to bed now."

"Daddy, I wanna stay up with you."

Stephanie intervened. "Go to bed, Damien. You can play with Daddy in the morning."

"Aw, man." The little boy reluctantly and slowly removed himself from the living room.

Corey went into the kitchen, and Stephanie followed him. She waited for him to offer an explanation, and when it was apparent that one was not forthcoming, she spoke up. "I called you twice tonight."

"I was busy."

"You couldn't have called to let me know you weren't coming home anytime soon or something?"

Corey opened the refrigerator and rummaged through it in search of his dinner. He ignored Stephanie's concerns. Unable to find anything to eat, he closed the refrigerator door with only a beer in hand. "I thought you cooked dinner."

She sighed. "Your plate is in the microwave."

Swigging his beer, Corey went over to the kitchen table and took a seat.

Assuming this was her cue, Stephanie walked over to the microwave and pressed the REHEAT button. Two minutes passed, and the microwave beeped. She took the plate of cubed steak and potatoes out and sat it in front of Corey.

"Smells good," he said. "Lemme get a fork."

She retrieved a fork for him and sat at the table beside him as he began to eat his dinner. He ravished the food, as if he hadn't eaten all day.

"So where were you?" she asked him. His left eyebrow rose and his nose flared up, and Stephanie quickly sat up straight in her seat. "I mean, I was worried, is all." She tried to clean up the question. "And Damien was asking for you. Like I said, I called you twice. . . . It went to voice mail. You didn't call, so I wasn't sure when to expect you."

"To expect me?" he repeated. "This is my house. I'm supposed to check in now? Let you know when I'm leaving and when I'm coming back?" He chuckled. "That's some family-type shit, huh? Lemme get some steak sauce."

Stephanie rose from the table and gathered his A.1. Steak Sauce from the cabinet. After placing it in front of him, she slid back into her seat. "I'm just saying. It's the polite thing to do so that I won't be worried about you."

"A'ight. Check it. You know when I gotta go to work, I gotta
go to work. I don't exactly punch in and out of no clock. You
know what I mean?"

"I know."

"But I tell you what. I'll do better. I'll hit you up to let you
know when I'm coming home from now on, a'ight? Just to
give you some peace of mind."

Stephanie gave a weak smile.

"Don't be worried about me, boo." He winked at her. "I'm
on my grind out here. I got niggas watching my back, front,
and sides. So don't be worried about nothing."

His cell phone chimed, and Corey quickly pulled it from the
holster. "Yo . . . yep. Bet. Come on." He replaced the phone
and gobbled down the last of his steak and potatoes.

Stephanie glanced at the clock on the microwave. It was
12:30 a.m. Who the hell could be calling him at this hour?

"The food was good, boo," he said, swigging the remainder
of his beer. "I got my mans coming through for a minute, so
go 'head and clean up and go to bed."

"Corey, it's the middle of the night. Who—"

There was a tap on the front door that was just audible
enough for them to hear it in the kitchen. Corey patted her ass
and headed toward the door.

"Clean up and go to bed," he called over his shoulder.

She sighed and hurriedly put the plate and fork in the dishwasher. She wiped off the table, threw his beer bottle in the
trash, and entered the living room en route to their bedroom.
Corey was sitting on the couch with a man Stephanie had
never seen before. Their voices were hushed, and the man fell
silent when he saw Stephanie. Corey turned to face her.

"Good night, boo." He made it clear that he wanted her out
of the living room and had no intention of introducing her to
his company.

She hurried from the room but lingered at the door to
their bedroom, trying to hear what the hell was so important
at midnight. She strained to hear bits and pieces of their
conversation.

"Where's his bitch ass now?" Corey asked angrily.

"The DEC . . . popping fly at the mouth." The DEC was the
name locals used for the city of Decatur and it was Corey's
territory.

"Into me for a ki . . . run it."

"Bet."

She heard the shuffling of feet and the click of the front door. Quickly, she hopped into bed and snuggled down into the covers. Just as she tried to regulate her breathing, Corey entered the room. He kicked his sneakers off and sat on the edge of the bed.

"I needa give you something," he told her.

Stephanie sat up, anxiety coming over her as she half expected her dreams to come true in the next moment.

"I can trust you, right?" His right eyebrow rose as he looked at her intently.

Speechless, she simply nodded.

"This is some serious shit, Steph. I'm giving it to you 'cause I trust that you'll ride or die with me. If I'm wrong about that shit, let me know now and I'll save myself the trouble later."

"Corey," she said, reaching out to touch his arm. "Baby, it's me. I've always been here for you, and you know that."

He reached into his pocket and pulled out a set of keys. Taking her hand in his, he placed the keys in the palm of her hand and closed his hand over hers. She looked at him in confusion.

"These are some important fucking keys," he told her. "Put 'em somewhere where they aren't easy to find and where you won't forget where you put them. Don't ever tell nobody where you put them, not even me, unless I ask you. Don't show 'em to nobody."

"What do they go to?"

"Don't worry about that. Just know that they're important. I'm trusting you with my life, Steph. Don't fuck up."

She nodded and clutched the keys tightly. When Corey told her to shut up about something, she knew better than to press further. She just nodded her understanding and said nothing. Corey rose from the bed and went into the bathroom to shower. Listening to the sound of the water, Stephanie stared at the keys in her hand, wondering what doors they were going to open in her future.

Chapter 23

Jada

The tune he was humming was completely random, and his movements were offbeat. Jada was doubled off with laughter as he shook his nonexistent booty in her face during his comical striptease. Jordan exaggerated his movements as he pulled his shirt off and tossed it in Jada's face.

"Oh yeah! Show Mama some skin, baby." Jada egged him on and could barely breathe as he enacted his version of a lap dance.

They both could hear her phone singing, and as she struggled to reach for it, Jordan lowered his 210-pound frame onto her lap and wiggled his behind to prevent her from moving.

"Stop . . . stop," she protested.

Jordan laughed at her and finally decided to spare her some mercy. The phone continued to sing. Jordan grabbed it and threw it at her. "Answer your punk-ass phone," he teased her.

She pressed the TALK button and could barely utter a salutation.

"Are you busy?" Alex's voice sounded a little frantic.

Jada tried to wave Jordan away and motioned for him to be quiet. She sincerely hoped that her girl was not stranded on the side of the road in the SWATS or something.

"Not really. What's up?"

"Okay, you have to promise not to tell anybody."

Jada sat up in the middle of her bed and struggled to regulate her breathing. "Okay."

"Definitely not the other girls."

"Okay, honey. What's up?"

"Not even Jordan, Jada."

"Oh my God, really? What is *so* secret that I can't tell Jordan?"

Jordan raised his hands up in the air, as if to say, "What gives?" Jada simply shrugged her shoulders and watched as her husband turned on the television. *White Chicks* was playing on USA again. Jada loved that movie.

"I'm pregnant."

"Shut up, Alex. Seriously, what's going on?"

"That's it."

Jada sighed, so not in the mood for games tonight. "Alex, you have to have sex to get pregnant."

"You don't think I know that? Why are you talking to me like I'm stupid?"

"I'm just saying. We *all* know that little Ms. Princess ain't giving up the drawers, so getting pregnant isn't really an issue for you." There was a pause as Jada considered the possibility. "Unless little Ms. Princess *has* given up the drawers! Did you have sex with someone?"

"Yes, Jada. Ugh. Why did I call you? You're not taking me seriously."

Jada covered her mouth in disbelief. "Are you serious? You're pregnant? For real, for real? Oh my God. Have you been to the doctor? How far along are you? What the hell is going on? You never told me that you did the do, girl. And with who? That admissions rep guy?"

"Why are you sounding happy?" Alex asked pitifully. "This is *not* a happy occasion. I'm miserable. I can't have a baby. I can't even take care of myself, let alone a baby."

"Well, boo, it's kind of too late to be having that frame of mind now, isn't it?"

"This wasn't planned. I didn't even mean to have sex with that punk."

"Wait a minute. Isn't he your boyfriend?"

Alex sighed. "At least I thought he was. I haven't heard or seen much of him lately."

"Have you told him?"

"He's coming over tonight, supposedly. Then I'm going to tell him. What am I going to do, Jada? My parents are going to kill me."

"You haven't told them yet?"

Alex began to sob into the phone. "I haven't told anybody. Just you. I'm so disappointed in myself. I don't want to have a baby. I wish to God that I could just erase it."

"Did you say you've been to the doctor?"

"Yes. I went today. I'm eight and half weeks. And sick to my stomach all the time. It sucks."

"Why did you wait so long to go to the doctor? You know you've got to tell your parents, right?"

"I can't. I've already made an appointment for a consultation. I can't have a baby. I waited so long to confirm it because I didn't want to deal with it. I don't want to be anybody's mama right now. I'm *not* going to be a mama."

Jada rubbed her temples. It was all going too fast for her. "Wait. You *just* found out. Are you sure you're ready to make that decision? Especially before you have the chance to even talk to Mario about it?"

"It's my body." Alex paused. "Don't judge me, Jada."

"I didn't say anything."

"Yeah, but I know you."

"You know me? Listen to me, girl. This is not going to be an easy decision to live with. Now, whether you do or don't, it's your business, but I'm just suggesting that you take some time to think about it."

Alex sniffled. "Okay. I better go get cleaned up before the butt hole shows up."

"Call me back if you need to, girl. I love you."

"I love you too."

Jada snapped her phone shut and looked over at Jordan, who was engrossed in the movie. She hit him playfully on the leg. "Did you catch all that?"

"I sure did."

She snuggled up to him, and they lay there in silence for a few seconds. She began to toy with his shirt and looked up at him. "Why does it seem like all my girls are getting pregnant but me? I'm the only one that's in a stable relationship. Well, minus Candace."

Jordan sighed and held his wife closely. "Because it's not our time, baby. Come on. Don't start stressing about this. It'll happen when it's supposed to happen. I promise."

"It's not fair," she said, pouting.

"Life isn't fair, babes." He shook her playfully. "Come on. We were having a good time. Don't stress, okay?"

She nodded in agreement, but the look in her eyes told him that she wasn't able to let the thought escape her mind.

Jordan kissed her forehead. "I love you, babes."

Jada smiled weakly. "I love you too."

Chapter 24

Miranda

It had been a long day at work at the store. Miranda's feet were throbbing from the overtime shift she'd just pulled. With Norris gone, she had to cover extra shifts to come up with the small portion he contributed to their household expenses. She was planning to find a smaller apartment, somewhere more affordable. As she climbed the steps to her apartment, she saw the figure of a man with his back to her standing in front of her door. She adjusted her glasses, and as she moved closer, she recognized him immediately. Her defenses went up, and she quickly scanned the area to see if anyone else was around. She considered running back down the stairs and hightailing it back to her car. Before she could make the decision, he turned around and spotted her.

"What's up?" he asked, as if they'd just seen each other yesterday.

She looked at him cautiously and grabbed her keys out of her purse. "What are you doing here, Norris?"

"I needa holla at you."

Approaching her door, Miranda glanced down at the ground next to the threshold. A bouquet of roses and a shopping bag were lying next to Norris's duffel bag. Miranda rolled her eyes and looked at her husband in confusion. "Holla at me about what?"

"Why you all tense?" He moved toward her, and she flinched. He began using a lot of hand motions and speaking softly. "Okay, check this. I know we've been through a lot of fucked-up shit. I know I haven't been the best husband. But I am your husband. All I want to do is come in, sit down, and talk to you for a minute. Let's see if we can work this out."

"I don't know. . . ." Her voice wavered.

"I'm not asking for a reconciliation. I just want to talk to you."

Miranda sighed. She walked past him, unlocked the door, and led the way inside. Norris, following suit, grabbed up his goodies and shut the door behind him. He handed the flowers to Miranda.

"Thought you'd like these," he said with a smile.

Her face was emotionless. "Thank you."

Norris walked over to the sofa, placed the roses and the shopping bag on the coffee table, and took a seat. He patted the space next to him, motioning for her to sit down beside him. She sat down, being sure to leave some distance between them.

"Where's your little girlfriend?" she asked him.

He waved her off. "Ah, man, that chick ain't my girlfriend. She's just a girl I know."

"Right."

"For real. We worked together. I've been crashing at her place since I left here. That's it."

"Uh-huh, and while I was in the hospital, you had her all up and through here, like her name was on the lease."

"Just kicking it. Look, I don't want to argue about the past. I just want to move forward and see if we have a future."

Miranda crossed her arms, and Norris gave her a hurt expression. "What? You don't believe me?"

"No." She shook her head. "I don't."

"Okay, okay. I deserve that. So I guess I've just got to show you."

She shook her head. "What do you expect me to say, Norris? Huh? You want me to just forget that you broke my rib, Norris? That you left me lying in here for dead?"

"Baby, I'm sorry. I fucked up. I own that. I fucked up."

"Damn right. And then you bring another woman up in my house, treating me like I'm some trash in the street."

Norris got down on his knees in front of her and placed his hands on her lap. He looked into her eyes pleadingly. "I can't take back everything that happened. I know that. I just want you to give me a chance to do the right thing. I want to try. I'm just a man, baby. I'm not perfect."

Tears welled up in his eyes. Miranda felt herself begin to loosen up. Norris noticed too and quickly grabbed the shopping bag off the coffee table.

"Here," he said, rummaging through the bag. "I bought you something I thought you'd like."

He pulled out a Coach purse with the tag still hanging from it. Miranda's eyes widened. She reached for the bag, turned it around to see if it was indeed real. It was. She looked at Norris in amazement. He'd never bought her anything just because, and certainly not anything as lavish as a Coach purse.

"You like it, don't you?" he asked. "Look inside it."

She looked inside the purse and found a diamond tennis bracelet inside a pocket. The bracelet was stunning, and Miranda couldn't contain the gasp that left her mouth as she held it in her hand. This was definitely not the Norris she knew.

Silently, he took the bracelet from her and placed it on her arm. She turned her wrist this way and that way, admiring the shine. Sighing, she looked at her husband, who was still kneeling on the floor in front of her.

"I need you to go to counseling," she said softly. "By yourself and marriage counseling."

He nodded. "I can do that. I can do that."

"And you will never, ever hit me again, Norris. Not so much as a slap on the ass."

"I won't, baby. I won't."

Her left eyebrow rose. "I mean it."

He reached up and touched her face gently. "Baby, I promise I will never touch you like that again."

Miranda simply looked at him, trying to get a sense of whether or not he was being truthful and sincere with her.

"Can I kiss you?" he asked.

She was hesitant but nodded her consent.

Norris rose to touch her lips softly with his. It was the most delicate kiss he'd ever given her. Miranda felt tingles inside of her as their lips joined. Perhaps her husband really was ready to be the man she needed him to be. Needing to be loved, Miranda was ready to give it a try and give her marriage a second chance.

Chapter 25

Alex

You can do this, Alex told herself. *Just tell him. Open up your mouth and tell him the words "I'm pregnant." It's simple.* Alex and Mario were sitting in her kitchen, eating a pepperoni pizza she had ordered just before he arrived. He had taken the liberty of helping himself to her dinner, and Alex hadn't felt compelled to stop him. Watching him eat two slices on top of each other at once, Alex felt her stomach turn. Surveying him, she began to question why she'd even started going out with him in the first place. Feeling her stare, Mario glanced up.

"What's up? Why you stop eating?"

She shrugged. "I don't really want it anymore."

"What's up with you? Since you were sick a while ago, your appetite has been, like, nonexistent. You don't want nothing."

Segue, stupid. Tell him.

She shrugged again and decided to change the subject. "Can we go to a movie?"

"I can't tonight. Already got plans to hit up this party."

"Oh, okay. I can just go with you."

He took a swig of his Coke and shook his head. "Naw, it's one of my boys. You wouldn't wanna go. You wouldn't even know anyone."

"I'd know you."

He reached for another slice. "We'll do something tomorrow."

"Yeah, right," she mumbled.

"What's with you?"

"What's with me? You're the one that doesn't ever want to do anything with me. You barely come over. I'm wondering if we're even dating anymore."

"Okay, you're tripping."

She crossed her arms and pouted. "I'm not tripping. You act like you don't like me anymore."

He laughed at her. "For real, Alex? Come on, man. Please don't start this little girl shit. Quit with that whiny voice and pouting routine. I'm not in the mood for that."

"Whatever." She rose from the table and started to walk out of the kitchen, but his words stopped her.

"You must be on your period."

She spun around, walked over to him, and slapped the back of his head. He dropped his slice of pizza and jumped up just as she finally found the nerve to voice her secret.

"I would be on my period if I wasn't knocked up with yo' baby!"

He grabbed her arm and froze as he processed what she'd just said. Quickly, he released her arm. "What?"

She sucked her teeth. "You heard me."

He looked her up and down before falling back into his chair. "Yeah, I heard you, but you've got the wrong one."

She glared down at him with her hands on her hips. "What's that supposed to mean?"

"That means that ain't my baby."

She gasped in contempt and looked at Mario in disgust. "That's some typical nigga shit to say."

"Watch your mouth."

"Watch yours. What? You trying to call me a ho now? You know good and well you're the only one I've ever been with."

He raised his left eyebrow. "You better calm your tone. I'm the only one, huh? We barely had sex, Alex. *Once*. And now I'm supposed to be your baby's daddy. Please. Try that high school shit on one of those young cats you're used to dealing with."

She pushed his head with her index finger. "It only takes once, dummy."

He rose once more and spoke in a threatening tone. "Don't keep putting your hands on me, Alex. For real, though."

He started to walk past her, and Alex stepped in his path.

"What? Are you seriously trying to leave? This conversation isn't over."

"What do you want me to say?"

The buzz of his phone vibrating caught their attention. He pulled the phone from its holster, looked at the caller ID, and silenced the call.

"Is that your other little girlfriend?" Alex asked, reaching for his phone.

He moved away from her. "Watch out. You talking crazy."

"I'm talking crazy? You're the one who just denied your kid. Let's be real, Mario. Clearly, you don't care anything about me. So be honest. I know you're messing with someone else."

"Man, you're on some other shit today, Alex. I'm telling you, you better go on with all that."

"So you're going to deny that too?"

"Whatever."

Turning away from her, he walked into the living room and grabbed his jacket. Alex followed him and quickly grabbed the jacket from his hands.

"You're not leaving!" She was close to tears. "You do not get to impregnate me, cheat on me, and walk out on me."

"Yo, you're way too dramatic for me today."

Finally, the tears began to fall down her cheeks, despite her attempts to control herself. She stared at her boyfriend defiantly. "I know you're cheating on me, Mario. I've read your text messages several times. You're busted."

"So now you're going through my stuff? Didn't realize you were so crazy."

"And I didn't realize what an ass you were."

They faced off in silence. Mario ran his hand over his head and sat down on the sofa.

"Look," he said. "This isn't working out."

"I'm pregnant." She said it blankly, as if saying it for the first time. "And it's yours."

He sighed. "I'm going to need some proof of that."

Alex grabbed her purse from the nearby lounging chair and pulled out a piece of paper. She handed it to Mario. He glanced over it and shrugged his shoulders.

"Okay. You're pregnant. But this paper doesn't say it's mine."

She cocked her head to the side. "Mario, you *know* it's your baby. You nearly forced me to have sex with you that night. If I wasn't ready to give it to my boyfriend, what makes you think I'm really sexing anybody else?"

Mario got angry. "You trying to say I raped you?"

"I'm trying to say we're pregnant. That's all."

Mario sighed and threw the paper down on the sofa. Wringing his hands together, he looked up at Alex and shook his head. "I'm going to need a minute, a'ight?"

He stood up and held his hand out to her, silently asking for his jacket. She didn't budge. He shook his head. "Come on now. I don't want to argue anymore. I'll call you later, or I'll be back. I just need some time to think about this, okay?"

Reluctantly, she handed him back his jacket. She watched him walk to the door and pause before he exited.

"I'll call you later, okay?" he said without turning around.

She watched him exit the apartment and felt herself fall to the floor in a fit of tears. Her breathing became uncontrollable, and she forced herself to calm down. Suddenly, she reached for her phone and dialed a familiar number.

"Yo!"

She sniffled and tried to fight back her tears so that she could respond. But she couldn't. All she could do was cry hysterically into the phone.

"Alex? What's wrong?"

She couldn't answer. The tears kept coming.

"Hey, I'm coming over, okay? Just stay on the phone till I get there. I'm coming."

It took a little over twenty minutes, but true to form, her friend came right over. Alex was disheveled, and her eyes were all red and puffy, by the time the knock sounded at the door. Sluggishly, she opened the door and fell into Clay's embrace.

"What happened to you, girl?" he asked jokingly. "You sounded like your best friend died. I'm alive and kicking, so it can't be that bad."

He ushered her into the living room, and they sat on the couch, with Alex lying in Clay's lap.

"I hate my life," she said softly.

Clay stroked her hair. "Please. Your parents pay your rent. Everybody loves you. . . . What about your life is so bad?"

She was quiet. Her tears were falling slower now, and each drop landed on Clay's pant legs.

"Okay, this is the part where you confess your sins."

She sighed. "I have to tell you something. And please don't make a joke about it."

"I won't."

"I'm pregnant."

Clay said nothing.

Alex noticed that he had stopped stroking her hair, but she continued with her confession. "I am, like, eight weeks pregnant, Clay. And when I told that jerk, he tells me it's not his . . . insinuating that I'm sleeping with everybody and their brother. Then he denies the fact that he's cheating on me. . . ."

Clay remained silent.

She hit his leg. "Say something."

Still nothing. Alex sat up and looked at her friend with pitiful eyes. His look was hard and uninviting at first. But as he took in the sight of her, sensing her turmoil, he softened.

"I knew you were sleeping with him," he stated.

"It isn't like you think. It happened only once, and it was horrible. I barely remember it. I was sick out of my mind, and he more or less forced himself on me."

"Come on, Alex—"

"You don't believe me?" Her feelings were hurt.

Clay grabbed her hand. "No, I believe you. But look at the dude you're talking about, Alex. Look at all the dudes you mess with. What did you expect from him? For him to ask you to marry him? You thought he was going to be happy? You already knew he was cheating on you."

"You're supposed to be making me feel better."

"Yeah, I'm here for you. But as your friend, I also have to be real with you. This isn't cool. Now you have another person to be concerned about. Forget that dude. Just make sure when the time comes that you get what you need out of him financially. Other than that, this is all on you, Alex."

Alex fell back into Clay's lap. "I can't do this. I can't be anybody's mama."

"Yes, you can."

"No, I can't. I can barely take care of myself. And I can't tell my parents about this. My dad would be so disappointed in me."

"You've got to tell them at some point."

"Ugh. I can't believe this is happening to me. This wasn't supposed to be me."

"Well, you know I'm here for you. Just call me Uncle Clay."

She slapped his leg. "Shut up, Uncle Clay." She sat up and gave him a weak smile. "I'm so glad you're my friend."

Clay nodded his head slowly. "Yep. That's me. Your good ole friend."

They were silent for a moment.

"So," Clay said, kicking his feet up on the coffee table, "where's your baby daddy now?"

"Ugh, don't call him that. To me, he's just a sperm donor now. I don't want him anywhere near me . . . the asshole."

"Okay, then. Where's your sperm donor?"

"He left, talking about how he needs time to think this whole thing over. I mean, you'd think *he* was the one with a baby in his body. Jerk. I should have stabbed him in the eye or something."

Clay laughed heartily. "You're nuts. That was your boo, though."

"Shut up. Speaking of boos, where's yours? You don't have some hot date to run off to?"

He shook his head. "Naw. I'm chilling. The chick I was seeing . . . well, it wasn't meant to be. Besides, I'm holding out for someone else."

"Oh yeah? You just move from one to the next, huh? You sure you don't have some babies out there somewhere?"

"Ha-ha. It's not even like that. I'm telling you, Alex, this girl is the one. It's just gon' take a minute to get her."

"What? She's not falling over herself, trying to get with Mr. Clayton Paul? What's wrong with her?"

Clay laughed. "I know, right? She's a little slow. But it's all good, pimpin'. I'll wait. I'm a patient man."

"Don't you want to get me some ice cream, Precious?" Alex asked in her sugary voice.

Clay bopped her on the nose. "Oh, you not concerned with listening to my saga, huh?" he joked.

"I'm sorry. I have a taste for it."

Clay rubbed her stomach. "It's all good," he said. "I'll make a run for the munchkin. Ain't nobody worried about you. Uncle Clay to the rescue."

Alex laughed. "You're killing me with that. Don't go growing attached to this fetus . . . embryo . . . whatever it is. I'm not planning to keep it."

Clay shook his head in disbelief. "You're just scared. Don't go making hasty decisions out of fear. I'm gonna get the munchkin's ice cream. Go fix your face or something." He playfully ruffled her hair and rose from the couch in pursuit of her snack.

Later that night, after she had taken a nice long bath, Alex surveyed her body in the mirror. She noticed a slight bulge in her tummy, which no one else would have caught. She viewed herself from all angles, trying to imagine herself with a more protruding figure. She couldn't see it. More to the point, she wasn't sure that she wanted to see it. Wrapping herself in a towel, she sat on her bed and dialed her parents' number. She hadn't spoken to them in a few days and had been trying to muster up the courage to get it all over with.

"Hey, baby girl." Her dad answered the call.

"Hi, Dad."

"What's going on? Haven't heard from you in a few days. Everything okay?"

"Yes. Just been a little busy, that's all. How's Mommy?"

"She's good. She's in there talking to your brother. He came over for a minute."

"Oh, okay."

"Mom wants to do a family vacation for Christmas, instead of the usual festivities. Like a cruise or something."

"Oh yeah?"

"Yep. We're going to pay for it, if you want to go."

Alex sighed. "That sounds fun."

"Your aunt Polly called yesterday. She was asking about you. Mom told her you were doing well in school. Mom's real proud of you, baby girl. Me too. Real proud of you."

Alex sighed again, her nerve totally gone. "Thank you, Daddy."

"Mmm-hmm. You wanna talk to Mom? I'll get her for you."

"No, I have to go study now, Daddy. Can you tell her I said hello and I'll call her tomorrow?"

"Okay, baby girl. You have a good night."

"Thanks, Daddy. Talk to you later." She clicked the phone shut and lowered her head, ashamed at herself. As she replayed the conversation in her mind, her phone rang in her hand. She looked at the caller ID and cringed.

"Hello," she said gingerly, preparing herself for more of his insulting behavior.

"What's up?"

"Nothing much. Getting ready for bed. So you done thinking it over?"

"I didn't call to argue with you, Alex," he said, catching her tone. "I'm done arguing. It's not productive, and neither one of us is getting anything out of it."

"Okay."

"So when's your next doctor's appointment?"

"In two weeks. They're going to do an ultrasound." She paused. "You want to come?"

"Let me check my schedule. I might be able to. What day?"

"Thursday."

"Yeah, I'll let you know by next week. Do you have insurance? I could add you to mine, but you know . . . we're not married."

"I have insurance through my parents. It's okay."

They sat on the phone in silence, each considering their own thoughts.

"You hurt my feelings, Mario," Alex finally said. "All that stuff you were saying about me and other dudes, and denying the fact that you're cheating on me."

"I just don't think we're on the same page. I mean, I'm sorry if I hurt your feelings, but a brother gotta be careful, you know? Girls pull this mess all the time, trying to get dudes caught up . . . trapped. Plus, I'm not ready for no kid."

"Neither am I. I'm still in school, trying to get my career going. How do you think I feel? I'm the one whose life is going to change. I'm the one carrying the baby."

"And I can respect that. But this affects me too. I have to look out for my best interests, you know?"

"Uh-huh." Alex touched her belly and quickly moved her hand. "I have to look out for mine too."

"For sho'."

"So I don't really think it's in my best interest to have a baby right now."

Mario hesitated. "So what are you saying?"

"I'm saying that when I go back to the doctor, I'm going to confirm my appointment for an abortion. I can't do this. I don't think I'm prepared to do this by myself like this."

"By yourself? You act like I just said, 'To hell with you, Alex.'"

"You may as well have. I'm not trying to be somebody's baby mama. When I have children, I want it to be in a stable family environment. Not some mistake with somebody who doesn't respect me."

"Oh my God. I was really trying to keep this drama free, Alex. For real, so you can stop with all the dramatics. We're not together anymore. So what? People have babies every day out of wedlock. It's not the end of the world. You're not going to kill my kid just because we broke up. That's some selfish shit."

"First of all, I didn't realize that we'd officially broken up."

"Stop playing."

"Second of all, who you calling selfish when you're the one messing around with God knows how many chicks? I guess I should be thankful that you gave me a baby and not an STD with your trifling self. Third off, now you wanna claim the baby? I'm gonna need you to make up your mind. This is the exact reason right here why we *don't* need to have a baby together. You can't be the baby's daddy one day, when it fits you, then disown the baby the next day just 'cause you feel like it, Mario. Now *that's* some selfish mess. Babies need stability. We don't have that. Well, you definitely don't."

"Lower your voice when you talking to me. You're getting a little bit beside yourself. If you think I'm going to let you just kill the baby, *if* it's my baby, and I'm not going to do anything, you can forget it."

"Really? Last time I checked, this was *my* body. Tell you what, Mario. When April twenty-sixth comes, I'll call you and let you know if the baby came or if I aborted it. Don't bother calling back."

She clicked the phone closed, ending the call, and fell back on her bed. Instantly, the phone began to ring again. She sent the call to voice mail. Two minutes passed, and the phone rang again. Once more, she sent the call to voice mail. On his third call, Alex answered without speaking, then immediately hung up. Before the phone could ring a fourth time, she powered off her cell and closed her eyes.

This is my body, she thought. *My body, my decision. Period.*

Chapter 26

Candace

Candace took a deep breath as she entered her home. From the doorway she could hear the video game blaring. Walking through the kitchen, she surveyed the dirty dishes in the sink and the half-empty pitcher of lemonade on the counter. She sat her purse and cell phone down next to the pitcher and clutched an envelope in her hand.

"Jehovah, give me strength," she whispered.

She walked into the living room and over to the big-screen television. Quincy barely noticed her. Without warning she pulled the plug to the television out of the wall, and the screen went blank.

"What the fuck!" Quincy yelled at her. "Do you know what you just did?"

She tossed the envelope at him. "How 'bout you tell me what you've done?"

"What the hell is this, and why the hell did you come in here fucking up my game in the middle of the damn season, woman?"

"Read the letter, Quincy."

He threw down his wireless controller, then looked at the envelope, which was addressed to him. "It's already open. You read it, already. What you want me to read it for?"

She put her hands on her hips, praying for inner strength. He pulled the letter out, and she watched as his eyes went over the words she'd already memorized. *Your home is scheduled to be foreclosed.* Quincy sighed deeply and leaned back on the couch.

"Uh-huh." Candace looked at him with contempt. "We are about to lose our house, Quincy. You care to explain that?"

"Don't worry about it." He waved her off.

"Don't worry about it?" she repeated. "Are you serious? That's all you can come up with? I've been busting my booty working, and you won't so much as lift a finger around here. And now you've lost our house."

"*My* house . . . and we ain't lost nothing. I said, 'Don't worry about it.' I'll take care of it."

"*Your* house? Oh, you getting technical now? What's wrong with you? Have you lost your mind? What have you been doing with your money, since you haven't being paying the damn mortgage?"

"Look, don't start trying to get in my shit. You ain't never been concerned about how the bills got paid before, so—"

"Hold up. Don't flip this on me! You are supposed to be the head of your household, financially and spiritually. So don't be acting like you've been burdened by responsibility."

"Whatever."

"In two weeks they are going to put us out, Quincy. So you haven't been paying the mortgage for a minute. And you didn't think that was something you're obligated to tell your wife?"

He didn't respond. He simply tossed the letter onto the coffee table and walked over to the wall to plug the television back in. She reached out to grab his arm, and he violently yanked it away from her. "Get off me!"

"You're just going to ignore me? Ignore our problem?"

He restarted his game.

"Quincy!" She was astonished by his silent treatment.

He chose his team again.

"Quincy!" She flailed her arms about, trying to get his attention. He continued to ignore her. "You know what? You're a sorry excuse for a man. You can't keep a job. You have no sense of responsibility. Can't even handle your own business. That's not attractive, and that's not the kind of husband I want."

"Shut up sometimes," he answered her. "Told you I'd take care of it, so leave it alone."

"How are you going to take care of it? Do you have all the money you owe them?"

He went back to ignoring her.

Candace sucked her teeth. "I didn't think so. Why did I ever marry your sorry butt? What kind of man can't provide for his wife? You make me sick."

She turned from him and hurried upstairs. In the heat of her anger, she grabbed a suitcase and began packing some of her belongings.

Quincy had the television blaring so loudly that she didn't hear her cell ringing in the kitchen. As he sat there playing his game, Quincy could hear the phone chiming. He ignored it. Then he heard the continued beeping of her text indicator. Intrigued, he went into the kitchen and grabbed her phone. He saw the missed call from Khalil.

Who the hell is that?

He clicked on the VIEW MESSAGE button to read the texts sent from Khalil.

Baby, are you still mad at me? If you can get away, text me so I can show you how sorry I am. I miss your sexy, sleek body, and I want to run my tongue down your legs the way you like. Come on. You know you want to.

Quincy bolted up the stairs and grabbed Candace as she was frantically packing.

"What—" The rest of her words could not escape her lips as he pinned her up against the wall.

"You bring your ass in here, talking about what kind of a husband I am, but what the hell kind of wife are you?"

"You are hurting me." She winced from the pain of his tight grasp.

He threw her cell phone in her face so hard that it bruised her cheek. "Who the fuck is Khalil?"

Her eyes grew wide, and she opened her mouth to speak, but he cut her off.

"Save it, you foul-ass bitch." He let her go and moved away from her. "Walking around here, talking about how spiritually superior you are. You're a hypocrite, a fuckin' joke. You think I'm supposed to bow down to your ass, like you're some rare dime piece or something. How fuckin' rare are you if you're opening your legs to every dick that points in your direction? Oh, my bad. Let's not forget every pussy that drips your way too."

She rubbed her face and bent down to pick her cell up from the place where it had fallen on the floor. She looked up at Quincy in fright, having never seen him so enraged.

"Stupid bitch," he shouted, turning away from her. He let out a piercing scream, which scared her; then he abruptly punched a hole into their bedroom wall.

Candace was stunned. She slid to the floor and watched him, afraid of what his fury would lead him to do next. A thousand thoughts flew through her mind, including an image of Miranda looking frail and hopeless. She was scared that she was about to be the next one in her girlfriend circle to be abused by her husband. She clutched the cell in her hand and stared at Quincy as he paced back and forth, punching the air and hurling obscenities. Once he tired of this, he turned his angry glare back to her. He eyed the suitcase she had been packing.

"What? You're leaving me? You think you hurting me by packing your sorry-ass bag and leaving? Fuck you!" He took her suitcase off the bed and threw it at her. "Fuck you and all the niggas you've been fucking and all the chicks you've been eating out. Fuck you."

She jumped.

"Get the fuck out of my house with your sorry ass. Think you're God's gift to a man? I hope you lay down and get gonorrhea in your ass and chlamydia in your mouth, you sorry cunt."

He kicked her suitcase, and Candace screamed. She was so sure that he was aiming for her body instead.

"Get the fuck up and get your fake ass out of my house." Quincy was beginning to cry now.

She blinked, not sure if she should move or not. Thinking it best to just go, she grabbed her suitcase, tossed a few more items into it absentmindedly, and hurried out of the room. She could hear Quincy throwing shit down the stairs behind her and cursing her as she scurried away.

"Don't bring your ass back here. I don't need you. Talking 'bout you need a real man. Tell Khalil's ass to buy you a house, you second-rate bitch. Think you got so much class. You ain't nothing but a hood rat with some typing skills. Flexing ass, you ain't even got a paralegal certificate, let alone a college degree. You ain't shit, your damn self. You one step away from flipping some burgers. Fuck you!"

She ran out of the house, neglecting to close the front door behind her. Quickly, she jumped into her car and sped off down the street. When she approached the first red light, she glanced at the text Khalil had sent. Damn his ass for texting her, instead of just approaching her at work tomorrow. She could have kicked herself for having the lack of vision to leave her phone downstairs. Unsure of what to do next, she pressed the CALL button to return his call.

"I'm glad you called," Khalil answered. "Are you coming over?"

"Actually, I am."

"I'll cook you dinner."

"Where's Sheila?"

"Where's Quincy?"

"We're getting a divorce."

"She's kinda gone away for a while. Let me go start dinner. I'll see you when you get here."

"Okay."

Candace wasn't sure if running to Khalil was a smart move to make. But she was determined not to return home to her parents and admit that her marriage was a mistake. They'd never let her live it down, especially after she'd fought so hard to convince them that she truly loved Quincy. As she drove in silence, she thought about the girls questioning her true feelings about Quincy. They too would never let her forget how much of a front she had put up about being married.

I tried to be a good wife, she thought, reasoning with herself. *I admit that perhaps I lost my way, but Quincy was never a good man for me, and a home is only as strong as its spiritual head.*

She soon reached Khalil's place and was almost ashamed to look at him as he opened the door and allowed her entry.

As she stepped into the light of his foyer, Khalil could see the bruise on her face. He slammed the door shut.

"What did that nigga do to you?" he demanded.

"Calm down," she urged him. "It's not that bad. He didn't hit me or anything."

"It doesn't look like he didn't hit you."

"He threw my phone at me after he saw your text tonight."

Khalil grimaced. He reached for her hand and led her into the living room and onto the sofa. Slowly, he lifted her legs onto his lap and removed her shoes. He used his magical fingers to knead the soles of her feet. Candace lay back on the sofa and tried to relinquish the tension she'd been feeling for the past hour.

"What did you say to him?" Khalil asked her.

She shook her head. "Nothing. He didn't really ask me any questions. He just yelled and cussed and punched a hole in our wall."

"What made him look at your phone?"

"I don't know. We had just had an argument. His sorry ass has let our house go into foreclosure, and he's mad at me because of his stupidity."

Khalil shook his head. "You need a real man, sexy. A man who knows how to take care of his woman and provide for her." He slid his hand up her leg and under her skirt. She squirmed.

"Khalil," she protested weakly.

"Hmmm?"

His fingertips slightly caressed the fabric of her cotton bikini briefs, which were already becoming soaked. It didn't take much to excite her. She felt him slip inside of her undies, and his thumb strategically brushed over her clit repeatedly. She relaxed her body and gave in to the intense sensation of his touch.

"You like it when a real man touches you, don't you?" Khalil whispered to her.

In seconds she was exploding in spasms against the back-and-forth motion of his finger. Her body shuddered and convulsed until the sensation passed her by. Satisfied with himself, Khalil removed his hand and licked his fingers seductively, making a great production of it. Candace looked at him as he dragged his tongue back and forth, lapping up all her juices.

"Great appetizer," he teased. "Now, let me go get your entrée, my dear." Without another word, he left the room in pursuit of their dinner.

Later, as they lay in bed, intertwined and damp from their lovemaking, Khalil ran his hand up her spine. The smell of incense burning relaxed her mind in the aftermath of him relaxing her body.

"You can stay with me for as long as you need to," he said softly. "I'm here for you."

She sucked her teeth. "And what would Sheila say?"

"She's in jail for the time being."

Candace was stunned. "What? Why?"

"Domestic dispute."

She turned over to face him. "Let me get this straight. You called the police on her and pressed charges against the woman?"

"She came at me with a knife. Threatened to cut my johnson off."

Candace laughed. "Shut up."

"For real. She's crazy. I was breaking up with her, and she went nuts. Rather than put my hands on the woman, I called the police."

"You couldn't just leave?"

"She wouldn't let me."

Candace lay back, looked up at the ceiling, and laughed uncontrollably. "Ridiculous. And how long is she going to be in there?"

"Until she makes bail. Or until her court date. I don't really care."

"You are something else." She sighed. "I can't stay here. As much as I need a place to stay for a minute, I don't think I should stay here with you, Khalil. If she comes home and finds me up in here . . . I don't want to hurt anybody if she clicks on stupid. And I damn sure don't want anyone running after me with a knife."

"She won't come back. She's not that crazy."

"Right."

Khalil kissed her cheek gently. "Let's get some rest. You can figure it all out tomorrow. Tonight just let me hold you." He embraced her, and she allowed herself to be cocooned in his arms.

Chapter 27

Jada

They entered the building quickly. Jada headed toward the elevator, and Alex followed her, dragging behind.

"Slow down, girl," Alex complained, leaning against the wall as they waited for the elevator to reach them. She clutched her left side and leaned over slightly.

"You okay?" Jada asked.

"Cramping. And you're killing me by moving all fast. Jeez."

They entered the elevator, and Jada pressed the button for the lobby. "You can use the exercise, girl. Gotta get you ready for carrying that baby weight around."

"Well, you can cancel that, because I'm not going to be carrying anything around."

Jada shot her friend a puzzled look. "Are you still on this?"

The elevator buzzed as they reached their floor.

"I'm telling you, I'm not having this baby."

They exited the elevator, and Jada slapped Alex on the arm. "What is wrong with you?"

Alex rolled her eyes. "What's wrong with you?"

"Don't do this."

"No, *you* don't do this. Don't lecture me. I know you want to have a baby, Jada, and you think the idea of being a mom is all grand. Good for you. You're married. You can do that. But I'm not, so I can't."

Jada stopped walking and turned to look at her prissy friend. "No, you can do it, all right. If you were woman enough to lie there and sleep with ole boy, then you should be big girl enough to own up to the responsibility. You kill me."

"What?"

"You're so freakin' spoiled and clueless. So . . . selfish."

"Because I don't want to share my body with a little person I made with a man that doesn't even like me? Where do you get off judging me?"

Jada noticed that Alex was leaning over and cradling her left side. "I'm not judging you. . . . What's wrong with you?"

"I told you I'm cramping."

"You're pregnant. You shouldn't be cramping. Come on. Let's take Jordan his lunch. You can sit down in his office for a minute."

Alex followed Jada through the corridor and into Jordan's office. The tall man was busy on a call when they entered. He waved at them, and Jada waved back. She motioned for Alex to take a seat. Sitting next to her, she whispered to her friend.

"I think you should think about this before making a rash decision. Trust me, you don't want to wake up years from now regretting the decision you make."

Alex began to rock. "Let it go, Jada. Okay. It's my decision."

"I know that. Okay, okay. Um, you're making me nervous, girl. You don't look too good. Is it painful?"

"A little worse than my menstrual cramps."

"You want me to take you to the hospital? It doesn't sound good, girl."

"No. We can just stop and get some aspirin or something."

"Hey, babes," Jordan called to Jada.

She got up and walked over to her husband, and they exchanged a quick embrace.

"You didn't have to come down here," he told her.

She shrugged. "We were in the area, so I thought it would be nice to drop a little something off to you."

"That was nice of you."

Jordan looked over at Alex. At this point she was leaning over, with her face in her hands. Jordan looked at Jada for an explanation.

"Call nine-one-one," she mouthed to him. She walked over to Alex, who was whimpering softly. She touched her friend lightly on the back. "Alex?"

Alex looked up at her in tears. "Something's wrong. I feel like I'm bleeding."

Jada looked over at Jordan, who was already on the line, calling for help. "Stand up," she ordered Alex. "Stand up just for a second. Let's check you out, okay?"

She assisted Alex to her feet, and sure enough, her jeans were stained with blood. Jada eased her back into the chair and held her hand. "Someone's coming to help us, okay? Just stay calm for me."

Jada rubbed her friend's back and looked over at Jordan, who was still on the phone, directing the emergency team on how to get to the building. Time seemed to stand still as the trio waited for the paramedics to come to Alex's aid. They were all relieved to see the two men enter the office with a stretcher in tow. A short, bald man approached the two women and looked down at Alex.

"Ma'am, can you tell us what's hurting you?"

"I have bad cramps in my left side," Alex cried. "And I'm bleeding."

The paramedic checked his computer device, which he was carrying in his hand. He peered over his notes. "You're pregnant? How far along are you?"

"Two months."

"Okay. We're going to get you on the stretcher and take you to the hospital, okay? Do you have a preference? Is there a particular hospital that you want to go to?"

Alex shook her head no.

Jada thought quickly. "DeKalb Medical."

"You're her friend or family?" the paramedic asked.

"Both," Jada replied.

The other paramedic unzipped the large bag he'd brought in with them. "You don't wanna take her vitals first, Parker?" he asked his partner.

Parker shook his head. "Don't want her to lose much more blood. We can do it in the truck."

"Does the cramping hurt worse when you move, hon?" Parker asked.

Another shake of her head.

"Okay. We're going to help you up here and ease you onto the stretcher, okay? On the count of three." Parker positioned his hand under Alex's arm and proceeded to help her up. "One, two, three."

Together the men eased Alex onto the stretcher, strapped her in securely, and covered her with sheets.

"How old are you, ma'am?" the second paramedic asked Alex.

Alex didn't answer him.

"She's twenty-one," Jada answered.

"Do you know her height and weight?" the second paramedic asked.

"Um, about five-eight, a hundred thirty-two pounds," Jada told him.

"Come on. Take her BP and temp in the truck," Parker ordered. He looked at Jada. "Are you riding with us?"

Jada grabbed Alex's purse and moved toward the door. "No. I'll meet you there."

She hurried out of her husband's office without so much as a kiss good-bye and sped down the stairs to the parking garage. She didn't want to take the elevator, because she knew they would be bringing Alex down that way. Quickly, she trotted to her car, climbed in, and exited the parking garage. As she drove through downtown Decatur, she could hear the sirens of the truck, which was following behind her. "They move quickly," she said aloud.

As quickly as she could, she reached the hospital, parked in the garage, and went inside the emergency room in search of her friend.

Alex looked at Jada with sad eyes when she entered the room. "Can you help me please?"

Jada helped the tall beauty over to the bathroom. Alex leaned on Jada and began to sob heavily.

"I didn't mean it, Jada. I didn't mean to say I didn't want my baby." Her words were barely distinguishable through her loud sobs. "God is punishing me. He's punishing me for being selfish."

Jada hugged her friend and tried to reassure her as best she could. "That's not true. Things happen, and we really don't know what's happening now. Come on. Pull yourself together, sweetie."

Together they managed to get Alex onto the toilet. Jada then helped her over to the exam table, where Alex removed her blouse and replaced it with the paper gown. By the time the nurse reentered the room, Alex was lying quietly on the exam table.

"Okay, dear, my name is Brenda. I'm your nurse. How long have you been bleeding?"

"Just today," Alex answered softly.

"And how pregnant are you?"

"Two months."

The nurse busied herself with washing her hands. "First pregnancy?"

"Yes, ma'am."

The nurse turned to Alex and smiled. "Aw, 'Yes, ma'am,' huh? Listen at you sounding all sweet as pie. How old are you, child?"

"Twenty-one."

The nurse felt around her stomach. "Tell me if it hurts worse in any particular spot." She mashed and pressed Alex's abdomen, and Alex just lay still, saying nothing. "Anything?" the nurse asked.

"No. It just cramps badly on my left side."

The nurse pulled a square package out of the storage cabinet under the sink. She smiled at Alex. "Okay, hon. The doctor is going to want to have an ultrasound and blood work done. I'm going to put this catheter in for you now and then draw your blood. Okay, sugar?"

Jada cringed, and Alex frowned at the nurse.

"What's that for?" Alex asked.

Nurse Brenda pulled a long tube out of the package and held it up for her to see. "We put this part into your urethra so that your urine trickles out into this bag." She held up the pouch for Alex to see.

"Why?"

"Need your bladder empty for the ultrasound, love. It's not that bad. When you had sex for the first time . . . I promise you that *that* hurt worse." Nurse Brenda laughed and patted Alex on the leg. "Relax, sugar." She turned to look at Jada. "Okay, baby. You can wait outside for just two minutes, while we put the catheter in."

Jada stood up, and Alex held her hand out. "No. Don't go." She looked at the nurse pitifully. "She can stay. It's okay."

The nurse shrugged, and Jada sat back down.

"Scooch up, baby, and bend your knees up," the nurse told Alex.

Alex did as directed.

"Now, move your legs apart for me." The nurse went about putting in the tube, and Alex winced from the discomfort. Nurse Brenda tried to take her mind off of it by keeping up idle conversation. "You two must be good friends, since you let her sit in here and see all your business like this."

Jada giggled a little.

"We're pretty close," Alex responded through clenched teeth.

"Mmm-hmm. I wouldn't even let my sister be taking in all my business. All right, you can relax your legs now."

Alex put her legs down and sighed.

"That wasn't too bad, now was it?" Nurse Brenda asked her.

"It was bad enough."

The nurse pulled her rubber gloves off and washed her hands again. She selected several tubes from a rack, a butterfly needle, and what looked like a large rubber band. "Okay, time to take your blood," she told Alex. "Which arm do they usually take your blood from, sugar?"

Alex held out her right arm. Jada watched as the nurse wiped her arm down with alcohol pads and proceeded to take her blood. In no time she was done. Tubes of blood in hand, the nurse patted Alex on the leg and assured her that a tech would be in soon to transport her to radiology for her ultrasound.

Alex sat up on the exam table and looked at Jada. "Thank you for coming with me."

"You don't have to thank me."

"You're always there when I need you."

"That's what friends are for, girl. You'd do the same for me."

"Yeah, well . . . I'd probably panic and not be much help to anybody."

"Do you want to call Mario?"

Alex sucked her teeth and crossed her arms. "For what? He can kick rocks."

"He should know what's going on."

"We don't even know what's going on, right?"

Touché, chick, Jada thought to herself. Before she could respond, there was a knock at the door, and in walked the tech with a wheelchair.

"Radiology?' he asked, rather than said.

Alex made an effort to get off of the exam table, and sensing her struggle, the tech assisted her into the wheelchair. He looked up at Jada and nodded. "You can stay here. She'll be back in about thirty minutes or so."

Jada watched him wheel Alex out of the room, letting the door close behind him. Staring at the bloodstains Alex had left on the white sheets of the exam table, Jada sighed. She sat back in her chair and closed her eyes, trying to relax her mind. A melody suddenly played, interrupting her attempt to unwind. She was holding Alex's purse in her lap, and she could feel a phone vibrating as the melody got louder. Realizing that it was Alex's phone ringing, she quickly pulled the cell out of the girl's purse and uttered a rushed hello.

"What's up? I was trying to reach Alex." The man on the other end of the line sounded confused. Jada looked down at the caller ID and saw that it was Clay on the line.

"Hey, Clay. This is Jada, Alex's friend."

"Oh, what's up? Where's your homegirl? In the bathroom?"

"Not exactly." Jada was unsure how Alex would feel about her disclosing her situation to Clay. "She's in the hospital, in the emergency room."

His tone told her he was panicked. "Hospital? What happened? Is something wrong with the baby?"

Jada exhaled. "I wasn't sure if you knew she was pregnant or not, but she was cramping and bleeding—"

"The baby? What's the status on the baby?"

"They just took her down for an ultrasound, so we don't know for sure yet, Clay." She sighed. "But I think it's pretty safe to say that she's having a miscarriage."

"Which hospital?"

"DeKalb Medical."

"I'm on my way."

Clay didn't give her a chance to respond or protest. He clicked off the line immediately. Jada was touched by how much the young man really cared for Alex. Too bad Alex wasn't able to see how he truly felt about her, she thought.

Chapter 28

Miranda

"Something's different about you," Norris commented as Miranda checked her attire in the mirror.

She stuck her nose up and straightened out her beautiful bracelet.

Norris was sitting on the bed, flipping through the cable stations and drawing on a blunt he'd just rolled. "You seem more chill than normal. You're not even bugging me about smoking in the house."

She shrugged. "Just have decided not to beat a dead horse."

"Uh-huh." He held the blunt out in her direction. "Want a hit?"

She looked over at him and raised her eyebrow.

Norris laughed and threw his head up at her. "Go on," he urged her. "You know you want to."

She took one step toward him, then stopped.

"Don't hesitate," he teased her. "Go on and take it. You know you want to."

"Stop playing," she told him.

He chuckled. "You stop playing wit' yo' self."

"What is your problem?"

He shrugged. "No problem. It's all gravy to me. I'm just saying, be real with ya' boy. I've been smoking for years, baby. *Years*. Trust me. I can smell the hint of the green from down the street. Especially if it's that good-good."

Miranda sat on the bed and began to put her boots on. "So what are you trying to say?"

Norris leaned forward and blew a puff of smoke in his wife's face. She barely flinched and didn't cough and choke, as she usually did when he did that.

"I'm saying I'm not tripping that you've been hitting the blunt. Hell, that's all right with me. This shit here is good for you. It's all natural."

"Whatever, Norris."

"All I'm wondering is, when did you pick up your new little pastime?"

She shook her head and rose from the bed. "Norris, I'm not entertaining this conversation." She grabbed her Coach bag and headed for the bedroom door. "I'll be back later."

"Where you going? Off to blaze? That's something else that's different 'bout you. You're always running off somewhere. Ever since I came back home, you stay gone. What's that about?"

"I'm just going to hang out with my girls. I'll be back in about an hour. Okay?"

"Yeah, all right. Least you could do is let a nigga hit whatever the hell you're sampling."

She waved him off and walked through the apartment, heading to the front door. "Whatever, Norris," she called over her shoulder.

She exited the apartment and began to descend the stairs. Suddenly it dawned on her that she'd forgotten her cell phone in the house. She turned around and walked back to her unit. Hesitating before unlocking the door, she wondered if she should just tell Norris the truth. Sneaking off to nurture her newfound bad habit was beginning to get on her nerves. Sighing, she turned the lock and reentered the apartment. She looked on the coffee table. The phone wasn't there. She looked on the kitchen counter and still no phone. She turned around and headed for her bedroom but suddenly stopped in her tracks when she heard Norris's voice.

"You know you miss me, girl. . . . That's your own fault. All you had to do was act right, and it woulda been all good. . . .I might just stay gone until you learn how to treat your man. . . . Watch your mouth now. . . . How you gon' be mad because a nigga is with his wife? You knew what it was when we first started. . . . Oh yeah? And what you gon' do for me if I do come over?"

Miranda couldn't listen to any more. She made the final steps into their bedroom, and Norris quickly clicked off his cell phone. She didn't say anything. Her eyes surveyed the room, and she spotted her cell lying on the night table. Slowly, she walked over to it, picked it up, and waved it at Norris.

"Guess it's a good thing that I left my phone, huh?"

Norris jumped up and walked over to Miranda. "Baby, look. That shit wasn't nothing—"

She held her hand up to silence him. She turned to leave the room, and he grabbed her arm. Instinctively, she screamed and snatched her arm away.

"Man, calm down," he begged her. "Nobody's going to hurt you, Miranda. I'm just trying to talk to you."

She shook her head and backed out of the room. "No, I don't want to talk to you. I don't have anything to say to you. Tell it to Tammy."

Quickly, she ran from the apartment and down the stairs to the safety of her car. Eyes filled with tears, she peeled out of the parking lot and down the road. Her cell began to ring, and she ignored it, sure that it was Norris calling to plead his case. Four calls and many tears later, she was at her destination. It was a place she'd been visiting often. She walked the familiar path up the sidewalk and to the door of the luxury apartment. Knocking two times but getting no answer, she leaned against the door frame, unable to control her tears. Suddenly she heard the lock on the door turn and stepped back just as the door swung open.

"Man, you're bugging," he said in a hushed voice.

Ignoring his reference to her dishelmed appearance, Miranda walked past him and entered the apartment. "I'm having a bad fucking day."

"What's wrong, girl?"

Miranda looked to her left abruptly, completely taken aback from hearing Stephanie's voice. There she sat on the couch, rubbing her belly, with her feet propped up. Miranda's glance flew over to Corey, who was standing by the front door, shaking his head. Quickly, Miranda returned her confused look to her girlfriend, who was looking at her with concern.

"Um, I . . . I don't know where to start," Miranda said, babbling. "I'm just so . . . in shock." She felt herself begin to shake from nervousness. Trying to get herself together and regain her composure, she drifted over to the couch and sat down.

Corey walked over to the ladies and smiled. "I'm going to leave y'all to your little girl talk. I'm going outside to clean my car out."

"Okay, babe," Stephanie said cheerfully.

Corey left the apartment, and Miranda leaned back against the couch. She placed her purse down beside her. Stephanie noticed it immediately.

"That's a nice bag, girl. Where'd you get it?"

"Norris," Miranda said without thinking. She bit her lip right after saying his name, knowing that this was going to lead to many more questions. She wasn't ready to tell any of her girls that she and Norris had reunited. Especially after what had just happened.

"Mmm-hmm. What is he doing? Trying to buy back your affection?"

Miranda was silent.

"I hope you told him to dream on."

Miranda rubbed her temples, so not wanting to have this discussion.

Stephanie leaned forward. "Miranda? Please tell me that you did not take that sorry-ass nigga back."

Miranda shook her head. "Don't judge me. He *is* my husband."

"Your husband is the same jerk who tried to kill you, honey."

Miranda sighed. "He wants to try to make it work. He's truly sorry. He agreed to go to counseling."

"How long?"

"How long what?"

"How long have y'all been back together?"

"I don't know. Two weeks."

Stephanie shifted her position. "Are you kidding me? What are you thinking? You were just telling us about the desperation of some women . . . you know, just wanting to be loved. Are you that desperate for love that you'd go back to a man who beats you like you're some nigga in the street who's stolen his money?"

Miranda grabbed her purse. "I really didn't come here to be berated."

Stephanie's brow knit as she looked at Miranda skeptically. "Oh? And what exactly did you come over for? I don't even remember you calling my phone to say you were on the way. Since when do you just do a drive-by? And how did you even know where the new apartment was? I haven't had y'all over since we moved in."

Miranda stood up and headed for the door, with Stephanie following behind her, in pursuit of an answer. "Forget this. I just needed to talk. I didn't know that I needed to make an appointment with my girlfriend to have a heart-to-heart. Thanks for the memo. I'll know who not to run to next time."

Before Stephanie could respond, Miranda quickly exited her friend's apartment and slammed the door behind her. She felt guilty for her defensive outburst but was relieved to be out of the apartment as she hurried to her car.

"Hey," she heard Corey call out as she was about to get into her car.

She turned around and watched him walk over to her.

"What the hell is up with you?" he asked.

'I . . . I didn't know she was here."

"I called you four times to tell you not to come through. And I sent you a text, man. What? You don't use your phone anymore?"

"I heard the phone ring. I thought it was Norris."

"Whatever. Tell you what. You can't come back to the house no more. I don't make it a habit to do business at my house with my ole lady and my kid here, anyway."

"I'm sorry, okay? It was an honest mistake."

"That's cool. Just know that whenever you need to cop something, you gon' have to go to the trap."

She nodded her understanding. "Can I get that, though? This time, I mean."

"Man, get outta here. I can't be doing that out here all willy-nilly. Have my neighbors all suspicious and shit. And you know your girl is probably looking out the window at us. I'll text you the address later, a'ight?"

"Okay." She felt defeated. Nothing was going her way today.

Chapter 29

Alex

Waking from a long slumber, Alex turned over in her bed and grimaced. She felt so tired. The knocking at her front door caused her to sit straight up. Slowly, she slid from the bed and walked to her bedroom door. The sound of two male voices alarmed her. Then she remembered. Clay had been staying with her since the day she returned home from the hospital. Like a true friend, he hadn't left her side without a great reason. He had been fixing her meals, keeping her company, even washing her clothes. Anything she needed, Clay was right there. She listened hard, trying to make out who the other voice belonged to. Then it occurred to her. It was Mario.

"Can you just wake her up and let her know that I'm here?" Mario asked Clay.

Clay popped his knuckles and hung his head. "Naw, bruh. I can't do that."

"What's your problem, man? Why you blocking?"

"Go on somewhere with that, man. Nobody's blocking. I'm telling you straight up, Alex doesn't want to see you. It's my understanding that ya' business together is over."

"As long as she's carrying my seed, our business is very much still on and popping."

Clay pointed his finger at the other man. "See, that right there shows just how out of touch you are. Alex isn't carrying your seed anymore."

"What the hell are you talking about?"

"It's been what? Two weeks. You haven't called her, haven't thought to come by. You've been ghost all this time. I don't even see why you're popping up now."

Mario rubbed his chin. "So the bitch went and had an abortion, anyway?"

Without thinking, Clay stepped to Mario, bringing the two men face-to-face. He was so close to Mario that their noses were almost touching.

"I'm gone say this one time and one time only, so I hope you catch it so that you won't catch my foot up your ass. Don't you ever, *ever* call her a bitch again, my dude. The only bitch in here is you, you bitch-ass nigga."

"Man, you don't want none of this, so you can get the fuck out of my face with your li'l preppy-boy ass. What? You fucking her now? All this time you're supposed to be her little BFF. The way she talked about you, I thought your punk ass was gay. I wouldn't be surprised if the baby was yours."

Clay shoved Mario, causing him to fall back against the front door. "Sorry-ass excuse for a man." He glared at Mario as he tried to regain his footing. "She lost the baby two weeks ago, probably because of your bitch ass stressing her out. And for the record, you should consider your ass lucky that you're not in jail for raping her."

"Man, fuck you. Nobody raped that girl. I'm a grown-ass man. I got plenty of chicks willing to give it to me, so why the hell would I want to take it from her young ass?"

"I'm giving you two seconds to raise up out of here, home-boy, before I catch a case."

Mario shoved Clay. "Get some, then."

Clay stood firm, with fists clenched and expression hard.

"That's what I thought," Mario spat out. He turned to leave. "Tell Alex she doesn't have to worry about me anymore. I'm gone."

Alex heard the front door slam and returned to her bed. She was more thankful than ever to have a friend like Clay by her side. She thought he was going to come to the bedroom to check on her, but the sound of the television in the living room let her know that he was not. Lying down on the bed, she stared up at the ceiling, deep in thought. Her cell phone rang from under her pillow. She retrieved it and answered the call.

"Hey, Jada."

"How are you, girl?"

"I'm okay. Just over here resting."

"Clay still there?"

Alex smiled. "Yes, girl. And he just chomped Mario off not even five minutes ago."

"For real? That Clay is something else."

"Yes, he is. My little knight in shining armor."

"So are you feeling any better?"

"Yes. I am. I'm just ready to get my life back to normal. This whole thing has been so depressing and difficult."

"Did you ever talk to your parents?" Jada asked.

"About what? There's nothing to tell now."

"Are you serious? You just had a traumatic experience and a surgical procedure, girl. You don't think that's cause enough to let your family know what's going on with you?"

Alex sighed. "I really don't see the point in upsetting them at this point. What they don't know won't hurt them."

"But it'll hurt you. You need all the emotional support you can get, girl."

Alex was silent.

Jada tried to convince her that she needed to tell her parents what had happened. "Okay then. Think about this. When they get their little statement from United Healthcare showing them the services you recently had that their insurance covered—you know . . . those little statements that say 'This is not a bill'—what the hell are you going to say?"

Alex was speechless. The thought that the insurance company would send them anything hadn't crossed her mind. Now she was going to be forced to deal with the disappointment and hurt she thought she was going to avoid.

"Let me call you back." Alex was anxious to end their conversation.

"All right, girl," Jada replied. "Just do me a favor and consider getting to your parents before they read about it in the mail. Okay?"

"Okay, friend. Talk to you later."

Alex disconnected the call and closed her eyes. If it wasn't one thing, it was another.

Chapter 30

Candace

It was definitely time to move on. Candace had been back and forth between Khalil's house and an older cousin's house while trying to figure out what her next move was going to be. It was becoming increasingly difficult to hide her separation from her parents. Work was becoming a challenge as well, because with all her personal issues, Candace was becoming more and more moody. She used to love getting away from the office with Khalil during lunch breaks, especially when there was tension in the office. But now that they'd been cohabitating, their afternoon trysts were no longer appealing to Candace. In fact, she tried to avoid him in the office building altogether. She was grateful for a place to lay her head, but she was getting sick and tired of his male chauvinist attitude and superiority complex.

Khalil liked to attribute everything he didn't agree with or like about her to the fact that she was so much younger than he was. He treated her like she didn't know her ass from a hole in the wall. As if his purpose in life was to give her a new direction. She was sick of him acting like he was her daddy. His charm and charisma seemed to come and go; he was never consistent. He was either belittling her or bewildering her—always going from one extreme to the very next. It was exhausting, never mind the fact that he could never take it whenever she called him on his bullshit. Again, he considered her perspective to be juvenile and childish.

"Candace, can you bring me Sylvia Peterson's case file?"

She was being paged by Pat, one of the firm's junior partners. Candace didn't care much for Pat, and she certainly was in no mood to play anyone's errand girl today.

She buzzed Pat's office back. "I can't leave the front. Sorry."

Her matter-of-fact tone didn't sit well with Pat. She stormed out of her office, past the receptionist's desk, and to the back of the suite, where the files were stored. It took her maybe five minutes before she returned and stood in front of Candace with the case file in her hand. She waved it at the young woman. "How difficult was that?"

Candace stared at her blankly.

Pat was further annoyed. "You're an assistant. Your job is to assist."

"No, I'm the receptionist and legal assistant," Candace said, correcting her. My job is to receive your clients, type your memos, arrange your exhibits, and update your files. I do that."

"It would behoove you to watch your tone. You should have a little more respect for authority."

Pat walked away and returned to her office. Candace rolled her eyes at the older woman's retreating figure.

"Dyke," Candace murmured under her breath.

Her eyes reverted to her message pad, which was lying on her desk. Rolling her eyes again, she realized that she hadn't given Pat her messages from earlier. Quickly, she ripped the message slips out of the book and walked to Pat's office. She didn't bother to knock. "Here are your messages from lunch," she announced.

Pat was standing by her bookshelf near the door. She walked over to Candace and without a word plucked the papers from her hand.

"Okay, now that was rude," Candace said loudly.

"Excuse me?"

Just as the exchange was taking place, the senior partner's executive assistant, Missy, walked out of her office. "What's the matter?"

Candace looked at Missy in disbelief. "I think Pat has a problem with me. She just snatched those papers out of my hand all rude like."

"I'm not entertaining this nonsense," Pat replied. "Get away from my office."

"Who do you think you're talking to?" Candace stormed. "You want me to exercise more respect for you, but you get to talk to me like I'm some trash?"

Missy placed her hand on Candace's arm. "Let's go back to the front. Come on."

"No. I want an apology," Candace asserted.

Pat laughed. "Are you kidding me?"

"No, I'm serious. You need to apologize to me."

Pat stepped forward. "And you need to get out of my office."

Candace refused to move, despite Missy's urging. Fed up with the whole ordeal, Pat slightly pushed Candace away from her threshold. It was just enough to allow her to close her oak door.

"Rude-ass bitch," Candace muttered, walking back to her desk in a fury.

Missy was right on her heels. "You know Bob is not going to like this, right? She's going to tell him about it."

"So?" Candace challenged. "You were right there. You saw her push me. Let her tell him, 'cause if she doesn't, I will as soon as he comes back. I'm not working anywhere where people get to yell at me and talk to me like I'm not shit. Hell, if they didn't know, slavery is over."

Missy gave a nervous laugh. "Well, calm down. You know how Pat is. That's just her personality. She's really blunt and straightforward. You know?"

"Uh-huh. And I can be real hood when someone messes with me. I'm not intimidated by her rude ass."

Shrugging her shoulders, Missy gave up on Candace and walked away. As if she needed any more aggravation, Khalil chose that moment to pop his head through the door of the suite.

"Hey, pretty lady," he said. "You didn't come out for lunch. Wanna go across to the Starbucks for a minute?"

She shook her head and tried to make herself look busy. "I can't. I'm swamped over here."

He looked disappointed. "Okay. I'll see you tonight, then."

She was relieved to see him go, as she was in no mood to listen to his bullshit this afternoon. She tried to focus her attention on her work but was finding it difficult to do. Within an hour Bob returned to the office. Candace handed him his messages and was not about to let him walk off without addressing the incident with Pat.

"Bob, I need to talk to you about something," she said.

He gave her a curt smile. "Pat called me already. We'll talk about it later."

He walked off before she could respond. Candace felt defeated and pissed. What part of the game was this?

The entire afternoon went by with no further mention of the situation between Candace and Pat. Candace closed down the firm and made her way back to Khalil's house reluctantly. He'd given her a key for her temporary use. When she arrived at the house, his car wasn't in the driveway. She was pleased about that. She figured it would give her the opportunity to take the few things she had there and find somewhere else to stay for a while. Coming in the door, she could hear rumbling in the kitchen. Puzzled, she began to walk in that direction and was surprised to be met at the kitchen door by a tall, slender woman with a short Halle Berry haircut.

"What the hell?" the woman asked. She held a knife in her right hand and what looked to Candace to be the remnants of one of her blouses.

"Who are you?" Candace asked, for lack of anything better to say. Truly, she knew the answer to the question before it even left her lips.

"I'm the bitch who's about to cut your ass for lying up in *my* house with *my* man." Sheila waved her knife in Candace's face and threw the fabric at her chest. Candace let it fall to the floor and slowly began to back up.

"You . . . you've g-got it a-all wrong," Candace stuttered.

"Do I?"

Candace nodded as she slowly moved backward into the living room.

"It seems to me like I've pretty much peeped game, sweetheart." Sheila's eyes never left Candace's face as she waved her knife in the air theatrically. "You trying to tell me those aren't your clothes in my bedroom? That's not your deodorant lying on my bathroom counter, next to your Summer's Eve, like you live here?"

"I'm just a friend." Candace was nervous. "Khalil was helping me out. My husband and I are having problems. He just let me stay here for a few days, until I could get myself together. That's all."

"That's all?"

Candace nodded.

"You really think I'm that naive? How old are you? Twelve? Your gullible ass." Sheila laughed and put her hands on her hips yet never released the knife. "Tell me how you have the audacity to shack up in another woman's house and then lie to save the sorry nigga's life. What? You that in love with Khalil?"

Candace looked up at the ceiling and took a deep breath. It just wasn't her day. If this crazy bitch was going to kill her, she would have done so already. Candace decided to just let the chips fall where they may. "I just came to get my stuff. I was leaving tonight. I swear."

"Let me ask you this. Did you really think that the man's wife would never show up, honey?"

"Wife?" Candace almost choked on the word as she spat it out in surprise.

Sheila's eyebrows knit up. "Oh, lemme guess. He didn't tell you he was married. With all these pictures of me around here and all my stuff, you really want me to believe that you didn't know he was fuckin' married?"

Candace was pissed now. "He told me you just *lived* together . . . that you've been living together for a while. In fact, he told me that you were in jail for a domestic dispute charge."

Sheila laughed. "And you believed that shit? I was in Augusta, visiting my mother for the last month and a half, honey. She was sick. But I told his sorry ass to pack his shit and get the hell out of my house while I was gone. And do you know why?"

Candace shook her head.

Sheila pointed the knife at her. "Because I'm sick of him pulling bullshit like this. You think you're the first piece of ass he's fucked with in the six years we've been married? Naw, baby, you're not that special. The last bitch had a baby by him, and he still isn't claiming that child. I had him served with divorce papers last month. Sorry bastard changed my locks. I had to have a locksmith come out so that I could get into my own fuckin' house, only to find your tramp ass prancing up in here with a fuckin' key."

No sooner had she uttered the last word than the two of them heard the front door open. Candace spun around, and the women watched Khalil enter the living room and take in the sight of them. Fear crossed his face, and then he quickly began to save his ass.

"Baby, when did you get home?" He focused his attention on Sheila, failing to make eye contact with Candace.

"Now I'm your baby?" Sheila asked him. "And who's this bitch? Your sugar?"

Khalil laughed and slowly walked over to the women. "No, baby. What are you talking about? This is my good friend from the office. Candace."

"Yeah, me and your good friend have already met and had a nice little talk." She pointed the knife at his chest. "And your sorry ass is busted."

"Baby, I don't know what she told you. But I swear I was only trying to help her out. She was desperate for a place to go. Her parents put her out and—"

"Fuck you!" Candace was livid. "I'm not desperate for shit from your sorry, lying ass."

"Uh-oh," Sheila interjected. "Looks like your stories aren't matching up. Surprise, surprise."

"Candace," Khalil said slowly, as if he were talking to an idiot, "you need to stop this."

Candace reached out and slapped his face. "Fuck you. You're the one who invited me to your house and then lied about your *wife* being in jail. Sorry bastard."

"His house?" Sheila asked. "No, ma'am. This house is owned by me and only me. Always has been and always will be. And I'm just about tired of these shenanigans. So I'm giving both of your asses five seconds before I start slicing and dicing a motherfucker."

Candace looked from her to Khalil and quickly moved toward the door. "I'm outta here."

From behind her, Candace could hear Khalil begging and pleading with Sheila to believe him. Sheila obviously wasn't playing, because before Candace even reached her car, she heard Khalil scream. She looked up and saw him running out of the house, holding his arm.

"You cut me!" he screamed. "You fuckin' cut me! Crazy, bitch."

Sheila stood in the doorway, flailing her arms every which way. "You want crazy? I'll show your ass crazy. Bring your ass back on my property, and I'll shoot you in the fuckin' foot. You and any of your tack head–ass baby mamas and your stank pussy–ass girlfriends."

Khalil ran toward Candace. "Call the police! Call the police! She cut me."

Candace tried to wave him off. "I wouldn't spit on your ass if you were on fire."

Quickly, she got into her car and hurried out of the driveway. In her rearview she caught her last glimpse of Khalil, running down the driveway, screaming, and Sheila, continuing to hurl insults at her wounded husband. What a fucking day.

Chapter 31

Jada

"Are you kidding me?" Alex asked in disbelief. She was sitting on the sofa in Jada's living room, munching on popcorn, eyes wide open as she listened to Candace give them a play-by-play of the encounter she had recently had with Khalil and his wife.

Jada propped her feet up on the ottoman and shook her head. "You better thank your lucky stars that woman didn't decide to play surgeon on your ass," she said. "What were you possibly thinking, laying up in that woman's house with that man?"

Candace was sitting next to Alex, holding the bowl of popcorn. "I didn't know they were married."

"But you knew that they lived together," Jada said. "So that was reason enough for you *not* to be laying up in that woman's bed every night. You're lucky as hell. I would have killed you."

"Y'all should have seen his sorry behind running around, yelling about how she'd cut him."

"Too funny," Alex commented.

"That shit isn't funny," Jada countered. "It's crazy. I swear. All of y'all get into the craziest situations. Y'all got issues."

Candace moaned. "Okay, here goes Ms. Perfect."

"I'm not perfect. I'm not even trying to front like I am. But I have the common sense not to be all up in another woman's place, playing house. That's just stupid."

"He told me she was in jail."

Alex laughed. "Wow."

Candace hit her. "Shut up."

"What about Quincy?" Jada asked.

"What about him? We are so over. My dad is going with me to meet him this weekend to get my stuff out of storage."

"So they really foreclosed on the house?" Jada was surprised.

"Yep. At least the fat bastard had the decency to put all our stuff in storage. He's just been giving me a hard time about getting my stuff out, though."

"You've been going through it," Alex said.

"Speaking of going through it, has anyone heard from Miranda lately?" Jada asked.

The other two girls shook their heads.

"Then, y'all don't know." Jada grabbed a handful of popcorn

"Know what?" Candace eyed her suspiciously.

Jada hesitated. "She got back with Norris."

"What!" Alex exclaimed.

"Are you for real?" Candace questioned. "You can't be for real."

Jada nodded her head. "Yes, ma'am. Steph told me that she came over to her house one day out of the blue and told her that she was back with Norris. They fell out, so Steph didn't really have much more to tell. But yep. That's the gist of it."

"After everything he did to her, why in the world would she take his sorry butt back?" Alex asked.

"I know I wouldn't have." Candace repositioned herself on the sofa. "Please, it doesn't matter what Quincy says or does, I'm never going back. Once it's over, it's over. You only have to mistreat me once."

Neither Alex nor Jada responded to this. Each woman just considered her own thoughts.

"So let's get to planning this shower," Alex said, breaking the silence moments later. "I know that Steph can't wait to not be pregnant anymore."

"I can imagine," Candace agreed. "I don't see how anyone ever *wants* to have a little parasite in their body to begin with."

"That's an endearing way to describe someone's child." Jada threw a popcorn kernel at her friend.

"I'm just saying. You'll never catch me destroying my body. My boobs are too perky for all that."

"You'll change your mind about that once you fall in love with the right man. You'll want to have his baby," Jada assured her.

"I'm surprised you and Jordan haven't got pregnant by now. You're all in love and shit. Why aren't you pregnant?" Candace said.

Jada smiled and toyed with her shirt. "It's just not our time yet. We've been trying, but you know. Sometimes it just takes time."

Alex silently munched on her popcorn. She wasn't in the mood to have this conversation.

"Well, good luck to you on that," Candace said. "You and Steph can have all of that. I'll just continue to be the fabulous friend while y'all chicks play Mama."

"Whatever." Jada grabbed a notepad off of the coffee table. "Come on, ladies. Let's get to it."

Chapter 32

Stephanie

Stephanie and Jada sat on Steph's couch, going through all the baby gifts from her shower. The room was filled with onesies, diapers, gift bags, and envelopes. The only noise in the apartment was the chatter between the girls. Damien was spending the night at a friend's house, and Corey hadn't been home since the baby shower. Stephanie was concerned but didn't want to let on in front of her friend.

"You got so much cute stuff, girl," Jada commented.

"Yep. It was a good turnout too. Thank you again for everything. You know you always throw a mean party."

"I try." Jada busied herself with folding up some long-sleeved T-shirts.

"But what was up with Miranda?"

"What?" Jada was clueless.

"After blowing up at me a while back, she strolls up in my baby shower without so much as two words to say to me. Like nothing happened. And did you see the way she was all cozied up to Corey?"

Jada smacked her lips. "Steph, stop it. They were not cozied up."

"Well, they were off to the side, whispering about something, and then she was ghost. Did she even bring me a gift?"

"Of course she did. And what is up with you? Why are you so fixated on Corey and Miranda? Nobody's trying to get with your boyfriend, girl. Especially not Miranda. She's too stuck on stupid with Norris."

Stephanie fidgeted on the couch, grunted a little, and rubbed the side of her belly. "I'm just saying. To me, it looked like something was up, and the way she just popped up at my house that time without calling first . . . If I didn't know better,

I could have sworn that she looked surprised to see me sitting in my own living room."

"Don't go starting any mess over your crazy, hormonal overreactions."

Stephanie grunted again. "*She* better not start nothing."

"Leave it alone. Where is Corey, anyway?"

Stephanie rubbed her side and laid her head back on the couch. "I don't know, girl. He hasn't been home since last weekend . . . since the shower, actually."

Jada looked over at her friend. "You okay, girl?"

"Yeah, yeah, I'm fine."

Jada looked at her quizzically and went back to sorting the baby items. "So is that normal? For him to be gone so long? Has he called at least?"

"He does that some times, but you know . . . What can I do about that? He's busy, so I try not to bother him."

"Busy? What is wrong with all my friends?"

Stephanie cocked her head to the side. "What?"

"You said he's busy, like he's flying back and forth to Wall Street or something, girl. Let's face some reality, shall we? Your baby daddy is the dope man."

"Jada, please don't start."

"I'm just saying. How long are you going to live this fantasy life with him? And now he just comes and goes as he pleases, leaving you here in his dope-house mansion."

"Stop it. There's no dope or blow or weed in this house. Corey wouldn't disrespect me like that."

"Hmm. But he'd leave his pregnant girlfriend alone frequently for days on end?"

Stephanie let out a sharp moan and bent over in a painful motion. Jada reached over and touched her arm.

"Girl, I'm sorry. I didn't mean to upset you. Are you okay?"

Stephanie shook her head. "No. No. I think I'm in labor."

Jada's eyes grew wide, and she began to speak slowly. "Are you absolutely sure?"

Stephanie looked up at her and grimaced. "No, Jada. I just wanted to scare you to death. Yes, damn it! I'm sure."

Jada jumped up. "Okay, okay. What do we do? Should I call your doctor or just take you straight to the hospital?"

Stephanie waved her hand in the air. "Calm down. I need you to calm down. Get my purse for me. We can call my doctor on the way to the hospital. And Corey too."

Two hours passed, and Stephanie found herself lying on the delivery bed, epidural in place, preparing to push, but the room was devoid of Corey. Jada stood by her side as the nurses busied about, prepping the area for the delivery.

"Did you call him again?" Stephanie asked her friend.

Jada brushed Stephanie's hair back and smiled at her. "I called him five times already and left two messages. Maybe he'll be here soon."

Stephanie's mind was filled with many thoughts. The stress of giving birth was intensified by the stress of worrying about Corey's whereabouts. But there was no time to focus on Corey right now. The nurses were instructing Stephanie to help hold her legs up so that she could attempt to push at the next contraction. She gave it all her might, which was a struggle against the effectiveness of the epidural. Her memory could retain only the sounds of voices urging her to push harder before she drifted off into darkness.

The room was quiet when Stephanie opened her eyes. She struggled to sit up and noticed the IV attached to her arm. Hearing her stir, a figure approached her bedside and turned on the light.

"Mom?" She could barely utter the word because her mouth was so dry.

Her mom reached over to the bed table, picked up a carton of cranberry juice, and held it to her lips for her to sip. Absentmindedly, she drank from it and simply stared at her mother in confusion.

"You need to rest," her mom ordered. "You've been through a lot today."

"Where's my baby?"

"In the nursery. She's fine. You just need to rest for now."

Before Stephanie could say another word, Jada walked in and was surprised to see her up.

"You're awake! That's good. How do you feel?"

"Tired. Very tired." Stephanie looked back to her mother. "What are you doing here?"

"I called her," Jada blurted out. "You really needed some family here, sweetie. So I called your mother after we couldn't get in contact with Corey."

Stephanie rested back against her hospital bed pillows and crossed her arms. "I didn't think you'd care to come see me, given that I was carrying another one of Corey's babies."

"No matter who their father is, these are still my grandchildren," Ms. Johnson replied. "And you are still my daughter."

There was a tap on the door to the room, and Corey strolled in nonchalantly with a big teddy bear and flowers. He sat the goodies on the guest chair and walked over to Stephanie's right side.

"What's up, Mama?" He kissed Stephanie's forehead.

Stephanie looked at him blankly, confused about how he could be so nonchalant after having been missing for several days. "Hi," was all she could manage to say.

"How you doing?" he asked.

"How does she look like she's doing?" Ms. Johnson was annoyed. "She's worn out. She had to have a blood transfusion after giving birth to your child *alone*. You would know that if you had been where you were supposed to be, tending to your family, instead of out there in the streets, destroying everyone else's with that stuff you push."

"Mom!" Stephanie exclaimed. "You're out of line."

"With all due respect, Ms. Johnson, you shouldn't assume you know anything about me. I'm taking care of my family twenty-four-seven. You can believe that. Everything I do is for my family."

"Is that right? Well, you forgot to do one thing, son. And that is be there *with* your family."

"Mom, please. If you only came down here to argue with us, then you should just leave. I can't handle this right now. I really can't."

Ms. Johnson looked from Stephanie to Corey with disdain. In a huff, she grabbed her purse and walked to the door. She stopped and turned back to look at Stephanie. "This fool is going to be the death of you." Without awaiting a response, she hastily left the room.

Jada was uncomfortable in the silence that followed Ms. Johnson's exit. "Um, maybe I should go too. I'll come back tomorrow to check on you and the baby."

Stephanie smiled at her. "Thanks for everything."

Jada hugged her friend tightly and whispered in her ear, "Watch the news, girl. I love you."

With a questioning expression on her face, Stephanie watched her friend walk out of the room. Why did Jada want her to watch the news?

Corey sat down on the side of her bed and grabbed her hand. "You a'ight?"

She nodded. "Where were you?"

"Taking care of some business and laying low."

"What does that mean?"

"Don't worry 'bout all that," he told her. "Daddy's home now. It's all good. I'm going to go see if the nurse will bring the baby up from the nursery. You need anything?"

"Can you get me something to eat? From the cafeteria maybe?"

Corey hopped off the bed. "I'll see what I can do, li'l mama."

She waited until he was out of the room for several minutes before using the bulky hospital bed remote to turn on the 6:00 news.

"DeKalb County officials are investigating the murder of a local man. The victim has been identified as Montae Stokes. Neighbors in the Decatur neighborhood where Stokes resided say that he was a well-known guy and a small-time drug dealer. Officials say that Stokes worked part-time out of a local club owned by Ernest Henderson. Henderson is offering no statement at this time, except to say that he has no knowledge of Stokes dealing drugs. Stokes's body was found by a group of teenagers in a creek behind some abandoned apartment buildings on Bouldercrest Road early Sunday afternoon. He suffered two bullet wounds to the chest and one to the head.

Stokes's family and some close friends have been interviewed to determine the motive for this crime. At this time, officials believe that Stokes's death is the result of a struggle of power in the drug community. DeKalb's deputy director stated that a full investigation will be conducted. At this time, they are not releasing the names of suspects or persons of interest."

Stephanie turned off the television and struggled to catch her breath. Her heart was telling her that Corey couldn't possibly be responsible for the man's death. But her mind was telling her that he very well could be. Apparently, Jada thought so too, otherwise why would she have encouraged her to watch the news? It was his territory they'd mentioned; she knew that much. She also knew that he had been experiencing some kind of beef with someone in the hood, based on the hush-hush conversation he'd had with his worker months ago in their living room. But Stephanie wasn't ready to face the reality of Corey's illegal activity. She loved him too much and desperately needed to hold on to the dream of being a real family. Sighing, she lay back against her pillows and said a quick prayer that everything would work out in her favor.

Chapter 33

Miranda

Several months came and went, with Miranda asking herself daily why on earth she had agreed to stay married to Norris. Sure, in the beginning he tried to play the considerate husband. But over time he began to show his true colors, acting more and more like the man she had come to despise. It was Christmas morning, and Miranda woke to find her bed devoid of Norris. She sighed, assuming he was gone. She rose from the bed and went into the bathroom to wash up. When she returned to the bedroom, Norris was sitting on the bed, shirtless, rolling a blunt.

"You have to do that in here?" she said as she walked past him.

"Merry Christmas to you too," he responded.

She ignored him and lay down on her side of the bed.

He lifted the blunt and licked it, smiling at her wickedly. "You know you want some."

"Shut up with that."

"Look, it's Christmas. Let's just enjoy each other and stop all the damn fronting. I'm not tripping. It might take the edge off if you smoke with ya' boy and chill the hell out. I'm just trying to chill with you, Miranda." He held the weed in her direction. "This is who I am. Take it or leave it. I wasn't born yesterday, wifey. I *know* you light up. You gon' tell me that you can light up without me, but you can't do it with me?"

He fell silent, allowing her the opportunity to consider the offer. Miranda looked at him and bit her lower lip. It was Christmas, so she knew there was no way she was going to be getting anything from Corey anytime soon. She took a deep breath, not believing herself as she reached out for the blunt being offered to her.

Norris watched as she inhaled and then exhaled slowly.

"Yeah," he coaxed her as she closed her eyes and took another drag. "That's what's up. Now pass that shit, babes. Don't be greedy."

They smoked the entire joint and soon found themselves giggling and playing around like old friends.

"Where's my Christmas dinner at, woman?" Norris joked, tickling her.

"I wasn't planning on cooking. I told my mom we would come over to my family's house for Christmas dinner this afternoon."

"Long as I get my smoked turkey and banana pudding. Somebody needa teach you how to make that good ole soul food."

Miranda lay back on the bed, feeling her head spinning. It was a sensation she had never felt before, and she wasn't sure where the rush was coming from.

"You 'bout to knock out on me?" Norris slipped his hand under her nightshirt.

She fidgeted at his touch and looked up at him. She could feel her heart pounding through her chest. "No, no. I feel weird . . . like woozy kinda."

He pulled his jogging pants down and began to nibble on her neck.

"Feeling like your adrenaline is pumping?" He nibbled on her ear. "Like you're about to spin outta control?"

She couldn't focus on his face, so she just closed her eyes and nodded. "What the hell?"

He mounted her and entered her moist opening. Every part of her was in overdrive. She was incredibly horny, gyrating under him as he moved inside of her.

"That's that PCP, baby," he told her between thrusts. "You don't know what's in ya' greens these days."

"Hmm?"

She couldn't focus on his words, but her body was focused on her orgasm, which was fast approaching. With no foreplay and very little sensuality, Norris pumped himself into her, abusing her G-spot until she climaxed so hard, she felt she was going to have a heart attack. The sensation was powerful.

Miranda screamed and grabbed his forearms so tightly that her nails dug into his skin. Her recovery seemed to never come, as her heart rate felt as if it was never going to decrease. Norris came soon after her, collapsing onto her fidgeting frame for a short time. Soon he got off of her and hurried into the bathroom.

Miranda continued to lie on the bed, clutching her chest, trying to slow down her rapidly beating heart. Her thoughts were all a blur. Norris reentered the room at some point, then mentioned something about fresh air. As she focused on calming herself, she heard a car peel out of the parking lot. Instantly, she sat up, trying to think clearly. She jumped off the bed, then sped through the apartment, stopping only to glance at the table where her keys had been resting. She threw open the front door and stood on her porch, looking out at her empty parking spot.

PCP. The memory of his words slapped her. She sauntered back into her home, curled up on her sofa, and buried her head in her hands. Perhaps he would return home soon.

The sound of her phone ringing woke her up. Her body was drenched in sweat. She looked at the cell phone buzzing on the coffee table and quickly snatched it up. It was her cousin, Myra.

"Hello." Her voice was harsh and her mouth felt cottony as she gave the salutation.

"Miranda, Merry Christmas, ma'am. Y'all aren't coming over with the family?"

"What time is it?"

"It's two o'clock. We're about to bless the food. Where are you?"

"Two o'clock?" Miranda rose from the sofa and went into the kitchen to pour a glass of water.

"Yeah. Are you coming?"

"I don't think so. . . . I'm not feeling well, and Norris isn't here."

"Okay, then. I'll let everyone know. I'll call you later."

"Uh-huh." Miranda disconnected the call and stared at the time on her phone. Nine minutes after two in the afternoon. Where the hell was Norris? He'd been gone all morning and apparently all early afternoon. She dialed his cell and waited for him to answer.

"He's busy, honey, and don't call this phone anymore, bitch."

The phone went dead. *Who the hell?* Miranda called the number back again and leaned against her kitchen counter.

"What, bitch? Are you slow?"

"Who is this?" Miranda demanded.

"Norris's *woman*. Something yo' ass ain't never been with ya' junky ass."

"Put my husband on the phone, trick."

"I got your trick, ho. Norris is busy. He's playing with his daughter. It's Christmas, if you haven't noticed."

"Daughter?" Miranda felt herself slide to the floor, overwhelmed by this new information.

"Yes. His daughter. So I'll tell him you called."

The line went dead. She was stunned. How could he have fathered a baby with someone else and she not know? Without much thought, she redialed his number once more. The call went straight to voice mail.

"You sorry son of a bitch. Who the fuck do you think you are, leaving me in this house, stranded, to go play house with some hood rat? Bring my damn car back now, Norris. I mean it. I want my damn car back now!"

She hung up and called right back. The call went to voice mail. She called again, and the line was quickly answered.

"Yo, I'ma call you back in a minute, a'ight?" Norris said hurriedly.

"No, hell, it's not all right," she retorted. "I want my—"

The line was disconnected before she could finish her sentence. She screamed and called back once more.

"What man!"

"What is going on, Norris? Who the hell was that bitch that answered your phone? Where are you?"

"I ran out for a minute. Visiting folk, man. It's Christmas. Calm all that noise down."

"Are you kidding me? Some chick just told me that you were playing with your daughter, Norris. What the hell?"

She could hear commotion in the background. He sounded like he was struggling with someone for the phone.

"Norris?" she called out.

She could hear a female in the background say, "Fuck that bitch. Fuck her ass. If you want that bitch, fuck you too."

"Norris!" Miranda called out again. "Norris! Answer me. What the hell is going on?"

His end of the line was silent for a moment, and then Miranda heard his heavy breathing. "What's up?" he said.

Miranda banged on one of her kitchen cabinet doors with her fist, pissed and frustrated. "What's up? What's up, Norris? You tell me what the hell is up."

"You're tripping. You still buzzing off that shit? I'm on my way home, man."

"Who are you with, huh? Who the hell is that saying to fuck me, Norris?" Recognition set in, and Miranda took a deep breath. "That's that trick you had up in my house, isn't it?"

He didn't answer.

"You have a baby with her?"

"Man, go on with all that. Look, I told you I'm on my way home."

"Answer me, damn it! Do you have a baby with that girl?" Miranda gripped the phone tightly. Her breathing was heavy, and her eyes began to tear up.

"Miranda—"

"No. Don't try to talk circles around me! Answer the fucking question."

"A'ight, man, you ain't gon' talk to me like I'm some pussy nigga. You don't be coming off of any information when I ask you questions about what *you* have going on. But you wanna question me and shit? Fuck all that, Miranda. You ain't running shit around here."

"Fuck you! You lying, cheating piece of shit."

"For real? I'm a piece of shit? A nigga chillin' on Christmas and yo' geeked-up ass blowing me up and starting shit. Okay, you want to know? Yes. That was Tammy. And, yes, I have a li'l girl with her. Now what? I'll see your ass when I get back."

He ended the call, and Miranda screamed long and loud until no more sound could come from her throat. Lying on the kitchen floor, she cried as her body convulsed in fits of frustration. She cried herself into an uncomfortable sleep, which was interrupted an hour later by the ringing of her phone. She answered without screening the call. Her voice was barely audible as she said hello.

"Merry Christmas, girl," Jada said cheerfully. "What are you up to?"

Miranda rose from the floor and looked around her quiet apartment. "Dying."

"I'm sorry. What?"

"I'm sorry. I'm just not having a very merry Christmas."

"Why not? What's wrong?"

Miranda walked over to the pantry and pulled out a pack of ramen noodles. "Norris left me."

Jada sighed. "And that's not a gift to you?"

"I mean, he left me stuck in the house. He took my car and is over at his baby's mama's house."

"Baby mama? When did that happen?"

Miranda threw the noodles in a bowl and poured a little tap water into it. "I don't know. I'm so tired of him. I'm so drained, Jada. I just can't take much more."

"He took your car, huh?"

"Yep."

"Report that shit stolen. That'll teach his ass. This isn't a community property state."

Miranda put the bowl in the microwave. "I can't do that."

"Why not? Miranda, that man is over there fucking that other woman, playing the family man with somebody else. Trust, he's not thinking about you or your feelings, so why are you giving so much of a damn about his?"

Miranda remained silent.

"Okay," Jada sighed. "Call me back later and let me know what you decided to do. I love you, sweetie, but you really need to stop being a doormat for this man and leave well enough alone."

"Bye, Jada." She pressed the END button and watched the minutes run down on the microwave. Taking a deep breath, she dialed 911 on her phone and closed her eyes.

"Nine-one-one. What is your emergency?"

"I'd like to report my car stolen."

Chapter 34

Alex

"You didn't have to get me a gift!" Alex exclaimed, snatching the small box out of Clay's hand. "But I'm glad you did."

Clay plopped down on the sofa and watched as Alex opened the jewelry box. Her eyes lit up as she removed the locket from the box.

"Oh my goodness! It's beautiful, Clay. Thank you."

He motioned for her to come over to him. "Here. Let me put it on for you."

She sat next to him, and he put the gold chain around her neck. She could smell the crisp, clean scent of his clothes mixed with the masculine aroma of his cologne. She smiled at the familiar scent, which always made her feel so comfortable.

"There you go."

She touched the locket with her fingertips and turned around to smile at her best friend. "You're absolutely the best. You really are. You're always there for me. I can always count on you. You're the best friend a girl could ever ask for, Precious."

He nodded and grabbed her hand. "I really need to talk to you about something."

Her eyebrows knit up. "Is something wrong?"

"No, it's just that I've been needing to tell you something for a long time, and I think that now is the time for us to have this discussion."

"Okay. What's up?"

Before he could speak, her cell phone rang. Alex jumped up to get the phone off the nearby table. Looking at the caller ID, she smiled at Clay. "It's my new boyfriend." She turned away from him to answer the phone. "Hello . . .? Tonight? Okay, I guess I can go. . . . I'll be ready. Okay, bye."

She threw the phone back on the table and winked at Clay. "I have a date."

"On Christmas night?" he questioned. "And since when do you have a new boyfriend? Last time I checked, you were just getting over the whole baby thing."

"He's not really my *boyfriend*. I just said that. I met him a couple of weeks ago at the mall."

Clay nodded. "So you're trying to make him your boy-friend?"

She shrugged. "I don't know. He likes me, and he's not a jerk like Mario was, so we'll see. I needa get ready. I'm going with T to the studio."

"T?"

"Yes. His name is Thad, but his friends call him T." She got up to go to her bedroom, then thought about it. "Oh yeah, what did you want to talk about, Precious?"

Clay shook his head and waved her off. "It's not important anymore."

She looked at him pensively. "Are you sure? You made it seem like it was important."

He shrugged. "Thinking about it, it isn't really that big of a deal to trouble you with it. Go on and get ready for your li'l date. I'm going to bounce."

She smiled at him. "Okay. And thanks again for my neck-lace. I really love it."

Clay smiled back as he rose from the sofa. "Glad to hear it. Be careful with your boy tonight, okay?"

"Always."

Chapter 35

Candace

Candace dragged herself from her car and then up the walk to Jada's front door. Taking a deep breath, she knocked with all her might. Jada answered immediately, clad in her underwear and a short bathrobe, which was partially tied. She ushered Candace in quickly. Candace sulked her way into the dining room and plopped down at the round table.

"Well, hello to you too," Jada said jokingly. "What was the big emergency that you had to see me today, girl? And take them damn glasses off. Ain't no sun in here."

Candace pulled off her sunglasses. Her eyes were red and puffy. "I'm late," she said.

"Late for what? This was your idea. I know that if I don't get out of here soon, I'm going to be late for Jordan's mom's birthday dinner."

Jada rummaged through her makeup bag while standing at the table. Noticing that Candace had not responded, she looked over at the smaller woman. She plopped down the makeup bag when she saw Candace's tear-swollen eyes.

"What's wrong, girl?" Jada asked gingerly, her voice laced with concern.

"Everything. I think I'm pregnant."

"Are you kidding me?" Jada sat down in the chair across from her.

Candace shook her head. "No. I would never joke about that mess. I haven't had my period in a month, Jada. I know my body. I'm telling you, I'm fuckin' pregnant."

Jada smoothed her hair down and stretched her neck. "Okay, so have you said anything to Quincy?"

"About what?"

"About your condition. What do you mean, about what?"

Candace shook her head, and Jada's eyes grew wide. "Please tell me you haven't said anything because you don't know for sure."

Candace shook her head again, then buried it in her arms on the table.

"Candace!" Jada exclaimed. "How could you be so irresponsible?"

"I know, I know," she muttered.

"Why would you be laying up with that man and not using protection? Are you crazy?"

"It was only once or twice. We were careful most of the time."

"Most of the time? You know it only takes once, right?"

Candace lifted her head, and tears streamed down her face. She looked at Jada pitifully. Jada had never seen her so distraught before. "What am I going to do?" Candace was flustered.

Jada raised her right eyebrow. "First things first, hon. You need to take a test. There's no point in sitting up here, crying about something that you're not even sure of. Stay right here."

Jada disappeared from the dining room and ran to the back. In an attempt to compose herself, Candace wiped the tears from her eyes with her hands. Jada reentered the room and handed Candace a slender box.

"What do I do with this?" Candace looked at the box quizzically.

Jada laughed. "Read the instructions, girl. It ain't rocket science. Pee on the stick and wait one to three minutes for your results. Simple."

Candace rose from the table with the box in hand. "Why do you just happen to have this?"

Jada shrugged. "We've been trying for a while. It's no big deal. I get them from the Dollar Store. Go on, girl. Don't prolong the inevitable. I've got places to go."

Candace walked the short distance up the hall to the bathroom and shut the door behind her. She read and reread the instructions before opening the package. Sighing, she eased onto the toilet and peed on the little stick. After positioning it on a piece of tissue, she laid the stick on the counter, finished her business, and washed her hands. The whole time she ignored the stick, not daring to look at it, not yet wanting to know what the answer was. She hurried out of the bathroom to find Jada standing impatiently by the door.

"Well?" Jada was anxious.

"I didn't look."

"You want me to?"

Candace nodded and returned to her seat at the dining-room table. "Jehovah, please don't let this be happening to me."

Jada entered the room, holding the stick and smiling. "It's a good thing."

Candace blinked, not fully understanding. "It is? Oh my God! I'm not pregnant? Woo. I am so freakin' relieved I don't know what to do with myself. I just can't—"

"Okay, okay. Pump your brakes," Jada interjected. "Maybe I should have said that it's not such a bad thing."

"What?"

Jada handed her the stick, and Candace's eyes fell on the unmistakable two red lines.

"I'm going to be an auntie," Jada singsonged.

"No," Candace said. "No. I cannot have a baby. Especially not like this. Okay, okay. Do you have another one of these things?"

"Um, yeah, but you know, it doesn't matter how many times you pee on these tests. They're all going to say the same thing, honey. You're gonna be a mama."

Candace threw the stick down on the table. "My life sucks."

"Oh, please shut up." Jada snatched up her makeup bag. "You should be thankful that all you got was a baby. It could have been much worse. That trifling *married* man could have given you an STD or, worse, AIDS. Hell, you haven't even been to a doctor yet, so you don't know for sure what else he could have left you with. For your sake, I pray that this is it. Some people out there are dying to have a baby, Candace. Be thankful that you're fortunate enough to be able to conceive. Stop looking at this as a punishment and get over it."

"But you don't understand," Candace whined. "My parents are going to be so disappointed in me. They're already in 'I told you so' mode about my separation from Quincy. My divorce isn't even final yet, and here I am, pregnant by another man. A *married* man."

Jada rolled her eyes. "And whose fault is that?"

"I'll be shunned by my congregation. This type of thing is seriously frowned upon."

"And yet none of these things occurred to you while you were doing your dread-headed boo, though . . . right?"

"Why are you being so mean?"

"I'm sorry, girl. I'm just being real with you. You need to take some responsibility for your actions and start making some wiser decisions."

Candace stared at the glass dining-room table, trying to get her thoughts together. Jada was right, but the truth definitely did hurt.

"I don't have health insurance," she thought aloud.

Jada sighed. "I'm just in the business of rescuing everyone around here, aren't I? Tell you what. First thing Monday morning I'll take you to the health department. They'll do blood work, an official pregnancy test, and they'll give you Medicaid all in the same day. After you get the Medicaid, you can go to any ob-gyn that accepts it."

"I don't have an ob-gyn."

"Okay. I'll refer you to mine." Jada looked at her friend and softened a little. "It's not the end of the world, babes. Really. It'll all work out."

Candace smiled. "Thanks, girl."

She tapped the phone, trying to decide if it was the right thing to do or not. Perhaps she should wait until Monday, when she would have some clearer answers. What if the number was disconnected? She had been avoiding him at work lately, and he had never come by the office after that incident with Sheila. Sucking it up, she dialed the number and waited for him to answer.

"Hello?" His voice sounded unsure.

"Khalil, it's me, Candace."

"Long time, no hear," he retorted. "Didn't think I'd ever hear from you again."

"Me either." She sighed. "I really need to talk to you, though."

"Something wrong, pretty lady? You need to come over?"

She laughed dryly. "Are you kidding me?"

Khalil sucked his teeth. "I'm just expressing concern, dear. Extending an open arm to you. And besides, Sheila and I are no more, so you wouldn't have to worry about her."

"I'm not going down that road with you anymore, Khalil. Fool me once."

"Nobody's trying to fool you. I've always cared deeply for you."

"Really? And is that why you lied to me and tried to make me out to be some kind of stalker in front of your wife?"

"Let's leave the past in the past, shall we? You can't deny that we had a special bond, Candace. I'm only trying to make things right moving forward."

"I'm not coming over, Khalil. In fact, I should have never come over to begin with and should have avoided this whole mess."

"What are you talking about?"

"Khalil, I'm pregnant."

"Okay . . ."

"By you, Khalil. I'm pregnant with your child."

"Candace, I haven't touched you in nearly two months."

"That's right. And I haven't had a period in nearly two months."

"Get the hell out of here. How are you so sure it's my child? I mean, you *are* married."

"You're such a typical dude. You know good and well I was separated from Quincy the entire time I was staying with you. Don't try to play me like I'm some skank."

"I'm supposed to just believe what you're saying?"

"Why would I lie?"

"For money."

"Fuck you, Khalil. I'm not so hard up for money that I'd scam a man into thinking I'm carrying his baby. Everyone who knows me knows that the last thing I've ever wanted was to be pregnant, so I damn sure wouldn't make a joke about it just to get at you."

"Okay, okay. Calm down. Have you been to a doctor? I mean, are you sure?"

"I go to the doctor on Monday. But I took a test and it was positive and I know my body."

"No offense, but it's been quite some time, Candace. If you knew your body so well, why are you just now determining that you're pregnant?"

"It's never been unusual for me to skip a period here and there, but skipping two is out of the norm. And I just feel different. Why am I explaining myself to you?"

"Because I should know *if* I'm the father of this child."

"Tell you what. I'll call you on Monday, after I come back from the doctor. Unless you want to go with me. My friend offered to take me, but she can just as well tell me where it is and we can just go together."

"I have to work. Just call me when you're done."

Candace sucked her teeth. "Fine. I'll talk to you then, I guess."

Frustrated, she disconnected the call and threw the phone on the bed. The hard part was yet to come. Reasoning with herself, she decided it would be best to go ahead and tell her parents. She took a deep breath and walked out of her childhood bedroom. Candace found her parents cuddled up on the living-room sofa, watching a rerun of *CSI*.

"Mom, Dad, can I talk to you?" she asked softly.

Mr. Lewis looked up at her and smiled as his wife clicked off the television. "What's up, pumpkin?" Her dad's eyebrows knit with concern.

Candace sat in the armchair close to them, searching for the words with which to disappoint them. "I know that you guys were not very happy with my decision to marry Quincy. And although that did not turn out the way I would have liked it, I had every intention of maintaining an honorable marriage."

"Okay." Her mom tried to coax her to get to the point.

"I know that I haven't been going to the meetings like I should, and I haven't kept Jehovah at the center of my life the way I should have. And I promise you that I intend to change that. I realize how important it is to have a spiritually strong foundation for your life."

"Not that I'm not glad to hear you admit all of this, dear, but I'm sensing there is something more prevalent that you wish to say to us." Mrs. Lewis was growing impatient.

"I'm pregnant."

She checked their faces for their reactions. Her mother gasped and stared at her with her hand over her mouth. Her father simply gripped the arm of the sofa and nodded.

"And how long were you going to wait to tell us this?" he asked.

"I wasn't waiting. I mean, I just found out today. I just realized earlier this week and—"

"Have you told Quincy? Not that I think a baby is a just cause to force a reconciliation, but the man has an obligation to take care of his family, nonetheless," Mr. Lewis said.

"Daddy, it's not Quincy's baby," she said, dropping the bomb.

"Excuse me?" Mrs. Lewis was astonished. "Just what is it that you're saying?"

"Quincy and I had problems long before I asked to stay with you guys. We were separated for a minute, and I was staying with a friend."

Her mother gasped. "And by *friend,* you mean a man?"

Candace nodded.

Her mother shook her head. "I could tell that something was up with you. Your body is changing. I was hoping that it was just my imagination. But I'm very disappointed in you, young lady. Whether or not you and Quincy were having problems before is not of importance. You were still very much a married woman. You *still* are a married woman."

"Your mother is right. Stepping outside of your marriage vows like that is not favorable, Candace. And what God-fearing man would have the gall to shack up with someone else's wife? Who is this man to you? Are you running from one relationship right into another one?"

Candace grabbed a throw pillow and hugged it for support. "No. We're not in a relationship. We just—"

"Were playing house and having sex just for the sake of it," her mom said, finishing for her.

"Mom, please don't judge me."

"We're not judging you, dear. Simply telling you the error of your ways," her mother replied.

"Do you think this young man has any respect for you, Candace?" Mr. Lewis looked at his daughter sternly.

Now was definitely not the time to tell them that Khalil was much older and was a married man himself. She simply shrugged her shoulders.

"You don't know?" Her father moved to the edge of his seat. "Certainly you know. If he did, he would have never laid down with you. Where is he now? Does he know?"

"He knows."

"Have you been to a doctor?" her mother asked.

She shook her head no. "A friend of mine is taking me to the health department on Monday. I think they do free testing or whatever based on income."

"I think this young man should be covering your medical expenses. Is he going with you?" Mrs. Lewis asked.

Another shake of Candace's head.

Her father stared her dead in the eyes. "You have disgraced yourself. You know that, don't you?"

Candace blinked through the tears. "I know that, but—"

"I encourage you to ask Jehovah for forgiveness and to repent immediately. But no matter what, you are still our daughter, and we love you regardless. I would have liked to think that your mother and I taught you to have a little more self-respect than this. Whoever this man is, Candace, I want to meet him. If you won't do it, I will . . . I will make sure that he understands that he has an obligation to take care of this child and that we, as your parents, expect him to step up to the plate."

Candace nodded her head in understanding.

"You're going to the doctor on Monday, right?" her mother asked. "Invite the young man over for dinner Monday night. We can all sit down and talk about this like adults."

"Okay. I'm really sorry to spring this on you guys like this. I really am."

"We're your parents, dear." Mrs. Lewis gave Candance a reassuring look. "You can always come to us."

Candace rose and hugged her parents before hurrying out of the living room. It had gone over much better than she had anticipated. But what was going to happen when her parents came face-to-face with Khalil?

Chapter 36

Miranda

It had been silent in the apartment ever since Norris left her on Christmas. It had taken only three days for the police to find her car. But upon finding it, they had also found Norris with less than an ounce of marijuana on him. Sure, he had been arrested, but they had not detained him. Miranda knew that he was out, and she was grateful that he had not come back home. But she was on pins and needles as she waited for him to eventually show up and retaliate for her setting him up. As she anticipated his violence, her habits progressively got worse.

Miranda felt uneasy as she rode around, looking for the trap. Corey had made it clear that she was not to come to his home for pickups anymore. They'd worked out a plan, which generally entailed meeting each other at a mutually convenient location. But today Corey was adamant that he couldn't get away and that she would have to meet him at the spot. So there she was, pulling up in front of a shabby ranch-style home in the depths of Decatur. She slowly dragged herself out of the car and to the front door. There was no doorbell, so she had to knock. The door was answered by a big, dark man who made her think of Willie B.

"Sup, Ma?" He looked over her shoulder toward her car and down the street.

"Is Corey here?" she asked.

"He expecting you or something?"

She nodded.

The man chuckled. "You sure you 'posed to be coming round here? You sure this what you want?"

She rolled her eyes and sucked her teeth. "Just tell Corey I'm here."

"A'ight, then, li'l mama. Come in."

She stepped inside, and instantly the man began to pat her back and legs.

"Excuse you!" she protested.

"Safety precautions," he said matter-of-factly. "A'ight, you clean. Come on."

She followed him through the living room and into the kitchen, where Corey was sitting, bagging up little packets of what looked like a pile of flour. He looked up at her and raised an eyebrow.

"Mannie, you got that dime?"

A short, younger guy wearing a baseball cap down low rose from his seat on the stool at the kitchen counter, where he'd been counting money. He walked over to Miranda and handed her the bag.

She took it and handed him a ten but addressed Corey. "I was wondering if you could . . . I mean, if I could try something . . . different . . . harder."

Corey kept bagging. "What I look like? A damn candy store? You wanna come up in here and taste test shit? Get outta here, man."

"Fuck you, Corey. I've been putting money in your pocket consistently. Don't talk to me like I'm a waste of your time."

"So I'm supposed to up and let you sample what? Some blow?"

She looked at him blankly, and he chuckled. "You don't even know what that is, huh?"

"Yo, she five-oh?" the big man asked Corey.

He shook his head. "Naw, she's a fuckin' mistake. Go on, Miranda. Get out my spot. Stick to what you know. This ain't for you. Don't make me sorry I put your ass on."

He went back to focusing on his work, and the big man gently guided her by the arm toward the front door.

"Bullshit!" She was pissed.

The man followed her onto the porch and closed the door. "Hey," he called to her as she walked toward her car. "I got something for you."

She turned around. "Huh?"

"You grown. Do what the fuck you wanna do." He flashed a tiny Baggie in his hand.

Miranda's eyebrow went up, and she clutched on to her purse. Slowly, she moved closer to him. "What am I supposed to do with that?"

The man tapped his nose and sniffed before covering his mouth quickly to cough.

Her eyes lit up. "How much?"

"For you, twenty-five dollars."

She took a deep breath, nodded, and reached inside her bra for the money that was resting there. Hesitantly, she pulled the money out and handed it to the man. He quickly snatched it from her and replaced it with his product.

"If anything, you didn't get it from me." He turned away and disappeared back into the house.

Miranda hurried back to her car and rode off down the street before looking at the Baggie clutched tightly in her fist. Sitting at a red light, she continued to clutch it in her hand, her heart racing from fear and an excitement she couldn't explain. Miranda had no clue what she was getting herself into.

Chapter 37

Alex

Dating an industry dude was a thrill for Alex. Being in the studio with T and watching as he and his boys did their thing was exciting. Alex was impressed by the way he was so passionate about his rhymes. She ignored the fact that all the other people in the studio were puffing away on one blunt after another. She coughed when the smoke got too thick for her, but continued to sit there, staring into the booth as T spat out his lyrics with conviction. She rocked to the beat, feeling it, just before he stopped abruptly.

"Yo, Ricky, this ain't working," he said into his mic.

Ricky, T's friend and producer, stopped the instrumental and waved T out of the booth. T joined his partner, plopping down into the chair next to him.

"It was good, Money," Ricky stated. "What you feel's missing?"

"That hook, man. It doesn't feel right with me just spitting on it. It needs some softness. I need a vocalist."

"You wanna put a chick on it, shawty?"

"Yeah, man."

"Who you got in mind?"

T shrugged. "I don't know, man. I don't really have anyone in mind. You know somebody? And not that chick that be hanging around during everybody's studio time. What's her name?"

"Erica. Yeah, I heard she let you hit it, man."

The men laughed, and Ricky elbowed T as Alex rose and walked over to him.

"Baby, are you done?" Alex leaned seductively on T's shoulder. "Are we about to leave?"

Although it was fun watching them create music, Alex was ready to get on with the date that T had promised her. Dinner and a movie, her choice.

"You might as well go on and kick it with ya' girl," Ricky urged T. "Our time is up in, like, seven minutes, so it's all good."

"A'ight then." T rose from his seat. "I'ma check around to see who knows somebody that can set this shit off, man. It has that whole *Hustle & Flow* vibe. You know that song I'm talking about, homie?"

"Yeah. 'It's Hard Out Here for a Pimp.'" Ricky began to sing the familiar hook.

"Yeah, man. Like dat there."

"A'ight, we 'bout to be out."

T ushered Alex out of the studio. He put his arm around her, and they exited the office building, walking into the crisp evening air.

"Man, I just wanna go somewhere and chill out, Ma." He kissed her forehead. "Let's grab something and go back to your place."

Alex couldn't contain her disappointment. "You said we were going to do dinner and a movie."

"Baby, I'm tired as hell. You can't feed your man and let him chill out? We ain't gotta always go out and spend a lot of money just to be together."

Alex bit her lip again. She didn't want to argue, but she wasn't happy about being conned out of a date. In the short time that they had been dating, Alex had noticed that T never wanted to do anything that involved him spending money. They spent most of their time either eating fast food at her apartment or sitting around the studio as he and his boys did their thing. Alex didn't want another boring date, but she also didn't want to piss him off and drive him away, leaving her alone for the night.

They rode in silence in T's old gray 1978 Chevrolet Camaro, listening to a throwback OutKast CD. Riding through downtown Decatur, getting closer to Alex's apartment, T reached over and massaged her left thigh. "What you wanna eat, baby? Chick-fil-A, huh?"

It was more of a directive than a question. Alex simply smiled and nodded. "That's fine."

T approached the Chick-fil-A drive-through and leaned back in his seat as they waited in line for their turn. His hand still caressing her thigh, T looked at her through slanted eyes. "Baby, you mind spotting this?"

What the hell? she thought. *Is he for real?* "I guess so."

Reaching into her purse, she grabbed a twenty and handed it to him. He ordered their food and drove them home. All the while Alex said nothing. Silently, she was debating whether or not this relationship was worth her time. The thing she liked the most about T was his passion for music. It was seemingly the only thing he took seriously and invested any real time, energy, or money in. Many times she'd watch him write his lyrics, tuning out everything and everyone around him. She admired his drive. What she detested was the fact that he still lived at home with his mother, never took her out, but was always sitting around her house, eating her food, spending her money, and expecting sex at the end of it all.

T was very rough around the edges. He was a real street dude in Alex's opinion. His hard, thug-like demeanor was also a turn-on for Alex. Although it irked her whenever he shut her down, she liked that he had such a domineering, aggressive personality. She wasn't scared of T, but she definitely found herself monitoring her words so as not to piss him off.

As they finished their Chick-fil-A sandwiches in the comfort of her living room, Alex decided to entice him with conversation about the subject that mattered most to him. "So you need a female singer, huh?"

He nodded. "Yep. Bitch gotta be bad too. Need her to have that confidence in her voice like whoa."

"You know, I can sing a li'l bit."

T laughed. "Oh, for real? You can sing?"

"Why you laughing at me?" She pouted and playfully slapped at his arm.

"Man, I been kicking it with you for over a month now, and you ain't never said nothing to me about being even remotely interested in being in the business."

"I mean, it's not something that I've always aspired to do, but I was just saying . . . just letting you know . . . making conversation, letting you know that I can sing."

"So, what? You wanna audition for me now? What is this? *T's Hood Idol?*"

T laughed heartily, and Alex rose to clear their trash from the living-room table. As she walked toward the trash can, T grabbed her arm. "You know I'm just fucking with you, right?"

"You play too much. I was just letting you know something about me."

"Aw, don't be salty, baby. You know how many chicks—and dudes, for that matter—get at me, only to try to get me to put them on?"

"So what? You think I was telling you that for you to give me my big break?"

"Man, go on with that. I'm done with groupie girls trying to get their two minutes of fame or landing a balling-ass rap star. That's why I was saying I don't even want my mans trying to put that leech Erica on. That girl be up in everybody's session, trying to be down."

Alex laughed to herself at the thought of him calling someone else a leech. She was about to leave the room, and he grabbed her by the waist, pulling her down into his lap.

"I just be messing with you, baby. I know you down for me." He kissed her abruptly, stealing her breath with his quickness and intensity. She let him run his hands over her breasts through her T-shirt. He squeezed her right breast like he was inspecting fruit. Pulling back, he looked into her eyes. Alex had to admit to herself that the chocolate brother was very cute.

"I can count on you, can't I?" he asked her as he looked into her eyes intently and seriously.

Alex touched his face and stroked his cheek lightly. "You know you can."

"I got some studio time booked for this weekend, but I'm short a hundred and fifty dollars. You know I wouldn't ask unless it's very important, and you know ain't nothing more vital to me than this music thang."

Alex was speechless. Here she was thinking that he was about to reveal something personal about himself, when all he really wanted was some money to invest in his dream. "You haven't asked me anything." She was making him work for it, since he had the gall to be going there, anyway.

"Come on, baby. Can your boy hold a hundred and fifty dollars? I'ma get it back to you as soon as possible."

She was reluctant to comply with his request, unsure of whether or not she'd ever see her money again. Optimistic, she hoped that his career took off and she'd be the dime piece on his arm. She desperately wanted to be in on all the hot parties in Atlanta, fly out to LA with other celebrities, and partake of that fast-paced life. Helping T out and holding him down on his rise to stardom could be considered her paying her dues. If she hung in there with him while he had nothing, surely he'd take care of her once his album dropped. T had talent, and Alex believed that he would make it. She just wondered how long it was going to take, because certain things about him were beginning to piss her off.

She sighed and kissed her boyfriend on the forehead. "I'll go by the bank tomorrow, okay?"

His hand found its way to the buckle of her jeans. "Thank you, baby. I'm so thankful to have met you. Let me show you how thankful I am."

Alex jumped out of his lap just as her cell phone rang. "Why don't you go watch TV, like you said you wanted to?" Looking down at her phone, she saw that it was her mother calling. She raised her eyes to the heavens and accepted the call.

"Hey, Mommy." Her voice was cheerful.

T raised an eyebrow, then rose from the couch and exited the room. He wasn't interested in hearing her girlie conversation with her mother.

"How are you doing, Alex?" her mom asked.

"Fine. How are you?"

"I've had better nights."

"What happened?"

"I got something very interesting in the mail. Usually, I don't open mail from the insurance people, because it's normally them trying to find a way to get more money out of us."

"Uh-huh." Alex had a sinking feeling in the pit of her stomach. She gripped the side of her chair and waited to see what her mother was going to say next.

"You want to tell me what kind of procedures you've been having? And why you were in the emergency room?"

Hell no, I don't want to tell you about that, she thought. "Um, Mommy . . . I was going to tell you about it. I mean, it's been so hectic lately."

"Stop it right there, young lady." Mrs. Mason's voice escalated. "I'm not slow, you know. I can read this statement of services rendered quite well. A D ad C, Alex? How could you have gotten pregnant and gone through all of that without saying anything?"

"I didn't want you to be disappointed."

"Disappointed? So you thought that hiding it from us and bottling up your emotions and issues was a better way to go? That we'd be less disappointed in that? You haven't even told me anything about a boyfriend, let alone that you were *that* close to someone that you allowed yourself to get pregnant. *Pregnant,* Alexandria. My goodness . . ."

Alex was silent as she listened to her mother's sniffles. She genuinely felt bad for causing her mother such frustration. This was exactly what she had wanted to avoid.

"Do you have any idea how hurtful it is for me to know that my baby, *my baby,* was laid up in some hospital, in pain, needing someone to be there for her, and she chose *not* to call me?"

Alex's eyebrows rose. *Huh?*

Mrs. Mason's voice was now laced with compassion. "I am your mother, Alex. I may not like your decisions in life, but it's your life. But at the end of the day, you are my baby, and I will always want to be there to support you. I can't imagine what it must have been like for you to go through that . . . losing a child alone."

Alex felt her own tears rolling down her cheeks as she listened to her mother's sobs. For all her good intentions, she'd still somehow managed to get it wrong. "Mommy, I'm sorry. I wasn't trying to close you out or anything. I just didn't want you and Daddy to be upset with me for getting pregnant in the first place. It was a mistake. The guy was a real jerk, and I was contemplating having an abortion, anyway. I never wanted to do anything to make you or Daddy think less of me."

"Alex, you're our daughter. Like I said, we may not like your decisions, but we're always going to support you and love you. We're your parents."

"Did you tell Daddy?" Alex was worried about what her father would have to say.

"You think I shouldn't?"

"He'll be mad, Mommy."

"Yes, he will be. Do you understand the seriousness of this? What if something had gone wrong during your procedure? No one wants to get an out-of-state call from some hospital, saying our child is in critical condition."

"I know."

Her mom sighed. "It's between us this time, Alex. But please don't ever sell your parents short like that again, baby. We want to be there for you always."

"Okay, Mommy. I'm sorry."

"I love you."

Alex could feel her mother's smile through the phone and wanted nothing more than to be hugged by her. "I love you too, Mommy.

Chapter 38

Stephanie

Since returning home with the new baby, Stephanie had found herself completely on edge. Corey had been spending more and more time away from home, not telling her where he was or when she should expect him back. She'd come to expect this from him, but with her uneasy feelings about the murder in Decatur, Stephanie wasn't sure if she could put up with Corey's shenanigans any longer. She respected the fact that whatever was going on, if anything, he kept it away from their home and their children. But still, she was his girl, and she had the right to know what the hell he was up to.

Desperate to figure some things out, Stephanie found herself rummaging through his things one night. In the top of their closet he kept many shoe boxes. Corey had a thing for sneakers. She opened and searched through each shoe box, finding nothing but the Tims, Jordanss, or Air Force 1s that belonged in them. She went through his bureau drawers, still finding nothing unusual. Going back to the closet, she rummaged through miscellaneous bags on the closet floor. Still nothing. Mindlessly, she began patting down the pants he had hanging up. She stopped when she felt a bulge in one pair. Quickly, she snatched the pants down and reached into the pocket. She pulled out a wallet and instinctively flipped it open. Her breath escaped her as she instantly recognized the name on the ID card staring back at her. Montae Stokes.

She reached over and grabbed her cordless phone, calling the only person she felt confident enough to confide in.

"Yes, ma'am." Jada answered the phone with a hint of attitude.

"I have a problem." Stephanie bypassed cordialities.

"Of course you do. Seriously, do you people call me only when something's wrong? No one ever calls me to say they miss me, to see how I'm doing, to tell me they love me. None of that. Y'all suck."

Jada laughed at her own joke, but Stephanie was in no joking mood. "This is serious, Jada."

"Okay, boo. What's wrong?"

"Remember the news story about the dude who was shot in the Dec, right?"

"Of course I do."

"I'm staring at Montae's driver's license."

"Say what?"

"I found Montae's wallet in a pair of Corey's pants."

There was silence on the other end.

Stephanie tossed the wallet on her bed and jumped up. "Jada!"

"What?"

"Say something, bitch. I'm panicking over here."

"Hell, I was waiting for you to tell me that you need me to come help you pack. What do you want me to say, Mama?"

"Tell me what I'm supposed to do. I mean, why the hell would Corey have this man's wallet?"

"Tell you what to do? I need to get a new set of friends, because y'all chicks are wildin'. What do you mean, tell you what to do? Clearly, your boyfriend is what? *At least* an accessory to a crime, and that's at best. What do you think you should do? Ask Corey about it? Give Montae's family back his wallet? I mean, come on, girl!"

Stephanie bit her lip. "You think Corey really killed that guy?"

"You don't? Everyone knows Corey is *the* dope man in the Dec, Steph. You're not oblivious to this. From what I hear, Montae must have been trying to push your boy out of business, and Corey had to show him who runs shit. I mean, that's the word on the damn street."

"But he wouldn't do that. Corey wouldn't hurt anybody like that."

"Okay, tell me again what you called me for?"

"To help me, Jada. Come on. This is serious. If Corey killed that man, my children's father may go down for murder. But worse than that, if this Montae had a street team, those niggas might try to come back for Corey."

"Here's some solid, loving advice, Stephanie. Get the hell out of there. This is not the situation to rear your children in. You need to run, girl."

Steph sighed and picked up the wallet. "I can't run out on him, Jada. I know you don't understand this, but I love Corey. I promised him that I was in this relationship to the end."

"I can't listen to this. Baby girl, things can only get worse."

Stephanie returned to the closet and stuffed the wallet back into Corey's pants pocket. "I'll figure things out. Thanks, girl. I gotta go." She clicked off the phone before Jada had a chance to respond to her statement. If Corey was in deep, Stephanie was dead set on helping him pull through and convincing him to move their family the hell up out of Atlanta before shit went too far.

Chapter 39

Candace

Since the day she'd broken the news to Khalil about the baby, he'd become more evasive than ever. They had agreed that he would come to her parents' place for dinner following her first doctor's visit. But weeks had passed before he'd finally committed to a date and time. Candace was nervous about how the interaction between him and her parents would go. Never had she imagined that her lover and her parents would come face-to-face. It was funny to her how things worked out sometimes.

Sitting in her parents' living room, she fidgeted as she waited for him to show up. Already, he was half an hour late. Her father, who was not a very lenient man, was not very pleased that Khalil would be so disrespectful as to stand them up.

Candace stared at her nails as she tried to avoid apologizing to her parents for Khalil's absence. Just as her father walked into the room, looking at his watch, the rhythmic sounds of hip-hop forced their attention to the window. Khalil was pulling up in their driveway, to everyone's relief.

Candace walked out the door to meet him at the bottom of the sidewalk. "You're late, you know."

He shrugged nonchalantly. "I got held up with something. I'm here now." He walked up to her and gave her a weak hug.

She didn't return the embrace but looked at him sternly while speaking softly. "My parents are not very understanding people, and they are already not happy with either one of us. So please, put your 'I don't give a damn' attitude in check."

"Look, I'm not going to sit up in here and be intimidated by you or your parents, so you can forget that, sweetheart."

"Don't sweetheart me. Please, just be respectful, and hopefully, this whole dinner will be over soon."

She turned away, and he followed her up the walk to the front door, where her father was awaiting them. She took a deep breath as her dad stepped back to let them enter the living room. Her mom was standing behind her father, waiting patiently with her hands clasped.

"Mom, Dad, this is Khalil. Khalil, these are my parents, Barbara and Walter Lewis."

Khalil held out his hand to her father, and the two men gave a firm shake.

"How are you, sir?" Khalil asked her father.

"Fine, son. Nice to meet you."

Khalil smiled at her mother. "How you doing, ma'am? You have a lovely home."

Mrs. Lewis smiled. "Thank you. Come on in and have a seat. Dinner will be on the table in about ten minutes."

"Oh, thank you for the invitation, but I've already eaten. Thank you."

Mrs. Lewis looked to her husband, whose lips were tightly pursed. She too was annoyed. "Okay, well, come on. Have a seat. Would you like something to drink? Lemonade or sweet tea?"

"Tea would be fine." Khalil sat down on the love seat.

Mr. Lewis took a seat on the sofa across from him and toyed with the remote that was resting next to him. Candace perched herself on the arm of the love seat and waited for her father's opening remarks.

"Candace did tell you that we were expecting you for dinner, right?" Mr. Lewis asked Khalil.

Khalil nodded. "She did. But my plans have changed a little bit."

"We were waiting for you. It would have been a little more considerate if you had let us know that you wouldn't be joining us for dinner."

"My apologies. Something came up with my son, and I ended up eating with him."

"Oh, you have other children?"

"Yes sir. Two sons and a daughter."

"How old?"

"Twenty-one, ten, and one."

"All with your wife?"

"The two oldest with my ex-wife and the one-year-old with an ex-girlfriend."

Mr. Lewis's left eyebrow rose. Mrs. Lewis entered the living room with a glass of tea for Khalil. She sat beside her husband as Khalil nearly drained his glass. Candace assumed he needed the hydration, since beads of sweat were forming on his forehead, no doubt as a result of the interrogation her father was giving him. Candace herself was in shock about some of the things coming out of Khalil's mouth. She knew he was married to Sheila, but she had no idea that he'd been married prior to her. It was hard to discern his truths from his lies.

"Do you see your children often?" Mr. Lewis asked.

"Oh, you have other children?" Mrs. Lewis was stunned.

"Yes, ma'am. And no, sir. I don't see them as often as I'd like. The two older ones live in Virginia."

"Exactly how old are you, son?"

"Forty-three," Khalil answered.

Mrs. Lewis looked to her daughter questioningly, and Candace simply looked away.

"Do you know how old Candace is?" her father asked.

Khalil nodded. "I do."

"You're six years younger than me. You're practically old enough to be her father. You couldn't find a grown woman to fool around with?"

"Dad!" Candace interjected. "I am a grown woman. Age is just a number."

Her father shook his head. "Is it? With age comes wisdom, and you're not there yet, dear. Consider this present situation you're in."

"That has nothing to do with my age. Everyone makes mistakes."

"Okay, we're losing sight of the point here." Mrs. Lewis held her hands up to calm everyone down. "Mistake, lack of wisdom, whatever. There is a new life we are all bound by now. It's a shame that this child has to come to life in this type of situation, but we need to figure out how we're going to handle this."

"Well, with all due respect, Mr. and Mrs. Lewis, I want you to know that I have every intention of taking care of this child and being there for it. I understand your concern for Candace and her baby. If the situation was reversed and it was my daughter, I'd be asking questions too. But don't worry. I know how difficult it is to raise a child and what all needs to be done. Trust me, Candace isn't in this alone."

"*It?* Candace and *her* baby?" Mrs. Lewis repeated Khalil's words with a sour look on her face. "Do you understand that this is *your* baby too?"

Khalil nodded. "I understand that."

"So don't say 'Candace's baby.' This is y'all's baby. As in we expect the two of you to handle whatever needs to be handled to care for *your* baby," Mrs. Lewis said.

"I understand that. By the same token, to protect myself, I will have to have a DNA test done after the baby's born."

"What?" Candace was unable to contain her contempt. "What are you trying to say, Khalil?"

Khalil raised his hand to silence her. "Calm down. I'm just saying it is the only reasonable thing to do. Let's be candid, shall we? I mean, you *are* married. It could just as easily be your husband's baby, right?"

"It's not Quincy's baby. You know that. I haven't had sex with Quincy in a couple of months. Why would you say that?"

"I'm just trying to be responsible, sweetheart. That's all."

Mr. Lewis chuckled. "Responsible? If either of you had been responsible, we wouldn't be having this conversation. But, speaking of spouses, have you advised your spouse of your new *expectation?*"

"My wife and I are separated. But, no, she doesn't know."

"Since you have children and you say you know what all needs to be done to care for a child, you understand that she'll have doctor's appointments to go to frequently, bills associated with health care, and that once the baby is here, he or she will need health insurance and things in general?" Mr. Lewis asked.

"I do. Once the baby is born and we've done the DNA test, I insist that the baby be placed on my health insurance. I'm sure Candace will get plenty of incidentals from baby showers or whatnot, but I don't mind purchasing the bulk of major items, like furniture, a car seat, or whatever."

"Okay, but what about living situations?" Mr. Lewis asked. "Candace doesn't have a home anymore. We're not exactly equipped to house a second family in our home. She and the baby will need their own space."

Khalil sighed and looked at Candace. "I guess I could assist with a deposit on an apartment for you. Just find one and let me know what I need to do." He looked back at her parents reassuringly and softened his tone. "Mr. and Mrs. Lewis, I know this isn't the most pleasant situation in which to introduce a new life into the world, and I know that you may not believe this, but despite what you think about the way Candace and I came to create a child together, I do care for your daughter. Candace knows that she has a place in my heart and that I'd do anything to help her and *our* child. In fact, Candace knows that she could stay with me if she wanted to, versus getting a place of her own."

Candace sucked her teeth and looked away. She couldn't stand to watch the show he was putting on for her parents' benefit. Perhaps he knew that she wouldn't tell them about the scene that had gone down between the two of them and Sheila. But this fake, loving persona he was fronting with was making her sick.

"Out of the question," her father told him. "Even though you are both separated, you are both very much still married. Either of you could decide to return to your spouse at any time."

"Highly unlikely on my end, sir. But I understand your conviction on the matter."

"What are you going to do about child support?" Mrs. Lewis asked.

"We can figure that out before the baby gets here," Khalil responded. "We don't have to involve the courts. Give me the DNA test for reassurance, and I will gladly provide for my child. I don't need any judge to tell me to take care of what's mine."

Mrs. Lewis touched her husband's arm. "It sounds feasible, Walter."

Mr. Lewis nodded. "Okay. As Candace's father, I'm hoping that you fulfill all the promises you made here today. As a man, I hope that you're as good a father as you're portraying yourself to be. Children need both parents in their lives."

Khalil nodded and gave Candace a sideways glance. "Yes, I know what a difference that makes. Candace can count on me." He looked at his Timex and smiled at Candace's parents. "I have to be going now. I have another engagement. Thank you for the tea and the talk. It was really nice to meet both of you. I guess we're all sort of like family now, huh?"

Khalil's attempt to make light of the situation didn't go over very well with Mr. Lewis. The older man simply ignored him and looked over at Candace. "When's your next doctor's appointment?"

"In three weeks. They're going to do an ultrasound."

Mr. Lewis looked back at Khalil. "I trust you'll make *that* appointment, right?"

Khalil nodded and rose from his spot on the love seat. He touched Candace lightly on the leg. "Just let me know when it is, Candace, and I'm there."

Candace moved her leg away. "I'll call you."

"Mr. and Mrs. Lewis, it's been a pleasure." Khalil moved toward the front door. "Perhaps next time I'll be available to have dinner with you. Whatever you've cooked smells delicious, Mrs. Lewis. You all have a good evening."

Candace followed him out the door. She stood on the porch and pulled the door closed behind her. Khalil turned to look at her before he went to his car.

"You know, if you need anything else before your appointment, you can call me for that too, baby girl."

She turned her nose up at his come-on. "That's not going to happen, dear. You can count on *that*."

Khalil chuckled and touched her face lightly. "I can guarantee you that it'll happen. Your hormones are about to be raging out of control, and I can tell you that pregnant pussy is the best, and you already know that I miss the taste of yours."

Candace was mad at herself for getting moist in response to his lewd comments and his gall to make them on her parents' porch. She shuddered at his touch and tried to keep up her hardened demeanor so that he wouldn't know she was turned on. "You're so cocky, it's a shame. Go home and tell Sheila I said hello. You know, after you call and check in on your three other children."

Khalil chuckled and walked to his car. "Yeah. Right."

She didn't wait for him to pull off before she went back inside and shut the door. Her father was sitting at the dining-room table, and her mother was in the kitchen, fixing his plate.

"You pick the most interesting characters to get involved with." Mr. Lewis laid his cloth napkin over his lap.

She shrugged. "He's not all bad, Dad. It's an awkward situation for all of us."

He didn't respond.

Candace sighed. "I'm gonna go wash up and help Mom." She hurried up the stairs to the bathroom, relieved to be alone. As she washed her hands, she thought about Khalil's statements and his touch on her skin. She hadn't had sex in a while, and she was horny as hell.

"Damn Khalil," she said, cursing his memory. She looked at herself in the mirror and touched her breasts. They were a little tender. Probably a combination of being horny and being pregnant. She resisted the urge to pleasure herself and hurried out to struggle through dinner with her parents.

Chapter 40

Jada

Jada took a deep breath, said a small prayer, and walked into the bathroom. Slowly, she reached for it with her eyes closed. She was too afraid to open it. Her heart raced rapidly. She wasn't ready for the answer. She wasn't prepared for the letdown. Sighing deeply, she picked it up and opened her eyes. *Only one. Only fucking one.* She began to heave, unable to control her breathing. She clutched her chest with the stick buried in it, trying to pull herself together. It didn't work. She couldn't breathe past the hurt or the feeling that overcame her. Slipping to the floor, feeling the cold tile against her bare legs, she leaned against the vanity and suffered through the panic attack she couldn't avoid.

She sobbed between gasps of air, her body convulsing with her struggle to breathe normally. She never let go of the object of her distress. She was so distraught that she didn't hear Jordan come into their home and call out her name. He walked through the apartment in search of his wife.

"Jada, baby, where you at?" His voice boomed through the apartment.

He walked into the bathroom after seeing that the door was slightly ajar. "Baby, you in here?" Jordan saw her sobbing uncontrollably on the floor. He kneeled down and reached for her, confused about what was going on. "What's wrong, baby? Baby, what's wrong? Talk to me." He put his arms around her, hugging her lovingly, and kissed her forehead. "Baby, what's wrong?"

He began to rock her in an attempt to soothe her and calm her breathing. He touched her hand that was still clutched to her chest. Realizing she was holding on to something, he tried to pry her hand open. "What is it? Baby, what happened? Did something happen?"

He finally pried her fist open, releasing her grasp on the stick. He looked down at it, trying to figure out what had made his wife so unstable and upset. Jordan's brain was trying to process what the hell he was looking at. He looked from the stick to his wife, and then back at the stick, and then it dawned on him. He threw the stick down and rose from the floor.

"Come on, baby, come on. It's okay. Lemme get you off the floor." He reached down and cradled her in his arms and lifted her up. Her breathing was relaxing, and she allowed Jordan to carry her into their bedroom and lay her across their bed. He disappeared briefly to get her a glass of water.

"Sit up, baby. Try to drink this. Please." He was trying his best to get her to snap out of it.

She forced herself to sit upright. He lifted the glass to her lips, and she took a few sips of the cold liquid. As she drank, she looked up into his eyes and felt a tremendous bout of guilt, shame, and helplessness. Tears rolled down her cheeks from her bloodshot eyes. Jordan shook his head, knowing immediately what it was that she was thinking.

"Don't think like that. It's just not our time." He sat the glass down on the nightstand and took her hand. "I love you, baby."

She lowered her eyes. "As much as I want to, as much as I've tried, I can't give you the one thing I know you want more than anything in the world."

"I have the one thing I want more than anything. I have you, baby."

"It's not fair." Her shoulders shook as she cried. "Everyone else is getting knocked up. Even the ones that don't want to be pregnant. It just happens for them with no effort. It's not fair, Jordan. It's not fuckin' fair."

"It's just not our time, baby." He rubbed her hand.

"I'm sick of hearing that shit," she shouted angrily. "Stop telling me that shit. When is the time, Jordan? Huh? We've been trying for over a year. It's not rocket science. It's clearly not a hard thing to do. *I* just can't fuckin' do it."

"Why do you think it's you? Maybe it's me. Something could be wrong with me, babes. I could go to the doctor and get the shit checked out. You know, try to see what's going on."

"It's me."

"I'm just saying, neither of us can be sure until we both get checked out, so—"

"It's me, Jordan."

"Let's just both make an appointment to get checked out."

She snatched her hand away from him and balled her fists up in frustration. "It's me, Jordan! It's fuckin' me! I know that it's me." She began to cry hard and looked at her husband with sorrow in her eyes. "The summer after I graduated from high school, I had a boyfriend. He loved me, he always told me he wanted to have a big family, and I believed him. I believed everything he told me. So I got pregnant. It just happened so quickly. But when I told him, he acted like a typical nigga, saying he didn't believe me. He stopped taking my calls most of the time, didn't want to see me, and one day, when I was sick and in the hospital, because I was having difficulty with the pregnancy, he practically abandoned me. I called him to tell him where I was and that I needed him. He told me that it was my own fault and that he wasn't coming out to the hospital, and then he hung up on me.

"I didn't want to spend my life being someone's unwanted baby's mama. I wanted a family. I wanted to be loved. I wanted the whole package. And I wanted to hurt him the same way he had hurt me. So I had an abortion and went on with life like it had never happened. They told me that one of the side effects could be that my uterine lining would be scarred from them scraping it to terminate the pregnancy."

Jordan sat silently as he processed her confession. His eyebrows were knit as he came to terms with what she was saying.

"So see?" she whispered. "It's me. This is my punishment for killing that baby. I can't give you a child of your own." She covered her mouth to muffle her crying, tears seeping through her fingers.

Jordan massaged his temples and stared at the floor, shaking his head. "God doesn't work like that, baby. He's not a cruel God. He's a loving and forgiving God." He leaned over and kissed his wife's tearstained cheeks. "What you need to do is forgive yourself, baby."

Jada threw her arms around him and held on for dear life, crying into his shoulder.

"I love you, and we'll have a baby when it's time, Jada," he told her. "Let's just stop focusing on it so much and just let it happen. And in a year, if you are still worried about it, we'll see a specialist. Hell, if push comes to shove, we'll adopt. It doesn't really matter to me. We'll be parents one day, one way or the other. It's all good, boo. It's all good."

She looked up at him and kissed his lips passionately. "Thank you."

"For what?"

"For understanding and for loving me."

He held her tightly. "The pleasure's all mine, baby love."

Chapter 41

Miranda

It had been a long day. Work had been extremely exhausting, and all Miranda wanted to do was go home, have a glass of wine with a cup of noodles, and knock out. Walking through the grocery store down the street from her house, she searched for the wine aisle. Just past the snack aisle she saw a familiar face approaching her. She quickly racked her brain, trying to figure out where she'd met this woman before. The chick stopped dead in her tracks and looked at Miranda with an intensity that caused her to take a step back. Then it dawned on her. She knew exactly who this skank was.

"Not so hard out in public, huh?" Tammy crossed her bony arms. "What you got to say now?"

Miranda rolled her eyes. This was the last thing she was in the mood to deal with. "Why don't you just go about your business? I'd hate to have to mop this dirty-ass floor with your lily-white jumpsuit."

"Oh, don't hate, bitch, just because your ass lacks taste and class."

"Class? What the hell do you know about class? Trying to start shit with me in a grocery store? I mean, really."

"I don't ever start nada. I'm the one that finishes shit."

Passersby were starting to take notice of their confrontation. Sensing the attention from the crowd, Tammy began to really feel herself. She waved her index finger around as she raised her voice and hurled more insults at Miranda. "And you got about one more time to say some flip shit to me before I rip that tongue out ya' big-ass mouth. You jealous, bitter-ass bitch."

"I'm not gon' be too many more bitches. Now, if you wanna get down, we can get down. You name the place and time, but I'm not about to get into this with you in this grocery store. That's some tacky shit you might do, but I'm not going to jail with or for you tonight."

Rounding the corner, Norris walked up to the two women, and Miranda felt her heart skip a beat. Her first thought was to run, but she was rooted to her spot. She quickly regained her composure. There was no way she was letting her husband and his tramp intimidate her.

"What's up, Miranda?" Norris asked sinisterly. "Didn't think I'd run into your ass, did you? You know, I should beat the shit out of you right here."

"Don't waste your energy on this mud duck, baby." Tammy stroked Norris's arm. "She ain't worth it."

"Listen to your girl, Norris," Miranda stated sarcastically. "She must be an expert on worthlessness."

"Fuck you." Tammy rolled her neck in complete ghetto fashion. "You're just mad 'cause he's not stuck under your homely-looking ass anymore."

Miranda gave a curt smile. "If you're done wasting my time, I'm going to go on about my business." She clutched her purse tightly as she moved to the right to walk past the couple.

"Watch your back," Norris warned her. "This shit ain't over."

Miranda waved her left hand in the air. "I'm done with you."

Tammy laughed. "Her ass is done in general."

Just after passing the girl, Miranda quickly turned around and clocked her with her heavy faux leather purse. "On second thought, maybe I'm not done!" Miranda swung her purse over and over again at Tammy's face and head.

The younger girl was caught off guard by Miranda's attack and stumbled to the side, twisting her ankle on her Baby Phat platform shoes. Her squeals of "Stop! Stop! Stop!" were muffled under the blows Miranda continuously put upon her. A crowd was growing, but Miranda couldn't stop herself. In her blind rage, she swung her purse repeatedly until the strap broke from the force. Norris was ineffectively pulling on her

arm and urging her to chill the hell out. Tammy lay curled up
on the floor, trying to protect her face from the blows. Tired
of the purse, Miranda dropped it and grabbed Tammy up by
her arm.

"Come on, bitch. Talk shit now," Miranda growled.

Tammy's lip was busted, and her left eye was beginning to
swell. She struggled to her feet and spat in Miranda's face.
Her blood-tainted saliva slid down Miranda's cheek. "Fuck
you, you shysty trick!" Tammy huffed and puffed, with her
fists balled up and resting at her sides.

On instinct Miranda threw a fist to punch Tammy, but
Tammy was too quick. Getting her moxie back, Tammy
stepped to the side, and since Miranda's energy was spent
from missing her punch, Tammy was able to grab Miranda's
arm and landed a punch of her own on Miranda's nose. Blood
dripped out of Miranda's nose from the impact. Miranda
struggled to free herself from Tammy's grip as the crowd
hooted and hollered. A manager ran over to the scene.

"Ladies, stop!" The middle-aged gentleman pleaded with
them, to no avail. "Ladies! Ladies! You have to leave the
premises with this. Call security!"

"Let her go, baby. Come on," Norris said to Tammy, tugging
at her arm. "Ease up, man. Come on. Y'all cut this shit out in
here before these folks call the damn police, man."

Tammy ignored him as she pushed Miranda into a Kool-
Aid display, gripping her arm with one hand and her face
with the other. "You dumb, bitch. You don't know who the
fuck you're messing with. I will fuck your shit up. You think
you're so smart and shit. You ain't shit. Ya' man don't want
you. Nobody wants your sorry ass. Put ya' hands on me again,
and I promise you won't put your hands on anyone else ever
again."

"Fuck, Tammy. Let her go!" Norris yelled.

"Come on, ma'am." The manager was now whining as he
continued to beg them to break it up. "Please . . ."

Miranda gave up trying to pry Tammy's hand away from
her arm and ignored the sting of Tammy's nails digging into
her skin. She reached up and roughly grabbed Tammy's Remy
weave track. She tugged with all her might, causing Tammy

to let go of her face. A bruise was forming around Miranda's chin, where Tammy's hand had been. She pulled harder, and Tammy screamed, letting go of Miranda's arm. Taking this as an opportunity, Miranda tackled Tammy to the floor, choking her neck, shaking the girl, and kneeing her repeatedly in the gut. When Tammy seemed completely defeated, Miranda allowed Norris and the store manager to pry her away from the younger woman.

"Bitch." Miranda glared at her beaten opponent. She looked at Norris and snatched her arm away from him. Looking back at Tammy, she shook her head. Several store clerks were helping the woman to her feet. Doubled over in pain, Tammy glared up at Miranda, who gave her an equally hateful look. Norris put his arm around Tammy so that she could rest her weight against him.

"It's only a matter of time before he starts kicking your ass too," Miranda told Tammy.

An officer was by her side. "Miss, come with me, please."

Miranda ignored the officer. "You popping off at the mouth, all happy 'cause you're with *my* husband. Stupid bitch. Yeah, you got him, and look what getting him got *you*. Get used to getting your ass kicked, because I promise you, the shit's just around the corner."

"Man, go on somewhere with that shit." Norris waved her off as he and a store clerk led Tammy toward the exit.

Miranda's vision was blurred as she was whisked through the crowd and out of the grocery store. She could only vaguely remember how they had got to this point. Her mind went blank as the officers spoke to her and advised her that she was going to be taken to the county jail. She watched in what seemed like slow motion as a paramedic attended to Tammy farther up the sidewalk. She felt herself being ushered into the back of a patrol car and stared at the spectators as she was carried off to a place she'd never thought she'd go. Her entire life was spiraling out of control.

"That was completely irresponsible of you. I can't believe this shit. Y'all's asses are going to give me high blood pressure in this bitch. I mean, damn! Whatever happened to turning the other cheek? Or just walking away? Hell, if you wanted to kick someone's ass, why not kick Norris's ass? He's the one that has fucked you over. Tammy is just a product of Norris's bullshit."

Jada was ranting and raving nonstop as she drove Miranda home from the DeKalb County Jail. Several hours of sitting in a holding cell with hookers and other women who seemed down on their luck was more than Miranda could take. Now listening to Jada lecture her was the perfect end to a perfectly fucked-up day.

"You should be glad that girl didn't decide to press charges." Jada turned down the street on which Miranda's apartment complex stood.

"She didn't press charges, because Norris probably thinks that I'd press charges against him."

"That's what any sane person would have done a long time ago."

"I'm not asking you to understand, so—"

"Good, damn it. Because I don't. Hell, I don't understand why y'all do half the things y'all do. No, what I really don't get is why the hell y'all call me *after* y'all do crazy shit and don't expect me to be real with you."

"Real or not, don't pass judgment on me, Jada. You don't know what I've been through, and this is one of those things that you'll never really understand until you've gone through it yourself."

Jada sighed and looked over at Miranda. Miranda sat with her arms crossed, staring out the window, waiting for Jada to put the car in park. Jada softened. "I didn't mean to come off as being judgmental. I'm just saying, some things you just don't *have* to go through, you know. You put yourself in these positions and . . ." Her thoughts trailed off.

Miranda turned and looked at her friend. She knew the other girl only had her best interests at heart. Her body was sore, her head ached, and her feelings were hurt. She couldn't get past her own issues to see how she was putting extra baggage on the ones who cared for her the most. "Thank you for everything." Miranda hoped she sounded sincere. "Thank you for being there at the hospital before. Thank you for bailing me out tonight. Thank you for always being such a great friend to me."

Jada reached over and hugged her tightly. "I know you'd do the same for me. But, Miranda, seriously, maybe you should talk to someone about how to deal with everything you've gone through. Maybe it would help you to make some healthier, wiser decisions to kinda get your life back on track."

Miranda gave a half smile. She knew that Jada meant well. "We'll see." She opened the car door and grabbed her broken purse.

"Call me tomorrow," Jada called out to her. "Alex is planning some kinda shindig for her birthday, honey, and you know she'll expect you to be there, so put it on your calendar."

Miranda nodded. "Okay. See ya later."

She shut the car door and hurried up the steps to her apartment. Once safely inside, she went to the kitchen and rummaged through the pantry. She knew there'd be no alcohol there, which was why she'd gone to the store earlier to begin with. Plopping down at her kitchen table, she buried her face in her hands and sighed, too exasperated and too pissed to cry. She needed something to take the edge off, something to help her through the emotions she couldn't control.

She rose and went into her bedroom, where she hid her stash. Pulling out the shoe box, she reached inside and grabbed the little Baggie, the one she hadn't been able to bring herself to explore until now. Turning it over and over in her hand, she debated whether or not she should try it. Once she crossed that path, there was no going back. She felt tension in her neck and moved her head from side to side. Glancing over at herself in the mirror, she saw the bruises, the dried blood, and the tired look in her eyes. She didn't even recognize herself anymore.

She took a deep breath and went into the living room, to the coffee table. What did she have to lose? She quickly rummaged through her purse and pulled out a dollar. She'd seen this on TV. Surely, it was this simple. Carefully, she rolled the dollar tightly. After opening the little Baggie, she stuck her finger into the white powder and tasted it. She grimaced at the taste, which made her think of biting into an aspirin. She poured the powder out onto the table, then pushed it around with one edge of the rolled-up dollar bill. She made tracks through it, separating it into two mounds.

"It must be like sucking through a straw," she said aloud, trying to brace herself.

She didn't know what to expect or even if she was going about this the right way. This wasn't exactly the kind of thing you could call someone up and ask about. She took a deep breath and positioned the dollar over one of the mounds. Closing her eyes tightly, she put her right nostril over the other end of the dollar and inhaled long and hard. She felt a tingling sensation at first. After snorting half of the first mound, she sat back and massaged her nose. She shook her head a little, trying to shake off the tickling inside her nose. Her heart was racing at the very thought of what she'd just done. Not yet feeling any effect, and no longer scared of any horrible side effects, she picked up the dollar and finished off the first mound.

Leaning back, with her head resting against the couch, she replayed the afternoon's events in her head. She couldn't believe that she'd allowed Tammy to take her to the level of engaging in a catfight in public. But she'd whupped her ass good! She was glad that she hadn't backed down or walked away, leaving Tammy or Norris believing that she was a punk. Miranda was tired of being a victim. It was time to fight back. She had a record now, but at least she had stood her ground. While feeling proud of herself, Miranda noticed that the tingling feeling in her nose had quickly been replaced with a burning sensation. She squeezed the bridge of her nose, willing the feeling to go away. Suddenly paranoid, she jumped up and hurried to the kitchen.

"What have I done?" she asked herself aloud. "What have I done?"

She went to the sink and splashed water on her face, desperate to try anything to cool off the stinging. When she felt minimally satisfied with that, she poured herself a glass of water in an attempt to calm down. After a while she felt a surge of nervous energy, which had her rummaging through her closets and throwing out any remnants of Norris. This high wasn't what she was used to, but she was rolling with it. She had the nerve and the edge that she needed to start closing this chapter in her life.

"Fuck Norris!" Miranda stuffed his clothes into a garbage bag. "I'm not taking any more of his shit. Fuck him and fuck Tammy. I'm not a fucking punching bag. I'm not a fucking victim anymore! Fuck him!"

The phone rang, and she practically jumped at the sound of it. She stared at the ringing phone, wondering if it was her abuser calling to taunt her. "Fuck you!" she yelled at the phone as it gave its final rings. "Fuck you! Fuck you! Fuck you!" She threw a pair of Norris's socks at the cordless and turned away to promptly toss his game system into yet another garbage bag.

Chapter 42

Stephanie

She wasn't sure what the hell she was doing, but Stephanie knew she had to do something. She considered her options, and this idea was the one that made the most sense to her. If anyone found Montae Stokes's wallet on Corey's person or in his possession, she knew her boyfriend would be tried for murder. Why he had chosen to stash it in their home was beyond her understanding. She wasn't completely sold on the idea that Corey had killed Montae, but she knew that whoever did had done so according to Corey's instructions. This wasn't the man she knew who hustled hard in the streets to make life easy and lavish for her and their children. Stephanie knew for certain only that she loved this man and wanted only to protect him and their family. Her plan was still to convince him to tie up his business dealings and move their family away from Atlanta to a place where they could have a fresh start in life. But first, she had to dispose of the evidence that could ruin that opportunity for them.

She waited until it was completely dark out so that no one would see her. The kids were sound asleep in their beds, and Corey hadn't made it home, which wasn't uncommon for him. Taking the wallet out of the closet, she divvied up the items in it and placed them in three different garbage bags. She stared at the wallet itself for a moment before tossing it into one of the bags. Then she divided the contents of all the wastebaskets in the house and poured them into the three bags. Quietly, she exited the apartment and went down to the trash receptacle. Disgusted, she tore into the bags of trash already in the receptacle and began to mix up that trash with the trash in her three garbage bags. Satisfied that the evidence was carefully concealed and its previous location was unidentifiable, she tied up her bags and took them down to her car. She prayed that Corey wouldn't come home while she was out.

Quickly, she rode down to the corner store and disposed of the trash in the store's large Dumpster. Returning home, she hurriedly checked in on the children, then took a shower to rid herself of the stink of trash and the twinge of guilt she felt. She wasn't sure that she had done a good job of getting rid of the wallet. Perhaps she should have taken it to a place that wasn't so close to their home. She convinced herself that she'd done a sufficient job. If the police wanted to pin Corey, they'd go through his trash, not the trash at the corner store, right? She wondered where the gun was that had been used to kill Montae. If Corey did it, would he have kept the gun? If so, where would he have stashed it? Stephanie wanted to believe that Corey wouldn't be stupid enough to hold on to a gun with a body on it. But then again, he had been foolish enough to bring the dead man's wallet into their home.

Nervous and scared for their family, Stephanie threw on one of Corey's white T-shirts and went into the kitchen for a drink. He kept a bottle of E&J in the cabinet. Stephanie wasn't too fond of brown liquor but was in desperate need of something to calm her nerves. She mixed the E&J with some cola and leaned against the counter as she drank the concoction and let the alcohol burn down her throat. She heard the front door open and close and jumped. Turning around, glass in hand, she watched as Corey sauntered into the kitchen nonchalantly, as if it was twelve noon instead of two in the morning.

"What's up, boo?" He headed straight to the refrigerator for a beer. "You in here drinking up my shit?" He slapped her on the ass and took a swig of his Heineken.

Stephanie fought back tears as she took a sip of her own drink. She lowered her head. She was an emotional wreck because of all the things she had been internalizing. Corey looked at her and noticed that something wasn't right.

"What's up? Why you not in bed?"

She looked up at him with tears in her eyes. "Where were you?" She was deflecting because she wasn't ready to address what was really bothering her.

"Working."

"This late, Corey?"

He chuckled. "You act like I punch a time clock or some shit. My shit ain't exactly your average nine to five, baby."

Stephanie bit her lip. "I know that. I just thought that you could have at least been home by eleven."

"I'm home now. Are we going to have this same argument every time I don't come home when you want me to? This is my house. I should be able to come and go as I please, when I please. I'm tired as hell, woman. Please don't start this shit."

He started to walk away, and she reached out to grab his arm. "I need to talk to you." The words came out rushed and panicky.

He looked at her and raised an eyebrow. "'Bout what?"

She took a deep breath. "I want you to get out of the game."

Silence hung in the air as Corey took in her words, and she held her breath, waiting to see how he would react. He studied her face, and she searched his eyes for a clue about what it was that he was thinking. Unable to gauge his feelings, she sat her glass down on the counter and pushed it back and forth from one hand to the other. Corey leaned against the counter beside her.

"What brought this on?"

She shrugged.

"Don't get silent now." Corey crossed his arms. "Speak on it."

"I'm tired of worrying about whether or not you're going to come home. When the phone rings, I'm scared that it's you calling to say you're in jail or someone else calling to say something's happened to you. When you leave home, I'm sick of wondering if you'll make it back."

"This is what I do, Steph. You're not new to this shit. You've known who I am and what I am from day one."

She nodded. "I know, but it's not just us now. We have kids we have to think about. I don't want our son seeing his dad on the news for . . ." Her words trailed off, and she looked up at him.

His eyebrow rose, as if he was daring her to say the unmentionable. She wanted him to know that she was privy to what was going on, but she didn't have the heart to utter the words and didn't want to upset him.

"You've made good money, baby." Stephanie's tone was now pleading. "We could take the kids somewhere quiet, away from Georgia. I could go to school, and you could too, if you wanted to. Maybe start your own legit business doing something. I don't know. I just know that it's time to get out, baby. You can't do the same shit forever. At some point it's got to come to an end. Why not be the one to say, 'Enough is enough,' and just let it go before something bad happens?"

His expression softened as he felt the sincerity in her words and registered the fear in her voice. "Do you feel unsafe, Steph? 'Cause you and the kids are here with me? You wanna go back to how it was? Living separately?"

She shook her head. "No, Corey. I don't want to be away from you. We're a family. I just want our family to be safe and stress free." She touched his arm lightly. "Baby, you have the potential to be so much more than this. You're a businessman."

He snatched his arm away and took another swig of his beer. "So much more than this expensive-ass, upscale condo you're in? None of your friends have half the shit we got, baby. You got steaks and shit in the freezer. You ain't gotta want for nothing. Ain't no regular job out there for me, Steph, that's gon' keep us in this type of lifestyle. It just ain't happenin'."

"We have money saved, and we don't need fancy food or a fancy apartment, Corey. That shit's not important."

He held his beer bottle up in her face. "If I wasn't ballin', you wouldn't have looked twice at me back in the day. You loved this thug shit and this money, Steph. Don't front. I know what the hell it's like to be poor. Don't know where ya' next meal coming from, don't know how you gon' pay the bills, or if you even gon' have a place to stay, period. I don't wanna worry about that shit for my family."

"We'll figure it out. We can figure something out. Please . . ."

He took another swig and eyed her before nodding his head. "Lemme think about this shit, a'ight?" Without another word, he turned to leave but then stopped and looked back over his shoulder at her. "You know I got you, right? I ain't gon' let nothing happen to you or my kids, Steph. I need you to believe that shit, okay?"

She nodded, unable to look up at him. Corey walked out of the room, and Stephanie released the tears she'd been trying hard to hold back. She turned up her glass and emptied it in one gulp. She knew his intentions were good where the family was concerned, but she also knew that nothing good could come out of this situation unless they got out immediately. She touched the chain of keys that had been hanging around her neck ever since the day he'd given the keys to her, and she wondered for the first time in a long time what other troubles the keys would open up for them. She felt defeated and didn't know what else to do or where to turn.

Chapter 43

Candace

Time was steadily passing, and Candace was still trying to adjust to the idea of sharing her body with a little person. Pregnancy was not fun for her. The morning sickness was getting on her nerves, and she was now starting to feel a change in the way her clothes fit. Having kids was never something she had planned on doing, and it was definitely putting a crimp in her diva-like demeanor. She constantly felt chunky and self-conscious about her appearance. If she wasn't puking or munching on snacks, she was incredibly horny. This was a feeling that sucked for her, because she had no one around to alleviate her frustrations. Khalil was out of the question.

In fact, Khalil's ass was MIA. All the crap he'd told her parents about being there for her, helping to get her a place, and stepping up to his responsibility had turned out to be as fictional as Sheila being his estranged girlfriend. Her parents frequently inquired about his whereabouts and about whether or not she'd heard from him. Each time that she had nothing to report, she could see the rage growing in her father. She knew her parents didn't want to get stuck with footing the bills for both her and a newborn. Candace wanted nothing more than to move out of her parents' place and have her own space again, free from their disappointed and disapproving glances.

She hadn't heard from Quincy at all. That was fine with her. She was ready to close that chapter of her life, anyway. Horny or not, she was not about to let him touch her body ever again, for any reason. She'd recently filed for divorce. Since their marriage was short lived and they had no shared assets, she was confident that it wouldn't take long for the papers to be ready for their signatures. The sooner the better. Candace was ready to move on. But most importantly, she was ready to get her freak on.

Stopping by a popular rib joint in the heart of the DEC, Candace was in the mood for a greasy rib sandwich and fries. Sauntering into the small hole-in-the wall in her black slacks and lavender blouse, she noticed a familiar face smiling at her. She turned up her nose, not wanting to give him any eye contact, and went on to the counter to place her order. As she waited for her food to be ready, she stared out the window at the rush-hour traffic crawling down Candler Road.

"What you doing round this way?" His Southern drawl was close to her ear.

She flinched, wondering where he got the nerve to approach her like that. "I work not too far from here." She looked at him, noticing for the first time ever how smooth his chocolate skin was. Her hormones were messing with her senses. "What *you* doing round this way? You moved on up, remember? To ya' mansion in the sky with ya' wife and kids."

"We ain't married."

"Might as well be. You know that girl loves you with a passion."

He ran his hand over his perfectly maintained waves and shot her a knowing smile. "Look like somebody been loving you with a passion."

Instinctively, Candace pulled down on her blouse and smoothed the fabric over her belly. "What are you talking about?"

"Ma'am, your order's up," the cashier announced.

Candace grabbed her greasy bag and headed out of the soul food joint. He followed her to her car.

"Hey, man. I didn't mean to piss you off or nothing." He stood next to her. "I didn't mean it in a bad way, ya' know. I was just saying. It looks good on you."

She gave him a questioning look. "How does being pregnant look good on somebody? It's synonymous with being fat."

He opened her car door and leaned in a little too closely for someone who was definitely off-limits to her. "Pregnancy is beautiful on chicks who take care of their bodies. Makes you phat in all the right places."

She watched as his eyes surveyed her body, and felt his hand lightly graze her ass as she got in the car. He shut the door behind her.

"You got my number?" he asked.

"Yeah," she said coyly. "Your house number."

"A'ight, you got jokes. Giggle it up now. I promise you, I'ma get that."

"What the hell ever."

"Mark my words, baby girl. A nigga knows which chicks he can and can't pull."

"You don't think you're being a little arrogant? You talkin' all this trash. How you know that I'm not about to get on the phone and tell your girl what type of dog you are?"

"'Cause you won't. And even if you did, she wouldn't believe you." He flashed his cocky smile, tapped her car, and turned away.

Candace pulled off and considered their conversation as she drove to her parents' place. It had been a while since she'd had some attention from a man. Her ego and her body were screaming for it. Since she knew her body wasn't going to get any of the satisfaction that he had alluded to, she figured there was no harm in allowing her ego to be stroked by his come-ons. It was just friendly, flirty banter. No one was harmed. Would she call him? Of course not, and not just because the only number she had for him truly was their house number, but because it would be completely out of line.

However, later that night, as she lay in bed alone, she replayed their conversation once more, remembering especially how his lips had curled when he smiled at her and how his hand had touched her lightly. She worked herself up so much over the memory of such a brief, trivial moment that she began to wonder what it would be like to have his hands stroking her bare ass, her sensitive nipples, and her aching pussy. Her fingers slid down to her kitty as she envisioned him entering her with his tongue. She wasn't surprised to find it slippery down there, because she stayed super wet these days.

Candace let her index and middle fingers enter her body as she toyed with the erect nipple of her right breast. With her eyes shut tightly, she could see him thrusting inside of her and holding her legs up in the air as he pounded away. "Uhhh." The moan escaped her lips as she imagined his climax. Her body began to shudder at the thought of him cumming violently in her massive wetness, then collapsing on her.

As if on cue, she felt her walls constrict against her fingers, and she thrust them deeper and harder into her pussy, opening her legs wider and raising her hips slightly off the bed. She felt her body cross over the edge into ecstasy and stopped herself from whispering his name into the stillness of the room during the throes of her own passion. Recuperating from her moment, she felt a twinge of guilt for masturbating at the thought of someone else's dude. But at least she wasn't actually off somewhere, creeping with him. Candace turned over on her side and cuddled her pillow. She missed having someone there to sex her, then spoon her to sleep.

Chapter 44

Alex

"I can't believe this." She swiped her card again. After punching a series of buttons, she was given the same result. *Insufficient funds.*

The clerk looked at her with annoyance written all over her face. "Would you like to try another form of payment?"

Alex sucked her teeth and looked over at Clay. He nonchalantly reached over her and swiped his own debit card to cover her purchase. Exiting Party City, carrying her bags for her, Clay said nothing. Alex bit her lip, embarrassed but so relieved to have Clay chauffeuring her around that day. He opened the door for her, and she slid into his black Honda Accord. As they peeled out of the parking lot, she smiled at him.

"Thanks so much, Precious. You know you're the best, right?"

Clay chuckled. "Yeah, the best at rescuing you, you spoiled little princess. You going broke trying to give yourself the birthday bash of the year? This party can't really be all that worth it."

Alex sulked. "No, I'm going broke supporting T's ass."

"Come again?"

"I loaned him money for a few things."

"Such as?"

"Such as studio time, a new phone, and a few clothes. But that was more like a gift, because I wanted him to look fly for this showcase he did."

Clay tapped the steering wheel as he waited for the light to change. He shook his head in disbelief at his friend's naïveté. "So when's ole boy paying you back?"

Alex shrugged and examined her nails. "Who knows? Hopefully, he'll get this deal locked and we can be on our way to seeing some real money soon."

"We?"

"Yeah." Alex looked at Clay questioningly, wondering where his sarcasm was coming from.

Clay simply shook his head again, wishing to drop the subject.

"What?" Alex challenged him, turning her body in her seat to face him full on. "You don't think my relationship with T is valid or something?"

"*Valid?* Man, go on, Alex. I'm not trying to go there with you."

"Go where? Uh-uh, come on, Clay. Let's go on wherever you're headed. What's your problem?"

"Kick rocks, Alex."

She slapped his arm. "Kick deez. Now, what's your *problem?*"

He made the left onto Alex's street and headed toward her apartment complex. "I'm not the one with the problem. You keep picking up these dudes that don't treat you right, and every time the shit falls apart, you have this deer-in-the-headlights reaction to it like you didn't know they were shit to begin with."

"So what are you saying? You think T isn't really feeling me? You don't even know him, Clay."

"Hell, you don't even know him, Alex. One or two dates in, and you're ready to put your name on his bank account and a marriage license. What type of intent has he shown you to make you think that you're gonna be walking down the red carpet at the Grammys with him?"

Alex sat with her mouth open, wanting to respond but not quite sure what to say. "I . . . I . . . I'm investing in him. I believe in him . . . and . . . and if any relationship is going to work, you have to believe in the other person."

"That sounds like a whole lot of BS." Clay parked his car. "You're investing in being a part of the glitz and glam of the industry. You probably don't even like this cat as a person.

And no doubt you're fucking him already. Giving him all your little money, your cookies, and your time in exchange for what?"

"A relationship is give and take. And while you're all up in my business, where's your better half, Clay?"

"Oh, my bad. I'm a li'l more selective when it comes to who I give my all to. I don't make a habit of trying to force myself into a relationship."

"Force myself? You think I'm forcing myself on this man?"

"I think you need to exercise a little more discretion when you're dating. And you need to inquire with dude as to when you're going to get your money back."

"Unbelievable," she muttered.

"You're right. It's unbelievable that he has any intention of giving you back a dime." Clay got out of the car, leaving Alex stewing in anger. He grabbed her bags from his trunk and stood beside the car, waiting for her to get out.

With her pouty face on, she slowly exited the car and stood in front of Clay with her arms crossed. "I can't believe that you are talking to me like that. What did I do to you? Why are you being so mean to me?"

"Mean? Alex, are you kidding me? I'm just trying to put you up on game. You keep picking these knucklehead-ass dudes. This isn't what you need. I mean T and Mario. Those types of dudes aren't for you."

"Who are you to tell me who I should and shouldn't be with? What gives you the right to—"

"Forget it." Clay cut her off and handed her the myriad of shopping bags. "Forget I said anything. Go 'head. Stick it out with your boy. I hope y'all get married and have lots of kids." He walked around to the driver's side of the car.

"Where are you going?" Alex demanded. "You're not going to stay and help me with the party?"

"You don't need me," he called over his shoulder. "Go call up your boy. Let's see how quickly he comes to your rescue." He slammed his car door and quickly backed out of the parking lot, leaving Alex standing speechless on the curb.

***

"He was tripping hard. I can't believe he left me like that, being all extra dramatic. I've never seen him act so funny like that."

Alex was venting as Candace touched up her makeup in preparation for her birthday party. Jada stood to the side, looking over her list, trying to make sure that they remembered everything that they needed to do for the evening ahead.

"He said that I force myself into relationships." Alex turned up her nose. "He insinuated that I'm dating T only so that I can have some kinda celebrity-by-association thing going on. Like I'm a gold digger or something. What kinda mess is that?"

"I don't think you're a gold digger," Candace responded, touching up the eyebrow powder she'd previously applied to Alex's brows. "Nothing wrong with wanting to be with someone who has something going for himself or has potential to be going places."

Alex nodded. "Exactly. Maybe he was having a bad day or something. If I didn't know better, I'd say that he was jealous."

Candace looked over to Jada, who made a smirk and turned away. She bit her lip and smiled at her clueless friend. "Well, girl, maybe he is."

"I don't see why. Clay is always dating a new chick all the time."

"Yeah, he never is with the same girl, right? Well, maybe that's because he's keeping his eye on one special chick and waiting for the perfect time to scoop her up," Candace observed.

"That's his business. He ain't gotta rain on my parade in the meantime."

Candace threw down her compact in defeat. "Ugh. Okay, girl, I'm done with you."

Alex stood up and looked at herself in the full-length mirror. She was stunning in her black tube dress. The fabric hugged her curves in all the right places. "Well, I hope he gets over his attitude and gets his ass back here to my party. He knows better than to bail on me on *my* day."

"Is your boyfriend coming?" Candace asked.

"Girl, yes! What kind of question is that?"

Candace shrugged. "Just asking. It would be nice if he came and helped us get ready."

Alex didn't respond. She had been thinking the same thing herself but didn't want to voice her concern to the girls. After Clay's blowup about her relationship, Alex really didn't want to hear what anyone else had to say about T. It bothered her that she hadn't heard from him. All the things that Clay had said bothered her too. But she desperately wanted to believe that things would work out with this guy. Alex just wanted to be loved and adored by someone.

"Okay, girl." Jada closed her notebook and looked at Alex. "I'm going to run home to shower and change. I'll see y'all back at the clubhouse in a little bit."

Alex smiled and hugged her. "Okay, friend. Thanks for everything."

"No problem." Jada rubbed Candace's tummy and left the room.

Alex turned to Candace and giggled. "Never thought I'd see you pregnant."

"Never thought I'd see me pregnant, either," Candace responded, sitting down on Alex's bed. "Girl, it's a major adjustment. Stay on your birth control, Alex. You don't ever want to be in this boat."

Alex gave a half smile and looked away from her friend. She went back to looking in the mirror and fooling with her hair, marveling over her beauty. "So what's the deal with your baby's daddy?"

"No deal. His ass hasn't called or come by the house. My parents are too through with his ass. I'm not worried about him. Trust and believe that I will be at the child support office as soon as this kid is out of me."

The girls shared a laugh, and Alex's phone began to sing. She picked it up and looked at the caller ID. It was T.

"Hey," she answered, giving Candace a lovesick grin.

Candace rolled her eyes and excused herself from the room.

"Where are you?" Alex could hear the commotion in the background where T was.

"With my boy Tony. We down here about to hook up with this producer he know that wanna talk about that track we did last month. You know that one, 'Tribute to the A.' He might wanna put us on, babes."

"That's so good, T. But do you have to meet him tonight? You know tonight's my party."

"I know, but the biz don't stop just 'cause you have a birthday, yo."

"But, T—"

"Baby, don't start all that whining and carrying on, man. I called you to let you know I'ma be late. I'ma still try to make it, but I gotta handle this business. You understand that?"

"Yes, but—"

"I'm making history out here, baby. I'm doing this for us."

Alex was silent. She wanted to believe him, but her instincts told her that he was just running game. Clay had placed a lot of doubt in her mind, which she didn't want to give in to. She sighed and bit her lip. "Okay. Call me when you're on your way."

"Bet. Later, baby." He hung up before she could say anything else.

She was disappointed and hoped that he made an effort to show up in support of her. Throwing the phone on the bed, she looked herself over in the mirror once more. *He'd be crazy not to come to this,* she thought with a smile.

Chapter 45

The Girls

The party was jumping, and the clubhouse at Alex's apartment complex was filled with lively partygoers. Wings, chips and dip, and mixed drinks floated everywhere as the sounds of the hottest music blasted through the room. Stephanie leaned against the wall next to Jada, who was watching the activity around them and nursing a vodka with cranberry juice. Stephanie's head bobbed to the music. She was enjoying being out of the house, away from the children and temporarily free of her concerns over Corey's business dealings. But the sight of Miranda approaching Corey across the room rubbed her the wrong way. She tried to read their facial expressions but couldn't tell what their exchange was about. She nudged Jada.

"Have you talked to Miranda much lately?"

"Somewhat." Jada shrugged. "I mean, she had an altercation with Norris and his li'l girlfriend a couple of weeks ago. But I haven't really talked to her since that whole thing went down."

"Yeah, she hasn't been calling or getting up with me, either. But she's looking real cozy and friendly with someone."

Jada followed her friend's stare and shook her head. "Naw, now, don't start that. Miranda wouldn't go there, and you know it. Stop tripping."

Stephanie took a sip of her drink and cocked her head to the side in disagreement. "I don't know. There was that time when she just showed up at our place out of the blue. I don't think she knew I was there, but she played it off like she was coming over to talk to me."

"Don't start being paranoid about something that's *not* going on. You have other real Corey issues that you should be concerned with. Trust me, nobody wants your little thug."

Stephanie cut her eyes at Jada and returned her attention to her boyfriend and her friend.

"Why you avoiding me?" Miranda glared at Corey. "I've been paging you nonstop."

"Yeah, and I wish you would stop." He helped himself to a plate of hot wings.

"What did I do to you? I keep money in your pocket, so why you acting like that?"

Corey looked around, trying to keep his cool. He caught Stephanie staring at him from across the room but wasn't about to feed into her insecurity. "I'm not having this conversation with you in here, man."

Miranda was oblivious to the people watching them as she moved in closer to Corey so only he could hear her, which was a challenge over the music. "Look, I just need you to hit me up with a little something. Just this once."

"What you talkin' 'bout, just this once?" Corey looked at her and took in her antsy disposition and the look of desperation in her eyes. There was a sullen hardness in her face, which he had never noticed there before but had seen in his business often enough. "I don't know who got you on, but that's who you need to go holler at. Steph ain't gon' kick my ass 'cause you playing in a big man's game. Fuck that shit."

Miranda sucked her teeth. "This ain't about Stephanie. This is business, right? You're a businessman, right? This is your business. This is *my* business. This ain't none of Steph's business."

Corey's attention trailed off as he slyly watched Candace enter the kitchen area to grab a bottle of water. She walked away and was heading past the dance floor when a tall dude in a black tee stopped her. He noticed her body language and assumed that ole boy was kicking some game to her as she giggled in response. Corey whipped out his cell, barely listening to Miranda's mantra.

"I could go anywhere, Corey." Miranda tried hard to convince him to help her out. "But I come to you because I trust you."

"You say that shit like you're doing me a favor. Like this is some ordinary 'loan you a few bucks, baby sit ya' kid'-type situation." He quickly sent a text and returned his phone to its holster.

"No, but it's about money. That's what you're in it for, right? The money?"

He looked at Miranda as she gave him a serious look. He could understand a junkie's need for the product, because he himself had an addiction—to money. "Twenty-five dollars a hit. Get me busted with my ole lady, I'm fucking your shit up."

He walked off and Miranda folded and unfolded her arms, unsure of what to do next. She had been hoping he'd slip it to her right then. Disappointed, she decided to mix herself a drink and head outside for some air.

Candace was feeling the music at Alex's party. She danced until her feet hurt and her forehead began to sweat. Taking a time-out, she went into the kitchen area to grab a bottle of water. As she walked away, a tall, dark-skinned brother approached her and touched her lightly on the arm. She looked down at her arm and back at the cutie.

"Sorry, Miss Lady, but can I holla at you for a minute?" He was yelling over the music and smiling hard.

Her brow frowned, and she cocked her head to the side, not having heard what he'd said. "What?"

"I said, can I holla at you for a minute?"

She shrugged. "What's up?"

"What's your name?"

"Candace."

"Candace, you're looking pretty fine tonight. You here with your man?"

Candace giggled as she watched the dark brother lick his lips as he spoke. "I don't have a man."

"Well, my name is Kevin, and I'd like to see how I can be your man."

She giggled again at his forwardness, repositioning her body and assuming a sexy stance to maximize his view of her figure in her jeans. It was nice to know that she still had it, pregnant or not. "You don't even know me to know that you wanna be with me like that."

He touched her face lightly. "With a smile like that, pretty mama, I don't need to know anything else."

She felt her cell phone vibrate as he spoke. She reached for it, and he grabbed her hand.

"Go 'head and put my number in your phone, 'cause I'ma be calling you later." He flashed her a confident smile.

She smiled back and quickly clicked off of the message indicator on her screen. She handed him the phone. "Here. Put your number in."

He punched his number into her cell, then called himself so that he'd have her number locked in too. Handing her back the phone, he gave her a once-over. "A'ight, stay cute till you hear from me."

She sucked her teeth. "That shouldn't be too hard."

He smiled. "A'ight, li'l mama."

She walked away from the cutie, being sure to put on her sexy walk, knowing that he was watching her retreating profile. Candace headed over to Jada and Stephanie, who were huddled up across the room, in the middle of a discussion of their own.

"Having fun? Y'all so lame over here in the cut, gossiping, instead of out there on the floor, shaking your asses." Candace bumped Jada, trying to liven her up.

Jada bumped her back. "Yeah, you shake your ass enough for the both of us, so I'm good."

Stephanie laughed.

"Ha-ha," Candace retorted. "Don't hate."

"Keep it up, girl. The next time you drop it like it's hot, you're gon' drop that baby right out on the floor," Stephanie joked.

"Shut up. Where's Alex?" Candace said.

Jada took a final swig of her drink and shrugged her shoulders. "Last time I saw her, she was talking to some of her coworkers."

"I was wondering if her new boo made it here yet. Has anyone even met him yet?" Candace asked.

Both girls shook their head no.

Candace sucked her teeth. "His sorry ass." She thought about her statement and shook her head, dismayed at herself. "Hell, I'm one to talk. My husband *and* my baby's daddy are some sorry-ass jokers."

"Hmm." Jada was in agreement.

Candace felt her phone vibrate again. She pulled it out and saw that she had two text messages. She read the first one, which had come in while she was flirting with Kevin. You know that lame nigga ain't what you want. She couldn't help but laugh. She went on to the next message. You looking phat in dem jeans. Feel like being tasted? "Are you for real?" She was in shock.

"I'm just saying, she's been acting real funny lately, not like herself," Stephanie said.

"Who?" Candace asked.

"Miranda!" Stephanie exclaimed.

"Huh? What are y'all talking about?" Candace was confused.

"Who got you all open in your text messages that you can't pay attention?" Jada joked. "Stephanie's tripping about Miranda's attitude. She's over here, trying to convince herself that Miranda is doing something that she's not."

Jada shot Stephanie an "I'm trying to tell you" look, and Stephanie waved her off.

"Something like what?" Candace asked.

Jada looked at Candace and laughed. "Nothing, girl. Go back to your texts. It's not even important." Jada turned to Stephanie. "Really, boo. It's nothing. So let that go, okay?"

Jada walked off in pursuit of Alex, and Stephanie looked over at Candace, who was still lost. "A woman's intuition tells her when shit ain't right. Mark my words, Candace. Some shit ain't right."

Candace bit her lip, feeling some kind of way about Stephanie's statement as the other girl left her alone with her thoughts. She looked back down at her phone, knowing that she should just delete the messages and go on with her evening. How did you get my number? she texted back, just out of curiosity. Several seconds later she got her response. I have my ways. Meet me tomorrow at that BBQ place. I wanna get up with you.

It wasn't a good idea, but she was starving for the attention. Most importantly, her body was dying to be touched by hands other than her own.

Two and a half hours into her party, and T still wasn't there. Clay was right. She seemed to gravitate to these men who did nothing but treat her badly. But never would she admit to him or to her girls that this relationship, like all the others, was going nowhere.

As she was talking to a group of her coworkers, Jada approached her and gave her a friendly hug. "Having fun, friend?"

She gave Jada a big smile and nodded. "Yep. Nothing better than being a real princess for a day."

Jada looked over Alex's shoulder at the door and gave a smile of her own. "Well, you're about to be even happier, 'cause look who's here."

Hoping that her mystery guest would turn out to be T, Alex felt her heart skip a beat. She turned around and was mildly disappointed to see that it was only Clay. She should have known better. Jada had never met T and so was unable to identify him. Clay approached them with a small black bag in his hand and a bouquet of pink and white roses. He gave Alex a tight squeeze and a kiss on the cheek.

"Alexandria, is this your boo you're always talking about?" one of her coworkers asked playfully.

Alex gave a polite smile and shook her head. "This is my best friend, Clay."

Clay waved to the group of women, then motioned to the kitchen area. "Let me talk to you for a minute, Alex."

Alex nodded her consent and followed him to the kitchen. Jada walked beside her. "Everything okay?" Jada whispered.

Alex shrugged. "I guess. He probably wants to apologize for being such a meanie."

Jada raised an eyebrow and fell back, allowing the two of them their privacy.

No one else was in the kitchen. Clay handed her the flowers and smiled at her. "You look nice."

She sniffed the flowers and cradled them in her arms. "Thank you. For the flowers and the compliment."

He sighed. "Look, I'm sorry if I hurt your feelings earlier, especially being that today is a special day for you. For that I'm sorry."

"Yeah, Precious. You're supposed to always be on my side. That's what best friends are for."

"I am on your side. Always. But that doesn't mean that I'm not going to tell you the truth, Alex. I just want the best for you."

Alex looked down at her flowers as she swayed back and forth, not wanting to tell Clay that he really had nothing to be sorry for, because he was completely right. In her heart, she knew that he would never intentionally hurt her. She knew that she could always depend on Clay to be there for her when she needed him and to have her back always.

"I know you're just looking out for me." She looked up at him and tried to keep a straight face to make her next statement convincing. "But I've got this, Clay. I'm a big girl now, and I've got this."

Clay looked at her knowingly. Alex could never fool him. But he didn't want to argue with her about it anymore. He only wanted her to enjoy her evening and to know that he was always there for her, no matter what.

"I got you a gift." He held out the little black bag. "It's no Tiffany diamond, but I worked mad hard to save up for it, so I hope you like it."

Alex reached out for the bag. "You know I *love* me some jewelry."

Before her fingertips could touch the handle of the bag, Alex's eyes were drawn to the figure heading in their direction. Her eyes squinted as she gazed through the crowd, but she would have noticed that physique anywhere. As he hurried into the kitchen, Alex dropped her hand and carelessly tossed the flowers onto the counter. T threw his arms around her, disregarding Clay as he stood there.

"It's going down, Ma!" T embraced her tightly and wildly. "Woo-hoo! It's going *down,* baby!"

Alex was overwhelmed and stunned. She just allowed him to bear hug her until he finally let go. In one hand he had a bottle of Hpnotiq; and in the other hand, a little gold box.

"I'm glad you came," Alex said excitedly.

"Yeah, baby! Fo' sho'. I know this your night. But, baby, I got the deal. Ya' man got the deal!"

"You signed with a label?" Alex was baffled.

Clay stood to the side, listening and watching their exchange while holding his gift in his hand. He didn't like the sight of T. Maybe it was the chains around his neck and his sagging jeans. Maybe it was his boastfulness. Or maybe he was just plain jealous and upset that the dude had burst in at a time when he was trying to get his nerve up to come clean with Alex.

T held the bottle of Hpnotiq up in the air and nodded his head repeatedly as he bounced around. "That's right. That's right. Ya' boy is about to fuckin' blow up. I'm in, baby! I'm fuckin' in!"

He grabbed Alex up again and kissed her ferociously. She barely had time to pucker her lips and kiss him back as his mouth crushed hers. Withdrawing from the embrace, he handed her the little gold box. "Happy birthday, baby. Nothing but the best for you."

She opened the box and pulled out a thin gold chain with a pendant displaying her name dangling from it. Clay surveyed her smile, thinking that she looked like she'd just won the lottery or something. He recognized the standard gold jewelry box and the cheap gold-plated chain she held on to lovingly. It was a typical item from a typical jewelry kiosk at North DeKalb Mall. The dude probably spent a total of twenty dollars for the gift.

Alex threw her arms around T and kissed him passionately. "Thank you, baby. And congratulations on your deal. I knew you could do it."

T grinned like a Cheshire cat and held the Hpnotiq bottle up once more. "That's right! Now let's celebrate off in this thang-thang. Yo, where the cups at?"

T turned away and busied himself with pouring a drink, never once acknowledging Clay. Alex didn't even bother to introduce her best friend to her new beau. The rest of her girls sauntered into the room and circled around her.

"T's here." Alex motioned over to her boyfriend. "But look what he gave me." She showed them the necklace, and they all gave polite responses as she hurriedly put the jewelry around her neck.

Clay, who was leaning against the counter, said nothing.

Alex beamed proudly. "Come on. Lemme introduce y'all to my boo. He's so crunk, 'cause he finally signed with a label tonight. I knew it would work out for him."

The girls walked over to T with Alex, and she began the introductions. Fed up with the scene, Clay nodded his head in defeat and sat the black bag on the counter. He was done playing second best to all the other dudes Alex had encountered over the years. Without a good-bye, he briskly walked out of the party and out of Alex's life without her knowledge.

Chapter 46

Alex

It took a lot for Alex to clean her apartment after the party. All the gifts, leftover food, and knickknacks that were left from the party had all ended up thrown haphazardly about Alex's living room. She and Kacey took their time going through each bag and each container until everything was perfectly in place. A small pile of gifts sat in the corner, untouched, but Alex was too pooped to go through them. She plopped herself down on the couch and watched Kacey enter the living room with a glass of lemonade in one hand and a wad of plastic bags in the other.

"Here, girl." She gave Alex the glass. "I'm telling you, you had the jam of the century, girl."

Alex giggled. "It was so fun. And did you see T? He was so crunk, right?"

Kacey gave a phony smile and cocked her head slightly to the side. "A li'l drunk, don't you mean?"

"He was excited. He's been working hard to get a deal. He deserved to wild out a little bit."

"A li'l bit? Girl, him and his boys were getting straight toasted up in there. Almost didn't know if it was your party or his."

Alex fingered the necklace dangling around her neck and shrugged. She had just been glad that he showed up. "It wasn't that big of a deal. I had fun."

Sensing that she was striking a nerve, Kacey let it go and balled up the already wadded clump of plastic bags in her hand. "Hmm." She scrambled to unwad the bags. "Something's in here."

Alex drained her glass and watched as Kacey pulled out a tiny jewelry box.

"This must be a gift you overlooked, girl." Kacey opened the box and gasped.

Alex's eyes widened with intrigue, and she jumped up and grabbed the box from Kacey. She peered inside and saw a beautiful solitaire diamond ring. A gift card was stuck to the inside of the box. She snatched it out and read the imprint. *A promise of everlasting friendship and whatever else is to follow*. She looked at Kacey, who was looking right back at her.

"Who the hell is that from?" Kacey's eyebrow rose. "And please don't tell me your broke-ass rapper boyfriend, girl, 'cause we all know what his idea of fine jewelry is."

Alex ignored the jab at T and returned her eyes to the beautiful ring in the box. The memory hit her instantly. Clay was trying to give her the gift just as T waltzed in and commanded her attention. She read the card again and felt chills tingling up her spine. What did he mean by "whatever else is to follow"? Where had he gone tonight? She didn't remember seeing him at the end of the party. Quickly, she pulled out her cell and dialed his number. She was stunned to hear an automated recording tell her that the number she had dialed had been disconnected. Thinking it was a mistake, she dialed the number again. She received the same message.

Sitting down on the sofa, she held the box in her hand and stared at the ring inside of it. She had ignored Clay when T came in. Perhaps that had hurt his feelings. Was that when he left? What was he going to say before T came in? What was he trying to say by giving her such a sentimental piece of jewelry? For the first time, Alex realized that Clay was actually digging her. For years she had seen him as just a friend and had been sure that he felt the same way. Sure, he was always there to rescue her. Sure, she felt extremely comfortable with him. But she had never really entertained the idea that he was in love with her. Or maybe she had known all along and had just chosen to ignore the signs.

She looked at her phone and then back at the ring. There was one thing she was now sure of. Whatever chance they stood was long gone. Clearly, Clay was tired of standing in the shadows and had decided to be done with her. His phone had never been disconnected before for any reason. It was no coincidence or mistake. He was gone. Alex snapped the ring box closed and covered her mouth with her hand to muffle the sound of her cry. Not only had she missed out on knowing what kind of future they could have had, but she had also lost her best friend.

Chapter 47

Candace

Her body was aching in ways she'd never experienced before. As time went on, her belly expanded, her mood altered, and her parents became increasingly annoyed with having her around. The feeling was mutual. She was tired of not having a place of her own as well. Her entire situation was stressful and unbelievable. At times, Candace felt like she was watching a Lifetime movie instead of living her own life.

Her divorce from Quincy was final now. She was glad to be rid of him and his antics. She hadn't seen him in the months prior to their court appearance for the divorce. When he saw the swell of her belly, he'd sneered at her knowingly. She'd expected him to tell the judge that she had obviously been unfaithful to him during their marriage, but he hadn't. When the judge had asked if she'd be seeking child support for their unborn, she'd just shamefully shaken her head no. Quincy had laughed, and the judge had commented on how irresponsible and naive young people were today. Although it was an uncomfortable situation, in the end Candace was glad to finally be done with Quincy's sorry ass.

Shaking Khalil's sorry ass was another story. Her parents had given up asking about his whereabouts and his intent, because it was clear to everyone that he had no desire to play an active role in their child's life. Secretly, for the child's sake, Candace hoped that he'd come around once the baby was born. She understood the importance of having a father in your life and didn't want her child to be cheated out of that necessity. Still, she couldn't force the trifling dude to do anything. At this point, she didn't care whether he called, came by, or what. She didn't feel like dealing with his nonsense, and she definitely wasn't trying to go back to sleeping with him.

Khalil swore that he had her open, but these days Candace had her eye on someone totally different—and totally wrong for her.

She knew going into the situation that it was a complete no-no. But sometimes the danger of a situation was what made it so hot and tempting. On this day, she managed to escape her parents' shameful glances and comments and was out of the house for the evening. Much like they needed a break from her, she needed a break from them. Pulling into a small, yet cozy apartment complex, she scoped the buildings, looking for building number twelve. Finding it, she parked, exited the car, and sashayed her pregnant body up the walkway to apartment 12B.

It felt a little secluded to her, the way she had to walk around to the back of the building to reach the unit. It was totally private, and so no one could see her comings and goings. She understood why he'd picked this place. Before she knocked on the door, she quickly applied some shimmering lip gloss and shook out her newly done kinky twists. She was ready for whatever was about to go down.

He opened the door, wearing nothing but a pair of black basketball shorts and socks. His killer smile was enough to make her melt right there in the doorway. "What's up?"

She gave a tiny smile. "What's up with you?"

He stepped to the side to allow her entrance, and she walked by, taking in the scent of his cologne. *Yummy.* He closed the door and walked up on her from the back. "Was it easy to find?" He spoke softly and seductively in her ear.

She nodded, turning her head a little, playing as if she didn't want him that close to her. She walked away and dropped her purse down on the single sofa in the living room. She turned and looked at him as he walked over to her.

He slapped her on the ass and sank down onto the sofa. "Sit down, Mama."

She took a seat beside him and looked around the scantly decorated apartment. Little more than the essentials adorned the place, but it was clean and had the perfect homey touch, thanks to the scented candles and the incense he had throughout.

"So what is this? Your home away from home?" she asked him.

He threw his head back. "Something like that. So what's good with you? What you got going today?"

"Nothing. Just really needed to get out of the house." She found herself rubbing her belly. He placed his hand on top of hers, and she quickly snatched her hand away. Not missing a beat, he began to rub her belly. Noticing her comfort with this, he pulled her shirt up and moved over to kiss her protruding stomach. The touch of his lips against her skin felt so soft. It had been a few months since she'd had someone other than her ob-gyn touch any part of her body.

"Take your shoes off," he ordered her.

His demanding tone sent a chill up her spine and turned her on. Following his instructions, she kicked her flats off quickly. She watched as he knelt down on the floor and began to massage her feet.

"Do your feet get swollen?" he asked. "Do they hurt?"

She shrugged. "They're not really swollen, but they do get sore. I definitely can't wear my heels anymore, and that sucks, because my heels are a part of my sexy swag, ya' know?"

He nodded. "You got some cute little fat feet."

"My feet aren't fat." Candace pouted playfully.

He massaged her heels, then each individual toe. She watched as he worked his magic, enjoying being pampered, even if the situation was completely foul. She leaned her head back on the sofa and gave herself over to the feeling he was giving her.

She didn't protest when he reached up to pull down her leggings, along with her underwear. She opened her legs for him when she felt him push them apart. He kissed the inside of each of her thighs as he ran his finger back and forth across her clit. Her juices were running down onto the sofa as she became more and more turned on by his touch. She moaned slightly when he put two fingers inside her. Her body arched as his fingers continuously hit against her G-spot. She couldn't control her orgasm. As quickly as the penetration began, she felt her pussy muscles contracting around his fingers. Just as she settled from the climax, he rose from the floor and dropped his shorts. She knew exactly what would come next.

"Turn around," he ordered. "Here. Put the pillows under you if you need to."

He was so matter-of-fact about it, but Candace went with the flow. She was eager to feel him deep inside of her. She didn't comment on the fact that he had neglected to put on a rubber. She just bit her bottom lip as she felt all nine inches of him sink into her body. She clutched a pillow, overtaken by his girth. He thrust into her wetness hard and forcefully, lifting her butt cheeks up and apart for greater depth. It was a sensation like none other that she had ever felt. And his shit talking drove her crazy.

"Oh, shit." He moaned as he pumped in and out of her. "This shit is wet. Throw it back, baby. Throw it back."

She moved her body to meet each of his powerful thrusts. He slapped her ass hard.

"Yeah, baby. Just like that. Throw that shit back."

She was into it, caught up in how good her pussy was feeling as he assaulted it and how dirty she was feeling with each word he spat out.

"Damn." He gave a deep guttural groan. "Mmm. Yeah, yeah. Wait. Hold up. Hold up. I can't do that, can't do that."

He grabbed her ass to cease her movements, and he stood still. She referred back to her Kegel exercises and began to squeeze his dick with her muscles.

"Shit!" He was losing control. "Fuck it."

With all his might and vigor, he pounded into her, holding her lower back with his large hands. Candace couldn't contain her own moans of pleasure as his speed increased and he finally pushed himself to the point of no return. He climaxed hard inside of her, reaching around to tickle her clit as he ejaculated. So turned on by his touch and the force of his thrusts, Candace found herself cumming right behind him. The two of them quickly tried to regain their composure as he pulled out of her and she flipped herself over to a more comfortable position. He sat on the couch beside her and threw his head back.

"Damn!" He patted her thigh. "I swear, ain't *nooo* pussy better than pregnant pussy. I swear."

Candace focused on his hard, chiseled features as he closed his eyes and regulated his breathing. Now that the deed was done, she felt a twinge of guilt creep into her heart. She didn't like him, but she was sexually attracted to him. She knew that she could have found any other dude to just fuck or even date. She knew that taking things to this level with him was something she would never be able to take back. But she also knew that this was a secret she would definitely take to her grave. With all her wrong acts lately, she knew that Jehovah would not be proud of her. She knew she was dead wrong. But for the moment, she just wanted to live a little bit free of the pressures of being presumably good and right in everyone else's eyes. Right now, as crazy as it was, she was enjoying being of the world.

Chapter 48

Stephanie

It was really bothering her, thinking about Corey's legal problems and her suspicions. Corey wasn't exactly the type of guy she could just flat out accuse of something and it blew over well. So she kept her mouth shut, much like she had done about finding the man's wallet in their bedroom closet. Sitting on the couch, folding clothes, she watched and listened as Corey walked around complaining about anything and everything. For whatever reason, he was in a foul mood. The baby slept nearby in a playpen, and Damien sat on the floor by the couch, playing with his cars, oblivious to his dad's antics.

"What the fuck do you do all day, man?" He stared at her and bitched at the top of his lungs. "All these damn clothes should have been washed and put away. You're at home all the damn time."

"Someone has to be," she muttered.

He knocked over a stack of towels. "Hey, watch ya' mouth, a'ight? I'm for real. When a man comes home, he expects his shit to be in order."

"I'm doing my best, Corey. The baby requires a lot of attention. It would be nice if you could help me more with her. Or with any of this."

"I'm doing what I'm supposed to be doing. Out there making that money so we can be living up in here like Weezy and George."

Corey laughed at his own joke and went into the kitchen. She could hear him slamming around in the fridge and the cabinets and simply tried to ignore him. She looked over at Damien as he rammed his cars into one another.

"When are you going to cook dinner?" Corey called out to her.

"I ordered a pizza," she called back.

He stormed back into the room, beer in hand, and stood next to her. "Pizza ain't no damn dinner. You too lazy to get yo' ass in there and cook? All that food that's in there spoiling and you want to go order a pizza?"

"It's something quick. What's wrong with that?"

"You feed his ass junk too much." He pointed the beer bottle at their son. "He needs some damn vegetables and shit. Not greasy-ass pizza and hamburgers and shit. Spending money on that bullshit all the time."

"It's not all the time. You act like I never cook."

"You rarely cook. I'm not saying you never cook. Yo' ass *rarely* cooks these days."

"Because I'm tired, Corey. Dang."

"From sitting at home with your kids all day? What kind of shit is that?"

They both heard the buzz of his text message indicator, and Stephanie watched as he pulled out the phone and read the message. He gave a quick reply and replaced the phone in its holster.

"If I could just get some help so I can rest—"

He promptly cut her off. "Call ya' girls over here to help you. I ain't never heard anyone say they need help being a parent."

"That's not what I said. Why are you jumping on me?"

"'Cause laziness ain't sexy, man. You act like you don't wanna cook, don't wanna clean, damn near don't wanna fuck. Don't wanna keep yourself up. Man, we was better off living in separate places. This ain't the type of shit I had in mind."

Stephanie fought back her tears. He was really starting to hurt her feelings, and she pursed her lips together to remain silent in hopes that he would catch on and shut up too. But he didn't.

"A nigga wants a bitch that's down for him. Someone that makes him feel like a king in this damn castle. A chick that's gon' to nurture his seeds, take care of him, and keep her shit tight. Don't nobody wanna come home to clothes all over the damn place and some greasy-ass pizza."

She arranged the children's clothes in an empty basket to take to their room. She kept her head low so that he couldn't see the tears that had managed to escape her eyes, despite her efforts to hold them back.

"Do you hear me talking to you?" he asked.

She didn't respond.

"You ignoring me now? What kinda shit is that? Huh?"

Still nothing.

He began to shake the contents of his bottle out at her. Drops of beer landed in her hair and on her shoulder.

"Stop it!" She jumped up and faced him. "What the hell is wrong with you?"

"You're the one sitting up here, acting like a damn baby, pouting and ignoring me. And what the fuck are you crying for?"

She grabbed a towel and wiped her face. "You're being mean to me for no reason. You haven't said one nice thing to me all day."

"I'm just telling your ass the truth."

"You think I'm lazy. You think I'm a bad mom. You think I'm not a good woman. Fuck you, Corey. I put up with too much of your shit, and I take care of your damn home, when any other bitch would have left you by now."

"Be any other bitch, then, Steph." He shrugged nonchalantly. "Fuck, you wanna leave, get the fuck on."

The baby began to cry, and Stephanie hurried over to soothe her and place the pacifier back into her mouth. "Stop yelling. You're scaring the baby."

"Be her damn mama and pick her up, then. You're not going to shut me up in my own house that I pay the fuckin' bills for. If you don't like it here, take your ass on somewhere. Trust me, there are plenty of badass dimes that would love to be up in here."

She shot him a look mixed with hurt and fury. "I bet some already have been up in here."

"What?" Corey walked up on her like he was about to swing, and Damien quickly ran to his mother's aid.

"Don't hit my mommy." His tiny face was laced with fear.

Corey looked down at his son and balled up his fist. "Nobody's gon' hit your mama. A real man won't hit a female." He took a final swig from his beer and stared hard at Stephanie. He plopped the bottle down on the coffee table and leered at her. "I'm fucking leaving."

He turned away and headed toward the door. Stephanie was fast on his heels.

"So, what? You're just going to disappear for two, four, six days and leave us here alone? Where do you go, Corey? Laying up with someone? Are you fucking around with someone else? Trying to guilt me into feeling like I'm not shit and not worthy of you, your money, and your house."

"Get the hell on, Steph, with all that bullshit."

"It's your bullshit, Corey! All your drama, your lies. I've been good to you. I have continued to be there for you through all the bullshit, and you treat me like shit whenever you fuckin' want to."

"I love your ass, girl. Nobody treating you like shit. I'm fuckin' tired of you walking around here, acting like you don't want to be with a nigga. Like some shit is bothering your ass. Go tend to your kids, Steph. I'm gone."

She grabbed his arm. "Don't you walk out on me! Don't leave me, Corey." She was crying pathetically. But she didn't want him to leave the house, because she didn't know what to expect of him once he was gone.

Corey shook her off. "Go on, man."

"Where are you going? Are you going to see some bitch? Huh? Are you fucking Miranda?"

Corey looked at her with a raised eyebrow, shook his head, and chuckled. "You don't know what you're talking about, man. You wanna know what the deal is with your homegirl, ask her."

He opened the door and left quickly. Stephanie threw herself against the heavy oak door and screamed at Corey.

"You bastard." She pounded on the door. "I hate you. I fucking hate you. I hope they catch your ass and you fuckin' rot in jail. Go fuck her. Go fuck her, you bastard."

She buried her face against the door and sobbed loudly, with Damien at her side, hugging her legs.

"Don't cry, Mama," he pleaded sweetly. "Daddy didn't mean it."

Her body shook as she tried to collect herself. She could hear the baby crying once more and knew that she had to get it together. With tears in her eyes, she reached down and hugged her son. "I love you, Damien. I love you more than anything. You're Mommy's big boy."

She released him from her embrace and hurried over to pick up the crying baby. Cradling her in her arms, she looked at Damien and was ashamed of herself for being so emotional in front of her children. She looked around the living room, at the mounds of clothes in disarray, and sucked her teeth. She wasn't a bad mother, like Corey had insinuated. But she definitely needed to get some things in order. Stephanie went to the kitchen and warmed a bottle for Mariah. Back in the living room, she changed the baby's diaper and began to feed her while Damien nuzzled up on the couch beside her. She kissed the top of his head and sighed deeply. She wondered if and when Corey would return home.

A brisk knock on the door interrupted her thoughts. Damien jumped, but Stephanie kissed him again and gave him a reassuring smile.

"It's just the pizza man," she told him, rising from the couch.

She placed the baby inside the playpen and headed for the door. Without taking a look through the peephole, she carelessly opened the front door and was quickly bum-rushed by a small group of men in dark suits.

"Stephanie Johnson?" one of them asked.

She was shocked and confused. "Yeah . . . yes?"

"I'm Agent Wilbur, and these are my team members. We're with the GBI. We're investigating a homicide."

Damien was scared. "Mommy, are we going to jail?"

"I don't understand." Stephanie was struggling to get her thoughts together and was afraid of what was about to happen next.

"No, son," one of the other agents answered Damien reassuringly. "We just want to have a talk with your father and take a look around your house."

"My house?" Stephanie turned to the consoling agent. "What are you talking about? Why do you need to look around our house?"

"Is your boyfriend, Corey Polk, home, Ms. Johnson?" Agent Wilbur asked.

Stephanie shook her head no.

The kind agent turned back to Damien and eyed him askance.

"Daddy's gone." Damien cosigned his mother's story. "Him and Mommy had a fight, and Daddy said he was gonna leave us. Then my mommy was crying and—"

Stephanie waved him off. "Damien, baby, go to your room, okay?"

"The police are our friends, Mommy. Maybe they can make Daddy come back."

"Go to your room!"

The baby was agitated by Stephanie's tone and began to cry again. Stephanie lifted the infant from the playpen and rocked her with nervous energy. She turned her attention back to Agent Wilbur. "Corey is not here. Why do you have to look around our home? I'm telling you he isn't here."

"Then you won't mind if we have a look?" The agent smiled at her.

"But why? Why? What is it that you're looking for? Corey isn't here."

"As I stated, we're investigating a homicide, and your boyfriend is a person of interest. We're looking specifically for anything that may tie him to the crime. So do you mind?"

"Yes, I do mind," she answered defiantly. "This is my home. My children are here. You can't just come up in someone's home and rip it to shreds. Don't you have to have some paper or something from the courts, giving you permission to do that?"

Agent Wilbur held up what looked to Stephanie to be a brochure. "What you're referring to would be called a search warrant. Yeah, we have one of those."

He handed it to her, and she took it absentmindedly, still halfheartedly rocking the baby back and forth. Her heart was racing, and she was half wishing that Corey's ass would walk back through the door at any moment and save her from having to deal with this humiliation.

"You take the back rooms. We'll look up front," Agent Wilbur ordered two of his colleagues. He looked at the nicer agent and motioned toward the kitchen. They proceeded. and Stephanie was right behind them, crying baby in tow and search warrant clutched in her hand.

"Please, don't tear my house up. Please."

The friendly agent turned to her and smiled. "This would go a lot smoother and quicker if you would just wait in the living room with your daughter, ma'am. I promise we'll try our best not to leave things in disarray."

Stephanie was speechless and helpless. With no recourse, she returned Mariah to her playpen and settled her down with her pacifier once more. She was tempted to pull out her cell and inform Corey of what was going down. But she thought better of it, knowing that they would just seize her phone and fearing that they would place a tap on it and find Corey's whereabouts. Even though she was pissed with him for being so mean to her and having an affair with one of her best friends, she still felt protective of him. The sad truth was that she simply loved the man and never wanted any harm to come his way.

Agent Wilbur reentered the living room and engaged her in a conversation that was akin to an interrogation as his colleague searched the room. "Do you know where Corey is, Ms. Johnson?"

She shook her head no.

He took a deep breath and nodded knowingly. "You know, if you're hiding information, you could go down with him as an accessory."

"To what?" She stared at him, daring him to refer blatantly to her as an accessory to a murder crime. "I didn't do anything, and I don't know anything."

"So you have no idea where your boyfriend has gone off to? Is there any usual place he goes to when he leaves the house? Do you know where his stash house is located?"

"Excuse me?"

"Don't play coy, Ms. Johnson. A man is dead, and I'm almost positive that your boyfriend can tip us off as to exactly how that happened. If you're aiding and abetting him, I'll have no remorse in taking you in too. That would leave your children in the custody of the state, and I'm sure you don't want that, do you?"

Stephanie looked down into the playpen at Mariah, who'd finally fallen asleep, despite the ruckus around her. "Please don't threaten me, Mr. Wilbur. I've told you that I don't know what you're talking about, and I have no clue where Corey went. Like my son told you, we had a fight and Corey decided that he'd rather not be with us. He's gone, and I don't expect him to come back."

The two men returned from the back of the apartment and shook their heads at Mr. Wilbur.

"Nothing," one of them reported.

The friendly agent joined the crowd. "Zilch."

Agent Wilbur took a deep breath. He nodded to the men, and the trio headed out the front door. Agent Wilbur reached into his pocket, pulled out a couple of business cards, and handed them to Stephanie with a half smile. "If you can think of anyplace we may want to look for your boyfriend or if you recollect any information about Mr. Stokes's death, please call me."

Stephanie looked down at the cards, moving them from one hand to the other. Wilbur noticed her nervous behavior and smiled. "Oops." He reached for one of the cards. "Gave you one too many, huh?"

She gave over one of the cards and cocked her head to the side. "Have a good evening, Mr. Wilbur."

He shook the card at her and smiled once more. "Same to you." He headed for the door and stopped short at the threshold. "Take care of those beautiful children, and we're sorry for any inconvenience."

She watched as he slowly closed her front door behind him. Quickly, she ran over to lock and bolt the door. Turning around, she saw a timid Damien lurking around the corner, looking at her with questioning eyes. She released a breath, which she didn't realize she had been holding. Going into her bedroom, she surveyed the damage done to her property. Clothes had been thrown about, papers were out of order, and miscellaneous items were all over the place. She sat on her bed and just stared at the mess. Looking into the closet, she saw the clothes left dangling from lone hangers, including a couple of pairs of Corey's jeans. Stephanie wasn't worried about their search. She knew they'd come up with nothing, because the one thing that could have nailed Corey was long gone.

She'd swallowed her pride and begged her mother to watch the children for a couple of hours. She'd made up some story about how Jada was sick and Jordan was out of town, so she desperately needed to go to the hospital with her best friend. Her mom had always liked Jada and appreciated the type of friend she had been to Stephanie over the years, so she agreed to watch the children for just a couple of hours.

With no intention of going to Jada's whatsoever, Stephanie mustered up her courage and drove deep into the Dec, to where she assumed that she would find her children's father. Although she willingly turned a blind eye to his shenanigans and illegal activity, Stephanie wasn't as naive and clueless as others thought she was. She knew the hood secret of where the neighborhood trap was really located, and she knew that her boyfriend was the dope man in the DEC. Watching cars behind her and around her, she drove cautiously, hoping to catch him there tonight.

Pulling up to the house, she surveyed the block. It was still and quiet. No cars were in sight, but that didn't mean that Corey couldn't still be hiding out in the house. She said a quick prayer and quickly got out of the car. Scurrying up the stairs, she tapped on the door and kept her eyes glued to the streets, watching for any suspicious or sudden movement. A big man came to the door, took one look at her, and stepped back, allowing her entrance. She silently passed him and walked into the house. The big man closed the door, and she looked to him for direction.

"Wait here," he ordered.

She assumed that he was going to go get Corey for her, and she was surprised to see his homeboy Antonio emerge from the back instead.

"Yo, what up, Stephanie?" he greeted her. "You know you really shouldn't be up in here, man."

She ignored his warning. "Where's Corey?"

"Hey, I don't know, but check it. I do know that dude wouldn't be too thrilled for his girl to be up in here. The block been hot for a minute, so this really ain't where you wanna be. If he comes through or hits me, I'll tell him to get at you. But you gotta leave, Ms. Lady. On everything I love, you gots to leave."

She studied his eyes, looking for some hint of foul play. But Antonio's expression indicated that he was dead serious. Before she could speak or make a move, there was a weak knock at the door. Antonio motioned for the big man to check it out. He looked through the peephole, then turned to report to Antonio.

"It's ole girl, the quiet chick."

It was as if they were speaking in code. Antonio shook his head. "Tell her ass to get on. We on ice around here, man."

The big man opened the door, and his frame prevented Stephanie from seeing who he was addressing.

"Hey, is he here?" the woman asked.

"Nobody's here," the big man answered. "We just coolin' it round here. We'll holla at you when we got that."

"Look, he's not answering my calls. If you could just hook me up, I've got the money."

"Man, go on, girl. I'm telling your ass we straight in here. A'ight? We'll let you know something."

"Why do y'all keep tripping like that?" The woman's voice turned whiny. "You get more money than a little bit from me, so what is the problem?"

Listening to the conversation, Stephanie felt uneasy. Hearing someone beg for some crack was sickening to her. But what was worse was that she recognized the voice.

"Yo, bye, man." The big man was putting his foot down.

"Tell Corey I said, 'Fuck you.' I'm sick of this shit. I'm fuckin' sick of this!"

Stephanie gasped and hurriedly brushed past the big man to come face-to-face with one of her closest friends. "Miranda!" She wanted to throw up immediately at the realization.

Miranda was stunned and nervously went about brushing back her hair and tugging at her clothes. She bit her lip, not sure what to say to Stephanie. She looked around, avoiding eye contact with her friend.

Stephanie stepped out onto the porch and touched her friend's face, forcing her to look her in the eye. "What's going on with you?" Stephanie asked her softly. She could hear the sound of the door closing behind her, the two men inside wanting nothing to do with this accidental intervention. "It all makes sense to me now." Stephanie brushed back Miranda's hair.

She studied Miranda's physique and body language. Her face looked harder than she ever remembered it being, and Miranda kept pinching her nose, although Stephanie could tell she was trying hard to appear like her normal self.

"All this time I thought that you were fucking around with Corey. But all this time you've been fucking up yourself with Corey's shit. I don't know whether to be mad at you for being so stupid or to pity you for being so obviously lost that you turned to this."

"Don't judge me." Miranda rolled her eyes. "Like you're perfect or something. Don't judge me. You don't know what my life is like, what I'm going through, or how I feel."

"All you've ever had to do is pick up the phone, girl."

"And call you, Steph? You're always too busy worrying about who Corey is under to be concerned with anyone else's problems." Miranda looked down at the ground and sucked her teeth. "You're probably gonna go run and get on your phone to tell the other girls what you think you know. Tell them, then, Stephanie. I'm dying on the inside, anyway, so nothing else really matters."

She looked back up and stared deep into Stephanie's eyes. Stephanie felt her skin crawl, and shivers ran up her spine.

"Then again, you practically said it yourself," Miranda stated. "You're really just glad to know that Corey isn't fucking around on you. Well, at least not with me."

Before Stephanie could respond, Miranda descended the steps and disappeared down the block, heading to where her car was parked in the distance. Stephanie took a quick look around and retreated to her own car. As she drove toward her mom's house, her mind was fixated on the memory of Miranda's thin body and her pitiful voice nearly pleading to cop a hit. Their circle had once been so close. But clearly, they were becoming distant. How else could all of them miss the fact that something was seriously wrong with Miranda? She felt herself crying as sheer memory led her back to her mom's house. Her focus was shot to hell. She sat in front of the house, crying on the steering wheel and feeling helpless for the second time that day.

It had been a long, rough day for her. She felt sorry for Miranda for feeling so alone that she had nowhere else to turn but to drugs. She also felt a kind of responsibility, because it was her boyfriend who had undoubtedly turned her out. How he could have done such a thing and not mentioned anything at all about it was beyond her. How could he have willingly allowed something like this to happen to someone whom she was so close to? Corey was clearly unscrupulous. Anything to make a dollar. Stephanie felt sick with disgust, pity, and shame. The very money he made off of Miranda was the very money that contributed to her lifestyle. In turn, they'd all become monsters associated with the game. She prayed that Corey would call soon. It was definitely time for them to make a grand exit. The signs were so clear to her. Miranda was already lost to her. Stephanie didn't want to risk losing anyone or anything else to this life.

Chapter 49

Jada

She wasn't sure if it was a good idea to invite all the girls over for dinner, but Jada felt it would be an opportunity for everyone to experience some release from all the things that they were going through. All the girls were experiencing some type of hardship, and none of them had seen much of each other since Alex's party. That, and she really wanted to unload all the stress her friendships were putting on her.

She and Jordan were still having problems conceiving, and her doctor seemed to believe that she was just under a lot of stress. Dr. Gregory had told them that once they both relaxed and stopped worrying about making a baby, it would happen for them eventually. The thought of not being able to give Jordan a child scared her. Before they got married, they used to talk about the type of life they wanted to live. They had agreed that they wanted to have a large family. Now it was time for her to make good on the agreement, and she was coming up short.

Dinner was ready, and she was waiting on the girls to show up, unsure of how the night would end. As she spooned seafood pasta into a decorative serving dish, she heard the chiming of her doorbell. Jordan had decided to meet some of his boys at the neighborhood Dugan's, so she and her girls had the run of the house. She wiped her hands on a dish towel and quickly went to greet the first of her dinner guests.

Standing at the door were Stephanie and Alex. The trio hugged before Jada allowed them entry into the living room.

"You got it smelling good up in here, friend," Alex complimented her.

"Thanks, boo. You know how I do."

Stephanie looked toward the kitchen as she sat her purse down on the coffee table. "Where are the other two?"

Jada shrugged. "On the way, I guess. Y'all want some wine?"

"You already know the answer to that." Stephanie was ready to get her drink on. She was going to need it to get through this dinner.

Jada headed to the kitchen and again heard the chiming of the doorbell. She turned to get the door, but Alex beat her to it.

"I'll get it!" Alex sashayed over to the door.

Jada continued on to the kitchen. She could hear the giggles and the oohs and aahs and knew instantly that Candace had arrived. She hoped that Miranda was with her, so that they could go ahead and start dinner. She walked back into the living room and put a smile on her face.

"Hey, girl." She gave Candace a hug.

"Hey, hon. How are you?"

"I'm good. I was hoping Miranda would be with you."

Candace's facial expression signaled trouble as she shook her head. "I called her to see if she wanted to ride with me, but I didn't get an answer. I assumed that she either didn't want to talk to me or was here already."

"Did she tell you she was coming?" Stephanie asked.

Jada shook her head. "I texted her, just like I texted y'all, but she didn't respond."

Alex clapped her hands together. "I say let's go ahead and eat. And if she shows up, great. If she doesn't, more for us."

"I'm with that," Steph chimed in.

Candace giggled. "Shoot me too."

The women filed into Jada's dining room, and Jada busied herself with setting out the food. There was seafood pasta, veggie lasagna, Caesar salad, and garlic bread sticks. An open bottle of white wine also rested on the table. Jada returned to the kitchen and came back with a newly opened bottle of sparkling cider. She placed it in front of Candace.

"I got that for you," she said and slid into her own spot at the table and smiled.

Candace gave her a sincere smile and poured a glass of the cider. "Thanks. You're so considerate."

"I try."

Everyone was helping themselves to the pasta dinner. There was clanking, shuffling, and the sound of chewing as the girls munched on their meal. Candace was the first to break the silence.

"So has anyone talked to Miranda at all lately?"

A series of head shakes. Stephanie cleared her throat, unsure of whether she should respond or not.

"I've seen her," Stephanie admitted.

Jada raised an eyebrow. "Oh yeah? When?"

"A couple of weeks ago." She was treading lightly because she didn't know how or if she should tell them the real deal.

The other girls looked at her, waiting for her to say more, but she just continued to eat her lasagna, avoiding eye contact.

Candace was annoyed. "Okay, sweetie. Can you be a little specific for us? A couple of weeks ago when? Where? How was she? And what did she say?"

"I saw her at this place I went to. I was out handling some business, and you know, we just ran into one another."

"Uh-uh." Jada chewed on her pasta and pointed her fork at Stephanie. "You're lying. What is it that you're not telling us? Don't sit up here feeding us no bullshit, Stephanie. What's the deal with Miranda?"

Stephanie pushed her food around on her plate, unsure of how to say what it was that she knew. A part of her didn't want to put Miranda out there. But another part of her was dying to share this secret. Besides, they were all girls, and it was apparent that Miranda needed an intervention or something at this point.

"Okay, fine." Stephanie threw her fork down on her plate. "I saw her at the trap."

"The what?" Alex asked.

"The trap, heifer. You heard me."

"The 'trap' trap?" Candace asked, using air quotes.

Stephanie nodded.

"Wait, what were you doing there?" Alex asked.

"Undoubtedly something stupid." Jada raised an eyebrow at Stephanie.

Stephanie sighed. "Corey and I are going through some things, and I was trying to find him."

Candace averted her eyes and took a gulp from her drink as the other girls gave Stephanie their full attention.

"I was desperate to find him, and I figured he would be over there, so I went to the spot, looking for him." Stephanie shrugged. "So . . . yeah."

Jada nodded her head. "Yeah, that was stupid. Girl, what were you thinking? What if it had been a bust or something while you were there?"

"All I knew was that I had to talk to Corey ASAP, and I was sure that that was where he would be. But he wasn't. So before I left, this chick came to the door, right? I could hear her voice, but I was standing behind this big dude, one of Corey's runners or somebody, so I couldn't see her. But the voice was so familiar to me, and after a minute I realized that it was Miranda."

"Okay, cut to the point now, girl." Jada was growing impatient. "What are you trying to tell us?"

Candace poured herself another glass of cider and continued sipping. Alex was eating and listening, intrigued, as if she were watching a movie play out right before her eyes.

"The writing's on the wall, hon." Stephanie paused. Once she put the words out there, she wouldn't be able to take them back. "Miranda is a crackhead."

Candace spat out her cider. Alex choked on her mouthful of pasta and bread. Jada's fist hit the table.

"That's some bullshit, Steph!" Jada shouted. "You're taking this shit a little bit too far."

Stephanie knit her brows. "I'm just calling it like I see it."

"Calling it like you see it, my ass," Jada stormed. "You have been gunning for that chick for a minute now. And now, the second she's not around, you're trying to paint some picture like the girl, *our friend,* is a fucking junkie. That's low, even for you."

"What you mean, gunning for her?" Alex asked between coughs as she tried to regain some composure.

"Stephanie has been assuming for a minute now that Miranda is fucking Corey's sorry ass," Jada explained.

Stephanie's right eyebrow rose. "So you think I'd make some shit up just to throw salt in another bitch's game?"

"I think that you're delusional," Jada replied. "Seeing shit differently from how it really is. The same way you're totally wrong about Miranda messing around with Corey."

"Why would you think they were messing around, anyway?" Alex asked. "We may not make the best decisions as a group when it comes to men, but I'm pretty sure none of us would go after any one of the others' man. That's just breaking the code, Steph. And we respect the code around here. Right, ladies?"

"That's what I've been trying to tell Sherlock Holmes over there." Jada shook her head and poured herself some wine.

Alex then looked to Candace for confirmation. She bit her lip and nodded, then tried hard to sell it. "Yeah, girl. That's just crazy. Besides, Miranda has her own issues with Norris. Why would she want a whole nother set of man problems?"

"I know she's not fucking around with Corey." Stephanie wanted to set the record straight. "I mean, I admit that I was a little curious about their interactions. Some shit just didn't sit right with me. But all the time that I was thinking they were getting up with each other, she was really just hitting up her dealer."

"I don't want to hear any more of this." Jada pulled out her cell phone. "I'm calling Miranda to see where the hell she is and what the hell is going on."

"I heard her ask the man for the shit with my own two ears, Jada. And when I stepped out to confront her, she basically told me not to judge her and that she knew I was going to run back and tell y'all."

Jada had already dialed Miranda's number, but the line just rang and rang until finally going to voice mail. As she looked into Stephanie's eyes, the truth she didn't want to face sank in. She knew Stephanie wasn't lying by the way she stared at her intently, unwilling to back down or take it back. Jada hung up the phone and focused on Stephanie's eyes.

"How did she look?"

Stephanie's voice softened now that she could sense that Jada had finally come to terms with the news she had shared. "Like she's living a hard life."

The room was silent. No one knew how to take this or what to say about it. Jada tried to picture in her mind how Miranda had gotten so far under her radar. Sure, she was sick of rescuing the girls and sick of all their unnecessary drama, but had she given her friend the impression that she couldn't come to her when she was feeling desperate and troubled? She couldn't understand how any person could one day just say, "Hey, let me try some crack."

"So how does that feel for you?" Alex asked, drawing Jada away from her own thoughts.

Alex was addressing Stephanie, who in turn gave her a questioning look.

"What do you mean?" Stephanie was defensive.

"How does that feel for you?" Alex repeated. "You thought she was screwing your man, but came to find out she wasn't. However, your man was, in fact, screwing her, or at least helping her screw herself. How does it feel to know that the very poison running through your friend's veins, which could possibly kill her, was placed in her hands by *your* boyfriend?"

Jada could sense the tension growing. She held her hand out, trying to run an early interference. "Wait. Hold up now. Let's not do this."

Stephanie ignored Jada's statement. "Corey didn't put a gun to her head and make her take a hit, Alex! That was a personal decision of Miranda's."

"How do you know that when you barely know where the hell he is or what the hell he's doing?" Alex retorted. "Until a few weeks ago your assumption was that he was doing her."

"He wouldn't force anyone to do anything, no matter who it is," Stephanie insisted.

"You talk about him like he's some saint or something. You kill me with that. Stephanie, your man is the neighborhood dope man. His job relies on your neighbors' and their neighbors'— and, hey, even your friends'—vulnerability, desperation, and naïveté."

"Alex, stop it." Jada knew that no good would come out of this conversation. "Stop it, please."

Stephanie shrugged and took a long swig of her wine. "They're not my neighbors."

"Oh, yeah." Alex smirked at her. "That's right. *Your* neighbors are the white people who your boo has moved you next to in order to get your family out of the hood while he continues to poison the hood."

Jada jumped up, went over to Alex, and grabbed her arm. "You need to take a walk now. This is going too far."

"Corey was right. You're jealous because you don't live the lifestyle we live," Stephanie retorted, then waved Alex off and took a bite out of a bread stick. "I'm not worried about ya' petty li'l comments. Go on. Keep being a hater. Trust, your little rapper wannabe boyfriend ain't gon' ever have the kinda paper we have."

Alex snatched her arm away from Jada. "Yeah? I won't have the guilty conscience your ass has, either." Alex leaned close to Stephanie's face, invading her personal space.

Jada was afraid that Alex was going to slap her. She had never seen Alex so riled up before.

"Your boyfriend's killing one of your best friends, Stephanie." Alex stared her dead in the eyes and spoke slowly. "And the money he makes off of each of her hits is the same money you put toward the steak you eat *alone* while your man's out dealing and whoring."

Impulsively, Stephanie threw the remnants of her wine in Alex's face, taking everyone by surprise, especially Alex. "Fuck you, Alex." She slammed the glass down on the table, causing it to shatter. She rose and walked out of the room as Alex wiped wine droplets from her eyes. "I don't need this shit!"

Everyone followed Stephanie into the living room, unsure of what to do or what would happen next. Jada ran back to the kitchen to get a dry dish towel for Alex to wipe her face and hair with.

"If you're waiting for me to take some responsibility for what's going on with Miranda, I'm not doing it," Stephanie told them. "That was her choice. *Hers*. And she has to live with that. Not me."

"Well, then why are you so defensive?" Candace asked, rubbing her belly.

Stephanie wanted to slap her, but she turned away instead to focus her attention back on Alex. "Because she's sitting up here, making me out to be the bad guy," she said, pointing at Alex, who was steadily blotting her head.

"No, your boo is the bad guy, honey." Alex wasn't backing down. "The problem is that you're so stuck on him, you don't see him for who and what he really is."

"Is that right? And you have such a great perspective on the men in your life? Where's Clay, Alex? You're so stupid and such a gold-digging opportunist that you don't realize that the only true man you've ever had in your life is Clay. But, no, you'd rather attach yourself to someone who you perceive has status and will upgrade your underprivileged-background ass."

"Wow," Candace said, reacting without meaning to. The conversation was getting pretty heated, and she was astonished by the things she was hearing tonight.

Alex stared at Stephanie blankly. She couldn't find the words to respond. Instead, she turned away and went to Jada's bathroom. Jada stood with her hand over her mouth, surprised at the low blows being passed out at her dinner party. She looked at Stephanie and shook her head.

Stephanie cocked her head to the side. "Don't give me that look. She had it coming. Acting like she's without fault."

"She was shocked, Steph. Just like the rest of us," Jada said quietly.

"Be shocked. Don't be spiteful."

Candace sat down on the couch, exhausted and exasperated by the turn of events. She propped her feet up on the nearby ottoman.

"As much as I would love to stay and be further insulted, I gotta go." Stephanie grabbed her purse from the coffee table and headed for the door.

Jada followed her. "Wait, Steph. Wait. Don't leave like this. You guys need to patch things up. Everyone is upset and not thinking clearly. Don't go."

Stephanie shook her head. "I have my own problems to deal with. I really don't wanna sit up here and be berated over someone else's issues. Later." Quickly, Stephanie exited the apartment.

Jada touched the door, wanting to go after her, but she was not sure about what to say to her. Everything had happened so quickly that she hadn't had time to process the information that had been shared with them. Taking a deep breath, she turned around and noticed that Candace had fallen asleep. She sighed and returned to the dining room to clean up the partially eaten dinner resting on the table.

Alex entered the room with the dish towel around her neck. "Need help?"

Jada shook her head. "I got it."

"You sure?"

Jada threw forks onto a plate and turned to look at Alex with her hands on her hips. "Yeah, you can help me with something. Tell me why you had to go and insult the damn girl and ruin my damn dinner?"

"That wasn't my intention." Alex looked hurt. "I was just mad. You know she acted like Corey was such a saint in this situation. I mean, Miranda is our friend, and Steph's man is basically pushing her over the cliff."

"Everyone's dealing with something. None of us have the right to throw stones at each other."

Alex sucked her teeth. "Really? You were pissed for a minute too, friend. Don't put it all on me. When you thought she was dragging Miranda through the mud, you were hot."

Jada nodded. "Yeah, I was. But you were trying to pick a fight with her. Getting all up in the girl's face. You asked for that drink in the face."

Alex sighed. "Okay, okay. Maybe you're right. We're all going through something, and I'm not exempt from that. And Steph was right. I was too stupid to realize how much Clay cares for me. But I'm not a gold digger. I'm not."

Jada rolled her eyes and went back to cleaning up the dining room.

"He gave me the most beautiful ring for my birthday, Jada." Alex was oblivious to the fact that Jada was only half paying attention to her. "Only I didn't even notice it until two days after the party. He left the sweetest note in the li'l ring box. Now he's changed his number, and I can't contact him. I may have lost out on my shot at true love, Jada."

"Shut up." Jada turned and looked at Alex once more. "Shut up. Y'all are fucking killing me. Y'all are so caught up in yourselves and your drama that I really think you've all become detached from reality. Seriously, Alex, it's hard to believe that you are really just now getting that Clay wanted you. A blind man could have seen that from ten feet away, girl."

Alex looked down at the floor like a child being chastised.

Jada continued to go in on her. "And even if you are just tuning in now, so what? He's pissed at you. And? It's not the end of the world, honey. Surely, he hasn't moved to another city or state since your party. You know where he lives. Stop waiting for some fairy-tale situation and carry your spoiled ass to his crib and apologize for being so freaking slow. End of story. There's your fuckin' happily ever after."

Alex scrunched her face up, offended by her friend's tone. "Why are you being so harsh?"

Jada sighed and picked up the stack of dishes on the table. "I'm tired, Alex. I'm tired of not being able to deal with my own problems, because I'm too busy dealing with everyone else's."

She left Alex in the dining room and went to the kitchen to load the dishwasher. She felt her breathing quicken and placed her hands firmly on the counter with her head down in an attempt to gain some composure. She could hear herself heaving, and she shook her head, warding off the panic attack that was steadily building. Jada was lost in her episode and didn't hear the front door open and shut as Alex left. She didn't hear Candace enter the kitchen and was barely able to answer her when the other woman called out her name.

"Jada, girl, I guess I'm going to get on out of here too and get out of your hair."

Jada tried to be silent as her body swayed.

Candace stood near the doorway and observed Jada. "Jada, you okay, girl?"

She nodded. "Mmm-hmm." But no sooner had the sound left her lips than her body went limp, she fell to the floor, and she began to struggle for breath as her body convulsed.

Candace's eyes grew wide from shock. Instinctively, she wobbled over to Jada and tried to sit her up against a cabinet.

"Don't touch me. Don't . . . d-don't touch. . . . Don't touch me," Jada stuttered nearly indecipherably. She curled her body up on the floor near the dishwasher and rocked as her chest heaved and her crying was hysterical.

Candace was unsure how to proceed. She whipped out her cell phone and started to dial 911. She wasn't sure if this was a seizure or what. Before she could press SEND, she heard the front door shut. Within seconds Jordan found them in the kitchen. Seeing both women on the floor, he knew something was wrong.

"Come on, baby," he coaxed Jada, who was now shaking uncontrollably. "Come on. Let me get you up."

He moved slowly so as not to startle or upset her. Gently, he lifted her from the floor and carried her off into their bedroom. Laying her down on the bed, he covered her up with a blanket as she balled herself up once more. Returning to the kitchen, he found a stunned Candace still sitting uncomfortably on the tile floor. He reached out to her and helped her up.

"What the hell was that?" Candace asked.

Jordan busied himself with getting Jada a glass of ice water. "She has a panic disorder."

"When did this start? I never heard her mention it."

"When did she have a chance to mention it? Every time y'all ring her phone, it's to get help with your problems. What? You thought she didn't have problems of her own?"

Candace was taken aback by the briskness of his tone, as well as the message he was conveying. She stared at him, as if waiting for him to say more.

"You can let yourself out," Jordan told her. "I needa go tend to my wife." Without another word, the man disappeared to the back of the house.

Chapter 50

Stephanie

Still pissed at Alex for what she'd said earlier, Stephanie drove home in silence, replaying the scene in her mind. How dare Alex try to pin Miranda's situation on her? She was tired of being looked down on because of Corey's business dealings. Besides, none of them had perfect men, so who were any of them to be judging hers?

Sitting in her living room now, downing a glass of Corey's liquor, Stephanie was filled with mixed emotions. Although she was pissed about being blamed for Miranda's bad decisions, she also felt sad for her friend. She had hoped that Miranda would show up at Jada's dinner. She was really hoping to see her doing well and looking better than before. The fact that she had not shown up at all only led Stephanie to believe that she was somewhere coked out of her mind or was simply hiding out, avoiding the shameful looks and the judgment of the girls.

She threw back the drink and pursed her lips as the liquor stung her throat. She massaged her temples and felt like she was about to scream from frustration. Faintly, she heard the muffled sounds of her phone ringing. Scrambling, she reached across the love seat to grab her purse. Buried deep inside, among papers, her wallet, her lip gloss, and other items, she finally found her phone. She rushed to answer before the caller hung up, praying that it was Corey.

"Hello," she said breathlessly.

"Where've you been?" His voice was angry.

She was caught off guard. "At Jada's." Then she realized that he was the one who had run out on her, and not the other way around. "Where have *you* been?"

"Locked the fuck up because of your stupid ass."

Her heart skipped a beat, and she sat up straight, trying to shake off the effects of the alcohol. "What the hell are you talking about?"

"What? You haven't seen the news, Steph? Shit's all over the fuckin' news tonight. What the fuck made you take the wallet out, Steph? Nobody knew that shit was there. Nobody. But with your jealous, snooping ass, I know it had to be you. Why couldn't you just stay out of it? Them motherfuckers said somebody tipped them off that you tossed that shit in a trash can. A fuckin' public trash can, Steph. What the fuck was that about? I almost think you wanted them to catch my ass. Is that where you're at with it? Don't you know they checked that shit for fingerprints, dummy? They got my prints, and guess what other idiot's prints are on that shit?"

The question was a bit muffled, but she heard it all the same, and a feeling of doom fell all over her.

"Where are you?" he muttered. She could tell his teeth were clenched as he spoke.

"Home," she said softly.

"Pack some stuff and leave the house. I need you to do a real solid. You got those keys?"

"Yes."

"Check your text messages. My dude texted you an address earlier, when I was first trying to reach yo' ass. Go there first. In the bedroom closet at that address are two garbage bags. Take the bags and yourself and the kids and go to North Carolina or somewhere else for a while, until I call you again."

"What?" She was having difficulty keeping up and understanding his directions. "Why are you sending us away? What the hell is in North Carolina?"

"This shit is bigger than the damn police and the GBI, Steph. They asses might arrest you, but the fuckin' cartel that's beefing with my distributor will kill you. Montae was from their sect. Shit is real in these streets, Steph. You did some stupid shit. So just do what the fuck I'm telling you to do and get the hell out of town."

"I don't want to leave without you," she cried into the phone as she frantically hurried to the children's room to throw some things in a duffel bag.

"Don't worry 'bout all that. Where the kids?"

"At my mom's."

"A'ight, I gotta get off this phone. Some dude in here got a cellie. I'll call you back when I can tomorrow. Be out of town by then, Steph."

"But why North Carolina? I don't— "

"I don't give a fuck if you go to South Hell. Just do what I'm saying and get the fuck out of Georgia. Stop asking questions you don't want the answers to, a'ight?"

Before she could respond, the line was disconnected. Tears blinding her, she threw clothes into a bag for herself. As she hurried into the living room to slip on her shoes and grab her purse, she looked at her phone. Four missed calls and two text messages. The entire time she'd been at Jada's, her phone had been left in the purse. She read the first text, which contained an address in Roswell and instructions on what to do when she got there. The second text was from Miranda's cell, much to Stephanie's surprise. Watch the news . . . only 'cause I think you should know.

She touched the chain around her neck and felt for the keys. Without giving it a second thought, she grabbed her things and quickly exited her apartment, just as Corey had instructed. In the car, she used the navigation function on her cell to direct her to the Roswell address. Her mind was racing with a million thoughts, and she was more fearful than ever. She wondered how the hell anyone had come across that damn wallet and how it had gotten tied back to Corey. If the police had figured out that Corey was responsible for the murder, she feared that they also knew that it was she who had disposed of the wallet. Perhaps she was just being paranoid, but she knew that Corey wasn't sending her and the kids away for no good reason.

This entire night had gone horribly wrong. She was unsure of what to expect once she reached the Roswell address. She prayed that it wasn't another trap house that he was sending her to at night. As frantic as she was, Stephanie tried to keep herself calm and maintain the speed limit so as not to cause unwanted attention. She had so many questions in her head, and she wondered if and when she would ever get the answers from Corey. How had she managed to get herself into this predicament? She desperately wanted to call Jada for comfort but thought better of it. After the blowup at her house, she got the feeling that Jada would not welcome any more of her drama as it pertained to Corey. Plus, she was a little pissed with Jada for not being more supportive of her when Alex was being such an ass.

Within thirty minutes she arrived at the address. The quaint apartment complex was quiet and still. There were few cars in the parking lot. Chills ran up her spine as she parked and exited her car. The scene just didn't feel right to her. But, as instructed, she walked around back to the appropriate unit, which seemed to her to be discreetly tucked away. Using the keys around her neck, she let herself into the apartment and quickly closed the door. Flipping on the light, she looked around the scantily decorated apartment. Instinctively, she knew that this was Corey's second home. A pair of his sneakers sat neatly near the couch, with an ashtray next to them. The room had the faint aroma of incense, a Corey trademark. Slowly, she walked into the kitchen. The only thing sitting on the counter was a half-drunken bottle of E&J.

She turned and went into the apartment's only bedroom. In the closet, just as Corey had stated, there were two garbage bags. She grabbed them, afraid to look inside, and turned to walk out of the room. But she quickly hesitated when she heard the sound of the front door closing. Someone was in the apartment with her. Her heart began to race, and she felt rooted to the spot where she stood. She looked behind her, as if searching for an exit, but there was only a narrow window. She considered using it to escape, but just as she was about to go toward it, she heard a voice call out.

"Corey, are you here? You left your door unlocked, hon."

Her nostrils flared, her eyebrows rose, and her eyes grew cold. She knew that voice all too well. Dropping the garbage bags to the floor, she burst out of the bedroom and into the living room to face the backstabber.

"No, bitch, but I'm here."

Chapter 51

Candace

She nearly jumped out of her skin. She could have kicked herself for not listening to her little voice earlier and not taking her ass home. But here she was, stuck in this unavoidable, unforgivable moment of truth. The two women stood staring at one another, each waiting for the other to speak. Candace couldn't begin to find words that she thought would smooth this situation over. She stood there, protruding belly and all, gripping her purse, with her eyes wide with fear.

Stephanie's fists were clenched, anger radiating off of her like heat. She stepped to Candace, and Candace placed her hand on her stomach, as if to brace her belly for the blow she was sure she was about to receive.

"You backstabbing bitch." Stephanie glared at her. "You trashy-ass ho! All this time you sat around listening to me complain about how I thought Miranda was fucking around with my man, and all this time it was your skank ass that was fucking him."

"It's . . . it's n-not what you think," Candace stuttered. She couldn't come up with a feasible lie. "Please—"

"What? You gonna tell me that you've been buying shit from Corey too? And that you drive your sadity ass all the way over here to get it instead of to the trap, like any other average crackhead? Fuck you, Candace. Fuck you if you think I'm stupid enough to buy that shit."

Candace shook her head, trying to convince Stephanie to believe her. "I'm telling you, it's not like that. It's not—"

"How long?" Stephanie interrupted her pleading.

"Nothing happened. Nothing happened, Steph."

Stephanie saw an extension cord plugged into the wall nearby. She snatched the cord out of the wall, quickly wrapped some of the length of it around her hand, then turned and swung the loose end, whipping Candace across the face.

"Ow! Ow!" Candace screamed and moved backward, grabbing her face with her hand. Blood dripped onto her fingertips.

"How fuckin' long!" Stephanie screeched.

Candace cried hysterically, still cradling her face. "Just a little while. Damn it, Steph. I'm sorry. I'm so sorry. I never meant to hurt you. I never wanted to hurt you."

Stephanie raised her hand to swing the cord again, and Candace flinched. Steph's eyes fell to the girl's stomach. "A little while," she repeated.

Candace looked up at her with sorrowful eyes and followed her stare. She shook her head, tears falling nonstop. "It's not his, Steph. I swear to Jehovah, it's not his. I was pregnant long before we ever hooked up. I swear it."

Stephanie dropped the cord and shook her head. She looked at Candace in disgust and frowned. "You're a sorry-ass excuse for a woman. You'll fuck anybody, won't you? You got married to a dude you barely liked, got pregnant by a nigga that barely liked you while you were still married, and now you're fucking your friend's man."

"I'm sorry." Candace looked away, ashamed.

"Damn right, you're sorry."

Stephanie turned away and walked back to the bedroom to get the garbage bags. Returning to the living room, she walked up to Candace, getting so close that she could feel the girl's breath on her face. "The only reason I'm not whupping your ass is because of that baby in your stomach. We're fucking through, bitch. I hope the next chick's nigga you fuck gives you AIDS." She walked away from Candace and headed toward the front door.

Candace turned to watch her and shouted out to Stephanie's retreating figure. "He came on to me, Stephanie! He came on to me more times than one way before I ever gave in. If he tried me, I'm sure he tried other chicks too."

Stephanie stopped walking and turned to face her former friend. "What the fuck is that supposed to mean? You want to hurt me, Candace? Well, you've hurt me."

"No," Candace interjected. "No, damn it! I told you I never intended to hurt you. It wasn't about hurting you."

"I don't give a fuck what it was about. Maybe Corey was fucking other chicks. Oh fuckin' well. But you know what the difference is between any of those bitches and your ass? *You* were supposed to be my girl. *You* were supposed to have my back. *You* should have fuckin' said no!" Stephanie turned away and proceeded to the door.

Candace trailed after her. "Steph, let me explain. Please, Stephanie. Please."

Stephanie ignored Candace's pleas as she opened the door to exit the apartment.

Candace approached the doorway as Stephanie stepped outside and headed around the corner. "Stephanie! I'm sorry. I'm so sorry." She followed her friend into the darkness.

Stephanie continued to ignore her as she walked through the stillness of the dark, stepping out of the cut of the apartment building. A dark sedan pulled out of a parking spot and lingered at the end of the sidewalk with its lights turned off. Without warning, shots sounded, and Stephanie's cries interrupted the silence of the parking lot. Candace saw Stephanie's small body fall to the ground as she was gunned down by assailants in two dark vehicles. It was as if she was witnessing the incident in slow motion. Her own screams of anguish, fear, and helplessness were drowned out by the noise of the shells being emptied into Steph's body.

Candace fell to the ground, sickened and petrified, as she was unable to help her friend. The offenders never even looked in her direction. She could hear herself crying aloud and screaming Stephanie's name in vain. No amount of screaming was going to raise her friend's body from the pavement. Suddenly silent, Candace crouched down near a bush and watched on in horror as one car sped away. Sirens could be heard faintly in the distance. Quickly, a figure jumped out of the remaining car and snatched up the bags that Stephanie had been carrying to her car.

Candace heard the man hissing at Stephanie's lifeless body. "That motherfucker thought he could just take what's ours and kill off our man with no repercussions?" The man tore a hole into one of the bags to check its contents. "We been waiting for the opportunity to catch his ass slippin', but now that he's facing that bid, offing his bitch and taking our dough, plus interest, is the next best thing. Thanks for showing up, Ma. Saved me from having to break into the spot. Hope your nigga gets this message loud and fuckin' clear."

To add insult to injury, the assailant then spat on Stephanie's body. As quickly as he had hopped out, the man hopped back into his vehicle, still not glimpsing Candace crouched silently on the ground, near a bush, frightened. The car sped off, and Candace began to cry again as she stared at her friend's body lying just a few feet away from her. Out of nowhere, a neighbor appeared by Candace's side.

"Honey, are you okay?" the woman asked.

Candace jumped. "My friend. My friend! My friend! They shot my friend."

The sirens were closer. Candace struggled to pick herself up off the ground. She waddled over to Stephanie, the nosy neighbor trailing behind her.

"The police are here, honey." The neighbor touched her arm lightly. "You can come inside my apartment to get yourself together, dear. Oh my! Are you bleeding?"

Candace lowered herself to the ground and threw herself over Stephanie's body. "Stephanie. I didn't mean it, Steph. I didn't mean it. Please. Please hold on. Please hold on."

"Ma'am, we need you to step away from the body."

She was unaware of the growing commotion around her. The police were trying to pry her from Stephanie's bleeding body, and a paramedic was off to the side, waiting. A few neighbors from the small community had begun to gather around, curious to know what was going on in their quiet little complex.

"Stephanie, please get up." Candace touched Stephanie's face and tried to will her to rise. "Get up, Steph! Get up! Get up!"

Her cries turned into screams just as a male officer was able to pull her away from Stephanie. She could barely stand upright. The pain of the shock and the horror was cutting into her abdomen. She felt sick to her stomach.

"Ma'am, are you bleeding?" The officer studied her intently.

She pointed to Stephanie. "They shot my friend. . . . They just shot her. . . . They just shot her."

"Ma'am, we need you to focus. Are you experiencing any pain?" A paramedic was now questioning her.

Candace simply shook her head no, yet her body swayed. She was finding it increasingly difficult to remain standing. The paramedic caught her as she wavered.

"How far along are you, ma'am?"

"I tried to tell her I was sorry." Candace was rambling. "I tried to tell her."

"She's delusional," the paramedic stated. "Get the gurney. I think this lady's having a miscarriage."

Chapter 52

Alex

The day after Jada's failed dinner party, Alex found herself seething with anger in her living room. She hadn't seen T in days, but today he finally called to say that he was coming by. His disappearing act was annoying all by itself, but it was the letter in her hand that was the true cause of her frustration. She tapped the pink envelope on her leg as she waited for T to pour himself a glass of juice without asking first and finally plop himself down on the couch next to her. He acted as if nothing was wrong and they were on great terms. Boy, was he mistaken.

"What's good, Ma?" He studied her and finally took in the attitude bouncing off of her.

She handed him the envelope. He didn't reach for it but looked at her quizzically instead. "What's that? A love letter?"

"It's a bill."

He pushed her hand away and finished off his drink. "Baby girl, I'm not in any position to pay off one of ya' bills right now. A deal don't mean instant dough, boo boo."

She threw the envelope at him and lost control. "You can't pay a bill for me? Let me be a little clearer. *That* is a collection notice for a purchase *you* made."

"I made?" He pulled the letter out of the envelope.

"Uh-huh. It seems that you bought some music equipment using my credit card and didn't bother to tell me, T! Then you had the audacity to *not* pay the bill."

"Oh, shit. Man, I meant to tell you about that, baby. It was an emergency. I had to get some shit to hook up a li'l studio area at my spot. But you never check your statements? You should have been known about those purchases."

She was stunned that he would have the gall to turn the situation around on her. She stared at him in amazement, wanting nothing more than to ring his thick-ass neck. "You're trying to make this out to be my fault? Negro, you basically stole from me."

"Stole from you? Man, watch out. You act like I took some money out ya' pocket or something."

"Uh, yeah! Basically, you did! You've jacked my credit up, and now I'm responsible for paying back this bill."

T said nothing. Alex was done. She rose from the couch and held her hand out. "I'm gonna need some money on this."

He looked her up and down like she was out of her mind. Seeing that she wasn't budging, he simply waved her off. "I ain't got it right now. Getting my new place and covering utilities and shit have tapped me out for a minute. I'll hit you up with some bread later."

"Later my ass, T! I'm sick of this shit. I have helped you, splurged on you, and let you straight up use me. This is over. I want every penny back for this bill, or—"

"Or what?" He stood up in front of her with an edge to his voice. "What? You not gon' give me none? You barely do that now. What? You not gon' help a nigga anymore? That's cool. That just let me know what type of chick you are or aren't. A real chick holds her man down."

"A real man wouldn't put his chick in a position to always have to make the sacrifice in order to hold his ass down. A real man doesn't steal from his woman. A real man does what he has to do to take care of himself and his woman, instead of the other way around."

Without warning, T hit her in the mouth with enough force to bust her lip and cause her to stumble backward. Instinctively, she covered her mouth with her left hand and looked up at him in fear. Thoughts of Miranda's words when the girls were all together at Candace's came back to her. She was not so desperate for love that she would let some dude beat on her.

"Another thing a real chick knows to do is shut the fuck up sometimes," T told her.

She spoke slowly, the tone of her voice even and deeper than usual. "I am giving you all of three minutes to get the hell out of my house before I call the police."

T chuckled and sat back down on the couch.

Alex pulled out her cell phone and dialed the three digits. "Don't test me, T. This shit is over."

He paused and tried to gauge her sincerity. Thinking better of it, he stood upright and walked past the tall, dark-skinned beauty. He turned back and whispered in her ear, "You're going to realize how big a mistake this is when you see me on the Grammys."

She snatched the gold-plated necklace he'd given her from her neck and turned to throw it at him. "No, you were the mistake, with your sorry ass."

T shrugged off her comment and pocketed the necklace. "Fuck you, then." He exited the apartment without any further discussion.

Alex quickly ran to the door to lock and bolt it. She touched her face, still in shock that the bum had had the nerve to hit her. Her phone was still in her hand, and it startled her when it rang. Thinking it was T, she pressed IGNORE without looking at the screen to check the caller ID. Tears began to fall slowly down her cheeks as she contemplated how her personal life had taken a horrible turn. She desperately needed to be comforted and consoled, but she was in no mood to hear "I told you so" or answer any questions from her girlfriends.

Alex grabbed her purse, jacket, and keys and headed out of the apartment. Taking the train and bus, she decided to try her hand at the one person who she knew always gave her great comfort and understanding—no matter what. She just hoped that he was in a forgiving mood.

It took nearly two hours on MARTA to reach Clay's apartment. By the time she arrived, her face was stained with tears, her eyes were red and puffy, and she was completely exhausted. Taking a deep breath, she knocked on his door and prayed to the heavens that he wouldn't leave her standing out in the cold. When he opened the door, she could tell that he was shocked to see her standing at his threshold.

"Alex?" He turned to look behind him. "What are you doing here?"

He didn't move to let her in, and Alex looked at him pleadingly. "I know you're mad at me, Clay. I get it. I really do, but I need you."

His eyes were sympathetic. He stepped back to allow her room to walk in. "I know it's got to be hard." He closed the door behind her.

Alex's phone began to ring again, and once more she silenced it. Her eyebrows knit as she considered Clay's statement. How would he know what had happened with T? Before she could ask, a short blond girl came down the hall and into the living room, looking at her questioningly.

"What's going on, Clay? You're not ready to watch the movie?" the girl asked.

"I didn't know you had company," Alex said softly.

The girl snuggled up to Clay and smiled nastily at Alex. "I'm Amanda."

Clay ran interference. "Amanda, this is Alexandria. An old friend. Alex, this is Amanda. We're dating."

"An old friend?" Alex repeated. "More like his best friend. In fact, there probably isn't even a word to describe what we are to each other."

Alex's tone was laced with anger, and Amanda looked at Clay for an explanation. "What's going on?" the blonde asked him again.

"Um, perhaps today's not a good time," Clay told Amanda.

Amanda stepped away from him and cut her eyes at Alex. "What are you saying? You want me to leave?"

Clay ran his hands over his head and looked over at Alex with compassion. He shrugged and gave Amanda a weak smile. "She's really going through a tough time and needs to talk. I'm really sorry. We'll do dinner tomorrow night. Your choice, okay?"

Amanda was hesitant but hopeful. "Okay." She grabbed up her belongings and placed a kiss on his cheek before heading to the door. Looking back at Alex, she gave her the same nicenasty smile. "I hope things get better for you."

Clay and Alex watched as Amanda exited the apartment. For a few moments they were silent, each looking at the other and searching for the words to say.

"Nobody knows me like you do," Alex told him. "Nobody knows how I feel, what I think, why I behave like I do sometimes. Nobody understands me but you."

Clay moved forward, took Alex's jacket and purse, and hugged her. Quickly, she melted in his embrace and cried. He held her tightly.

"I'm sorry," she said. "I'm so sorry."

"It's not your fault, Alex. You shouldn't beat yourself up about it."

"It *is* my fault. I should have paid closer attention. I should have never been with T."

Clay pulled back and looked at her face. For the first time, he noticed her lip. "What the hell?"

Alex lowered her head in shame. "He hit me. That bastard. He ran up my credit card bill and hit me when I was asking for the money back."

Clay shook his head. Alex's phone rang again. She silenced it again.

"You came all the way over here to complain to me about T?" Clay asked in astonishment.

"Yes . . . I mean no. . . . I came to say I was sorry." She grabbed his hand. "I came to tell you that you were right. That I don't belong with any of those other guys. That it's always been you who's been there for me. I came to tell you that I love you."

"Then you don't know?" Clay asked her, confused.

She held his hand tighter and stared into his eyes with her own puffy, tear-blinded eyes. "I *do* know, Clay. I found the ring you bought. I read the card, and I get it. I know how you feel, and I'm sorry I didn't get it sooner. I—"

"Alex, I have to tell you something."

"No, you've been telling me all this time in your own way, but I get it now, Clay. Really. You have to believe me."

He dropped her hand and grabbed her firmly by the shoulders. "Alex, shut up please. I need to tell you something."

She shook her head no, not wanting to face the reality that the opportunity had passed. She didn't want to hear him tell her that she was too late and that there was no happily ever after for them. "No. Don't say it. You don't mean it, Clay. You don't mean it. I love you. I really love you. Please don't say it."

Clay grabbed her hand and led her into his bedroom. Quickly, he changed the channel on his television to the early evening news. They'd been running the same story all day, and he knew that it would be covered now, if not in a few moments. Alex was still crying and protesting, not understanding what was going on or what Clay was trying to do. He listened to her rambling and crying until the story popped up again on the TV screen. Turning up the sound on the television, he positioned her right in front of it.

"Shut up," he ordered. "Shut up and listen."

Alex tried to focus on the newscaster, but each word that was spoken knocked the wind out of her, and Alex felt as if her spirit was floating above her body and watching as she fell apart.

"Officials are calling last night's homicide a message to neighborhood drug lord Corey Polk. Polk's long-term girlfriend and the mother of his two children, Stephanie Johnson, was gunned down in a small Roswell apartment community in the middle of the night. Johnson was leaving one of several of Polk's homes when witnesses say a car arrived out of nowhere and proceeded to empty bullets into the woman's small body. Johnson was DOA at DeKalb Medical. Officials have no leads as to exactly who her assailants were. But inhabitants of Johnson's neighborhood in Decatur have told authorities that they believe cohorts of Montae Stokes took her life in retaliation for his death.

"One eyewitness is said to have provided a statement to officials, offering only that the assailants were in a dark sedan and robbed Johnson of garbage bags believed to contain drug money. That witness was unharmed but is currently hospitalized at DeKalb Medical due to pregnancy complications caused apparently by trauma. Officials have not yet released the witness's name.

"Earlier on Friday the GBI announced that Polk had been picked up for questioning for the murder of Montae Stokes, which occurred earlier this year. A spokesman for the GBI told us that new evidence of Polk's involvement in the murder had been found, including his fingerprints on the wallet and identification of the deceased man. The fingerprints of Polk's deceased live-in girlfriend, Johnson, were also found on the items. No further information has been released regarding whether or not Polk has been formally charged with the murder yet."

Alex swayed, but Clay was right there to catch her. He eased her onto the bed and cradled her in his arms as she wailed and screamed. He kissed her forehead and continued to hold her tightly until she had no more tears left to cry. Sitting in silence, she laid her head in his lap. Her body tingled with grief and an emotional pain she'd never known before. Memories of T hitting her, her anger from earlier, and her fear of losing Clay were all replaced with the terrifying knowledge that she would never see one of her best friends again in life. Her phone rang again, and this time Clay reached for it.

"It's Jada," he told her.

Alex shook her head, realizing that it must have been Jada all along, calling to tell her the news. She wasn't ready to grieve with the girls yet. She wasn't ready to listen to Jada pull it all together and try to get them all composed, but she knew that if there was ever a time when her girls needed her, it was now. She looked up at Clay with swollen eyes. "Tell her I'll meet her at Steph's mom's house. I need you to take me there, Precious. We gotta do something."

Clay nodded and relayed the message. "She said to meet her at Ms. Johnson's. Yeah, we'll stop and get some food for the kids or something. See you in a bit."

Alex was in shock, but she sprang into action as she followed Clay out of the bedroom and out of his apartment. It was time to woman up and put her own feelings and issues aside. Stephanie was gone. The girls were going to need each other to get through this loss.

Chapter 53

The Girls

Three weeks after the funeral they all agreed that it was time. They had each been there to watch their friend be placed into the ground. Several of them had gone back to Steph's mom's house to help with the children. But they hadn't had the opportunity or the strength to come together and grieve for their girl by themselves, in their way. Today it was time.

They met at Alex's place for a change, for wine and cheesecake. Jada and Candace arrived together. The three of them were surprised when Miranda showed up at the door fifteen minutes later. Although she had texted saying that she would be there, they still hadn't been too sure. During Stephanie's funeral, they had spotted her in the very back. Why she had decided not to sit with the rest of the girls was unknown to them, but they were definitely glad to see her with them on this night.

There hadn't been much dialogue between any of them since their last meeting at Jada's and especially since the funeral. There was an uncomfortable, unusual silence between them as the women sipped their wine and savored their dessert. Really, what did a group say when they lost one of their members?

"This cake is really good." Alex licked her fork after taking another hearty bite. Leave it to her to mention something about food.

Candace giggled. "You know I love my New York–style cheesecakes from Publix."

Jada laughed this time. The feeling was therapeutic to her soul. "Something is seriously wrong with the two of you." She took a sip of water from her glass.

"What? I'm just saying." Candace said.

Alex refilled her wineglass and offered the bottle to Miranda. "Have some, girl?"

Miranda knew that she should say no. Alcohol was just another drug, and she'd promised herself she would get her act together. But tonight she desperately needed to take the edge off. She took the bottle and poured herself a glass. "Sure. Why not?"

A sigh fell over the room as each of them remembered what had brought them there tonight.

"It doesn't feel the same, does it?" Jada asked.

A series of head shakes ensued.

"I feel so horrible still," Alex confessed. "For the rest of my life I'll have to deal with the fact that my last interaction with her was an argument. I didn't really mean to come at her the way I did."

"I know you didn't." Jada looked at Alex, hoping to get her to end it there, versus continuing with this subject and embarrassing Miranda.

"I was just shocked, you know. And mad. Mad at Corey, really, but I was pissed that she couldn't see how poisonous he is," Alex added.

Miranda looked up at Alex. "What were you arguing about?"

"You."

All eyes focused on Miranda to see how she would react to this. She simply nodded her head in understanding. Surprisingly to the rest of them, she didn't appear ashamed or embarrassed. "So Stephanie told you, huh? I figured that she would. I knew she would. And it's okay." She looked at her friends and smiled. "You don't have to look at me with pity, you guys. I'm good."

"Even if she hadn't told us that night, the sight of you at the funeral and even now would be a dead giveaway, sweetie. Can I ask a question?" Alex said. "And please, excuse me if it's a little bit abrasive, but I just have to know."

"Shoot."

"What made you do it? Crack, I mean. I mean, I can't understand what would make any sane person *want* to shoot some shit into their veins or up their nose. I just don't get it."

"And I don't expect you to. You're right. No *sane* person just jumps into it. It's a progression. I didn't start off with that shit."

"You were on some other shit too?" Candace was intrigued.

Miranda shrugged. "I was smoking weed consistently, every day. After a while, I needed it to get through the day and all the shit I was going through with Norris. After a minute it started to not be enough. I felt like I had to go harder."

Alex shuddered, not wanting to hear any more and not wanting to picture her friend laid up somewhere, coked out of her mind.

"Do you still do it?" Candace looked at her friend for signs that she was coming down from a high.

Miranda shook her head and failed to make eye contact with Candace. It wouldn't do to tell the group that she'd had a hit several hours before arriving at Alex's. "I decided I'm going to go to a rehab center. Voluntarily. Do I think about it? Yes. But since Steph . . ." Her thoughts trailed off, but the others understood.

"I don't want to be a junkie," Miranda told them. "Nobody wants to be trapped in this addiction shit. I don't want people looking at me the way y'all are looking at me. I just have to make better decisions. This clinic, they're teaching me new ways to cope with my feelings and stress. So that I won't get high, you know?"

They all nodded, ready to put this uneasy discussion behind them.

"The day Stephanie saw me at that house, I knew she was ashamed of me." Miranda looked down at her hands. "I knew she was going to go back and tell y'all and that you all would be ashamed of me too. That's why I stopped calling and coming around. I didn't want to look at the shame and pity in your eyes."

Jada toyed with her water glass. "Are we really judgmental like that?"

Miranda nodded. "You're human."

They sat in silence, considering this thought. Again, forks clanked against porcelain as the girls devoured their cheese-cake.

"What about Norris?" Alex asked.

Miranda shrugged. "I gotta worry about me right now. Norris is probably off somewhere with his new bitch. They can have each other. Once I get me right, I'll deal with him. I just can't do it all right now. That cheating fuck." Miranda took another sip of her drink. "Did y'all know that Stephanie thought Corey was cheating on her with me?" Miranda questioned the group.

The question stunned them all. To tell Miranda the truth that they'd all been discussing her behind her back was hard to do, but today was a day for honesty. Jada nodded, and Alex followed her lead. Candace took a sip of her wine and looked at the group.

"So I guess it's my turn to confess," she said.

Alex raised her eyebrows. "Uh-huh. When I found out that you were there the night Stephanie was shot, a few questions came to my mind. . . ."

Candace hadn't been with Jada and Alex at Stephanie's mom's house the day after Stephanie's murder, because she'd been in the hospital, dealing with her own issues. There had been so many questions they wanted to ask her, but they'd felt the timing just wasn't right, considering what she was going through and the fact that they needed to be strong for one another at the funeral. But now was the time to lay some concerns to rest.

"I'm sure . . . so I'll just say it," Candace stated. "I was fucking around with Corey. Briefly. When I left your house that night, Jada, I went to that apartment in Roswell, where I'd met him before to . . . you know. . . . I didn't realize that Steph was there and Corey wasn't until I actually went inside."

"That's so foul." Jada abandoned her cheesecake and shook her head in disgust. "So foul. Why would you even go there, Candace? To mess with your girl's dude like that?"

"I don't know. I was feeling so rejected and disappointed in myself from messing with my series of losers. I just got caught up in the attention he kept throwing my way. He was the one always coming on to me."

"That still doesn't make it right," Alex interjected.

"You're right. It doesn't. And if I could take it all back, I would. But I can't. Alex, you feel bad that when you last saw her, y'all had a petty argument—"

"Which you could have helped end by admitting that you were the one screwing her baby's daddy. I'm just saying," Alex interrupted.

"Well, I have to live with the fact that she died hating me and that I had to watch her die so horribly," Candace declared.

They were silent again, each of them considering Candace's mixed emotions. As a group, they had all been through so much, hurting one another in ways they had never imagined they would.

"I know that isn't an easy thing for you to deal with." Alex reached over and offered her hand for support. Candace gave it a squeeze and fought back her tears.

"It was like watching a movie, I swear. And there was nothing I could do. Nothing. I didn't even realize I was losing the baby, because I was so fixated on losing her."

Alex hugged Candace, and Jada patted her leg.

"But the saving grace is that there is a God, Candace," Jada offered. "A God that knows your heart and gives you just what you need when you need it. Zoe may be fighting for her life, but at least she is still here to fight."

Candace hadn't lost the baby. The doctors had informed Candace, who was at just seven months at the time, that she was going to have to give birth to the child prematurely. There was no way that they could keep the baby from coming. The trauma she had endured had caused her to go into labor, and she was hemorrhaging from the blow she'd taken when she fell to the ground in fright as the guns began to blaze.

Her daughter, Zoe, weighed two and a half pounds now and was being cared for in the newborn intensive care unit at Emory University Hospital. The entire ordeal was tiring and stressful for Candace, but she was ever so thankful that Jehovah had pulled her and the baby through and had brought them thus far. Khalil still hadn't been to the hospital to visit his daughter, but Candace wasn't going to press the issue. She wasn't about to school the older man on how to be a good parent. Instead, she had decided to let child support enforcement deal with getting her the money she would need to care for Zoe.

"The thing that really eats at me, though, is how the dudes knew that Stephanie was even over there at the apartment," Alex stated, bringing the conversation back to the particulars of the murder.

Candace shrugged. "Like I told the police, I heard the guy say something about breaking into the place and having been trying to catch Corey slippin' for a minute. My guess is that they had been watching Stephanie too, to know that she was his girl. Maybe they'd planned to break into Corey's place that night, but Steph kinda made it easy for them by showing up and practically handing them the bags of money."

"How do you know it was money in the bags?" Jada asked.

"'Cause dude told her he was taking back his dough, plus interest." Candace shook her head. "This is never going to end. The GBI has interviewed me up and down about this. They think this is more than some petty local dope boys beefing."

"More like what?" Alex asked, raising her eyebrows.

Candace shook her head. "I'm not sure, but they made it seem like there were other folk involved. They kept asking me if Stephanie ever mentioned the names of Corey's associates and if he ever ventured out of the state or the country to handle his business. Their investigation is still open. Hell, they're liable to call me up anytime to ask a random question."

Miranda chugged her wine and poured another glass. "I bet if she could do it over again, Steph woulda never got rid of that damn wallet."

Jada's eyes darted over to Miranda instantly. "How do you know that Steph knew about the wallet?"

Miranda took a slow sip of the wine and tried to get her thoughts together quickly. "Well, they said on the news that her prints were on it."

"But that don't mean she threw it away," Jada replied.

"She . . . um . . . she told me." Miranda looked away and took another sip of her wine. It was best for her to just remain silent now in order to avoid spewing out more lies.

"You knew about the wallet, Jada?" Alex asked.

Jada nodded. "I told her to leave his ass the day she found it. If only she had listened." Tears welled up in her eyes.

"Don't cry, J. She's in a better place now." Candace placed her arms around Jada.

Alex and Miranda joined the other two girls, and they all embraced in a group hug. So many emotions flowed through them, and so many memories were shared between them. Shaking off the moment of nostalgia, Miranda poured herself another glass of wine and exhaled.

"We are one fucked-up group of chicks," she joked. "I don't know about y'all, but I desperately need to hear some good news."

Alex cleared her throat and put on her best princess voice. "I've got some good news."

Candace and Jada shared a look and laughed.

"Everybody knows your good news, Alex," Candace replied. "It's written all over ya' face."

"Yeah, girl." Miranda's smile extended past her lips to her eyes, brightening up her otherwise dull face. "I saw Clay escorting you around at the funeral."

Alex beamed and threw her head back against her chair. "He loves me."

Jada threw a pillow at her lovesick friend. "And it took you only forever to realize it."

Alex reached for her glass. "Hey! Don't shit on my happily ever after."

The girls laughed.

"We are definitely not," Jada told her. "We're glad you've finally got a good man so you can cut down on your drama, boo. Kudos to you."

"Ha-ha." Alex smiled.

Miranda went around refilling their glasses with a bottle of Riesling. She reached for Jada's glass, and Jada put her hand over the top. "None for me. Thanks."

"What's up with you, Jada?" Candace asked. "You giving up alcohol, girl? Isn't it a little early for you to be starting a New Year's resolution?"

The others chuckled, but Jada smiled nervously. "No. It's just that I peed on a stick the other day, and I don't want to mess anything up."

Miranda looked at her quizzically, and Alex scratched her head.

But Candace got it immediately and sat up straight in her chair. "Are you saying what I think you're saying?"

Jada smiled. "Jordan and I are going to be parents."

The girls enveloped her in hugs and kisses, each equally and sincerely excited for their patient and deserving friend.

"I was wondering when y'all were gonna put a bun in that oven," Miranda commented.

"I'm so happy for you, girl." Candace squeezed her extra tight. "I really am. You truly deserve it, and you're doing it the right way. I'm so proud of you."

Jada smiled, wanting to tell them how much of an accomplishment this truly was for her and Jordan given everything they'd been through. But she didn't want to taint the moment. Instead, she just relished the joy of being with child and having her friends be happy for her. She looked around at the girls. Things seemed to be reaching some level of normalcy for them. But she felt the void of Stephanie in the room. They all did. It was a feeling she was sure would take time for them to overcome, perhaps forever.

Their group had been through so much in the past year. They had had happy times and sad times. They had gone through births and death. They had seen each other through breakups and new unions. They had also discovered that each of them had areas to work on in order to be better friends to one another. But one thing was definite, one thing that none of them ever wanted to change. They were girls, and that was a bond they intended to keep for life.

Chapter 54

Jada

Six Months Later

People always say that you should be careful what you ask for. Jada was beginning to understand that more and more with each day that passed by. Pregnancy was kicking her ass. Now, in her second trimester, she was grateful to be getting over the all-day sickness but was struggling to find clothes that fit, foods that didn't disgust her, and a mood reminiscent of the way she used to feel on good days. As much as she wanted to have this baby, getting used to the changes was quite an adjustment. Standing there looking at the profile of her newly protruding belly in the dressing room mirror, she smiled. She was growing a person.

"Damn, girl, can you hurry up? It didn't take them this long to make the damn dress." Candace was growing impatient as she waited in the cramped maternity boutique surrounded by waddling women. She was glad that her maternity days were over and had no intentions of reliving them.

Jada rolled her eyes at her reflection and began to peel off the floral dress she'd picked out. "Just a minute. Geez." She didn't know why she'd even bothered to invite the girl shopping with her in the first place. If only Jordan hadn't had to go into work for a few hours this morning. Thinking of her husband, she pulled her phone out of her bra and sent him a quick text.

What do you want for dinner today?

She quickly tucked her phone back into her bra and hustled to redress in her blouse and khakis before Candace could voice her impatience yet again. Things had been pretty strained among all of them since the day she'd announced her pregnancy. In fact, it was the last time the girls had all been together. Alex was living a new life given her relationship with Clay, Miranda was in rehab, and Candace was being Candace. Since having her daughter, she'd been dating a series of guys, none of whom seemed particularly special to her. But Jada was willing to bet that her friend had been doubling back to her former habits and sexing her baby's father. To avoid listening to her lie, Jada chose not to ask the girl about it. The last thing she needed right now was to be caught up in any of her homegirls' drama at this point in her life.

Walking out of the dressing room, she noticed that Candace had stepped out of the store to make a call. It was just as well. At least it gave Jada an opportunity to pay for her purchases in peace. She decided to get the floral dress as well as a maroon dress and a pair of blue jeans with the belly panel. A few minutes later she walked up on Candace as she was finishing up her call.

"Are you sure your folks won't mind?" *Who the hell was she talking to?* "Okay. I'll call you when I'm on my way. It won't take long."

"What? You're about to ditch me?" Jada spoke into her friend's ear, nearly scaring the life out of her.

Candace quickly flipped her phone shut and shot Jada a look. "Girl, you know that's how folks get shot, right? Just rolling up on someone like that. You better watch it before you and mini-you gets got."

"I ain't scared of you, chica. Now, who you ditching me for?"

"Nobody's ditching you. But after we leave here I'm going to stop by my homeboy's house for a minute."

Jada's eyebrow rose as the two of them began to walk toward Macy's to exit North Lake Mall the way they'd come in. "What homeboy?"

"He's like my best friend from high school, girl. I've known him forever, but we lost touch after I hooked up with Quincy. I ran into him a week ago when I was over at that strip mall off Rainbow where my sister works. Man, we go way back."

Jada looked away. She'd known Candace for a minute now and never once had she heard any tales about some long lost best friend that happened to be a male. It was all sounding like some bullshit to her. "What's his name?"

"Rico. And he's so sweet. He's good with Zoe too."

"You've had that man around your baby?"

"Yeah. What's wrong with that?" Candace turned her nose up as if Jada had said something completely out of line. "I'm telling you, me and Rico used to be inseparable, girl. He's like my brother. I trust him with my daughter."

"Y'all *used* to be inseparable. That was in *high school*." Jada stated high school with as much sarcasm in her tone as she could muster up. "But the real is that you've obviously not been in contact with this dude for a hot minute, so you don't know who or how he is now."

"True friendship transcends time and is not affected by distance or lapse of time."

Jada gave her friend the side-eye. "You read that on a greeting card or something?"

"Ha-ha." Candace held the door open for her pregnant friend as they exited the mall. "But anyway, you know I wouldn't have nobody around Itty Bitty that might click on stupid. I don't play that."

Jada smiled at the girl as she sauntered out of the door past her. What she knew was that Candace was likely to paint the prettiest picture of someone she had no business dealing with as long she was caught up in them. But once the magic of the moment passed away and she was tired of them, Candace's description of and references to them would become less than favorable. Jada wasn't buying this homeboy that was "like a brother" story at all. But if that was the story Candace wanted to stick to at the moment, so be it.

"Well, all I'm saying is be careful, love." It was the soundest advice she could give her without going into depth about her association with this dude.

"Of course." They approached Candace's car first, and the girl promptly turned around and embraced Jada in a heartfelt hug. "Let me get out of here so I can get home in time for my mom to get to her meeting tonight."

"Oh, she kept Zoe today?"

"Yep. I'm trying to find a babysitter that I can afford and trust. I'm not ready to send her to a day care yet."

Jada felt her phone buzz inside her bra. She had a bad habit of storing her phone there so that she wouldn't have to fish through her purse for it. She pulled it out and saw that she had a text message from Jordan. "Well, you'll find somebody. I'm sure it's hard to leave your kid with a stranger, whether it's a day care center or a private sitter. I think . . ." Jada's voice trailed off as she read and reread the text that she'd been sent.

But will you swallow it if I let you?

The message had nothing to do with the question she'd asked him earlier. She stared at the screen trying to decide how or if to respond. Candace was speaking, but she couldn't make out what she was saying since she was lost in her own thoughts.

Candace slapped her arm. "Look, you and Jordan can go on and have you sex-text convo. I'm out, girl."

Jada looked up and nodded. "Uh-huh. Okay, boo. Be safe." She walked in the direction of her car without looking back. After getting inside and starting the engine she returned to the text message. Reading it again she shifted from confusion to annoyance. Her little voice was telling her that something wasn't right. She didn't know what the hell was going on, but one thing was for sure, that damn text message was certainly not meant for her.

Chapter 55

Jordan

It felt good to be away from home for a minute. Everything about home was a constant reminder of how their lives were about to change. The myriad of baby clothes and paraphernalia, the *Atlanta Parent* and *American Baby* magazines that covered the coffee table and the magazine rack in their bathroom, and the calendar in their kitchen which marked Jada's doctor's appointments and the number of weeks she was all served to taunt him. He was going to be a father, and it seemed as if he couldn't escape the reality of that one thing. Even watching the way Jada's body was changing was beginning to take a toll on him. Jordan knew that his personal hang-ups and gripes were selfish and wrong so he tried his best not to show any of his feelings to Jada. But in order to keep her at bay of his true emotions he needed a break.

He'd lied and told her that he had to go into the office just so that he could get out of going shopping with her for maternity clothes. He'd never been fond of trailing her around on her shopping expeditions, and he surely was in no mood to peruse maternity shops. Instead of going into the office he decided to hook up with one of his oldest buddies from college for a little one-on-one.

Jordan met Martin at Midway Park. As usual, Martin was late. Jordan had been waiting twenty minutes for his homeboy to show up and was just about to call it quits when the shorter, balding guy finally appeared across the court.

"Late as usual, nigga. You gon' miss out on your own funeral, watch," Jordan said giving his boy a pound.

Martin Hood was a portly, light-skinned dude who got much love from the ladies during college because of his loveable and quiet demeanor. His boys knew that that "quiet" business was just a front. Once you got to know Martin he was full of life and jokes. The thing that Jordan liked about him the most was that Martin, although chronically tardy, was one of the most reliable dudes he'd ever met. Jordan would go so far as to call Martin his best friend.

"Man, I had to go with Ashley to check out this bakery," Martin stated tossing his gym bag to the ground and pulling out his baseball cap.

Jordan tossed his basketball at Martin. "What's up at the bakery?"

"Trying out cakes for the wedding."

Jordan stopped dead in his tracks. "What wedding? You never told me that you asked Ash to marry you, bruh."

"Ahh, bruh, you haven't been paying attention." Martin dribbled the ball and smiled at his boy. "I posted that shit on Facebook, and I e-mailed all the homies an announcement."

"You know I'm not on Facebook. I don't even know nothing about no Facebook, and I ain't seen no e-mail either, bruh. Not to mention Jada hasn't said anything about receiving an invitation in the mail."

"Come on, man. Bring some offense." Martin began to run to the hole while dribbling the basketball. "Invites are going out next week. You gon' get one. Make sure you text me your mailing address."

"What?" Jordan said reaching for the ball and missing by an inch. "You not gon' have your boys be in the wedding?"

"Naw, we keeping it as simple as we can. Just me, her, the preacher, and family and friends can watch as we do our thing."

"Can't see how I missed this, man. Ole baby-face-ass Martin getting married!"

Martin shot the ball from the three-point line and was amazed that he actually made it. "Yeah, you been so caught up in baby-land you probably missing a whole lot of shit."

Jordan ran for the ball. "Man, it's a little overwhelming. It's like the whole relationship just shifted. Everything is about the baby. I mean, *everything*. From the food she cooks 'cause the doctor put her on a diet to control her blood sugar . . . right down to the way we have sex, *if* we have sex, so that she can be comfortable."

Martin laughed. "It can't be that bad, man. Y'all both getting what you wanted, right? You wanted to have a baby."

Jordan shrugged. Martin wasn't even married yet so he didn't have a clue how crucial this whole thing was. "Yeah, man. I'm excited about the baby and all . . . It's just a little overwhelming."

Martin knocked the ball out of Jordan's hand. "You'll be all right, man. You need to go ahead and shake it off 'cause it's affecting your game."

"Nigga, you wished you *had* game," Jordan countered.

"Bring it then."

"Man, shut up and run me that ball."

Once their friendly game of 21 was over and both men were exhausted and sweaty Martin reached for his water bottle while Jordan reached for his cell phone. He checked the time. 2:30 p.m. He wondered if Jada was home or if she was still out shopping. The thought of going home right away didn't appeal to him much. He checked his Yahoo! Messenger mindlessly and saw that he had an instant message from one of the interns at the radio station where he worked as a DJ during the week.

Mona: What you doing, Boss Man?

Jordan liked it when she called him that. At first he thought it was sign of respect, but then he realized over time that she was really doing it flirtatiously. The attention he was getting from her was enough for him to entertain her random instant messages and e-mails.

Jordan: Just finished playing ball with my boy. What's up?

It didn't take longer than a second for Mona to respond.

Mona: Nothing. Just saying hi . . . Couldn't tell if you were really online or not. Why you didn't invite me to hoop? I'm nice.

Jordan: Yeah, right. Girls don't hoop like dudes do. You don't want none of this, youngon.

Mona: What you know about what I want? Anyway, I can ball. I'm real good with my hands . . . and other things too.

It was the furthest she'd ever crossed the line with him. Feeling that they were just engaging in harmless banter, Jordan didn't feel compelled to put an end to the direction their conversation was going in.

Jordan: What else you good with?
Mona: My mouth. Can I show you?

Jordan's phone buzzed in his hand as a text message came through. As he clicked to read it Martin pulled him out of his daze.

"Whatever you over there talking 'bout sho' got you grinning like a dang Cheshire cat," Martin joked. "Jada musta said something you like."

Jordan glanced down at the text that had just come from his wife asking about his dinner choice. Figuring he could just call her in a minute to let her know, Jordan pressed a button and looked up again at Martin. "Don't worry 'bout what's going on over here with my phone. You just worry about making sure you get my invitation to me on time. Next time some important shit happens with you try picking up the phone."

"Like *you* ever pick up a phone," Martin argued. "You stay more busy than anybody. Between work and being booed up with Jada you don't never have time for jack. Shoot, I'm surprised you even called me up to ball today."

"Sometimes you need to get out with ya' boys," Jordan said as he struggled to send his reply to Mona while keeping up with the conversation with Martin.

"A'ight, man," Martin said rising from his seat on the concrete. "I gotta get back to the house. We have plans, and I don't want Ashley to get pissed with me for being late. You know how that goes."

Jordan pressed the send button quickly, rose from the ground, and stuffed his phone into his pocket. "Yeah, bruh. I know exactly how that goes."

They gave each other a half hug and a pound before each headed toward their respective cars.

"Aye, congrats, man," Jordan called out to Martin. "If I ain't tell you, I'm happy for you. I know you and Ashley been through a lot. It's good to see y'all hanging in there."

Martin nodded. "Yeah, you and Jada are our inspiration." He laughed.

Jordan shook his head. It wasn't the first time someone had referred to him and his wife as such. Especially in Jada's circle, they were the only couple that was able to sustain. On the outside looking in, it probably seemed as if they had it all. But on the inside just trying to make it, Jordan was starting to feel more and more like he'd made a mistake in marrying so young. They had their whole lives ahead of them. They both were at the beginning of lucrative careers. As much as he loved Jada, the thought of the dynamics of their relationship changing when they were still so newly married scared him.

"A'ight, man. Be safe," he told his boy as he reached his car. What else was there for him to say? The moment he admitted to anyone that maybe he wanted out he'd seem like the biggest asshole in the world. Perhaps it was just best for him to continue to suffer in silence. Jordan realized that relationships went through stages. Maybe they were just in an awkward stage that would soon change. In the meantime, he was content with using his disappearing acts and increasing mindless flirting habits as his defense mechanism.

He hadn't gotten a response back from Mona. After the game with Martin, Jordan drove to his mom's and chilled there for a bit. He was stalling for time because he knew that once he got back home to Jada there was no way he was going to be able to get away should Mona decide to resurface. He wasn't completely sure that he wanted to get up with her, but the possibility of it excited him. The shit-talking was giving him life. It helped him escape the routine he and Jada had fallen into, which was driving him crazy.

Reluctantly, he returned home in the early evening. Part of him hoped that Jada would already be asleep even though it was only 5:00 p.m. That pregnancy fatigue was real, and it seemed to strike Jada more often than the nausea. He let himself into their quaint little cottage home apartment and knew he was going to be in trouble the moment he closed the door behind him. He could smell the scent of onions and garlic and could hear the sizzling from the doorway in the quiet of the house. Although the smell was pleasant, Jordan's stomach wasn't ready for it.

He threw his gym bag on the ground and walked into the kitchen where Jada was placing a large juicy steak onto a platter surrounded with baby potatoes, tricolored peppers, and broccoli sprouts. She was barefoot and dressed in a simple blue slip dress. Her hair was pulled away from her face as the sweat beads formed around her forehead and the nape of her neck. She had a look of intense concentration on her face as she worked.

"Hey, you," Jordan greeted his pregnant wife. He leaned in to kiss her and she offered her cheek instead of her pretty pink lips. "How was your day?"

Jada placed the cast-iron skillet she'd sautéed the steak and veggies in into the sink and ran warm water into it. She shrugged her shoulders as she poured dish detergent into the pan. "Typical Saturday. Went shopping with Candace. Came home and washed clothes. Watched a movie. Cooked dinner."

"Eventful," Jordan joked as he pulled a bottle of water from the refrigerator.

"You know what I didn't do?" Jada asked turning off the water and beginning to scrub the skillet clean.

"What?"

"Receive a return text or a call from you."

Jordon guzzled his water before responding to her. Judging by the tone of her voice she was in a bad mood, and he didn't want to escalate it into a horrible mood by starting a petty argument. Her emotions were raw these days due to the pregnancy. She bugged out over every little thing, and he wasn't in the mood to go there with her today.

"My bad, babe. Martin was hating 'cause I whooped him so we had to run it back," he lied. "Then we got to talking 'bout him and Ashley getting married. I got your text, and I meant to hit you back, but I was talking to bruh and I just forgot."

"And when you left the park?" Jada asked in a scarily calm-before-the-storm-type of tone.

"I rode by Mom's place. Hadn't seen her in a minute and I just wanted to see my mom. Is that okay?" He shouldn't have caught an attitude at the end, but the interrogation was grating his nerves.

"That's fine," Jada said picking up the skillet to dry it with a dish towel. "But I'm just wondering if ol' girl actually did swallow whatever you put in her mouth or was that something that was going on at your mom's house?"

Jordon tossed his water bottle into the trash and frowned at his wife. "What you talkin' 'bout, babe?"

Jada took her time wiping dry the skillet as she looked at Jordan with piercing eyes. Her nostrils flared as she spoke. "You know, today actually was a little more eventful than I put on. You see, you *did* text me, asshole. Only I'm quite sure that the text you sent me wasn't meant *for* me. Your question was 'if I do will you swallow' and I'm asking you now . . . Did the bitch who the text was meant for actually swallow whatever the hell you put in her fuckin' mouth?" Her tone grew louder as she finished her question.

Jordan's heart pounded. He remembered the text all too well, and now he understood why Mona hadn't responded. She'd never gotten the message. He wanted to kick himself for getting their messages mixed up and creating this entire mess. Now he stood there watching his wife basically caress a cast-iron skillet like some psycho. He was pretty sure that there wasn't going to be any happy ending from this.

"I'm sorry." He didn't know what else to say. He couldn't possibly tell her that he hadn't sent the message because she had the proof sitting in her inbox. "I was just messing around online . . . talking trash. I guess I got your message mixed up with whoever I was talking shit to. It was nothing."

"You're *sorry?*" Jada asked, narrowing her eyes.

"I'm very sorry," Jordan replied sounding pitiful.

"You were just *messing around* online?"

Jordan nodded.

"It was *nothing?*" Jada asked, tossing the towel onto the counter and grasping the handle of the skillet tightly.

"Yeah, babe. It wasn't shit. Just talking shit on somebody's Facebook wall. That's it."

Jada nodded and remained silent for a moment before moving closer to him with a scary smile on her face. "Do I look like I'm stupid?" The second the word *stupid* escaped her lips she swung the skillet with all of her might.

Jordan ducked in the nick of time and quickly backed out of the kitchen.

Jada kept swinging the skillet, all the while ignoring the horrible pain she was feeling in her wrist. "You stupid son of a bitch! You think I'm stupid? Or are you actually that dumb to be putting this type of shit on some slut's public Web page for all the world to see it?" She swung and finally grazed the side of his arm.

"Fuck!" Jordan hollered. "I said I was sorry. Put that shit down, babe," he said jumping up onto their sofa.

She pointed the skillet at him and shook her head. "I don't know what's wrong with you, but you had better fix it. I'm not putting up with this shit from you, Jordan. You wanna fuck around with some skanks out in the street and do stupid shit to ruin your career like posting dirty comments on hoes' pages, then you go right ahead . . . but you gon' have to do all that without me. So you better make a decision, brother, 'cause I will leave your ass before I stick around for this shit."

Jordan held his hands up in defeat. The thought of her leaving him scared him. Jada was the best thing that had ever happened to him and even though he was feeling some kind of way, he knew that he didn't want to be without his wife. "I'm sorry, bae. It was stupid, and I was wrong. I'm sorry. You know I love you, and you know I didn't mean nothing by it."

Jada cocked her head to the side and surveyed her husband's shaken demeanor. She could see that he felt guilty and that she'd put a little fear in him. She needed him to know that she meant business. Shaking her head she turned away and returned to the kitchen.

Jordan could hear her fumbling around with dishes. Taking a deep breath he lowered himself to the ground and took a seat on the couch. Quickly he pulled his phone out to make sure he'd deleted any and all messages, including texts and instant messages. It wouldn't do to have her scroll through his phone in the middle of the night and find any more incriminating stuff.

"Come eat!" Jada called out.

From the sound of her voice he could tell that she was in the dining room. He tossed his phone onto the sofa and buried his face in his hands. He had a decision to make. Should he be honest with his wife fresh off this argument and tell her that he'd already eaten at his mom's house, or should he keep the peace and force himself to eat the meal she'd prepared? He rose from the sofa and took his time washing his hands at the kitchen sink before making his way into the dining room. Jada was already seated, and his plate was waiting for him at his usual spot. He took a seat and smiled at his wife.

"It looks good, babe." He meant it. The potatoes au gratin and the steak and veggies looked very appealing to his eyes. He loved his wife's cooking, but his stomach still hadn't fully digested the fried fish, okra, baked beans, fries, and hush puppies that his mom had whipped up.

Jada blessed the food and started to eat. The air in the room was stale as they both remained silent. Jordan took small bites of his food and was hoping that he'd be able to find a way to excuse himself without pissing her off. Jada was still fuming over his foolish behavior. She looked over and noticed that he was pecking away at his food verses devouring it the way he usually did.

"You don't like it?" she asked.

"Huh?" Jordan looked up at her. "Why you say that?"

She rolled her eyes. "Because you're barely touching it, like you think it's nasty or something."

Jordan shook his head. "You know everything you touch is the bomb. I'm just not that hungry."

Her eyebrow rose. "Why not?"

"I ate a little something at Mom's," he finally admitted. "But it's cool. This is good, boo. You know I'm gon' eat it."

"Don't bother!" she snapped. "I specifically asked you what you wanted for dinner. Instead of answering me, you out flirting with some trick. You knew I was gon' be cooking dinner for you, but you went and fed your face at your mom's house. You're an inconsiderate ass."

Jordan knew that he'd pissed her off this evening, but he was still the man of this house. He was just about sick of the way she kept berating him. This wasn't the Jada he'd come to know and love. Pregnancy was not a good look on her. "A'ight, you can chill now," he told her in a stern voice. "You don't have to keep bringing up the shit we just squashed. If we done with it, be done with it. And I told you I'm gon' eat the damn steak so you can let that go too."

Jada looked at him in shock at his tone. She couldn't believe his nerve. How was he going to come home and ruin her whole day, then turn around and try to put her in her place? Suddenly her appetite was gone. She rose from the table, and Jordan jumped up after her.

"Where you going?" he asked, only half-worried that she was about to actually leave the house.

"To my room," she told him. "I don't have the appetite to sit here with you and pretend that everything's all good. So you can suffer through your second dinner by your own damn self." She left the dining room and wobbled to the bedroom.

Jordan let out a loud sigh and sank back into his chair. He just couldn't win with her these days. It was really beginning to affect their relationship. He pushed the food around on his plate for a little while longer and tried his best to eat half of the meal. Once he realized that he wasn't going to make it, Jordan rose from the table and took both of their plates back to the kitchen to put in storage containers. He cleaned the kitchen and dining room up, figuring that Jada would appreciate the assistance.

There was nothing but silence coming from the bedroom, and he prayed that she had finally calmed down. He carried a lit frankincense incense into their bedroom and placed it in the usual spot on the dresser. Jada was lying in the middle of the bed surrounded by pillows and reading a book. He didn't say anything to disturb her. He pulled a pair of boxers out of his drawer and went to take a shower. As the water ran over his body he huffed. He was horny, but he knew that following their blowup there was no way that she was going to give him any tonight. But he was becoming used to that. Jada rarely ever felt like being intimate these days. It was just another thing that was affecting their relationship negatively.

After getting out of the shower and drying off he returned
to their bedroom. Jada had put her book aside and turned out
the light, signaling that she was going to bed. Jordan's eyes
darted over to the clock on the dresser. It was only a little
after 7:00 p.m. He wasn't ready to go to sleep so early so he
grabbed the remote and plopped down on the side of the bed
where she'd left very little space for him.

As the light from the television brightened the dark room
Jada slapped one of her pillows. "Do you *mind?*" she asked
with an attitude.

"What?" Jordon asked. "It's too loud?" He lowered the
volume.

"No, I just don't want to be disturbed by the TV. Period."

"What you want me to do, Jada? It's not even 8:00 o'clock.
Just because you're turning in super early doesn't mean I
have to, babe. If I do that I'll be up in the middle of the night,
and that's really gon' piss you off."

"Go watch TV in the living room," Jada suggested. "In fact
. . . here." She sat up, struggled to reach the bottom of the
bed to retrieve the spare blanket, and then handed it to him.
"Take your pillows too and you can just sleep out there."

"*Seriously?*" He looked at her as if she was crazy. "You're
punishing me now?"

"No. You want to stay up, and I don't. Plus I'm not comfortable all cramped up in the bed together."

"Cramped up?" This was news to him. "Since when do you
feel like we're cramped up?"

"Why do you think I have all these pillows everywhere? I'm
trying to get comfortable, and it's just easier when I have the
whole bed for that instead of trying to keep me and my belly
on one side of the bed."

Jordan swore under his breath and clicked the television
off. He threw the remote onto the nightstand, then grabbed
the blanket Jada offered him, along with his two pillows. This
was the most ridiculous thing he'd ever heard, but he couldn't
argue with her any longer tonight. Rising from the bed he
rolled his eyes and hoped that this pregnancy would speed by
quickly. As he left the room he heard her shifting around and
knew that she was repositioning herself in the middle of their
bed.

"Can you close the door?" she called behind him.

Jordan pulled the door closed without saying a word. Jada was officially getting on his nerves. He made up the sofa and turned on the TV, settling upon a rerun episode of *The Game*. No matter which way he maneuvered his body he just couldn't get comfortable on the couch. If someone had told him that having a baby meant no sex, a moody wife, and he'd be on the couch for God knew how long, he would have never agreed to it. Married life was turning out to be depressing.

Chapter 56

Miranda

Flashback

Fuck them, Miranda thought as she sat in her Nissan Maxima just outside the entrance to Stephanie and Corey's apartment complex. Corey was bugging about hitting her off and Stephanie had the audacity to be judgmental. She had half a mind to find a gun and go up in there and shoot them both dead in the fucking head. She was sick of people treating her like she wasn't shit. It was time to start showing these muthafuckas that they couldn't mess with her. The only flaw in her plan was that she didn't own a gun. But that was okay. She knew that she could cop one from any booster or crackhead on the street. Getting a piece would be the easy part. Executing the plan would be the hard part.

"What the fuck am I doing?" she asked herself. "I'm not about to put a bullet in nobody." She was tripping, and she knew it. She was just so pissed with the couple for how they were treating her, and she was in desperate need of a hit. Her mind was playing with her. It was time for her to go home before she did something stupid, but the thought of her empty, lonely apartment only made her angrier and more depressed. Before she could turn the ignition and get out of there she noticed a car exiting the open gate. Her eyes grew wider once she realized that it was Stephanie's Nissan Sentra speeding down the road. Where the hell is she going this late? Miranda wondered. There was only one way to find out. Quickly she put the car in gear and moved to catch up to a safe distance behind her friend.

They didn't go far. Stephanie parked her car at a convenience store right down the street and hopped out. Miranda parked her car across the street in the parking lot of an all-night Laundromat and killed the lights. There were no other people in sight. She squinted hard as she watched Stephanie pull a couple of trash bags out of the car. She felt her stomach turn the moment her friend began rummaging through trash bags in the Dumpster. What is she looking for? Miranda wondered. Surely they weren't starving. Corey and Stephanie had plenty of money to blow so Miranda knew the girl couldn't have been Dumpster diving. Finally she realized that Stephanie was pulling trash from the Dumpster and placing it into the trash bags that she'd brought. The rationale of it escaped Miranda's understanding. Once Stephanie was satisfied with her work she tossed the bags in the Dumpster, got back in her car, and made a U-turn toward home.

Miranda didn't follow her. There was no reason to. She was pretty sure the answers to her questions could be found in those garbage bags. She popped the trunk, and then hopped out of her car. After rummaging around for a minute she found a pair of work gloves that Norris always kept in the truck. She closed the trunk, then slid her hands into the oversized gloves as she crossed the street. It was clear that Stephanie had a secret, and she was about to find out what it was. After quickly looking over her shoulder to ensure that no one was watching she peered inside the Dumpster and pulled out the bag on top. The smell of garbage was repulsive, but Miranda was on a mission. She'd gone through two garbage bags before feeling as if she'd hit the jackpot.

Her fingers felt the thin plastic of what she knew was a card. Thinking that it was a credit card she pulled it out, only to see that it was a driver's license. Unfazed, she tossed it back into the pile and kept digging. Then it clicked. The name on the license was familiar. She doubled back through the garbage and pulled the ID out again. Montae Stokes. She thought for a moment, then realized just why the name was so important. It all made plenty of sense now. It wasn't Stephanie who had something to hide. It was Corey. But like a good wifey, Stephanie was doing the deed for him. Miranda wanted to kiss the license, but the thought of the germs crawling on it encouraged her not to. This was it. This was how she was going to get back at Corey's sorry ass and Stephanie's judgmental ass. She stuffed all the trash back into the garbage bag and made sure to place Montae's ID on top before carefully placing the winning bag back into the Dumpster on top of all the others.

She yanked the gloves off of her hand and whipped out her cell phone. Tonight she was about to be an anonymous Good Samaritan.

"DeKalb 911. What's your emergency?" the operator asked.

"Um . . . This isn't exactly an emergency," Miranda stated. "I mean, I think I have a lead on the Montae Stokes murder."

"Hold on, let me dispatch you to our tip line."

Miranda was placed on hold for a few moments before hearing another voice in her ear. Carefully she gave her location, then advised that she was a homeless person Dumpster diving and saw who she knew to be Corey Polk's girlfriend disposing of garbage at the convenience store. She told the interviewer that she'd gone into the bag hoping to find remnants of steak or something from the wealthy drug dealer's home but found Montae Stokes's ID instead. Before the interviewer could ask any questions she encouraged them to get someone out there quick before the evidence was gone, then disconnected the call.

Quickly she returned to her car and waited in the still of the night to see if anyone would follow up on her tip. Just when she was about to curse the justice system she saw an unmarked car stop at the Dumpster. She knew they were officers by the make of the car and their disposition. Her heart rate quickened as she watched them pull out trash bags with their noses turned up. They didn't have to look far or for long. What they needed was right there on top. She saw the taller cop wave the card in the air with his gloved hands.

"Gotcha," Miranda said out loud. "Y'all fucked with the wrong one this time."

Current Day

"How are you feeling today?" The therapist looked at Miranda with eyes of concern.

Nervously, Miranda wrung her hands together and rocked. The last thing she wanted to do was sit here and discuss her feelings. Her body felt like it had been hit by a truck. She ached all over and desperately wanted to crawl into the bed she'd been assigned by the rehabilitation facility. Unfortunately, she'd also been assigned to this whack-ass therapist and had to talk to her twice a day: once for a private session and once in a group session later in the day. Either way, Miranda wasn't feeling it.

She'd agreed to the rehab program once the reality of Stephanie's death had hit her. It was a sobering moment, and the girls had been so proud of her for committing to it. Although she said she'd do it, it had taken her three months to actually do it. Truth be told, it had taken Jada coming by the apartment and finding her passed out on the floor of her bathroom for her to get there. She'd been taken to the hospital, and from there she'd been shipped off to rehab. Whatever the reason and however the transition she was here now, but all she wanted was a hit to take the edge off. Since she obviously wasn't going to get that she would have settled for being left the hell alone.

"You know this session is really whatever you make it, Miranda," Doctor Dunham told her.

Miranda shrugged. She wasn't studying this woman. This was her fourth solo session and the fourth time she'd spent the hour and a half saying nothing. What the hell was there to say? The woman knew everything there was to know about her. It was pointless. Miranda knew that no one really gave a damn about her feelings.

"I want to help you, Miranda," Doctor Dunham stated. "But I can't do that if you don't do your part. This program was designed to . . ."

The therapist was talking, but Miranda checked out. She could see the woman's lips moving, but her mind was elsewhere. Honestly, her mind only stuck in one place when she wasn't craving a hit to put her out of her memory. Sleep never came. Insomnia forced her mind to replay the scene over and over again, never giving her a moment to be free of the living nightmare. Any time she tried to close her eyes it was as if she was standing in that funeral home again, staring at the still, lifeless body of the girl she'd once called her friend. That image only forced her to remember that Stephanie was placed in that casket because of her. This was something she couldn't discuss with anyone, including the therapist. Hell, she could barely stomach the memory and the reality herself. Doctor Dunham's constant inquiry about her feelings annoyed her. Miranda didn't want to feel the feelings she was experiencing, much less talk about them. The incident and her feelings haunted her daily. All she wanted was to escape it all.

Chapter 57

Corey

"You have nothing to worry about," Attorney Greg Phelps said to his client as they conversed in the private room at the DeKalb County Jail.

Corey threw his head back. "Aye, be straight up with me. Don't give me no bullshit, man. Tell me the real, ya' feel me?"

Phelps held his hand up. "If you have no evidence you have no case. It's as simple as that."

"Simple?"

Phelps smiled. "Simple," he reiterated.

Corey jumped up from the table and shoved it forcefully, penning his attorney in his chair with the table against his abdomen. Corey glowered at him. He was in no mood for any legal bullshit that this penny-pinching cocksucker was trying to feed him. He had too much on the line to be getting fucked around by the system. "Those bastard-ass GBI men in black fucks have Montae's ID with my prints on it. I'd call that evidence."

"Circumstantial," Phelps said nervously. "Means little to nothing. Just places you as a person of interest. Shows you were connected to him somehow, possibly there at the scene, but doesn't say you murdered him. Please . . ."

Corey frowned at the attorney and released the force he held on the table.

Phelps pushed the table away and cleared his throat. "A little trust'll go a long way here."

"Trust?" Corey asked. "You start trusting everybody that smiles at you then you're fucked, ya' feel me? So tell me, if this shit is so circumstantial, why the fuck have I been locked in this bitch for the last three months?"

"They had an eyewitness."

"What?"

"They had someone who said they saw you do it."

"Bullshit!"

"Must have been because that person is now MIA."

Corey shot him a look. "What?"

"GBI can't find their witness. Person just vanished so they have no one to testify against you."

Corey shook his head. "So, if they lost their witness, then again . . . Why the fuck have I been locked in here for the last three months?" his voice resounded through the room, raising the attention of the guard who poked his head into the room.

Phelps waved the guard away. "Because although the feds can't pin this on you, the state still intends to try, so they're holding you without bail until your court date."

Corey was livid. "This is some bullshit. When's the court date?"

"Two weeks," Phelps answered. "But I'm telling you that it's all circumstantial. With no eyewitness to present, you're as good as off. You'll be a free man."

Corey wasn't so sure about that. Maybe Phelps was telling the truth. Maybe they would dismiss the case and let him walk on the murder charges, but he knew it was only a matter of time before he'd have to face the music of the streets. More was going on than others truly realized. While Montae's folks were sure to come gunning for him once word got out that he was let off, *if* he got let off, there were others that would be looking for him too. He was going to have to explain a lot of shit to Castello and his crew. Surely the GBI had started sniffing in their direction once they hit his stash house and his place out in Roswell. Thinking about the Roswell crib made him feel emotions he wasn't ready to deal with. It reminded him of Stephanie and the fact that he hadn't even been able to say good-bye to the love of his life.

If he was getting out, it was time for him to start putting together a plan. He needed his crew's ear to the ground to see what kind of moves Montae's crew was planning to make. He needed to get his story straight for Castello and a plan so he'd be prepared for whatever the fallout was going to be with him. His business was very much a concern, but the most important thing he needed was to find out who exactly put the bullets in Stephanie. Once he found those bastards, they were going to have to feel the heat of his wrath. A lesson had to be taught in the streets. He was still the king, and no one was going to fuck with his family.

Corey looked over at Phelps. "I hope you right about this."

Phelps nodded his head. "I'm telling you . . . It's open and shut. Simple."

If it was one thing Corey knew from the dangerous life he led, it was that nothing was ever quite that simple. But he was down to take whatever stroke of luck he could get. He had things to do on the outside, and sitting in that cell waiting on some fucking suits to conjure up a case against him wasn't helping matters. In two weeks, let Phelps tell it, he was going to be able to get some shit popping. Until then, he planned to spend every moment getting his strategy together.

Chapter 58

Clay

"What the—" Clay tripped over the six-inch stilettos lying in front of the door as he tried to make his way into his apartment. Slamming the door, he kicked the shoes and rolled his eyes. He should have been used to coming home and tripping over heels by now. Ever since Alex moved in with him she'd taken the liberty of leaving her things wherever she pleased. It was one of the differences between them. He was organized and orderly, whereas Alex was creative and thrived in dysfunction. Maybe leaving her stuff everywhere had been okay when she lived with Kacey, but it was irking him that his girlfriend was becoming an apparent slob.

He sauntered into the kitchen and noticed that there was a bag on the stove. He took a sneak peek inside and found two takeout cartons of Chinese food. They usually took turns being responsible for dinner. It had been one of Clay's ideas. Since Alex was off on Fridays, today was her day to get dinner. She didn't exactly have any culinary skills, so it was so like her to order takeout. It was clear to Clay that she'd opted for delivery tonight.

As he pulled out a lukewarm egg roll, his beautiful, tall, ebony girlfriend skipped into the room. "Hi, precious!" she planted a big kiss on his lips. "I got you shrimp egg rolls this time."

He took a hearty bite of the appetizer and smiled. "Thanks, babe. How was your day?"

"It was okay. I mostly worked on my project for school and talked to Candace."

"How's Zoe?" Clay asked, inquiring about Candace's little girl.

"She's good, I guess. We didn't really talk about the baby. Candace has this new boo thang that she was going on and on about. You know how she does."

Clay raised his eyebrow. He certainly did know how Candace got down. Clay didn't want to come off as judgmental, but it was fair to say that Candace was one of Alex's friends that he liked the very least. He didn't trust her and didn't want her negatively influencing the woman he'd come to love so much.

"So did you finish the project?" Clay asked her, changing the subject.

Alex shook her head as she pulled his takeout carton out and placed it in the microwave. "Not yet. Almost though. Wait 'til you see this dress, precious. It is too hot."

"How hot?" He knew that Alex was all about fashion. Sometimes her fashion statements were a little over the top, but he loved how passionate she was about her craft.

She wrapped her arms around his neck and stuck her tongue inside of his mouth seductively. Over the last few months they'd gotten to know each other very well and very intimately. The transition of taking their relationship from friendship status to lover status had taken no time at all.

Clay reached behind her and tossed his egg roll into the plastic bag it had come out of. He then held her tight and darted his tongue against hers. He could feel his nature rising as he caressed all of her curves. He'd been waiting years to feel her, to experience her body, and to show her how deep his emotions ran for her. Now that she was his he made sure to show her how he felt about her every chance he got. He never wanted Alex to forget how much he loved her. She'd spent a lot of time chasing after paper and dudes that had very little real interest in her. He wanted her to be very clear what it was like to have a completely attentive, reliable, and accountable man in her life.

The microwave dinged as his hands reached up under her tank top and gently slid up and around to cup her free-hanging, perky feminine mounds. Feeling her nipples harden against his touch he pulled her shirt over her head so that he could lick each nipple purposefully.

"I thought you were hungry," Alex said, giggling at the way he was devouring her breast.

"Um-hum." Clay squeezed her round butt as he continued to fondle and lick her beautiful breasts. "I'm hungry for you."

The faint sound of music hummed from the bedroom. Alex popped his head playfully indicating that he should let her go. He shook his head and grabbed her tighter. She squealed with delight but was serious about answering her phone.

"Precious, let me see who it is," she said pushing away from him.

He watched her scurry off to grab her phone. He couldn't believe that she'd rather yap on the phone with who he was sure was one of her girls instead of making love to him. That just wasn't going to work out. Clay exited the kitchen, rounded the corner, and walked the short distance to their bedroom. Alex was standing in front of the vanity mirror of their dresser talking on her pink, bedazzled phone. She looked up in the mirror and saw him standing in the doorway behind her. She held up a finger indicating that he should give her a minute. A minute wasn't the only thing that he planned to give her.

Clay wasted no time coming out of his button-up shirt and crisply starched jeans. He completely undressed himself as she continued to chatter on.

"That would be good," Alex said. "We haven't hung out in a minute and that gives me plenty of time to get my project finished so I won't be goofing off . . . oh, that's nice. I'll have to ask Precious about it though."

"Ask me what?" Clay whispered in her left ear before kissing the sensitive area of her neck.

Alex flinched. She hadn't even noticed him creeping up on her. Looking up into the mirror now she could see that he was butt naked and obviously was in no mood to hear the word no. She smiled at the image of him reaching around and grabbing her breasts while she tried to maintain some composure while talking to Jada on the phone. Jada was saying something, but Alex's mind was gone. The feel of Clay's hands all over her body and his lips attacking her hot spot rendered her speechless.

"Hello? Hello?" Jada hollered on the other end.

"Tell her you have to go," Clay ordered.

Alex shook her head and tried to focus. "Umm . . . okay, girl. So . . . ummm, next Saturday is cool with me and I'll check with—"

Clay took the phone right out of her hand. Her mouth gaped open as he put the phone to his ear to bid Jada farewell. "Alex can't talk right now. She'll call you later." He pressed the end button and tossed the phone onto the dresser, daring Alex to say something to him about it.

She shot him a "well, okay then" type of look and reached out for his manhood. Clay smiled and smothered her lips with his. They enjoyed a sensual kiss before he led her over to the bed.

"I'm about to put something serious on you," he told her.

"Oh yeah, rudeness?"

He slapped her ass and guided her onto the king-sized bed. "We'll see how rude I am in a minute."

No further words were necessary. Together they created a magical moment all their own. Alex appreciated how gentle and attentive Clay was. Being with him was much different from the sordid sexual experiences she'd had with her old boyfriends T and Mario. Clay made her feel like she was the most beautiful and important woman in the world. She loved him more and more every day.

Their Saturday morning ritual was becoming more and more like second nature to Clay. They started the day with breakfast prepared by him, then did their laundry together. After that, they'd go out and catch a movie, do some shopping, or run errands. He enjoyed the time he spent with Alex, but he had to admit that her princess mentality seemed to be expanding. That morning alone he was fuming on the inside because instead of helping him fold their clothes she was engrossed in one of her many fashion magazines that she refused to ever get rid of. The box of magazines she had in their living-room closet bothered him, but he never complained.

"That is not cute," Alex said pointing to an unhealthy-looking thin model in a multicolored asymmetrical dress. "They should not have ever placed that monstrosity on that girl's body."

"Babe, can you give me a hand with these towels?" Clay asked, referring to the small stack of folded towels sitting on the floor directly below where she was currently balled up with her magazine. He rose from the couch with a basket full of their clothes, then headed toward their room to put it up. He noticed that Alex hadn't moved or responded to him. He stopped and turned back to look at her. "Alex?"

"Hmmm?" She didn't even bother to look up.

"We're going to get massages in an hour right?" he asked her.

She nodded. "Yes, precious one."

"Then can you help put the clothes away so we aren't late for our appointment."

Alex waved him off. "Oh you can just get those when you come back from putting the clothes away."

That was it. Clay couldn't take it anymore. He dropped the laundry basket onto the floor, then walked over to Alex and plucked the magazine out of her hands. She sucked her teeth and looked at him in disbelief.

"Okay, that was sexy when you did it with the phone last night, but for real, for real, you being a little rude," she told him.

Clay threw the magazine onto the stack of towels, then pointed to it. "Here. Read it all you want so long as you pick these towels up and put them away while you're doing it."

Alex reached down to grab her magazine. "What's wrong with you?"

"*This* is wrong with me, Alexis." He held his arms out-stretched.

Her eyebrow shot up. "What? You feeling some kind of way about the apartment? What does that have to do with your crappy attitude?"

"No, I'm feeling some kind away about *your* inability to help maintain the apartment."

"*Excuse* me?" Alexis couldn't believe that her boyfriend was standing there berating her.

"We've been living together for a few months, and I swear, you get lazier and lazier."

"I am *not* lazy," she argued. "Why would you say that?"

"Because you don't want to do anything, babe."

"I go to work and school. I think I do plenty, thank you very much." She rolled her eyes and flung open her magazine with a flare of attitude.

"I'm talking about doing stuff in the house. You don't wanna help do the clothes, you'd rather sit here flipping through magazines you've looked at a thousand times." He pointed to the heels that were still sitting on the floor near the front door. "And you won't even bother to put your shoes where they go. Those have been there for *three* days now!"

Alexis glared at him. "What? You're my daddy now?"

"Would your dad be able to push you to clean up after yourself?"

Alexis jumped up from the couch and stared at her boyfriend. Clay was sexy, but she wanted to tear his head off at this moment. "I don't know why you're trippin'. Just 'cause I didn't jump when you asked me to put the towels up? You all hyped up over some shoes? If it's that serious here . . ." she walked over to scoop up her heels, "I'll move them. You happy?" she asked cradling the shoes in her arms.

"What about food?" Clay asked.

"What about it?"

"We're going broke trying to maintain bills and your lavish takeout expenses all because you won't get in the kitchen and fry some chicken when it's your day to do dinner."

"I don't really cook like that," Alexis pouted. She was over being talked down to. "You knew that when you got with me, so I'm not seeing why it's a problem now."

Clay didn't like to see her face all distorted and ugly. He knew he'd hurt her feelings, but if he couldn't be honest with her, then they were never going to make it. "The problem isn't that you're not a good cook. The problem is that you won't *try* to cook. You know how to make some things. I mean, it ain't like you were sitting over there starving when you lived with Kacey."

She shot him a look. "Like you don't remember the many times I called you over to bring me dinner."

Clay shook his head and pulled her into an embrace. "Look, I didn't mean to come at you harshly or whatever, but we're a team now, so we both gotta act like it."

"Fine," she mumbled.

He kissed her on the forehead. "And if there's anything that I do that bothers you, you should let me know. I want us to be able to talk about anything. We're still cool like that, right?" He tweaked her nose.

Alexis looked into his eyes and smiled. "I guess so."

"Good." He pulled away from her and smacked her playfully on the butt. "Now put them shoes and towels away before we're late for our massages, woman."

Chapter 59

Candace

Things were starting to look up. Candace was finally back to work at a new law firm, Regal & Snyder, located on Peachtree Street downtown. She was enjoying her legal assistant position and had plans of going back to school to secure a paralegal certificate. She had her own spot and her daughter was happily cared for by a sitter during the week while she worked. Her divorce from Quincy was long since finalized and her fling with Khalil would have been a distant memory if it wasn't for the fact that she was caring for his daughter. It was a fact that Khalil only copped to when it was convenient for him.

Candace was seeing someone new. Rico Perry was a dude she'd gone to high school with and running into him at Stonecrest Mall a few weeks ago had brought back many old, fond memories. They'd been cool in school, but Rico had chosen now to admit that he'd had a crush on her back in the day. He'd been a grade level behind her, and she assumed that that was the reason he'd never said anything then. She had originally decided that it was best to keep him a secret from her girls. No one really trusted her judgment in men these days, given her track record. She couldn't blame them, but she also didn't care to hear any of their opinions about who she was spending time with and why. But things were starting to get serious between the two of them, and Candace was thinking more and more about completely coming clean. She'd started with Alex, who hadn't seemed all that enthused about two high school chums reconnecting. Alex's despondence encouraged her to put off telling Jada for the time being, especially since she was the more critical one in the group.

Candace checked her reflection in the mirror as she applied gloss to her lips. She was pleased with her round shape and alluring curves. Dressed in a fitted racer-back tank top and tights, she knew that Rico was going to find her figure inviting as well. The baby made a loud slurping sound, which caused Candace to turn around to look at her. She was lying in her playpen playing with her toes. Feeling that it was a supercute moment Candace picked up her cell phone off of the bed and clicked a couple of pictures of Zoe. If anyone had told her a year ago that she'd be a mother Candace would have laughed at them. But looking down into the playpen at Zoe she knew that she really couldn't imagine life without the precious little gift.

Being a parent forced her to think differently, and it definitely changed her routine. Everything she did now was for the sheer benefit of her angel. At least that was what she told herself and anyone else that would listen. She hadn't been dating much, partly because she didn't want to have just anyone around Zoe, partly because she was having a hard enough time keeping her vajaja in check and not giving it to Khalil whenever he decided to slide by, and partly because she hadn't encountered anyone worth being bothered with. At her new job there were several older men, all attorneys, that sniffed around her way now and again, but Candace was adamant about not falling into an office romance. She'd had enough trouble with having Khalil so close to her work environment previously.

Candace reached down and caressed Zoe's head. The fine hairs felt like silk against her fingertips. She finally understood what people meant when they said there was no love like a mother's love. She'd never loved someone so much with all of her being before. Zoe kept her grounded and had completely changed her life. She kissed the baby, feeling that sense of relief that the little one had lived through the unfortunate event that had occurred the night of Stephanie's death.

She shook off the memory. It occurred to her at least once a day. The role that she played in the whole mess made her ashamed of herself, but she knew that whether she'd been messing around with Corey or not, it would not have necessarily changed what happened. Whoever shot Stephanie had done so intentionally and were going to murder her that night whether Candace had been there under shady pretenses or not. It was the worst outcome possible. She'd tried over the months to envision other possible scenarios for how the whole encounter could have played out. Anything would have been better than the reality of Stephanie exiting Corey's secret apartment only to be massacred. Even Stephanie walking in on Candace and Corey in the act of their ultimate betrayal and them sitting there fighting and arguing it out until they were all spent would have been better than not having still among them the friend, mother, and sweet spirit that defined Stephanie.

The doorbell rang, bringing Candace out of her trance. She looked down at her cell phone to make sure she hadn't missed a call. No one ever just showed up at her house unannounced and unexpected. She left the baby in the playpen and hurried out to the living room where she took a look through the peephole to see who dared to just pop up on her. *What the hell is he doing here?* she wondered. *Certainly he's not here to bring diapers.* This was confirmed by his empty hands. She wanted to ignore him in hopes that he'd just turn around and go away, but she was sure that he'd already scoped out her car in the parking lot. She cursed her luck and reluctantly opened the door.

"What are you doing here?" she asked with her left hand on her hip and her right hand holding the doorknob, itching to slam the steel door in his face.

He smiled at her as if everything between them was cool and easy. "Hello to you too, beautiful. Are you going to let me in?"

She turned up her nose. "For the purpose of what?"

"Come on now, with the attitude. Let me in." Those hazel contacts covering his eyes only added to the effect of the fake look of innocence he was giving her. He licked his lips and smiled at her again. "Come on, sweetheart."

She rolled her eyes and stepped back against her better judgment. She didn't really have time for whatever bullshit stunt he was up to. She needed to drop Zoe off so that she could swing by and pick up Rico for their date. She needed some time outside of the house and away from Zoe for a little while. Although she loved her daughter with every fiber of her being, she still greatly appreciated the little adult time she was able to get.

She watched Khalil as he made his way over to her couch and comfortably took a seat. *Great,* she thought. *Obviously he intends to stay for a minute.* She wasn't too thrilled about that realization.

Khalil looked around the room and then craned his neck to look back toward the bedroom. "Where's Z?" he asked placing his hands on his knees.

"In the back in her playpen. Here, I'll go get her." Candace began to walk toward the bedroom.

"Hold up for a minute. Can we talk?" Khalil asked. He motioned for her to join him on the sofa.

Candace wanted to tell him to fly straight to hell on a one-way, first-class flight but tried to mask her contempt for him. They were coparenting, and although Khalil was sucking at it, Candace felt that it was her obligation, as Zoe's mother, to make sure that her father was welcomed into her life. Now, whether Khalil actually handled his business was on him, but Candace didn't want to have to explain to her daughter a decade from now why she'd let their personal differences affect her and Khalil's father-daughter relationship, so she tried to remain cordial at best. Slowly she walked over and sat on the sofa, making sure to leave some distance between them. The last time he'd come over she'd made the mistake of leaving herself way too open, and before she'd known it, Khalil was going down on her like it was his first pussy feast. If he thought that was going to happen again he could go fuck himself. Candace was tired of peddling backward with the man.

"How you been?" he asked her nonchalantly.

"Busy," she told him. "Just like I was busy before you just popped up over here."

"Busy doing what?"

"Taking care of your daughter." She crossed her arms. "That's something you should try to do more of."

"Now what's that's supposed to mean?"

"Exactly what I said. She's a baby, Khalil. She has needs. Like diapers, wipes, formula, clothes . . . all that good stuff. You promised me and my folks that you were going to be a responsible father—"

"I don't need anyone's parents to mandate me to do anything for my seeds," he commented cutting her off. "I'm a grown-ass man, Candace. I don't have anything to prove to your mom and dad."

Candace's eyebrow rose. "What about me and Zoe? You have anything to prove to us?"

He shook his head. "I do the best I can, sweetheart. Trying to take care of these other three kids, deal with this mess with Sheila—"

"Well, you created that mess," Candace interjected.

"And I'm trying to work on this book thing."

Candace was surprised. "What book thing?" This was the first she'd heard about any literary endeavor.

"I'm writing a book," he said. "Based on my life and my experiences. It's about all the stuff I've learned from various women in my life."

"Women you've fucked?" Candace asked.

"Why you have to have such a filthy mouth?" Khalil asked, frowning. He reached over to touch his fingertips gently against her lips. "You're too beautiful to be having such a foul mouth. Plus I don't want my daughter picking up on that type of language."

Candace slapped his hand away and chuckled. "Right."

He shook his head and crossed his right leg over the left while leaning back. "Anyway, the book is about some of the different relationships I've had with women and the things I've learned from them. Like each chapter covers a different relationship, starting with my mom in chapter one."

Candace was curious. "Am I in the book?"

"It's full of the women that have impacted my life, beautiful. Of course you're in it."

She didn't know how she should feel about that. "And what kind of light did you paint me in?"

He grinned devilishly. "You'll have to read the book to find out."

Candace's phone buzzed. She looked down to see that she had a text from Rico.

Where are you? You on your way?

She knew that she had to hurry up and get Khalil's ass out of her house so that she could get over to Rico. "I'm going to go get Zoe for you now."

She left him in the living room and returned to the side of the playpen in her bedroom only to find the little angel fast asleep. She started to leave her there, but realized that she had to move her anyway to get her in her car seat so she could take her to her parents. Candace stuffed her cell phone into her bra and smiled at her daughter adoringly. As she reached over into the playpen she felt strong hands grab her from behind and pull her back. "What the hell!" she exclaimed out of shock.

"Shhh," Khalil whispered in her ear. "Let her sleep. Don't disturb her."

"It's fine. We were getting ready to go anyway." She wiggled a little to encourage him to release his hold on her.

Khalil had one arm across her chest and the other around her waist. He held her close to him and knew that she could feel the rising of his nature against her round ass. He leaned down and kissed her ear seductively before speaking. "You're not going anywhere."

"*Excuse* me?" She was becoming enraged. "Let me go, Khalil."

"You don't want that. You know you don't," he said gyrating against the back of her body.

"Get off of me." She grabbed at his arm covering her chest.

Khalil ignored her. He took his left hand and squeezed her right breast with just enough force to make her wince for all the wrong reasons. Over time he'd come to learn exactly what to do to get Candace where he wanted her. Her body was his playground, and he knew which openings to tunnel through in order to get her to submit to him completely. His charm and his sexual expertise were the key attributes that lured her into his bed time and time again despite all of the drama they'd been through over the last year.

Candace didn't want to fall prey to it tonight, but she could already feel the stirring between her legs. She'd had sex with Rico only a few times at his parents' house, and she had to admit that his dick game was nothing in comparison to Khalil. Khalil fell short as a father and as a boyfriend, and she used that term very lightly where he was concerned, but he never once left her feeling disappointed or dissatisfied sexually. Just the thought of the way he pleased her made her want to throw herself on the bed and open her legs for him without protesting further. But she didn't want him to see her as a punk. She didn't want to be conceived as a pushover, thus encouraging his behavior. She needed him to know that she wasn't his sexual slave and that he couldn't just run through and hit it real quick when it was his daughter that really needed something from him.

"You need to stop," she said, slowly losing her resolve. "I have a date."

"Forget that nigga," he said kissing the side of her neck while squeezing her nipple through her tank top.

"Khalil," she said in protest as she tried to turn her head away to ward off his advances. "Stop. This isn't right."

Her cell phone rang from its spot in her bra. Before she could reach up to pull it out Khalil grabbed it and pressed talk. Candace knew that it was either her mom or Rico calling to see where she was. Either way, she was afraid that Khalil was going to say something stupid and embarrassing to the caller. The last thing she needed was for anyone to know that he was up in her house like he lived there, answering her phone. She found the strength to knock his arm away and reached for her phone before he could say anything.

"Hello?" she answered breathlessly while shooting him an angry glare.

"Aye, where you at?" It was Rico. He sounded perturbed.

Candace looked over at the time on the clock on her dresser. She should have been gone thirty minutes ago. She cleared her throat. "I'm still at home. Got behind a little bit."

"We're not going to make that movie," Rico said. "So you might as well just come get me and we chill there."

"You want me to drive all the way back here?" She was further irritated now. Rico's parents lived in a beautiful, spacious home out in Snellville. The thought of taking Zoe to her parents' in Decatur, and then driving out to Snellville, only to make it back to her apartment in Doraville didn't sound very appealing to her.

"Yeah. You want to be alone, don't you?"

She could hear his background and understood why he was trying to get away. Rico had two younger sisters. Erica and Ebony were seventeen-year-old twins. She could hear their cackling in the background and the sound of loud music, which she was sure was some cheesy boy group that had the young girls going crazy these days. Between the twins and Rico's parents, Felicia and Rico Sr. who argued with each other day in and day out, the house was never silent. The times she'd hung out with the whole family she'd left with a massive headache. She preferred the visits when they were all at work and school, giving Rico and Candace the freedom to have sex or just chill in silence.

Khalil watched the frown lines in her face deep and knew that whatever dude she was fucking with wasn't handling his business. He toyed with the string of her jogging pants and she slapped at his hand. He ignored her and struggled with her to pull the pants down. He dared her to say something to give herself away.

She held her right hand out as if to tell him to stop, but he wouldn't listen. She bent over and tried to back away from him before he could successfully get her clothes down. Her voice sounded strained and muffled as she tried to continue her phone conversation despite Khalil's trifling behavior. "Um . . . I don't know . . . I don't know about that."

"What you don't know?" Rico asked. "I'll shoot you some gas money, just come on and get me, please."

"Um . . . I . . . I still gotta take Zoe. Ugh!"

"What you doing?" Rico could tell that something wasn't right. "What's all that noise you're making?"

"Nothing . . . nothing. I dropped something. I was picking it up."

Khalil smiled wickedly as she fell back on her bed. He grabbed her pants and snatched them off.

"No!" she exclaimed. She couldn't help it and immediately became infuriated with Khalil for putting her in this position.

"No what?" Rico asked. "What the fuck?"

She didn't like him cursing at her, but now was not the time to go there with him. She tried to push Khalil away with her free hand, but he still managed to slip his strong hand between her thick thighs and stroke her kitty with his long, slender fingers. She knew that it was a wrap at this point. No longer able to fight him off she lay still as he parted her legs and fingered her while she stared at the ceiling. "I'm trying to do something," she said weakly into the phone. "I can't . . . I can't concentrate."

"Are you coming soon?" Rico just wanted to get to the bottom line.

"Mmm . . . not tonight," she purred. "I gotta go, Rico. Call me tomorrow." She ended the call before he heard anything further slip from her lips to belie the excuse she was giving him.

Khalil smiled victoriously. Whoever the hell Rico was, the brother wasn't getting any tonight. Instead, Khalil knew that he would be tapping this ass all over Candace's bedroom until his dick just couldn't rise anymore. He reached over and turned off her bedroom light. He didn't want his daughter to wake up and see what he was about to do to her mother. The sounds of Candace's pleasure filling the room were going to be detrimental enough. As he lowered his face to suck the cum that was slowly beginning to slip from her heated core, Khalil realized that he had a serious hold on her. No matter what Candace ever said or did, he knew that he could always get this pussy anywhere, anytime.

Chapter 60

Miranda

"I think my family understands," Bobby said. "I mean, they've always wanted to help me, but I just wasn't ready, you know? I wasn't ready. Nobody can help you when you're not ready."

Miranda rolled her eyes and huffed as she rocked in her chair. This shit was driving her crazy. They'd only been in the group session for twenty minutes and already she wanted to jump out of her chair, pounce on Bobby the meth addict, and scratch his eyeballs out. Some of the things they said in group session really annoyed her. Sure, she contributed nothing to the conversation ever but listening to the bullshit they were peddling between themselves was worse than sitting in the individual session with Dunham begging her to share her feelings.

The group was used to Miranda's silence and discouraging noises and facial expressions. On several occasions she'd been asked to respect the other members of the group, but it didn't change anything. Nothing they said could change the way she felt. She didn't understand why the others were fronting like these meaningless, empty words they were exchanging were really having some kind of effect on their mental and emotional states. It was bullshit. It was depressing. It made her want a hit to escape it all.

"When my sister caught me sucking her boyfriend's dick for that rock it, was over," Missy said from beside her. "She knew that I was using, and she was always trying to talk to me . . . see what was going on with me . . . But she had no idea that it was her boyfriend that was putting me on."

Miranda couldn't help but laugh. It was the most ridiculous thing she'd ever heard. The nervous laughter escalated as she replayed the words in her mind. Quickly the laugh turned into sobs. It was so ridiculously stupid and reminiscent of her own tragic story in a way. Missy's sister was like Stephanie. The memory of Stephanie finding her at the trap begging Corey's runner to let her cop something was probably one of the most humiliating moments of her life. The way she'd looked at her with pity and disgust made Miranda's stomach turn even now. Remembering that in the end her friend was dead made her tears fall faster. She'd never cried in group before, and the others were genuinely stunned.

Miranda closed her eyes and remembered Stephanie's judgment and tone. Although the girl was dead, Miranda knew that if she could go back in time to that moment on that stoop of that trap house in Decatur that she'd wring Stephanie's neck for making her feel like shit. Her fists clenched as anger replaced her despair. It wasn't fair. It wasn't fair for any of them to judge her. They didn't know shit, and they had no idea no matter what they ever said or did.

"Miranda?" Doctor Dunham called her name softly as the rest of the group watched her have her moment. "You have the floor . . ."

Miranda felt a hand on her shoulder, and she jumped.

"You'll feel better if you let it out," Missy said.

With her eyes still closed Miranda felt herself grow annoyed yet again. Who the hell were they fooling? She had no idea how discussing all the crap they did to themselves and others was going to make any of them feel any better. Besides, some of the shit she'd done to her friends was not anything she cared to discuss for various reasons. She swatted at her shoulder. She could still feel Missy's touch although her hand no longer rested there. Missy was a crackhead. Why was she supposed to take advice from a crackhead?

"We're all here to support you," Doctor Dunham tried to encourage her.

Miranda opened her eyes slowly and stared at the wall over Bobby's head. She focused all of her energy and emotions into that one tiny space on the ugly pale yellow wall of the community room they frequently met in for group. "They don't understand," she said slowly.

"They?" Doctor Dunham asked.

"They don't understand," Miranda repeated. "They may want you to be okay, to be like them, but they don't understand what's going on, where you are in life . . . mentally, emotionally. Not your family. Not your friends. Not your counselor. Not your doctor. No one. Unless they've been there. Unless they've scrounged through trash, been on their knees doing shiesty shit, abandoned all of their inhibitions and integrity just to get a hit, they don't understand. Unless they've been hurt more times than a few, physically and emotionally, they'll never ever ever understand. I don't give a shit what they say. And they can pretend to not know what the fuck's going on, but believe me, that's bullshit too. They know. They just choose to ignore it unless it begins to directly affect them. Damn what it's doing to you." She turned to the right to look at Missy with tears streaming from the corners of her eyes. "Your sister ain't stupid. If her man was dealing crack, she knew that shit. She was just hurt that you were in her house giving him head. That's all. The fact that he was feeding you junk was a secondary thing, so spare me the regards for her fuckin' feelings."

Missy jumped up and glared down at Miranda, and Doctor Dunham hurried over to restrain her. Miranda didn't budge. She'd lived in fear for so long that she was over it. She wasn't afraid of a little scrapping if it came to it.

"Don't talk about my fuckin' family!" Missy shouted, pointing at her. "You don't know me and you damn sho' don't know them."

"Missy!" Doctor Dunham was trying her best to pull Missy away and direct her back into her chair.

"I know you," Miranda responded in an even tone. "I know you, and I know them."

"Fuck you, Miranda! You sit up here acting like you're above us and shit. You ain't shit, bitch. You just a junky like the rest of us. You ain't no better."

Miranda shrugged. "Y'all delusional as hell. Sitting up in here singing 'Kumbaya.' This is a joke."

"*You're* a joke!" Missy spat in Miranda's face, and Doctor Dunham swung the eighteen-year-old around.

"That's enough!"

Miranda finally jumped up. All of her crazed energy exploded the moment her feet hit the floor. She quickly snatched Missy's arm pulling her away from Dunham's protective hold. She pulled the girl by her shoulder-length, unruly cornrows with her left hand. The other group members hooped and hollered over the scene playing before their eyes. Some were scared, some were excited about the moment of raw emotion, and others were disturbed. Dunham's small shrill voice hollered for Miranda to release the girl as she tried her best to pry her fingers away from Missy's hair. Missy reached her hands out and grabbed Miranda's neck attempting to squeeze for dear life. While Miranda could feel the pressure, Missy's grasp wasn't strong enough to cut off her air supply. Her state of withdrawal was having an adverse effect on her body so Missy's physical strength was a lot weaker than she thought it was.

"Girls, please!" Doctor Dunham begged. She blew the whistle that was around her neck that she used to calm the group down during heated moments. No one was giving a damn about that whistle today, and Dunham was rapidly losing control. "This is unacceptable. They will lock you in confinement for this, ladies! Please."

Miranda didn't care about confinement or any other consequence that might come her way. She needed this bitch to know that she was not to be fucked with. Miranda was tired of people taking advantage of her emotionally and physically. The last time someone had disregarded her feelings they ended up dead. Miranda fully intended to show Missy that she was not the one. Miranda stuck her index and middle fingers of her right hand as far up Missy's nose as she could, and then yanked. Missy screamed out in pain as her nose ring came undone. She let go of Miranda's neck and stared into her dark eyes.

"Miranda, no!" Doctor Dunham was now tugging on Miranda's arm. "Bobby, run and get Poncho and Captain."

Poncho was the head of security, and Captain was the head of the center. Miranda knew that once they arrived she'd surely be in trouble, but she didn't care. All that mattered was this moment. Blood trickled down her arm as she continued to hook Missy's nose despite the girl's futile attempt to remove her hand and Doctor Dunham pulling on her. Missy was growing light-headed and had begun to waver back and forth. Within five minutes Poncho was behind Miranda grabbing her from her waist and pulling her away, forcing her to scratch the insides of Missy's nostrils as her fingers were ripped out of the girl's nose.

A nurse was there to attend to Missy, who instantly passed out. Miranda looked on emotionless as everyone crowded around the girl while the nurse tried to bring her back. Poncho forced Miranda's hands behind her back and placed them in restraints. She knew what was coming next but didn't care.

"Let's go!" he said pushing her out of the room.

Together they walked down the hall to the far end of the building where the female dorm-style boarding rooms were. They walked past room 106, which was Miranda's room that she shared with another girl, Alicia. She knew that it would be at least two days before she saw the inside of that room again. They turned right at the end of the hall and headed to one of the two isolation rooms.

Poncho opened the door, removed her restraints, and then pushed her inside. "You better hope that girl's not seriously injured," he said before slamming the door shut.

The sound of the lock made Miranda realize that she was alone. She was stuck in her own horror story, held captive by her addiction and the memories of how her life had spiraled out of control. They could lock her away forever in this empty room; it wouldn't matter. She was already locked in her own hell long before today.

Chapter 61

The Girls

"Has anyone heard from Miranda?" Candace asked as she wiggled her toes in the warm water of the pedicure foot bowl.

They were congregated at a nail salon in the heart of Decatur having a much-needed girls' day. Jada had decided a week ago that they all needed to get together and hang out. It was her way of trying to restore and strengthen their friendship following all the things that they'd gone through. Later they would be meeting their significant others at the Hibachi restaurant on Memorial Drive for an early dinner. They were all like family, and it was time for them to start coming together as such.

"I haven't," Jada answered. She stared at a bottle of hot pink polish trying to decide if she really wanted to add color to her nails. "But I think they said that they encourage them to not connect with anyone from the outside for a minute while they're there."

"That makes sense," Candace said nodding. "I mean, she's there to work on her. Reaching out to us and talking 'bout everything we have going on probably won't help her much."

"I don't know," Alex said, changing the setting on her massage chair. "If I was away somewhere and going through something, I'd want to call my girls and have visitors. I'd want someone to show their support for me, you know? I'd want someone to be there for me."

"You want someone to be there for you when ain't nothing wrong with you to begin with."

"Ha! Don't hate just 'cause I'm lovable, boo-boo."

"Loveable? Yep, that's the word I was thinking of."

Alex frowned at Candace and stuck her tongue out.

Jada remained silent. She was concerned about Miranda as well, but the issues going on at her home plagued her more. It wasn't something that she'd ever feel comfortable sharing with the girls. They'd either jump all over Jordan in her defense, or they would mock her since they felt that her relationship and life were so perfect. She was still feeling funny about her marriage and wasn't sure what was going on with her husband. Until she had something concrete to put on the table she figured it was best to keep her feelings and misgivings to herself.

"So we're finally going to get to see this new boo thang today, huh?" Alex asked Candace, changing the subject.

Candace smiled. "Yep. He's supposed to meet us there, so I want y'all to be nice to him."

"Why wouldn't we be?" Jada asked.

Candace eyed her friend. "Girl, you know you. You don't like nobody."

"That is not true. Y'all just be coming with some real trifling dudes. Don't blame me. Blame yourselves for your questionable taste."

"Ewww," Candace shot back. "Attitude! Calm down, girl. I'm just saying I like this man, so be nice."

"Uh-huh." Jada focused in on the nail tech that was beginning her pedicure. "So is this the same guy that you tried to convince me was your homeboy?"

Candace smiled innocently. "He was, sweetie. A relationship won't work if you don't start off as friends first. You have to have some kind of solid foundation."

"Listen to you," Jada said. "That's what you learned after three trifling relationships?" She giggled. "I'm just messing with you, girl."

"Not funny," Candace said.

"Candace does have a point, though," Alex commented. "Just look at me and Clay."

"Poor Clay," Jada said. "It took forever for you to see that man, girl. Bless his little heart."

"He's a good boyfriend," Alex admitted. "He's a little controlling though."

"Controlling?" Candace asked sounding surprised. "Clay? He's cool as hell. How can he be controlling?"

"Not like a supernegative way. He's just like . . . you know . . . obsessive-compulsive, extremely organized, and überfocused."

"That's got to be quite a change from what you're used to," Jada said. "Don't be going around calling the man controlling. You're just not used to structure and having a man that's on top of his business. It's a good thing."

"Right," Alex said sarcastically. "You and Precious probably have more in common than I ever noticed." She laughed. "Anyway, Candace, go on, friend. Tell us about your new boo."

Candace smiled. She was more than willing to talk about her new beau. "Well, y'all already know that we went to high school together. He's a year younger than me and is really sweet and attentive. He makes me feel like I'm the most beautiful woman in the world, y'all. It just feels right when I'm with him."

"What does he do?" Alex asked as she handed the nail tech her left hand so she could start her manicure while another tech attended to her feet.

"Umm, well, he's looking into going to school for music production. He's really talented."

"That's cool. But where does he work?"

"He's between jobs right now. I'm trying to help him fix his résumé so that he can find something decent."

Jada's eyebrow went up, and she looked past Candace who was seated in the middle. Her eyes locked with Alex, and they both shared a look of concern.

It was Jada that spoke on their sentiments. "He don't have a job, girl?"

Candace shook her head. "Not right now. But he's looking."

"Did he have a job when you met him?"

Candace shook her head reluctantly. She really didn't want to discuss this with her girls, but she knew that it was going to come up eventually. "It's only temporary, so don't trip. He has potential. I know he'll find something soon. Sometimes you gotta stand by people you believe in and climb the stairs of success together."

"Who are you, and where is our friend?" Alex asked. "'Cause, honey, I have seen you walk away from a dude that didn't have a car, much less a job."

"Does he have a car?" Jada asked.

Candace shook her head again. "He's had some credit and license issues. He has some things to work out. That's all."

"Yeah, he needs to work out his life 'cause he has nothing to offer you," Alex said candidly.

"Don't go there," Candace warned. "I'm not so materialistic that I'm gon' pass on a really good guy just because he doesn't have a car."

"Right." Alex shook her head. "He don't have no job to buy one, either."

"All right, y'all, stop," Jada intervened. "If Candace is happy with her unemployed boo thang, then let her have that."

"I'd say thank you if that wasn't laced with sarcasm," Candace retorted.

Jada laughed. The thought of Candace laying up with a dude that had nothing was unbelievable. *Maybe she's growing*, Jada thought. *Maybe she's becoming less superficial and materialistic, which is a good thing.* But it was one thing to not be superficial and a completely different thing to be responsible with standards. Jada wondered if maybe her girl's standards were starting to slip. It would explain why she'd opened her legs to Corey months ago, being so unscrupulous as to have sex with her best friend's drug-dealing, shady-ass boyfriend.

"Where does this guy live?" Alex asked, still probing for information to prove that this guy was a loser.

Candace resented her for digging so deep but couldn't fix her mouth to lie about it. "With his parents," she said. "Just until he can get on his feet."

Alex was done. She'd had her share of bums, and if Candace couldn't see this guy for what he really was, then that was her problem.

Jada shook her head. *No standards,* she thought to herself. But who was she to judge? She was sitting there feeling that her husband was cheating on her yet hadn't made a move to find out or to do anything about it. She couldn't possibly school her girls on the status of their relationships when hers was falling apart at the seams.

Candace's phone rang. She pulled it out of her purse to check the caller ID. She didn't recognize the number and decided to send it to voice mail. The others noticed her action.

"What?" Alex asked. "Is that your boo telling you that he needs a ride?"

"I'm going to thank you to shut up," Candace snapped. "And anyway, he had a session at the studio with one of his homeboys. They're going to drop him off at the restaurant."

They each sat in silence thinking their own private thoughts. The salon workers spoke among themselves in their own language commenting on how catty the girls were to be friends.

"So how's Jordan?" Candace asked Jada, changing the subject.

Jada felt the tension seep into her body the moment she was asked about her husband. "He's fine. He'll be at dinner." It was all that she had to offer them.

"And the baby?"

"Fine," Jada stated. "We find out the sex next week. I'm hoping for a girl."

"I'm so happy you got the baby you wanted, Jada," Alex gushed. "If anybody deserves to be blessed with life it's you."

Her words were touching to Jada. "Thank you," Jada said smiling down at her feet as the nail tech filed her toenails. "I'm excited."

Candace noticed that she didn't say "we're excited" but decided not to say anything about it. "Yeah, you're more the mother type than me," she said instead. "I'm sure this will be a breeze for you, Martha Stewart. You're the homemaker, soccer mom type."

Was that an insult? Jada wondered.

"Uh-huh," Alex cosigned. "I know Jordan is living the life. He probably gon' be giving everybody and their neighbors cigars when you drop that baby."

Jada felt her chest tighten. If only Jordan really was that excited about the birth of their first child. She could feel an

anxiety attack coming on and prayed that she did not embarrass herself in the nail shop. She wanted them to change the
subject. Talking about it definitely was not going to help her
to feel any better.

"Choose your color," the nail tech said to her.

Jada looked at the bottle of hot pink polish again, then
decidedly picked up the white polish. "French tips, please,"
she said. It was better to be safe and not deviate from the
script. She felt the same way about her relationship. It was
best not to say anything to her girls right now. She just needed
to go on as if everything was normal until she knew for sure.
For now, it was best for her to just not think about it.

The girls stood in the waiting area at the restaurant as they
awaited their other halves. The aroma from the buffet was
enticing Jada. She was on the verge of saying screw it and
asking to be seated despite the fact that their whole party
hadn't arrived. As time went on in her pregnancy she noticed
that she was becoming hungrier and hungrier. Thinking that
it was normal she didn't see anything wrong with feeding her
face the moment hunger struck. Lately she'd been eating large
bowls of Fruit Loops and calling it a snack.

Candace's phone rang. She pulled it out of her purse and
hoped that it wasn't Rico calling to say that he couldn't get
a ride out. She'd just stood up for him back at the nail shop.
It wouldn't do for him to bail on her and give her friends
more trash to talk about the man they'd never met. Much to
her relief she saw that it wasn't him calling. It was the same
number that had hit her up earlier at the shop. She sent the
call to voice mail yet again.

"Somebody's trying to get up with you," Alex commented.

"Yeah, well, I don't answer numbers I don't recognize,"
Candace said placing the phone back in her purse. "So if they
really want something they better leave a message."

Alex opened her mouth to respond, then her focus shifted
when she saw Clay enter the restaurant. "Precious!" she called
out to him.

Clay sauntered over looking like the suave gentleman that he was in his classic khakis, blue, green, and white plaid button up, with matching plaid Skip's. "Hey, babe." He greeted Alex with a hug and a kiss before throwing his arms around Jada and Candace. "Hi, ladies. Good to see you again."

"Good to see you too, hon," Candace said smiling. She was happy for her friend. She'd finally hooked a guy with some manners and husband potential.

"How you doing, Clay?" Jada asked.

"Doing well," he responded. "I can't complain. How's the baby?" He smiled at her baby bump.

Jada rubbed her stomach. "Absorbing every bit of food I ever consume and pressing on my bladder nonstop. But other than that, thriving very well. We find out the sex next week," she repeated for him.

"That's exciting. I'm happy for you and Jordan." Clay put his arm around Alex. Seeing expectant parents made him feel some kind of way. It was what he wanted for him and Alex in the future.

"Thank you," Jada said softly as she felt her own cell phone vibrating inside of her bra.

Clay laughed as he watched her pull it out. "Convenient pocket," he said playfully.

Jada smiled and shrugged. "At least I never lose it up here." She pressed talk on her phone and walked away from the group to answer the call.

The trio chattered for a bit before the doors of the restaurant flung open and a short, almond-complexioned young man made his way inside. His neck was covered by chains that were cheap replicas of those donned by rappers. His black T-shirt did very little to cover up his blue plaid boxers that were exposed due to his army fatigue pants sagging. Alex tooted her nose, disgusted by his tacky demeanor. Clay was turned off by the way the young man had made such a display of entering the door by flinging open both doors. Candace, on the other hand, looked thrilled to lay eyes on him.

As the guy approached the group Candace held her hand out to him. "Guys, I want you to meet my boyfriend Rico."

Alex wanted to fall to the floor. She was dismayed by the sight before her. This guy was nothing like any of the qualities that Candace usually sought in a man. She wondered what in the world attracted her friend to him.

"What's up?" Rico asked. He held his hand out to Clay. "How you doing, man?"

Clay shook his hand respectfully. "Good. How you doing, bruh? I'm Clay, and this is my girlfriend Alex."

Alex forced her lips into a smile, but she knew that her eyes were dancing with confusion. "Hi," she said weakly.

Candace tightened her grip on the short man's hand. "How did it go at the studio?"

Rico shrugged. "A'ight I guess. Dre made a beat that goes hard, but you know my lyrics gon' make it sick."

Listening to him talk was making Alex sick. Looking at Rico she felt as if she knew him. Not personally, but she knew his type. Dating her ex, T, a proclaimed rapper who had nothing, she knew what it was like to be in a relationship with Rico's type. She made a mental note to pull Candace to the side later or call her up for a one-on-one to hip her to some game. Whatever she thought she saw in this joker was some bullshit and Alex didn't want her friend to get caught up in any of the drama she'd gone through with T.

Jada returned to the group with a solemn look on her face. This whole thing had been her idea, and now she had to change it up on them. "Hey, guys." She was about to break the bad news to them but was immediately taken aback by the appearance of Candace's guy. He was nothing like the other men Candace had been involved with.

"Jada, this is Rico," Candace said catching her friend's glance. "Rico, this is my girl, Jada."

Rico smiled. "How you doing?"

Jada gave a polite smile in return. "I'm good. Nice to meet you. Umm, ladies, I'm sorry, but I'm going to have to leave you. Jordan's not able to make it, and I just remembered that I promised my mom I'd do something."

Alex frowned. "Seriously, friend?" It wasn't like Jada to forget anything.

Jada nodded. "Yeah. I'm sorry. But you guys enjoy dinner, and I'll get up with you soon. I promise." She gave both of her friends tight squeezes before moving to leave.

"Call me, girl," Candace said. She was eager to get Jada's opinion about Rico even though she wasn't sticking around to actually get to know him.

"Okay," Jada said. She waved to the group and walked out of the restaurant.

Chapter 62

Jada

She was angry. She'd planned this outing a week ago, but Jordan picked the hour that he was supposed to show up to let her know that he couldn't make it. She felt humiliated and disappointed. Her little voice was speaking to her again. As she slid into the driver's side of her car she felt her breathing escalate to irregular spurts.

No, she thought. *No, I can't do this now.* She held on to the steering wheel and tried her best to remain composed, but it was not to be. The panic attack was coming no matter how much she willed herself to get it together. She heaved uncontrollably and wrapped her arms around herself. Her eyes grew wide as her body spazzed out. She hadn't even been able to close the door upon getting in the car before the attack took over her. Shaking and trying hard to fight against her panicked breathing, Jada didn't notice the older woman getting out of the car beside her.

The woman was initially annoyed that Jada hadn't bothered to close her door. But as she was about to try to squeeze past the open door she heard the sounds of trouble coming from inside the car. The woman peeked in and saw Jada convulsing in her seat. "Ma'am!" the woman called out concerned. "Ma'am, are you okay? Are you having a seizure, sweetie? Are you okay?"

Jada heard her but couldn't respond. All she could do was sit there feeling her body shaking and her tears clouding her vision. The woman could see Jada's belly and realized that she was with child. She figured that since she was still sitting upright that a seizure could be ruled out. Her spirit spoke to her, and the woman rounded the front of Jada's car and got in on the passenger side. Without saying a word the woman threw her arms around Jada. She could feel her body quaking under her embrace but held her as tightly as she could. She'd seen this on an episode of *Grey's Anatomy*.

Within a matter of minutes the woman could feel Jada's shaking lessen to a mere tremble and her breathing was becoming more relaxed. The technique was working. Now that the crisis had been averted Jada felt ashamed and distraught. Her feelings now became released in the form of a hearty cry.

"It's okay," the stranger said to her. "It's okay. You just let it out. Sometimes we have to just let it out."

Jada didn't know who this woman was, but she was glad that she'd been there to get her through the emotional moment. It was funny to her how God worked. None of her friends had realized that she was falling apart, but the second she lost it in the parking lot this stranger, an angel, came from nowhere to assist her.

"Thank you," Jada said pulling away from the woman who smelled like lilac. "I'm so sorry."

The older woman smiled at her. "There's no need to be sorry, honey. You can't help that you were having a moment. It happens to the best of us. I'm just glad that I could be here with you. You're having a baby," she said looking down at Jada's belly.

Jada nodded. It was feeling more and more awkward sitting in her car talking to a complete stranger.

"Your emotions are probably all over the place now," the woman said. "Bless your heart. Whatever it is, suga, you gotta pray on it and let that go. That baby feels everything you feel and the worst thing we can do is fill our impressionable, innocent beings with the anguish of us adults."

"Yes, ma'am."

The woman smiled. "Do you go to church, dear?"

Jada shook her head. "I haven't in a while."

The woman pulled a card out of her handbag and handed it to her. "Take this, baby. I'm Evangelist Betty Peters, and I started my own church. We're just two months old, and we meet at my house, but the Lord goes wherever He's called upon. I want you to consider coming and joining us one Sunday. You and your husband. We're down-to-earth folk, come as you are. We're just interested in getting to know the Word and praising God for all He's done for us."

Jada took the card and nodded.

"My brother died this morning," the woman told Jada. "I been crying all day. Me and my siblings decided to meet up here for dinner so we could shake off some of this somberness surrounding us. Plus we needed to eat," she said chuckling. "But I know what it's like to be consumed with stress and hurt, honey. Just feeling the way your body was trembling and hearing the vigor of your sobs I can tell a hurt spirit. Anyway, I hope you'll come out and worship with us, but if you don't, I want you to remember that whatever's going on, God's with you, baby. This is a happy time in your life. He didn't mean for you to be consumed with sadness when He's given you such a great gift."

Jada looked into the woman's eyes and felt herself about to start crying all over again. The woman reached over and squeezed her hand lovingly. "I'ma be praying for you, suga. What's your name?"

"Jada," she said. "Jada Presley."

"Beautiful name. I'm gonna pray for you, baby. I'm gonna pray for you by name. I'm not going to hold you up now. Please get home safely and I hope you'll come on out and see us." She exited the car and gently closed the door behind her.

Jada pulled her own door shut and watched as the woman disappeared into the restaurant where she was sure her friends were happily eating and not giving her a second thought. She looked down at the simple black-and-white business card and considered the idea of visiting the woman's in-home church. She knew that Jordan would never agree to it. She placed the card in her purse, put on her seat belt, and then turned the ignition. It was time to go home and deal with her problem.

Standing in her bedroom she didn't know where to start. Something was going on with Jordan, and she was going to get to the bottom of it. When he'd called her at the restaurant to say that he'd gotten caught up out in Riverdale with his cousins she knew that they were headed down a dark path. He'd never stood her up in the two years that they'd been together. Calling her while she was there with the whole group and forcing her to apologize on their behalf was rude. If he hadn't wanted to go he should have been honest a week ago when she'd first brought it up to him. The fact that he canceled on her at the last minute really made her question the sincerity of his excuse. Was he really with his family or was he somewhere else? With the problems they'd been having lately Jada wouldn't have been surprised.

She began to go through his underwear drawer, and then his T-shirt drawer. She wasn't sure what she was looking for but was certain that she'd know it once she found it. Moments later she opened the smaller closet that housed only his things. She looked inside of shoe boxes, pants pockets, and felt around on the top shelf. Nothing. His laptop was sitting on the table in the living room. She took a seat on the sofa and lifted the top of the computer. The log-in screen appeared, and it dawned on her that she didn't know his password. She'd never had a desire to know it before. She made a mental note to demand the password the moment he returned home.

Frustrated, she lowered her head into her hands and sighed. She was running out of outlets to find the explanation for her husband's current behavior. The baby fluttered, and she remembered that she was hungry. She could have stayed with the others at the hibachi grill, but she hadn't wanted to feel out of place or answer subsequent questions about her husband's absence. She shook her head and looked in the direction of the cabinet where Jordan hid his liquor. She really could have used a drink at that moment but knew that it was a definite no-no. Thinking about the fact that he was hiding the liquor in that cabinet made Jada wonder what else her husband was hiding from her in there.

She rose from the couch, walked over, then bent down to open the cabinet. Sitting on the floor in front of it she pulled out the half-drunk bottle of Crown Royal that stood in the front. Next she pulled out a bottle of Golden Grain. She smiled at the thought of the liquor's potency. But once she reached her hand inside again . . . Her smile dropped. She pulled out a black notebook and looked at it questioningly. She'd never seen the book before. Opening it to the first page she immediately realized that this was his journal. *What grown man keeps a journal?* she asked herself. She breezed through the first entry and concluded that it was about work, his goals, and how much he loved her. The next couple of pages were the same, and then the entries stopped. The rest of the pages were blank.

She was a little relieved to have found nothing and was about to put the notebook back . . . until she noticed a slip of paper hanging from the bottom toward the back of the book. She turned to the page and removed the orange slip of paper. It was a flyer for a sale at some store, but Jada was disinterested in it. Her attention was stolen by the first words on the entry that rested on that page.

There's just something about her. I can't describe how I feel when I talk to her. It's nothing like I've ever felt before. She understands things, and I don't have to apologize for my feelings or thoughts when I talk to her. I can just be myself. And she is so beautiful. I can't wait until I get to see what she feels like.

The entry stopped there. Jada couldn't believe her eyes. She flipped the pages one by one until she was completely through the book. There was nothing else written. It was clear to her that he'd placed that entry way in the back just in case she ever decided to open his little journal. The entry was dated. May 12, 2011. That was a little less than a month ago. Jada remembered the text message that Jordan had sent her by accident and his lame-ass explanation for it. *Online shit-talking, my ass,* she thought as she struggled to get off of the floor. She was furious. She pulled her cell phone from her bra and quickly dialed his number.

"What's up, babe?" he answered sounding annoyed.

"You have about thirty minutes tops to get your ass home before I start burning some of your shit," she warned him. "Then what's left will be sitting outside when you get here."

"What? What are you talking about?" The noise in his background was loud, but Jada was sure that he heard her loud and clear.

"If you value your marriage you'll get your ass home now or you can kiss my ass good-bye." She hung up. There was nothing else to say. Pissed, she waddled back into her bedroom and pulled her suitcase out of the closet. If he thought she was going to just sit there and ignore the fact that he was cheating on her he could go fuck himself. She wasn't that docile little housewife that everyone assumed she was.

As she threw random articles of clothing into her bag, tears of anger began to drop. She felt like she'd cried a river today. She thought about where she was going to go. She couldn't go to Alex's because she didn't want to disturb her and Clay. She didn't feel comfortable asking Candace if she could stay over because she assumed that her new boyfriend would already be there squatting. She refused to go to her mother's because she didn't want her to know that she and Jordan were having problems. The second she got wind of that the whole family would be in her business. Pulling out her cell again she dialed another number.

"What's up li'l sis?"

She knew that her brother would give her good advice. "I'm pissed," she said.

"Why? What happened?"

"I want to kill Jordan."

"What he do?" Antwan's voice was filled with concern.

"I think he's cheating on me."

"Why you think that?"

Jada stuffed a shirt into her bag angrily. "Because I found his little journal detailing his bullshit."

"You over there going through dude's stuff?" Antwan asked sounding amazed.

"Well, I knew something wasn't right," she explained. "I didn't expect to find the journal, but I did. So I read it."

"That nigga slippin' on his pimpin'. Writin' shit down. That's one of the first rules of doin' dirt. Don't leave no communication trail."

Jada huffed. She didn't call him to listen to him run down rules of the game. She needed somewhere to go. "Where are you? You at home?"

"Why?" he asked suspiciously.

"What you mean why? 'Cause I'm leaving. I'm not staying around for this crap."

"You can't live with me, and I know you're not going to Mom's house. Stop being silly."

Jada pouted. "I'm not being silly. What do you expect me to do?"

"Is that your house?"

"Yes!" she barked into the phone. "So?"

"So why the hell are *you* leaving your home in the middle of the evening with that baby in your belly? If somebody gotta go let his ass leave. But, Jada, on everything I love, if you leave that house I'm going to whip your ass."

Jada was confused. She plopped down on the bed next to her bag and stared at the wall. None of this was making any sense. "So I'm supposed to just sit here?"

"I give a damn what you do, and you better not do it outside of that house."

"Gee, thanks."

"I'm sure you'll figure out how to handle the situation without losing the upper hand."

Jada was feeling defeated. She sighed and ended the conversation. "Fine, but if I kill him you better bail me out of jail."

Chapter 63

Jordan

His heart was racing as he tried his best to save face and remain calm in front of his cousin Tony. He'd been playing spades with the fellas and drinking a few beers when Jada had called to threaten him. He knew that she was pissed about him bailing on their little group date, but this behavior was irrational and unlike his wife. If all of this was about his failure to show up this evening then he was going to suggest that she get counseling. Over-the-top behavior was not attractive to him. He started to pull out his cell phone and tell Mona about the drama he was dealing with but decided against it. He wasn't going to be able to respond once he got in the house, and it didn't make sense to start a conversation he couldn't finish. Besides, he didn't even know the full extent of the drama he was about to walk into so he figured it was just best to sit tight and wait to see what happened.

"You a'ight, bruh?" Tony asked glancing over at him as he pulled into Jordan's complex.

Jordan nodded and tried to appear unfazed. "Yeah, man. I just needa see what's going on with Jada. Everything's cool." He suddenly wished that he'd driven himself verses riding out with Tony earlier. He could have called Jada back in private to try to diffuse the situation or at the very least not have to worry about being scrutinized by his cousin. Jordan knew that he had to keep himself in check because he didn't want his marital issues being the talk of his family the moment Tony pulled out of the parking lot.

Tony parked next to Jordan's car in front of his cottage-style apartment home. "You want me to come in with you, bruh?"

Jordan sucked his teeth. "Man, stop playing. I'll get at you later. Thanks for the ride." He hurried out of the car before Tony could make another joke about his situation.

As he hopped down the stairs leading to his private sidewalk to get to the front door he took a deep breath. Whatever he was about to walk into he hoped that it was not going to end horribly. He felt it was a good sign when he didn't smell smoke coming from inside and didn't see his clothes strewn about outside like she'd threatened to do nearly an hour ago. He let himself inside the house and was surprised to find the house dark minus the row of candles that started at the front door. He'd nearly knocked the first one over when he stepped in. Jordan closed the door behind him and carefully followed the pattern of the first four candles. He was confused. If Jada was pissed, then why the romantic setting?

"Babe, I'm here," he called out. He stood still to see if he could hear any movement. Hearing nothing he continued to follow the row of candles all the way to their bedroom where he found his wife sitting on the bed dressed in a black nightgown and holding a candle. "Hey," he said from the doorway.

"That took longer than thirty minutes," she pointed out, referring to his trip home.

"I was riding with Tony. Had to wait a minute 'til he was ready. You okay?"

She shook her head. "No, I'm not okay." She reached behind her and pulled out a black notebook that looked familiar. "And this is why."

As Jada waved the leather-bound book in the air it hit him. That was his journal. He'd written some things in there that he'd never intended for Jada to find. He thought he'd been smart about it by putting the true stuff in the back of the book. He wasn't sure if she was mad that he was keeping a journal or if she was smarter than he thought and was mad because she'd found his secret.

"What you doing with that?" he asked nonchalantly.

"Learning about my piece of crap-ass husband," she answered. "You know, I didn't know that you had an interest in writing. All this time and I just didn't know that."

"Nothing wrong with jotting your thoughts down," he said shifting his weight from one foot to the other.

"Hmm. Let me share my favorite part with you." She laid the book down on the bed and turned to a back page that she'd dog-eared.

Jordan swallowed a lump in his throat and began to run down a list of excuses in his head as she read his words out loud. He had no idea how he was going to get out of this one, but he knew that no matter what lie he handed her, he was going to be in the doghouse for sure.

"And she is so beautiful. I can't wait until I get to see what she feels like," Jada said reading the last sentences of the entry. She turned and looked at him. "What the fuck was that?"

"I was starting a story." The lie just rolled off of his tongue.
"What?"

"I made it up. I was starting to write a story."

Jada's eyes grew wide with anger. "Do I look stupid to you? Do I look like some stupid-ass woman that doesn't know the difference between sugar and shit?"

"Come on, babe. I'm trying to tell you it's nothing. Either you believe me or you don't."

Jada was feeling his attitude. "Uh-huh." She held the book up over the flame from the candle. "Well, your story stinks and should be burned."

She lowered the book and the page caught the fire. Jordan leapt forward, snatched the book, and quickly put out the flame before things got out of hand. Jada set the candle on the nightstand and rose from the bed. She walked out to the linen closet and retrieved a blanket and pillow. Jordan followed her to the living room, carefully stepping around the candles.

"What are you doing?" he asked her.

She tossed the linen onto the sofa and turned to face him. "I'm putting you out of the bedroom indefinitely." She crossed her arms. "Now I'm going to ask you again. What the hell is going on?"

"Babe, I told you already," he said giving her a pitiful expression.

"Yes, you told a lie. Now try the truth."

"It is the truth."

She walked past him. "I'm leaving you," she said nonchalantly.

He turned around in a panic. "What?"

She stopped in front of the wall where their marriage certificate hung. In the blink of an eye she snatched it down, slapped the frame against the wall causing it to shatter, pulled the certificate out of the fragmented glass, and dropped the remainder of the frame to the ground. She held the certificate up for him to see. "You and me . . . us. We're over. You can't even be bothered to be honest after you've been caught. I'm giving you two weeks to find yourself somewhere else to live." She looked at him as if she expected him to say something.

"Come on," he begged. "Why are you doing all this? This is crazy."

"This is crazy?" she questioned. "You put your dirt in ink and told me it was a story in your defense, but *I'm* crazy?"

"Look, I'm telling you the truth, woman! It was nothing. I didn't even finish it. You saw that for yourself."

"You're a bad liar, Jordan," she said seething. "You're a bad liar, and I'm sorry that I ever, ever met you." She dropped the paper, and it landed on top of one of the burning candles.

They both watched as the marriage certificate went up into flames. Jordan grabbed the blanket from the sofa and hurriedly smothered the flames. His breathing was uneven, sweat dripped from his forehead, and his heart was racing by the time the fire was out. The marriage license was barely legible. A black mark smeared their names and only fragmented edges remained where their wedding date used to be. It was a symbol of how their relationship was now marred by his dishonesty and creeping.

"You trying to set the damn house on fire?" he asked Jada as he wiped sweat from his eyes.

"Why not? This marriage has already gone to hell; you might as well follow on behind it." She turned to leave the room.

Jordan grabbed her arm. "Bae, really? What the hell?"

She snatched her arm away and screamed at him. "You tell me what the hell. I'ma ask you one more fuckin' time, Jordan. What the hell is going on?"

Jordan was stuck. He knew she wasn't buying it. He thought that if he stuck to the lie long enough, no matter how weak it was, she'd give in and just believe him. He didn't expect her to go Carrie on him and try to set the place on fire. He walked over to the sofa and slumped down on the scorched blanket.

"You're little entry wasn't made up, was it?" Jada challenged from across the room.

Jordan shook his head no.

Jada crossed her arms. "You've been messing with someone else," she stated rather than asked.

Jordan shook his head again. "I've only been talking to her. I ain't fucked nobody. I haven't gone to see her. Nothing. Just talking."

"I read your words, Jordan. You marveled on and on about how beautiful this woman is, how good you feel with her. All while your pregnant wife walks around here taking care of your sorry ass and nurturing your unborn kid. What the fuck is that?"

"It was a stupid thing," he admitted. "It was stupid and thoughtless. But, baby, I swear it means nothing. All I want is you."

"All you want is me, huh?" she asked sarcastically.

"Yes, bae. I love you. You know I love you. There's no other choice here other than you. You're all I want."

Jada shook her head. "You stole my choice," she said softly feeling her eyes fill up. "I wanted to be married to a man that I felt would always protect me and love me, causing me no pain . . . Instead, you've got me married to a man who won't hesitate to lie to me. Why should I believe anything you ever say?"

Jordan shrugged his shoulders. "I don't know what you want me to say, babe. I'm telling you the truth. I'm coming clean here."

"Clean, my ass. Look how many times you lied. And you're still not being completely honest."

Jordan stared at the floor. *Damned if I do, damned if I don't,* he thought to himself. Now it was probably best to just remain quiet. Anything else he said would only be turned against him.

"We're broken, Jordan," Jada said after a long pregnant pause. "We're broken, and I don't know how we can ever be fixed."

Jada disappeared into the bedroom closing the door behind her. Jordan exhaled. He was glad that Tony hadn't come in to witness this psychotic scene. He knew that Jada was a force to be reckoned with, but this was the first time that he'd seen how crazy she could get. He knew that she was hurting, and it hurt him that he was the cause of her pain, but how could he tell his wife that their marriage had changed the moment she discovered she was with child? Sighing, he rose from the floor and blew out the candles. So much for the romantic mood he thought that she was setting. Jordan looked over at his blanket and pillow lying on the sofa. Apparently this was going to be his home for however long it took to get back in Jada's good graces.

Chapter 64

Corey

"On the charges of first-degree murder, we, the jury, find Corey Polk not guilty. On the charges of conspiracy to commit murder, we, the jury, find Corey Polk not guilty."

A mixture of emotions ran rampant through the courtroom as the juror issued the verdict. The mother and uncle of Montae Stokes were livid. They had been certain that justice was going to be served, but yet, they'd just heard the worst news ever since learning about Montae's death. Some concerned citizens who were also in attendance hoped to hear a guilty verdict but were surprised to hear that things had turned around in Corey's favor. They now feared that their neighborhood would once again be taken over by Corey's team. In Corey's absence, the hustle lessened but hadn't completely stopped.

Corey was elated to hear the verdict. His dick of an attorney had been right after all. He was about to be a free man. It was time to handle a lot of things that couldn't have been done successfully while he was in jail. The citizens had a right to attribute the change in their community to Corey's absence, but what they didn't understand was why. Although Corey's right hand was still sending out runners, they had to do this on a smaller scale due to the lack of money to invest in the business, thanks to the dudes that had robbed Stephanie.

At the back of the courtroom sat a man that no one recognized. They shouldn't have. He was as nondescript and unnoticeable as they come. He had a vested interest in the outcome of this case being that the dope Corey was pushing massive amounts of hailed from his family. The Black Dope

Mafia was hitting Atlanta hard, and Corey was a key player in getting things moving. BDM originated in New York around the time that the Junior Black Mafia was nearing the end of its reign in Philly being the feds stepped in and indicted their founders and key runners. In an effort to take over the Eastern drug game, BDM was steadily working to build powerful hubs in Atlanta, Florida, and New Jersey. Founded by Thomas "Tommy" Castello, the organization was making moves and putting out prime product with direct imports from authentic cartels in the heart of Bolivia. No one had purer cocaine than Tommy was bringing in to the States, and the dealers were taking notice. The problem with that was that Emilio Martinez, a rival kingpin, was trying his best to make his mark in the city and make BDM a thing of the past. Even worse, the Drug Enforcement Administration was paying attention as well and with BDM's entrance into Atlanta, the GBI was conspiring with the DEA to bring the organization down.

Johnny "Knuckles" Lyles was sitting in the courtroom taking in the entire experience so that he could carry the information back to Tommy. They were a private group. They tried their best not to have their faces out and about too much, but today was a big day. They needed to know how to deal with Corey and what moves to make next. Thanks to his fallacy in getting rid of Montae Stokes, a punk runner who was moving for Emilio Martinez, the feds were looking at them harder. Given the way Corey had botched up the job by leaving behind evidence, the heat was on. They needed to ensure that Corey wasn't going to talk, locked up or not. And now that they'd lost their key witness, BDM feared that the feds would go harder at trying to pin an indictment on any other players. Corey could be the fuckup in their plan.

Now that Knuckles knew that Corey was getting out, things needed to be done, discussions needed to be had, and moves needed to be made. As the trial proceeded with the formalities to adjourn all parties, Knuckles rose and made his way quietly out of the courtroom. There was no need to communicate with Corey with so many eyes and ears around. He knew where to find him, and he knew when would be best. He just hoped that things would go smoothly and that any further bloodshed could be spared. Corey was a thirsty kid, and he possessed great potential, but Knuckles had no problem eliminating him if his association with BDM continued to be problematic.

"How's it feel to be a free man?" Phelps asked, biting into an apple.

Corey had just walked out of the back doors of the jail after being processed out. Breathing in the crisp fall afternoon air made him grateful for every moment spent outside of the stale, stifled atmosphere of the Fulton County Jail.

"Feels like I need a decent meal, a blunt, and some head," Corey said honestly. "If you can't help me with that, then we best be parting ways now."

"Can I drop you somewhere?"

Corey shot him an astonished look. Where the hell did he think that he was going to drop him off to? He didn't want anyone in the streets catching him with dude. Everything he needed to do he needed to ride solo. Corey peered down the street and noticed an old-school Mustang idling. He knew that Mustang.

"I'm straight," Corey told Phelps. "Anything else I need to know?"

"Yep. Don't leave the country."

"What the fuck?" Corey wasn't in the mood for fuckery.

"Don't leave the country. You're exonerated of that murder charge, but you're going to be tried for possession with the intent to distribute. Lucky for you the judge allowed us to post bail."

Corey shook his head. His troubles never seemed to end. "Yeah, so when that happens get at me. I'm not leaving the country or the state so you can relax."

"I'll be in touch," Phelps said.

Corey rolled his eyes and waved him off. "Yeah. Later." He looked at him and waited for the man to catch a clue.

Phelps raised his eyebrows and pursed his lips in an "excuse me" manner before nodding his head and taking off toward his modest Toyota Camry. Corey shook his head as he watched the man pull off. *Where the fuck did he think he was taking me in his wife's car?* Corey thought. Putting his hands in his pockets and surveying his environment without appearing too paranoid, he hurriedly opened the passenger door and slid into the awaiting Mustang. The moment the door closed the Mustang peeled off.

"Where to?" Antonio asked as the jail grew smaller in his rearview.

"My mom's house. I need some food and a long fuckin' shower," Corey responded. "Put ya' ear to the ground and find out where them muthafuckers hiding at. Somebody's gon' answer for the shit that's gone down. What your stash looking like?"

"Man, we dry as hell, bruh. Not one bit of powder. Got that mid running all day but powder is a no-go. You know only you got the line to the connect," Antonio said sarcastically.

Corey nodded. He wasn't so sure that the connect was going to want to fuck with him after the way things went down. For the life of him he couldn't figure out why the hell Stephanie threw Montae's wallet out and how the fuck the feds were able to find it in the public Dumpster she'd put it in. What he did know was that the BDM, the connect that he answered to, was going to feel some kind of way about the ceasing of dope from his stash house and the money that was taken from Stephanie. Some of it was his, but most of it was owed to BDM for fronting him with the dope he'd been putting out at the time. Tommy Castello had trusted him and now because of his dead baby mama's futile attempt to help him and his inability to do a proper job of getting rid of Montae, Corey knew that he was going to have to come up with something to appease BDM. In the meantime, he needed to make sure that he put the word out that his family wasn't to be fucked with. There was only one way to do that.

"I need a new phone and some steel by tomorrow," Corey ordered.

Antonio nodded. "I got you. You already know."

Corey looked out of the window as they rode through the familiar streets of the neighborhood he ran. *I'm home, niggas*, he thought to himself as they passed down Memorial Drive. *Bring it!* Thinking about the fact that he wasn't returning home to Stephanie made his blood boil. The streets were about to be live. Corey was ready for war.

Chapter 65

Candace

The phone rang three times before going to voice mail. This was the seventh time she'd called him today. It was just like him to go silent and be MIA the moment she truly needed him. Candace wanted to kick herself for her moment of weakness weeks ago. She should have never let him into the house, much less into her body. She cursed his sexy lips, talented tongue, and probing hands. The man was definitely bad for her.

"Khalil, it's me again," she said to his voice mail. "I really need you to call me back. Or if you want to stick to the script and do what you usually do, can you just pop up over here and this time bring some diapers with you? Zoe's running out, and I don't get paid until the end of next week. Please." She disconnected the call and tossed the phone onto the bed.

She hated having to ask him for anything, but he was Zoe's dad. The least he could do was pitch in on the diapers. But, no, even that was too much for him to be bothered with. She wished that she could pick up the phone to call his other baby mamas and ask them how they dealt with his trifling ass because it was clear to her that she was getting nowhere fast with him. Maybe she should just start demanding cash from him whenever he had the nerve to do a drive-by. At least then she'd have a reserve for when times were hard. Now that she had to cover her own expenses, including childcare for Zoe, which wasn't cheap, she had to be more and more creative with stretching her dollars. It didn't help that she was putting more money toward gas these days with her frequent trips to Snellville to pick up Rico. It was all starting to become a bit too much. She prayed for the day that her boyfriend would find a job so that he could do what a man was supposed to do and help his woman.

Her phone rang, and she dove for it instantly. Thinking that it was Khalil finally calling back she pressed the talk button without paying any attention to the caller ID. "Hello? Hi."

"I'm trying to reach Candace Lawson," the unfamiliar male voice announced.

Standing at the foot of her bed Candace pulled the phone away from her ear to survey the number. It was the number she'd been dodging for the last couple of days because she had no clue who it was. How could she have made the mistake of answering now?

"This is she," Candace responded slowly.

"This is Agent Wilbur from the GBI."

Candace's heart felt as if it had plummeted into her stomach. She took a seat on the edge of the bed and was grateful that Zoe was peacefully napping. She knew that this phone call was going to have the potential to be unnerving. "How can I help you, sir?"

"We're calling to do a follow-up with you."

"Why? I told you all that I possibly could remember. There's nothing else to tell."

"Are you aware that Corey Polk has been freed?"

Candace was genuinely surprised. She hadn't been watching the news lately and none of the girls had called to tell her anything. But then again, Corey's affairs had nothing to do with her. She wasn't his girlfriend. "I didn't know, but what difference should that make to me?"

"I'm very clear on how street violence works, Ms. Lawson. I assume that you're not ignorant of it yourself. If Corey is half of the thug the streets make him out to be, then the death of his girlfriend isn't going to be something he takes lightly."

"So?" Candace still had no clue what any of this had to do with her.

"So he's going to be looking for some of the same people we're looking for. I need you to think long and hard. Is there anything that you may have forgotten or overlooked when you first told us your account of how the incident happened?"

Candace was silent for a moment. She hated being forced to relive that moment, especially when it already came back to her so frequently to begin with. "No," she said. "There's nothing else."

"Nothing specific about the car the perps were in? No names mentioned?"

"Nothing!" Candace snapped.

"Okay. Well, what about your relationship with Corey?"

This was getting a little too personal to her. "I don't have a relationship with him."

"But you'd showed up at the apartment to see him, correct? Not the victim."

"Right, yes. But I don't have a relationship with him . . . It's . . . It's complicated."

"Complicated? Hmmm . . . During any of your visits with Mr. Polk do you recall having met any older guys that may have been said to be a part of an affiliation?"

"Huh?"

Agent Wilbur took a deep breath over the phone. It pained him to have to talk to these young girls who acted like they knew nothing when it came to their street punk boyfriends. Their little acts didn't faze him one bit. "Has he ever introduced you to any of his colleagues?"

"No, of course not. Why would he do that? I wasn't his girlfriend."

"If we showed you a series of pictures would you be able to identify anyone that you may have seen Mr. Polk with?"

"No," she said annoyed. "I can't because I've never seen him with anyone. Again, Corey wasn't my boyfriend, Mr. Wilbur."

"Agent Wilbur," he corrected her. "I hope I haven't caught you at an inconvenient time, Mrs. Lawson. We're just trying to tie up some loose ends and put away anyone that was involved in the incident and anyone that may be doing any illegal trafficking. You're a big help to us."

Candace wasn't falling for the way the investigator was trying to butter her up. "There's never really a convenient time to discuss this." Her nerves were getting the best of her as her hand shook while holding the phone to her ear. "And for the love of Jehovah, please, please, please, stop referring to my friend as the victim and her death as the incident. I don't know what else you want from me, Agent Wilbur, but I've told you everything that I possibly could. There's nothing left. Now if you don't mind I have an infant I need to tend to."

"Certainly, ma'am. We'll be in touch."

Candace hung up without saying good-bye. *I really wish that you wouldn't,* she thought as she looked over at Zoe who was now beginning to stir. It was time for her to be changed and fed. Candace laid the phone on her bed and walked over to the changing table where she kept the pack of diapers. She reached inside and pulled out a diaper, realizing that the pack was now empty. She was sure she had at least three more to get through the afternoon. Taking a deep breath, she did exactly what she didn't want to do. Knowing that she couldn't call her parents and ask for anything she dialed the only other number that she knew she'd get a response from and help without hesitation. The phone rang twice before there was an answer.

"Hello?"

"Jada, it's Candace. I need a favor, hon."

Chapter 66

Alex

Alex had been hanging with Jada when she mentioned that she had to make a stop real quick by Candace's house. They were dropping off a case of diapers. Alex didn't mind because she'd wanted to give Candace her two cents about her boyfriend ever since the day that he wandered into the Hibachi Grill with his pants sagging, looking like a fashion misfit. Her girl needed to hear some unfiltered truth so that she could hurry up and kick ole boy to the curb before either of their feelings got too invested in whatever it was they were doing.

"What's up, chicks?" Candace greeted them at the door. It was always good to see her girls, even when it was in a time of despair.

Jada hugged Candace and carried the case of Pampers inside the cozy apartment. "I'ma go put this in the back, okay. The baby's awake?"

"Yeah, she is," Candace answered hugging Alex and closing the door. "What's up, booskie?"

Alex smiled. "What's up with you, honey?"

Candace shook her head. "You wouldn't believe the kind of day I've been having. It's rough right now, girlie. I can't even lie."

Alex walked over to the couch and took a seat. "Well, I've been meaning to get up with you for a minute now."

"About what?" Candace said sitting in her only armchair.

Jada entered the room with Zoe in hand. She was in awe of how adorable the little girl was. "There's your mommy. There's your mommy right over there," she said to a fuzzy Zoe. "Is she hungry?" Jada asked Candace.

Candace shrugged. "I swear she eats like a grown man. I just gave her a bottle less than two hours ago."

Jada paced the living room and walked the baby in an effort to calm her down.

Alex got back to the conversation at hand. "So, um, about your dude."

Candace immediately became defensive. "What about him?"

"How deep into this thing are you?"

"Why?" Candace crossed her arms.

"Because you need to save yourself while you can, honey. One look at him, and I knew that he was not the man for you."

"And what makes you such an expert on who's right and wrong for me? Hell, up until earlier this year you couldn't even see the good man standing right in your face."

Jada looked over at the two and wondered where the hell the conversation was going. She could feel the hostility growing in the room.

"Say what you want but I'm telling you that ya' boy ain't no good for you, friend."

"Well, thank you for your concern, but no one asked you for your opinion."

"Isn't that why you wanted us to meet him?" Alex asked.

"No. I wanted you to meet him because he's my man, and as my friends, I thought y'all should know him. But I'm grown, boo-boo. I don't need either of your approval."

"Hey!" Jada exclaimed feeling insulted. "Don't put me in this. I didn't even venture my opinion."

Candace waved her off. "Knowing you, it was coming sooner or later."

"You're tripping," Alex commented.

Candace rose from her seat and placed her hands on her hips. "No, boo. *You* trippin'. Please don't run up in my house thinking you're going to school me about my man. You ain't never got nothing nice to say about anybody's relationship. You don't never like nobody's boo thang, but the second you hook up with someone, your head's all up their ass and in their pockets that you don't see them for the jerks they really are. Hell, I'm surprised that Clay is even with your ass. You're about as deep as a damn puddle of water."

"Candace!" Jada called out walking over with the baby. "What the hell?" She had no clue that today's visit was going to turn so ugly.

Alex rose from the couch. "Nuh-uh, Jada. Let her speak her mind. Let her get it all out because the truth of the matter is that she's jealous. Li'l miss thing out here fronting like she got her shit altogether when she knows that it's killing her that she's somebody's tired ol' baby mama and the only dude she could pull is a lame with no skills, no job, and no business about himself. That puddle of water, boo, is much like your boyfriend. Useless and will evaporate as soon as the sun shines, just like all the other dudes you've been with. He'll be gone when he's done fuckin' with you."

"No," Jada intervened. "No, we're not going to do this and certainly not in front of Itty Bitty."

"Give me my baby," Candace demanded.

"What?" Jada asked. She didn't understand why Candace was catching an attitude with her.

"I said give me my baby, please."

Jada handed Zoe over carefully, then looked at Alex accusingly.

"Thank you for the diapers but I think it's time for y'all to go now," Candace stated.

Alex shook her head. "I'm just trying to help you, girl. I know what it's like to be stuck with a broke-ass dude who claims he's going to be the next Jay-Z. It isn't going to happen, Candace. That boy is going to use you until you have nothing left to give. You see, you don't even have money to get your kid some diapers." Alex knew that the last statement was a little below the belt, but she felt that Candace needed to hear the real right now. The last time they let a girlfriend get below their radar, she slipped into depression and addiction. Alex didn't want Candace to suffer any unnecessary hardships when all she had to do was just listen.

"Bye, ladies," Candace said turning away and heading to her bedroom. "Please let yourselves out."

Jada cut her eyes at Alex. "You just *had* to go there, *didn't* you?"

"What? You know I'm a straight shooter, friend."

"A little tact would have been nice. I get what you were trying to do, but your delivery just then . . ." Jada shook her head and headed for the door as her words trailed off. "Let's just go before you do any more damage."

"If we're friends I should be able to tell my homegirl the truth, right?" Alex asked, following her friend to the door.

Chapter 67

Clay

Clay tapped his foot lightly as he sat on the couch waiting for Alex. She'd promised him that she'd be home in time for them to make it to his supervisor's birthday dinner. Alex hadn't understood why he wanted to hang out with any of his coworkers after hours and had shown resistance against going to the party to begin with. Clay had explained to her that Anthony was more than just his supervisor, he was his mentor. Clay's job as an entry-level accountant was lucrative, but he wanted more: more money, more control over how he made his money, and a greater position at a higher-grossing company. He was certain that if he learned all that he could from people like Anthony, who had his own consulting firm on the side, he'd get where he wanted to be. That type of rapport could only be built by networking outside of the office.

Clay looked at his watch. They were already thirty minutes late. He considered leaving her a note and going on to the party without her, but the gentleman in him just couldn't leave her behind. He wished that she'd give him half of the consideration he gave her. He considered calling her phone but didn't feel it was necessary to remind an adult of where they were supposed to be and when. Besides, he'd texted her once already asking about her ETA and had gotten no response.

His stomach growled as he sat in the quiet of their apartment. There was no use trolling through the cabinets or refrigerator. There was nothing there to eat because he hadn't gone grocery shopping. He'd purposefully refrained from shopping the week prior because it was a task that Alex rarely ever did unless he dragged her along with him. He wanted to see how long she'd go with nothing in the house before finally getting off of her ass and going to the store. He loved her, but Clay couldn't believe how soiled his little diva truly was. He took some responsibility in that fact as he remembered the numerous times he'd jump to her aid the moment she requested the slightest thing. He'd done it because he was in love with her. Now he was trying to help her gain a sense of independence because he loved her and wanted her to be a responsible person for herself and for the sake of their relationship.

No longer able to take it Clay rose from the couch and grabbed his blazer. He'd given Anthony his word, and there was no way that he was going to renege on it because of someone else, even if it was the love of his life. He headed for the door and was nearly knocked over backward as Alex came bolting in.

"Hey, precious! I know, I know, I know." She blew him kisses as she threw her purse on the sofa and ran toward their room. "Let me just slip into my black dress and we can go!" she called over her shoulder.

Clay stared into thin air. *This woman drives me nuts*, he thought as he closed the door quietly. He leaned up against it and crossed his arms. He wondered how long he was going to have to wait for her to get herself together. Much to his surprise she ran right back out with her black dress slipping down her shoulder, heels stuck under her arm, and body leaning slightly to the left as she tried to put in a silver earring.

She walked over and turned her back to him. "Zip me, please."

Clay complied silently.

"Ugh." She dropped her shoes to the ground and slipped her feet into them as she struggled with the clasp of her other earring. "Sorry it took so long. I didn't know that we were going to stop by Candace's house, and then that turned into a big thing. You know, she had the nerve to catch an attitude with me because I told her that her new dude was not a good look. I mean, come on, precious. You saw that dude. He was not Candace material at all. Talkin' 'bout he's a rapper. He probably can't even read yet, alone come up with some lyrics.

And did you see how Candace whipped out her card and paid for both of them at dinner? Who does that?"

Alex was talking sixty miles per hour as Clay continued to stand in front of the door with his arms crossed, waiting. He was fuming on the inside, but Alex had yet to realize that anything was wrong. She checked her reflection in the mirror that hung on the back wall of the living room and pinned her hair up into a loose yet fashionable ball. She grabbed her purse from the sofa and headed toward the door, finally ready to head out.

"Okay, I'm ready," she said approaching Clay who was not budging. She stared at him blankly wondering what his problem was. "Come on, precious. We're gonna be late."

He smiled at her. "We're *already* late. We were late nearly an hour ago before you decided to put in an appearance."

Alex touched his face lightly and gave him her sincerest pouty face and innocent tone. "I said I was sorry. It was beyond my control, precious. Jada was driving. I was just riding."

"You could have let her know that you had somewhere else to be."

"What difference does it make?" Alex asked becoming annoyed with the discussion. "I'm here now. We're both dressed. Let's just go."

Clay was done. It was one thing for her to be inconsiderate. It was another thing for her to be inconsiderate *and* unapologetic about it. Her attitude was turning him off. Sure she'd said, "I'm sorry," but her tone and attitude belied her words.

"How about I go and you stay?" Clay commented coolly.

"*Excuse* me?" Alex asked with her hands on her hips.

"I'm just saying, you didn't really want to go in the first place, and I don't want you to do anything you don't want to do."

"But I rushed home and got dressed. Now all of a sudden it's all good if I don't go? You're tripping."

"No, I'm tired," he corrected her. "Tired of trying to redirect you."

"*Excuse* you! I'm not your child, precious. I don't need redirecting."

"Yeah. Well, you can just spend the evening at home with the person you care most about. You. I'm sure that'll make you happy." Clay turned around, opened the door, and then let himself out.

Seasons Lounge was filled to capacity. Anthony and his wife had gone all the way out to make the man's fortieth birthday celebration spectacular. Drinks were flowing, food was set out on platters in abundance, the music was easygoing and not too loud or rowdy, and beautiful women were everywhere. Any heterosexual man with class and a healthy sex drive would have been in seventh heaven, but Clay was miserable. Despite all of the buzz around him, all he could focus on was the fact that Alex was not giggling beside him.

"Clay! My man!" Anthony was on his third Cîroc on ice and was feeling no pain. He gave Clay dap for the second time that evening and frowned at him. "Didn't anybody tell you that this is a party?"

"Yeah, man. It's cool," Clay responded.

"Then why you over here looking like you 'bout to cry?" Anthony looked around. "Where's your lady?"

"She didn't come," Clay said taking a swig of the rum and Coke he'd been nursing for the last half hour.

"Y'all having problems?"

Now was not the time to talk about his relationship issues. He smiled at his mentor. "Nah, man. Why you over here worried about me and mine when it's your birthday? You should be standing on a table somewhere going buck wild."

"Man, when you get as old as me, 'bout the only thing you really wanna do on your birthday is have a good drink, a good meal, a good fuck, then be left the hell alone."

Clay laughed. It was the first time he'd heard his boss speak so candidly.

"Look, I got a lead on something I think you'll be interested in," Anthony said changing the subject briefly.

The DJ turned the track up as 50 Cent belted out the lyrics to "It's Your Birthday."

Clay leaned into Anthony in an effort to hear him better. "What's that?"

"Come . . . Monday . . . opportunity." Only every other word of Anthony's statement was audible to Clay over the blasting from the sound system. Anthony patted him on the back. "I got you." The man hurried off with his glass raised in the air.

Clay set his nearly empty glass on the counter and mindlessly watched as Anthony and his wife danced their hearts out. Others joined them on the dance floor seemingly without a care in the world. Clay's mind was elsewhere. He was intrigued by the opportunity that Anthony had mentioned and couldn't wait for Monday morning to roll around.

"Excuse me?" A sultry voice was in his ear as a beautiful, curvy, Dominican woman dressed in a revealing white Bodycon dress placed her left hand on his shoulder. "You look like you could use a friend."

His eyes tried to remain trained on her face but the exposure of her well-endowed cleavage was begging for attention. "Is that right?"

She smiled and caressed the side of his face gently. "Um-hum."

"And you want to be my friend?"

"If that's okay with you." She removed her hand. "Please forgive me if I'm a bit aggressive, but I'm the kind of person that sees what she wants and goes for it."

"Sounds like my kind of person."

She moved in closer and lowered her eyes seductively. "I was hoping you'd say that. You wanna dance?"

The woman's body was calling to him, but Clay wasn't down to give into temptation. As much as he was upset with Alex, he wasn't ready to throw away what had taken forever for them to start building. He smiled politely at the woman and rose from his seat. "Actually, I was just about to go."

She made a face indicating that she could barely hear him.

He leaned into her. "I'm leaving but thanks anyway," he said a little louder.

"Not before we get the chance to know one another."

"I'm sorry, pretty lady. You have a good evening." He moved to walk away.

The exotic beauty grabbed his hand and whispered into his ear. "You don't even wanna know my name?"

Clay laughed nervously as the sweet smell of the woman's perfume became intoxicating. "I don't really want to waste either of our time."

She placed her arms around his neck, and for the first time he could smell the alcohol on her breath. It was amazing what liquid courage could do. It clearly had provoked this very attractive woman to be so unattractively forward with a complete stranger. Any other guy would have taken her to the lounge's restroom and given her exactly what she was aiming for, not caring to know her name at all. Before Clay could pull the inebriated woman off of him without embarrassing her completely she forced her lips against his and tried with all of her might to slip her probing tongue past his lips while reaching down to grab his dick with her left hand. Others around them only thought they were an open freaky couple living in the moment. It was a moment that was going to last with Clay forever.

"So *this* is why you wanted to leave me at home?" Her voice was loud, shrill, and unmistakable over the loud music.

Time felt like it froze for a moment as Clay turned and came eye to eye with Alex. The chick hanging from him stood there with one arm still around his neck looking at Alex as if she was confused. Alex shot the chick a nasty look and crossed her arms in classic ghetto girl fashion.

"Is there a problem?" the beautiful stranger asked Alex.

"Uhhh . . . yes, ho. And *you* would be the problem," Alex responded.

Clay had never seen her get so turned up. He knew that it was time for them to get out of there now before an ugly scene ensued. He untwined himself from the other woman and stepped up to Alex holding out his hands. "Babe, calm down. Before you go off—"

"Before I go off you might want to tell me who the hell this bitch is holding your dick in her hand in the middle of this bar."

"Watch your mouth," Clay stated.

"Bitch?" the drunken woman piped up. "Oh, honey, trust me . . . You don't want none of these."

"You right, and neither does my man, so you can get to steppin'," Alex retorted smirking at the other woman.

The drunken bombshell eyed Clay as if she expected him to come to her defense. When he didn't she sucked her teeth and shook her head. "Forget both of you. I can have any man in this bar. I was just trying to make your day," she said to Clay.

"He doesn't need you to make his day," Alex retorted.

"Humph. Judging by the way his dick jumped when I touched him, he obviously did."

"What?" Alex asked, hyped up. She looked at Clay. "What the fuck did she just say to me? Honey, you don't know me. Please don't let the bourgeoisie fool you. I will mop the floor with your cheap-ass mail order dress on. Thirsty bitch!"

Clay grabbed Alex's arm. It was time to go. "Come on, man. This isn't the place for all that."

"Yeah, get out of here, you low-budget-model skank," the woman retorted. She laughed and turned toward the bar to signal the bartender for yet another cocktail.

Alex snatched away from Clay, grabbed his glass of rum and Coke from the counter, and tossed the contents onto the side of the woman's face, wetting her hair and staining her white dress. The crowd was now in an uproar, and they were the center of attention.

"You stupid bitch!" the woman called out turning around to swing on Alex who ducked just in time for the chick's mediocre punch to land upon Clay's jaw as he tried to pull Alex away yet again.

"Damn it!" he exclaimed.

Security was quick on the scene. Two big burly men approached the bar. One was holding on to the Dominican troublemaker and the other was standing before Clay and Alex.

"Okay, you two gotta go," the officer said in a brisk manner.

"We're leaving, sir," Clay stated, grabbing Alex's hand and heading toward the door. He was embarrassed beyond belief. He knew that on Monday he was going to have to explain to his supervisor why his girl had turned up and showed out.

Once they hit the pavement Alex snatched her hand away from Clay and slapped him upside his head with her clutch bag. "You dog!"

Clay shrugged it off and looked around at the line of folks waiting to get into the lounge as they checked out the scene Alex was causing. "Chill out and let's go to the car," he told her.

"No! I can't believe you, Clay. You're no different from any of the other trifling dirty dogs. Why don't you go find your li'l girlfriend and take her ass home."

"You're acting crazy. I don't even know that girl."

"Yeah? Well, she was sho' familiar with you with her tongue all down ya' throat and your junk all in her hand. What the hell was that?"

"That was a misunderstanding that I would have explained to you if you'd given me a chance."

"Right. I know what I saw."

"Can we go home, please?" Clay was over making a spectacle of themselves in public. This shit was for the birds.

"You go. I'm done with you."

"Alex, come on," Clay tried to appeal to her despite her edginess. "Let's just go home and talk about this."

Black tears ran down her cheek. "Fuck you, Clay. Fuck you and the bitch you left me at home for." She turned away and walked in the opposite direction.

Clay didn't know where she was going, but he wasn't about to chase her. The woman he loved should have listened to him and believed him. He was bending over backward to be the man that Alex needed, and she was giving him opposition at every turn. Tonight she was just going to have to be mad because he wasn't about to kiss her ass. Sadly, he turned in the direction of his car and prayed that she made her way home soon and safely.

Chapter 68

Miranda

"You said something that you were very passionate about," Doctor Dunham stated. "You said that they don't understand. Who is the 'they' that you were referring to?"

It was yet another tedious one-on-one session in Dunham's office. For the last couple of days Miranda had been confined for attacking Missy. During that time Miranda had cried herself to sleep, cried herself awake, and cried to be let out. She was going crazy. She was a prisoner inside of her own mind of hurtful memories and painful truths. It didn't help matters much that once she was able to return to the common area, she'd seen a news update stating that Corey was found not guilty for the murder of Montae Stokes. She'd figured that that was going to happen considering the fact that the witness the state claimed to have had disappeared. Now she wondered how long it would be before Corey figured out what happened and if he was going to come for her once he did. But it didn't matter. He could kill her if he wanted to. Her spirit had died a long time ago. Her body might as well follow suit.

Five Months Earlier

Now that she'd fucked them by providing the police with the slightest bit of evidence against Corey, it was time to take things one step further. The GBI had made no secret about the fact that they were looking for information about the murder of Montae. She'd given them the circumstantial tie to Corey, now she needed to make it stick. She sat in the middle of her living room holding her cell phone in her hand and getting high off of some weak-ass product she'd copped from a dude in Decatur. She'd been stalking the stash house for a minute, and the guy must have been watching her because he approached her with an offer that she couldn't refuse. He'd given her exactly what she'd been begging Corey and his boys to give her. Or so she thought. The feeling and taste of the dope was nothing like what Corey provided. It pissed her off even more that he'd forced her to run to some knockoff dealer instead of just doing his job.

Infuriated, she looked down at the phone and pressed talk to dial the number she'd pressed in nearly twenty minutes ago. The line rang twice before an unenthused female voice greeted her.

"GBI hotline. How can I help you?"

"I need to speak to Agent Wilbur," Miranda said covering the phone up with her T-shirt to try to muffle the sound of her voice. "I needa talk to him right now about Montae Stokes and Corey Polk."

"Ma'am, are you calling to provide a tip?"

"Better than that, honey. I'm calling to offer to be their star witness. But I needa talk to Wilbur. That's the only person I can talk to."

The attendant wasted no time tracking down the agent and patching him through. This was a high-profile case for whatever the reason and Miranda knew that they were going to be dying to hear what she had to say. That was the thing. She wasn't exactly sure what she was going to say, but she sure hoped that they bought it enough to act on it.

"Agent Wilbur," a deep male voice boomed on the line. "Who am I speaking with?"

"No names," Miranda said getting a little nervous.

"Ma'am, I was told that you had information about the Stokes murder. You are aware that this is a serious matter?"

Miranda didn't like the way that he was talking down to her. "Of course I'm aware. I called you, remember? I'm down to tell you whatever you need to know, but not before I know that I'm going to be safe when I do so. I don't want Corey coming back for me."

"Ma'am, I can assure you that once we convict Polk and his associates you won't ever have to worry about him *again. So, you're telling me you have solid proof that Polk murdered Stokes?"*

Miranda was a little caught off guard. Who the hell are Corey's associates? *she wondered.* "Um, something like that. I saw him do it with my own two eyes. I saw him kill that man at that club in the DEC." Miranda could hear the man murmur "Yes" under his breath.

"So you're an eyewitness? I need you to tell me exactly what happened."

"I was in the back. Corey came in with some other dude and shot him. Then they drug him out the back door of the club so nobody could see them on the street, and I ran out the front while they were moving the body."

"And you're willing to do a recorded and written statement, as well as testify?"

This lie was going on forever. "Yes, yes. Of course."

"May I have your name now, please?"

She considered giving him a fake name but didn't feel like committing to it. "I'd rather remain anonymous."

"If you're going to testify, you can't be anonymous. That's very difficult."

"Look, I have to look out for me here—"

"Okay, okay . . . I understand . . . The people we're dealing with here are very powerful so you're perfectly valid in wanting to maintain some anonymity."

Miranda was baffled. She couldn't understand for the life of her why the agent felt that Corey and his little street team were such a force.

"Tell you what, you give me your word that you'll have yourself in my office tomorrow afternoon and I'll make sure that we take every precaution in keeping you safe. Deal?"

"Deal." Miranda wasn't really sure what was going to happen now. "But in the meantime will he stay on the street?"

"Ma'am, now that we have you on our team and something tangible with Polk's prints on it we're going to bring him right on in. We can detain him for a while until we get your official statement, and then an indictment will certainly follow from there."

Miranda was feeling empowered. Corey was about to be arrested, and he wasn't going to know what hit him. Even if they only held him for a short while Miranda felt that she'd done something major. Payback's a bitch, she thought, imagining how Stephanie would lose her mind the moment she learned that her man was in jail.

"So you'll come in tomorrow afternoon?" Agent Wilbur asked.

Miranda's phone buzzed in her ear. She looked at the screen noticing that she had a text message from Jada. Quickly she read the message: Are you coming to dinner tomorrow night, chica? Get back to me. Get back to me. *Miranda had no intentions of going to that damn dinner. She was sure that it was nothing more than an intervention because Stephanie couldn't hold water. Truth be told she was surprised that the girls hadn't been swarming around shortly after her encounter with Stephanie at the trap. But it was just like Jada to put together some organized sit-down to try to tell her about herself. They could all kiss her ass.*

"Ma'am? Hello, ma'am? Are you there?" Agent Wilbur asked frantically, worried that he'd lost her.

"Yes, yes, of course," Miranda said laying out a line of her subpar coke, anxious to get the pig off of her phone. "Tomorrow midafternoon. Ask for you, right?"

"Yes, ma'am. Do you need the address?"

"No, I'm good. See you tomorrow." She ended the call and set the phone on the floor beside her. She snickered, knowing that she had no intention of ever visiting the GBI building. She was just ready to sit back and watch the news awaiting word that Corey had been picked up. She didn't even plan to pick up the phone to place a return call to the agent to advise that she wasn't coming. They'd figure that out soon enough.

Miranda's phone call did more than she'd ever intended for it to. Agent Wilbur was convinced in his belief that her testimony was exactly what they needed to bring Corey in and get to the heart of the BDM. The moment the GBI had learned that BDM was infiltrating Atlanta, Agent Wilbur was assigned to the case. The DEA was waiting to swoop in and put an end to the whole syndication of the organization.

Agent Wilbur was just concerned with keeping his territory clean of this type of criminal, poisonous activity, and having this indictment placed on his résumé so he could soon move up in rank.

Agent Wilbur wasted no time in getting on the phone and working his magic to secure an arrest warrant for Corey. He was itching to pick up the two-bit punk, and quickly. His energy was manic the moment he'd gotten off of the phone with his mystery witness.

"Hey, trace the number she called us from," he said to Royce, the agent beside him who was one of their information specialists.

Royce had been going through some computer files for another case he was assigned to but had been listening intently as Agent Wilbur got hyped over his conversation with the informant that had called in. He'd gathered just enough information from Wilbur's end of the conversation to know that this was about to be an open-and-shut quick conviction should the informant really waltz through their doors tomorrow with her detailed eyewitness account. Royce also knew the magnitude of the conviction and how it would be detrimental to BDM. He put his current project on hold and tapped into the agency's phone line to retrieve the last number Wilbur's line had been connected to before he'd called down for his warrant.

"No problem," Royce said cooperatively. "404-555-5111." He tapped his keyboard, surfed through some screens, and smiled victoriously as he found what he was looking for. "T-Mobile number registered to Miranda Wilson-Cox."

"My man!" Agent Wilbur said as he scribbled down the information. If she didn't come in as promised he was going to her. There was no way he was going to risk letting this conviction slip out of his grasp.

"Anytime," Royce said as Agent Wilbur walked away. Royce looked around to make sure that no one else on the floor was in close enough range to hear him. He pulled out his cell and dialed a familiar number. "Hey, it's Roy. You've got a major problem coming your way."

Current Day

Miranda rocked in her chair. Nothing she said and nothing she did ever seemed to work out right. Nothing she felt ever seemed to matter so she didn't see the point in discussing anything with anyone. But despite Miranda's disinterest in the program's mandated counseling, Doctor Dunham kept pressing. She could feel that the woman was about to break soon.

"There must be someone that you've always been able to count on," Dunham said. "Someone that's always been in your corner. There must be at least one person that you feel you can trust."

Miranda shook her head. How many times did she have to tell these people that in life you're all you really have? She strongly believed that no one could understand her and no one was ever really there for her. "No," she responded quietly. "No one."

Doctor Dunham was thankful just to hear the sound of her voice in comparison to the usual unproductive silence of her previous sessions. "When was the last time that you felt like someone was on your side, Miranda? When was the last time that you felt like someone cared about you?"

Miranda thought back. It had been an awfully long time, and her history was so filled with disappointment and pain that she could barely recall any positive moments. She closed her eyes and remembered that it had been Jada who was there in the hospital with her when Norris had beaten her. It had also been Jada who had found her in her apartment passed out from an overdose. But where had her friend been the whole time she was spiraling down the road of self-destruction?

"I had a friend," Miranda stated opening her eyes. "I had a friend that sat by my bedside when my husband beat me and when I'd nearly killed myself . . . Jada."

"Tell me more about Jada."

Miranda shrugged. "She's very ambitious. She's probably more focused than anyone I've ever known. She's having a baby. She always wanted to have a baby. Jada has this perfect life . . . a career, a husband who loves her, the baby she always wanted . . . no drama. She's so picture-perfect that it's like watching TV with her. It's hard walking in the shadows of a person so different from you."

"But she's been there for you," Doctor Dunham countered.

Miranda nodded slowly. "Every time things were at full mass . . . every time it could have ended for me."

"Well, that sounds like someone who loves you to me," Doctor Dunham stated. "But I'm curious as to why you originally said you *had* a friend instead of have."

"Junkies don't have friends," Miranda said with tears in her eyes. "Because no one wants to be associated with someone who's engaged in something they don't understand . . . something that scares them. I had a circle of friends that distanced themselves from me because they didn't understand."

Doctor Dunham tilted her head over in thought. "Hmm. Is that what happened, or do you think that perhaps you may have distanced yourself from your friends? Especially this one who seems to always be your saving grace?"

A tear fell from Miranda's right eye as she stared at the psychiatrist. "All the more reason for them to try harder to hold on. When you really love someone you don't turn your back on them, no matter what. You don't judge them, you don't ignore them, and you don't leave them to kill themself."

"You feel like Jada left you to kill yourself even though she was the one that got you to the hospital when you overdosed?"

"I feel like she wasn't there for a while before that moment. Saving me from me didn't fit into her picture-perfect life, I'm sure, not that I'm her responsibility or anything. Doctor Dunham, I've been killing myself for a minute now. It didn't just happen the night I passed out in the bathroom."

Chapter 69

Jordan

They went on for weeks, barely speaking and ignoring the issues that they were having. Home life was so hostile that Jordan didn't even want to go back after work each day. He lingered around the office as long as he could, doing meaningless research or paperwork just so that he could avoid having to sit in his living room while his wife lay on the cushiony bed in their bedroom pretending that he did not exist. Worst of all, he was horny. Although he knew he was the cause of his home being turned upside down he still felt that she owed it to him to forgive and forget. If anything, their current situation was making him want to reach out to any one of the several women he often chopped it up with on Facebook or via text.

"What are you still doing here?" Mona asked, poking her head into his office.

He looked up from his computer screen and smiled. He'd been trying his best to avoid her all day, especially considering the fact that his interaction with her was what had sparked the tension in his marriage.

"Messing around, wasting time," he told her honestly.

Mona entered the office with her long honey-blond Brazilian weave flowing freely down her back. She stood in front of his desk and smiled seductively. "You know there are other more fun ways to waste time, rather than sitting here playing on the company's Internet."

"Like what?" he asked feeding into her dirty talk.

"Like playing with something else."

"What you got for me to play with?"

She giggled. "Why you been on silent lately? You ain't hit me up or nothing."

"Close the door," he told her realizing that they were still at work.

Mona turned around and shut the door. For good measure she turned the lock before turning back around to face Jordan. "What's good?" she asked.

"You claim you are."

She giggled again. "I'm trying to tell ya', but you act like you don't really wanna find out."

He licked his lips. It had been so long since his dick had been touched by a hand that it wasn't his fault that he couldn't control the throbbing that was now occurring. He was already in the doghouse. If Jada assumed that he'd already fucked someone else, he might as well go ahead and do it. There was no sense in being blamed for something that hadn't happened.

Mona rounded the desk in slow, sexy strides. "So, what you down for?" she asked.

"Who was out there?" Jordan was down for whatever, but he didn't want to risk the chance of losing his job for a meaningless fuck.

"Jazzy J's show just started," Mona answered, moving to stand in front of Jordan as he turned his chair away from his desk. "All the other interns are gone for the day. It's quiet on the floor. Everyone's in the studio."

Jordan nodded. His body temperature increased as he reached out and grabbed her right breast through the soft fabric of her shirt. She moaned a little at his touch, giving him the courage to grab both of her breasts with his large hands. The young girl was thrilled by the fact that she was being lusted after by the popular afternoon show radio DJ. She reached over and unbuckled his jeans. Jordan lifted up a little and helped her to ease his jeans and boxers down. Mona lowered herself onto her knees and took his erection into her mouth without a word.

Jordan's eyes closed, and his head flew back to rest on the top of his office chair. The sensation felt so great that he felt as if he was going to bust one in her mouth immediately. Jada never gave him head like this, especially after becoming pregnant. Every little thing made her nauseous now, and he knew not to even ask her. Before the pregnancy she tried her best to do it whenever she felt in the mood to do so. It really wasn't her thing, but it was such a big thing to him. Jordan valued head over most other wifely duties. If he had a woman that was putting it down on a regular basis, like Mona was at this moment he would definitely feel like the man of his castle. He wouldn't have ever had a need to talk shit to the chicks he encountered online or flirted with around the office. He loved Jada, and she was a good, loving, and nurturing woman. She just wasn't the freak he needed in his life.

As Mona worked her jaw muscles and squeezed his balls gently, the tension built up greater. He reached for her head and pushed her down, encouraging her to take the dick all the way to the back of her throat. The sound of her gagging turned him on. His cell phone buzzed on his desk. He didn't give a damn who it was trying to get at him. He was on his way to a much-needed orgasm. He bucked a few times into the heated moisture of Mona's mouth and felt himself begin to erupt slowly at first, and then a series of sporadic involuntary jerking occurred as he released the evidence of his excitement into the girl's mouth.

Mona pulled away with come dripping from her lips. She smiled at him shyly as she wiped her mouth with her fingers. Jordan didn't smile back. He wasn't sure if the sight of her on her knees with his come all over her lips and fingertips turned him on or disgusted him. His phone buzzed again and he quickly grabbed it up. Guilt set in immediately once he saw that it was Jada that had been texting him. **Emergency**, her text read. Jordan took a deep breath. He knew that he was going to be in deep shit.

He raced to DeKalb Medical Hospital the moment he'd gotten off of the phone with his mother, Vivian Presley. By the time he'd gotten Mona out of his office and himself cleaned up he'd called his wife back but was surprised when her phone was answered by his mother. Vivian had informed her son that his wife was in the emergency room because of some pains she was having in her lower back and abdomen. The entire drive to the hospital had been nerve-racking for him.

All he could think about was how traumatic things were going to be if she lost the baby.

"I'm trying to find my wife, Jada Presley," Jordan said to the nurse sitting at the reception desk of the ER.

The woman nodded without speaking to him and checked the admissions database to see where his wife was. "Hmmm, she's no longer in the ER," she said. "She's been admitted and is in the main hospital on the third floor in room 320."

"The third floor?" Jordan asked.

"Yes, sir. Labor and delivery."

Jordan wanted to fall to the floor at that moment. Time stood still for a second. He wanted to cry out into the bubble of anguish that was clouding around him. This wasn't happening. Jada was only five months pregnant. There was no reason she should have been in the labor and delivery ward at this point in her pregnancy. At least there was no positive reason that he could think of.

Frantically, Jordan rounded the corner and walked the long hall toward the main hospital. He located the elevators and rode up to the third floor feeling nervous and shaky. He should have been home hours ago instead of sitting at the office avoiding his wife. He should have been right there with her instead of sitting in that office with his dick in Mona's mouth. How was he going to live with himself if something happened to his child or his wife when he'd been getting head by a woman that shouldn't have even been close enough to breathe on him?

He found room 320 and entered, fearing the worst. Jada was lying on her left side gripping the side of the bed and crying softly. His mother was sitting in a chair on the right side of the bed holding her hands together tightly. Even his sister, Ressie, was there, leaning over the right side of the bed rubbing Jada's back.

"There you are," Vivian said looking at her son with sullen eyes. "You okay?"

Jordan nodded, confused. "What's going on?"

"What's up, li'l bro?" Ressie asked, looking up at Jordan.

"Shit . . . wondering what's wrong with my wife." He walked over to the left side of the bed, kneeled down to be eye level with Jada, and rubbed her head. "Hey, babe."

"Your son is trying to come early," Vivian stated, watching her son interact with his wife. She knew this man, and she could read him well. Something was going on with him.

Jordan reached down and touched the side of Jada's belly feeling a bit of relief knowing that the baby was still inside of her. "Who told you you could do that, li'l man?" They'd learned the sex of the baby just a couple of weeks ago, and Jordan had been elated to know that he was having a son although the thought of parenthood still scared him.

Jada closed her eyes, not wanting to focus on his face as he kneeled before her pretending to be so attentive and caring. *Where the hell has he been when I'd originally texted him to say that something was wrong?* she wondered.

One of the machines beside her began to beep loudly as a long strip of paper continued to flow to the floor. Jordan looked up at it and knitted his eyebrows. Jada was also connected to another machine via a long tube that was inserted into her arm. It all looked complicated and very serious to him. The door opened, and a nurse came in to check on things.

"Hello, everyone," the nurse greeted them. She looked at Jordan. "Are you Mr. Presley?"

Jordan stood up and moved back to get out of the nurse's way. "Yes. Can you tell me what's going on with my wife specifically?"

The nurse pressed a button on the fetal monitor and took a look at the strip of paper that it was providing. "She's trying to have this baby too early," the nurse reiterated what Vivian had just told him. "But her doctor is right down the hall and is about to come in now to talk to you." She made a mark on the strip and let it fall back to the ground. "Okay, Mrs. Presley. We're doing shift change now, love, so I'll see you if you're still here tomorrow." She looked back at Jordan. "Her new nurse should be rounding in just a few minutes as well. You all have a good night."

"You too," Vivian stated.

"Thank you," Jordan replied.

No sooner than the nurse walked out, Jada's obstetrician, Doctor Henry, entered the room. "Mrs. Presley!" she called out cheerfully. "What's going on in here? Good evening, everyone," she said acknowledging the family.

"Good evening," Vivian said in her dainty tone.

"Hello," Ressie said, amused by the doctor's upbeat personality.

"How you doing, Doctor Henry?" Jordan asked as the doctor walked past him to get to Jada.

"I'd be better if our girl was lying up on this bed right now." Doctor Henry smiled at Jada. "Turn over on your back for me, sweet pea," she instructed.

Jada moaned and slowly complied. Doctor Henry took her vitals for herself quickly, and then listened to the baby's heart rate. "What's been going on with you?" she asked Jada. "Are you doing anything strenuous at work?"

Jada shook her head no.

"You been sticking to your diet to manage the gestational diabetes?"

Jada nodded.

"Anything stressful going on?" the doctor asked.

Jada blinked through her tears and nodded slowly. Vivian's interest was piqued, and she shot a look over at her son who donned a guilty expression. Something was definitely going on between the two of them.

"Okay, here's the deal," Doctor Henry said, scanning the room and looking at everyone present. "This baby is nineteen weeks old gestationally. The idea is for us to make it at least to thirty-seven weeks in order for the baby to be full term and safe to be delivered. I don't have to tell you that going into preterm labor is not a good thing, especially this early in gestation. The survival rate . . . well, we're not going to even get into that."

"Is this going to force her to miscarry?" Ressie asked.

"I'm going to administer Terbutaline . . . It's a tocolytic medicine that she'll get through her IV to help relax her uterine muscles and stop the contractions. So we're going to keep her here for about two days, give her the Terbutaline, and observe her to make sure it works. By law and medical regulations we can only give her this for up to seventy-two hours."

"So what if it doesn't work?" Vivian asked.

"Then we'll try something else. But I feel confident that this will work." Doctor Henry took a breath and continued. "The other thing is that I noticed her blood pressure is up, another sign of high stress level. So . . . I'm going to prescribe something for that as well as do some testing for preeclampsia. We want to take all precautions because with hypertension this medication can be fatal to both mommy and baby."

"What the flip?" Ressie interjected. "There's no other option then? I mean, if it's risky . . . she's already in a risky situation as it is with the preterm labor and the high blood pressure. Why would we want to risk making matters worse by giving her a medication that could . . . be fatal?"

"It's the best course of action," Doctor Henry stated. "Given the gestational age of the baby it is the most effective course of action. And we'll give her minimum dosages of the Terbutaline. Don't worry. If we see things going south at any point we'll reconvene and go a different route." She looked at Jada who had long since turned back on her side and closed her eyes. "Any other questions?"

"I think you pretty much covered it all," Jordan stated slumping over against the wall.

"Okay, the nurse will be back with the Terbutaline and the Labetalol for the blood pressure." She patted Jordan on his arm. "Don't worry. We're going to take good care of your wife."

Jordan nodded. He wished that he'd done a better job of taking care of her emotionally and maybe then they wouldn't have been in this predicament.

Chapter 70

Corey

He'd been out for a minute and was trying to get things back together. Staying with his mom had been a temporary thing, and he couldn't have stuck it out a moment longer. Being business minded, he'd had an account opened in his mom's name a long time ago and every so often he'd given her money to stash in it. Now that he was starting over he was able to draw from that account. Money talked in this city so he'd had no problems getting set up in an apartment in Five Oaks located on Montreal Road in Tucker. It was a one bedroom with a loft and was good enough for Corey. He just needed his own space so that he could work some things out, and he had to move fast.

His boy had gotten him the gun and phone he'd requested so now he was mobile and strapped. His ride had been seized after he was picked up, and the judge wasn't freeing it from the impound because of his pending drug charges. This meant shit to Corey. He simply fronted the cash to buy a 2001 black Cadillac Deville from the dude that owned the used car lot on the corner of College Avenue and South Columbia Drive. Now he was waiting for the word on who popped his girl so he could pay their ass a visit before he was paid a visit by his BDM friends. It bothered him that they hadn't surfaced yet. Corey wasn't a procrastinator. He preferred for them to just go ahead and bring whatever heat they had in mind instead of feeling like he had to look over his shoulder every second of every minute. The shit was killing him.

Getting out of his car and taking a quick look around Corey walked down the long, steep driveway of the house he thought he'd never have to visit again. He'd waited as long as he could, but now it was time to have the confrontation that was inevitable. He rang the doorbell and waited patiently wondering just how this was going to go down.

Ms. Johnson opened the door slowly and stared at the dark-skinned young thug in disbelief. "When I heard you was out I prayed that God wouldn't bring you to this door," she said with a scowl. "How dare you come here!"

He wanted to tell her that she could trust and believe her house was the last place he wanted to be but getting buck with her wasn't going to help matters. "I came to see my kids," he said calmly.

"You think I'm going to let you in here to disrupt these babies' lives? You're even dumber than I thought. These children are better off never knowing you exist."

"You can't keep me from my kids, Ms. Johnson." He was starting to lose his patience.

"Were you thinking about your children when you was out in the streets selling your drugs and taking innocent lives?" Ms. Johnson shot back. "Were you thinking about your children when you got their mother shot?"

His jawline tensed as he tried to exercise some restraint and self-control. "You think I wanted that to happen to Steph? You think I'm happy about that? You think that I don't feel some kinda responsibility for how that went down?"

"You should!"

"You act like I pulled the trigger!"

"You pulled the trigger the moment you pulled her into your lifestyle!" Ms. Johnson shouted emotionally. Her tiny fists balled up in frustration, and her face suddenly made her look older than she was. The stress and anguish were more apparent than ever. "That girl loved you, and all it got her was dead."

Corey was hurt and angry. "Believe it or not, Ms. Johnson, I loved your daughter with all my heart. I loved that girl. This shit tears me up every time I think about it, and you best believe I'm not gon' sleep on this like nothing happened. I'm gon' handle it."

Ms. Johnson shook her head and covered her ears. "You watch your mouth! And don't . . . don't come 'round here talking this nonsense. I don't wanna hear nothing about your illegal activity."

Corey sighed. What the hell did she want from him? "Look, I just wanna see my kids."

His voice boomed loud enough to reach Damien's little ears. "Daddy! Daddy!" he shouted from inside the living room.

Corey's eyes lit up as he tried to peer over Ms. Johnson's shoulder. He looked at her and cocked his head to the side. "My son wants to see me," he said in a threatening tone.

Reluctantly she stepped back and allowed him to enter her home. As he walked in Damien ran into his arms. Ms. Johnson shut the door, not noticing the dark sedan that slowly pulled up in front of her house beside Corey's car. She crossed her arms and watched the interaction between father and son. She'd purposely been keeping Damien away from the radio and television so that his image of his father wouldn't be tainted by the ugly truth. She didn't want her grandson to know what kind of monster his father really was or that he had any link to his mother's death. It had been hard enough to explain to the child that he wouldn't see his mother again until he reached heaven.

"Where you been, Daddy?" Damien asked innocently holding on to his father for dear life. "Mommy's gone. She's dead now. Did you know that?"

Corey squeezed his boy and felt his heart aching. "I know, son. I'm sorry." He pulled back and looked his son over. He hadn't seen him in so long. The boy was growing up quickly. "You taking care of your sister and your grandma?"

Damien nodded. "Ariel cries too much. Grandma cries too." He paused and looked at his grandma whose head was held down in despair. "Mama used to cry too. She cried because you were gone all the time. I thought you weren't coming back," he whimpered. "I thought you was in heaven too with Mommy."

Corey grabbed the boy back into a tight embrace and fought the urge to release tears himself. He hadn't cried in ages, having been taught that real men didn't shed tears. It broke his spirit to hear his son's fear and feel his emotions.

Stephanie's death affected everyone, but most importantly, their children were going to suffer because of her absence for the rest of their lives. He couldn't not do anything about it. He couldn't wait any longer. He couldn't bear to see his young son in such turmoil. Just the thought of his toddler daughter shedding tears constantly made him want to place a bullet in somebody's skull. Ariel could obviously sense that something was wrong. She was far too young to understand life and death, but she was human, and she knew she was missing the connection she shared with her mother . . . She was missing her scent, her voice, her touch, and her face.

Corey felt Damien's body shaking as he cried. Looking up, his eyes caught a picture of Stephanie. It was her high school graduation picture. He remembered that day. Seeing her short brown-skinned face smiling back at him was torture. He'd failed her. He'd failed their whole family. Kissing his son on the head he pulled away from their embrace and rose up. He turned to look at Ms. Johnson. "Ariel?" he asked.

Ms. Johnson sighed and led him to the back bedroom that used to belong to Stephanie. The kids now occupied the room indefinitely. Ariel was sound asleep in her crib that she seemed to be outgrowing. Corey's eyes misted over yet again as he touched the curly hairs on his daughter's head. He'd help to give these children life, only to have placed them in a fucked-up situation. He leaned over and kissed the baby's cheek gently before turning to face Ms. Johnson.

She shook her head. "This is their home," she said feeling that she knew what he was thinking. "The courts granted me custody, and the fact remains that *this* is their home."

"They safe here with you right now," Corey stated.

"Right now?" she asked confused. "What you mean right now? What? You think whoever you've gotten yourself involved with is looking to hurt these innocent kids?"

The thought hadn't occurred to him before she voiced it. He'd been thinking about getting custody of his kids once he cleared up all his other drama. But now a new fear was etched in his heart. He didn't want to alarm her further. "Y'all good. I'll be back to see my kids." He moved to walk away.

"You can't keep running over here bringing trouble to my front door. I might not like you, Corey, but I'm thinking about these children. You need to think about these kids too . . . don't bring us no trouble around here," she begged him, feeling herself running out of fight.

Her request was valid no matter how hurtful the reality of it was. Corey walked out of the bedroom with Damien at his heels.

"Where you going, Daddy? I wanna go with you," Damien pleaded.

Corey patted him on the head. "You gotta stay with Grandma, buddy. I'll get you later." He didn't want to shatter the boy's world any more than it already was by telling him he wasn't coming back any time soon.

"Don't go! Please, Daddy. I don't want you to be dead too." Damien began to cry.

This was the life he'd exposed his children to: having the fear that any time their parents walked out of the door they'd be dead. Corey remembered all of the times that Stephanie had asked him to get out of the game so they could go to some other city and start over. She wanted to have a safer, happier life. He'd been so money and power hungry that the idea wasn't even an option for him, although he'd told her he would consider it. If only he'd listened.

"Stop crying," he told his son. "Be a big boy and take care of Ariel and Grandma for me. Can you do that?"

Damien nodded although his sobs continued.

Corey looked back at Ms. Johnson. "I'll call you," he said before letting himself out of the house. He closed the door behind him and pulled out his cell. The moment the line connected he didn't even give Antonio the opportunity to say hello. "Nigga, you better have a name and location for me right now!"

"I mean, I got a location for where they trap at," Antonio stated nervously. "But that ain't no guarantee that the dudes that pulled the trigger on Steph gon' be there, man. You know you gotta think this one through, bruh." He could sense that his leader was getting a little hotheaded and feared that he'd act recklessly, bringing him along for the ride. He was down to push dope for his dude, make moves for him, and he'd even been with him when the job was done on Montae, but he wasn't about to do a bid because Corey wanted to act without a real plan. That shit wasn't going to fly. He was growing tired of playing the flunky.

Corey climbed the driveway at record speed. "Tired of sitting around, my dude. We gotta move on this. Can't nothing else be done until this is taken care of." He opened his car door and slid into the driver's seat. What he saw almost made him drop the phone, but he handled it with a calmness that surprised even him. "Aye, man, I'ma call you back. But you get at me if you can get that. Time is of the essence," he said as he closed his car door.

"A'ight, man," Antonio said skeptically. "Doing my best, bruh."

Corey ended the call, tossed his phone into the cup holder, and started up the car. He took a deep breath without looking over to his right. He prayed that time was on his side and that he would get to handle that business he'd just discussed with Antonio. "Where to?" he asked.

"The W downtown," Knuckles replied. "Hit the ground floor of the parking deck."

Shit was about to get real.

After traveling through the hotel's service entrance, the kitchen, and then taking the service elevator up to the tenth floor, Knuckles and Corey finally made it to their destination. Corey was nervous as hell. He assumed that Knuckles was taking him there to kill him ruthlessly in the bathroom of a lavish suite so that housekeeping would find his bloody body laid out in the tub the next morning. During the two years that he'd been doing business with BDM he had only met with Knuckles on two occasions: once when the organization had first recruited him, and then again when the shit with Montae started popping off. Knuckles had advised him that he needed to handle the situation the way street punks handled their beef, but that they needed some proof that he'd done the deed. That was why he'd kept the man's wallet; for some kind of tangible proof that he'd pulled the dude's card and had disposed of him. It turned out not to be the kind of proof BDM was looking for, and they certainly were not pleased with the fact that the police had picked up on him so soon.

The duo entered the hotel room and Corey gasped the moment his feet hit the carpet. Sitting on the comfortable posh sofa in the sitting area was the head of BDM himself. Tommy had a grim look on his face as he sat next to a young dude who Corey had encountered on several occasions. He was the one that kept the police off of Corey's ass as well as the one who actually passed the dope and cash between Corey and BDM. He was the middleman.

"Sit," Knuckles told Corey.

Corey obliged, taking a seat across from Tommy and his middleman.

"I'd offer you a beverage but this shit here isn't a social call," Tommy said in his raspy voice as he gripped the arm of the sofa.

Corey nodded. He wasn't in a position to say anything. All he could do at this point was listen. Talking would probably only push the nail further into his pending coffin. Besides, his heart was in his voice box now and there was no way he could formulate words with the fear that was running through him. Knuckles stood behind Corey's chair with his arms by his side ready and waiting should a move need to be made. Feeling the heavyset man towering over him made Corey sweat.

"Surely you understand why we couldn't communicate with you during your recent jail stay," Tommy stated.

Corey nodded.

"You also know we have much to communicate about. I'm out of several kilos and $40,000, Corey. I'm not very happy about that."

Corey nodded again.

"I also have the DEA throwing a precelebration party with the GBI, thinking they're about to bring my ass in behind your stupidity. I'm not very happy about that either," Tommy advised.

Corey swallowed hard.

"I should whoop your ass, then skin you like the pathetic doe you look like right now," Tommy told him. "I should let Knuckles hang you from the ceiling and set you on fire from your balls. But that's not going to get me back my money or my dope, is it? And it certainly isn't going to get the feds to stop digging up shit in my backyard."

Corey felt himself growing lightheaded from holding his breath waiting for the moment that Knuckles capped him. But Tommy's last words made him think that he actually stood a chance of getting out of that hotel room alive to accomplish his primary goal.

"First things first, where's my dope and my money?"

Corey cleared his throat. "I'm not sure. I mean . . . I know where the stash house is so I think it might be there."

"You *think?* You think your adversaries are stupid enough to keep that kind of cash sitting in the hood where they can be knocked over by 12 and that shit be seized? All dumb fucks like you keep money at your homes and operation bases?"

Corey shrugged.

"Look who the fuck I'm talking to," Tommy huffed. "The more I teach your ass the dumber you seem. Keep up, boy! I need my money to make it to me, or there's going to be more problems than a few. It's the principle of the matter."

"Yes, sir," Corey said weakly. "And I'm working on handling that. I lost something too."

"You comparing the breech in my business to the loss of your bitch?" Tommy asked. "Money is greater than pussy any day, son. Pussy will get you fucked in the game . . . but of course, you already know that, don't you?"

Corey had mixed feelings. From a business standpoint he could understand Tommy's position. The feds had seized his dope, and Montae's crew had stolen a great chunk of his money from Stephanie. Additionally, it didn't help that Stephanie's dumb-ass idea had gotten them into the hands of the feds. But on the other hand, Stephanie was his family. He'd lost his family, his woman, and Tommy had very little sympathy for that fact.

"Get out your fuckin' feelings," Tommy said, "and focus! Let's talk about the job. Did anyone see you?"

Corey shook his head. "It was just me and my lieutenant. I swear I didn't see nobody else around."

"Just because you didn't *see* them doesn't mean that they weren't there. Did you check to make sure you weren't being followed and that no one was there?"

Corey knew where he was going with this. "No . . . We didn't."

"Thanks to my nephew and the good ole' media we all know that a witness came forward. That is no good."

Corey was afraid for his life again as Knuckles shifted his weight behind him. "But whoever it was . . . They're ghost. My attorney said they just vanished. Charges against me were dropped, witness is history . . . We're good on that."

Tommy shook his head. "Dumb ass! Do you think they're really going to let that ride? You got off. Great. But they're not walking away from this. Not as long as this witness is still living and breathing and able to talk. If they can get up the slightest dirt that makes its way back to me in the slightest bit, *that's* a problem."

"But they don't even know who the person is."

"While you were taking a vacation my nephew was working. Royce, tell 'em what you know."

The middleman looked at Clay. "The witness is Miranda Wilson-Cox, whose previous address was 2117 East Chadwick. She was friends with your girlfriend."

Corey's head began to spin. What the fuck did Miranda have to do with any of this? "She's a fuckin' crackhead!" he spat out. Suddenly it dawned on him how salty she'd been when he'd had to shut down servicing her. He was worried that she was going to run her mouth to Stephanie and he hadn't wanted to deal with any of the unnecessary drama. Had the bitch been stalking him? Had she actually been there the night they took out Montae? Was she on some get-back shit?

"Seems like you have quite a mess here," Tommy stated. "The GBI went to pick her up after she failed to show up for her planned meeting with them. She was already gone, of course."

Corey was confused. "Gone? You mean . . ."

"Knuckles had a talk with her. She was ghost after that. But don't worry . . . He didn't kill her. He encouraged her to kill herself. That didn't exactly work out either."

"What?"

"Seems she made her way to a rehab center where she's currently under lock and key. The GBI is trying their damnedest to find her. Royce has tried to put them off by erasing information about her from the Social Security database and Georgia's vital records department, If that bitch was there and fingers you after all this, *you're* gonna have a problem . . . *We're* going to have a problem now that she's met our friend here."

Corey gulped. "So what are you saying?"

"I'm saying that your client, friend, or whoever she is needs to be dealt with."

The thought of having to murder one of his girl's closest friends was disturbing but Corey knew what he'd signed up for the moment he got involved with BDM. They were all about the money and if blood had to shed to keep their paths clear to make the money, then so be it. Corey wasn't as coldhearted as some thought. Compared to Tommy and Knuckles, Corey was a teddy bear.

"I don't have to tell you what would happen if you decided to switch sides, do I?" Tommy asked.

Corey shook his head. "I'm not a snitch. I wouldn't do that shit."

"I don't want to have to see you again," Tommy told Corey. "I see you again, that means you and I have a problem."

Corey nodded his understanding.

Tommy motioned toward the door. Their meeting was over. Corey jumped from the chair and brushed past Knuckles to get out.

"Corey," he heard Tommy call behind him before he could turn the knob on the door.

He turned around slowly wondering if it had all been a bluff and if the big man was about to shoot him dead in his face the moment their eyes made contact.

"You don't have long, my friend," Tommy warned him. "Get it down and get it down quickly."

Corey nodded and hurriedly escaped the room. He rushed to the elevator, dying to be as far away from the BDM members as possible. This was turning out to be a lot more than he'd bargained for.

***

"You think he has the heart to do it?" Knuckles asked Tommy as he took the seat Corey had previously occupied.

"You shitting me? I'd be surprised if he even finds the fucks that shot his bitch. But he better hope he does and gets me my money. Keep your eye on him."

Knuckles nodded. He knew exactly how this story was going to end.

Chapter 71

Candace

"Come on, woman. I'm hungry," Rico barked.

Candace was in her kitchen trying to keep her mind occupied. So much was bothering her, but she didn't feel comfortable telling Rico about any of it. He wouldn't have understood. She scooped out a hearty helping of her lasagna and placed it on a plate for her boyfriend before taking the plate out to him. "Eat up," she told him.

"That's what I'm talking about."

"And when you're done fill this out," she told him, motioning to the packet sitting in the middle of the table.

"What's that?" he asked.

"It's a job application," she said sliding into the seat across from him. "They're hiring debt collectors at my job. It's an easy, breezy position, and I'm in good with the hiring manager, so you're as good as in there."

"For real?" he said taking a bite of his dinner and reaching for the application. He'd been putting in applications here and there for the longest and nothing had worked out for him yet.

"Yeah, so make sure you fill it out completely, okay?"

Rico smiled. Hooking up with Candace had been the best decision he'd made lately. It gave him somewhere to go to get away from his parents and their dysfunctional relationship, wild sex because Candace was a freak with it, and plenty of food because the woman liked to cook whether she was good at all the dishes she tried or not. Now here she was helping him get money in his pockets. There was no way he was ever leaving her. She was exactly what he needed.

"Let's get married," he said to her taking a bite of his salad.

Candace poured herself a glass of wine and laughed. "Yeah, right. So now you want to be a comedian, right? You're something else." She looked over at the swing that Zoe was dangling in happily.

"Naw, I'm for real. You love me, don't you?"

Candace looked up and studied his face. Was he for real? "I love you," she said out of nowhere. They'd never really discussed their emotions like this before. She'd assumed that he was really digging her, but never had they discussed being in love or the possibility of getting married.

"And I love you too, so I don't see what the problem is."

She still wasn't convinced. "You think it's just that simple?"

"It is. When two people love each other and want to spend the rest of their lives together it don't get no simpler than that."

"I have Zoe," Candace said bluntly. "It's more complicated than one and one makes two."

"I love Zoe," Rico shot back. "Zoe's not an issue. I treat her just like I would my own kid."

Candace conveniently forgot about the way he hadn't bothered to lift a finger to help her get provisions for the child not even a month ago when her own father was MIA. "Um, you do realize that with Zoe comes Zoe's father."

"No, it doesn't. That nigga ain't ever around. So he might as well keep doing what he's doing. I'll be her daddy."

It all sounded like music to Candace's ears. As much as she kept harping on being an independent woman doing it for herself she had to admit that she was growing tired of struggling alone. The thought of having a helpmate was appealing, but she wasn't sure that marriage was the right move for them to make right now in their relationship. "I don't know," she said cutting her lasagna slice into pieces.

"What you don't know?"

"I mean, we haven't even been dating that long. I've been married before, and it didn't work. That was mainly because we had no business getting married as quickly as we did. We didn't really know each other."

"Don't compare me to that nigga," Rico snapped. "I'm not dude."

You ain't lying, Candace thought. *Quincy came with a house, a car, and no debt. You come with just about nothing.* "I know that. I'm just saying that I don't want to make the same mistake twice."

He was sold on his decision and wasn't about to backtrack now. He was determined to get Candace to see things his way. "You think being with a man that loves you for you no matter what happened in your past is a mistake?" he asked reaching across the table and taking her hand.

During the time they'd been together Candace had been honest with him about everything. She had no secrets from him and despite everything she'd shared with him he was still there. She knew that any other dude would have bailed on her once they'd gotten wind of even half of the drama that came with her. Rico had a valid point. He obviously loved her no matter what. But were her feelings for him deep enough to make such a sacred commitment? She'd vowed to herself that the next time she got married it would be a truly for-better-or-for-worse, no-way-out situation. Did they have what it would take to sustain a marriage?

"I know you're the one for me," Rico said, laying it on thick. "The way that I feel when I'm with you, man . . . I've never felt this for anyone else. You make me wanna be a better man, Candace."

Her eyes lit up at his words. She was making an impact on him. "Well . . . If we do this there are some stipulations that cannot be overlooked," she told him slowly, beginning to sway. "You know me. I'm a chick with standards. Either you're down or we can't do this."

Rico nodded and gave her his full attention. "Go."

"The smoking."

"Huh?" he frowned at her.

"The smoking, Rico. I mean, you don't ever do it while you're over here, and I respect that, but I'm not stupid. I know you be smoking weed, and I just don't want to live with or be married to a dude that smokes. Especially weed. I don't want my daughter around that."

Rico's nostrils flared slightly. "Wow . . . I didn't expect that."

She gave him a matter-of-fact facial expression. "I'm not backing down off that."

He picked up his fork and took a bite. "I been smoking for years, babe. That's like asking you not to go shopping. That's some shit you like to do. Some shit you're used to. Your hobby. The shits the same for me and smoking."

"That's a habit you have, not a hobby," Candace corrected. If he didn't want to agree to her terms then he could just kiss his proposal good-bye because she wasn't going to accept it.

"Fine, habit, then. So you know it takes time to break a habit."

Candace nodded. She understood that. "Okay, yeah . . . So you get a period of two months to withdraw from it."

"Before we get married? Come on, Candace. Work with a brother."

"Two months after it's over. No matter what. Not even a cigarette."

He shrugged. "Done."

She smiled. "Cool."

"Anything else?" he asked.

She bit her lip. "Yes. Two more things. First, we need to join a congregation."

"A what?"

"A congregation, baby. At the Kingdom Hall."

"And when was the last time you went to the Kingdom Hall?"

Candace shot him a dirty look. "That's beside the point. I mean, I know that I need to get back into the Word. I can admit that. But if we're going to do this then we need a solid, spiritual foundation."

Rico's mouth went to the right as if he wasn't buying what she was saying. "You want me to be a Jehovah's Witness? I'm not 'bout to be going out knocking on folks' doors trying to give them no pieces of paper telling them if they don't get right they going to hell."

"We don't do that!" Candace protested, feeling offended.

"I know you don't. You don't even go to the services."

"*Excuse* you! I'm saying we don't tell folk they're going to hell. Who does that? And don't try to make this out to be about me. I can admit that I've been slipping. But I want to be a better believer, a better woman, and a better mother for

Zoe. So if you want to get with me, then you're gon' have to get with it."

"My family's Christian."

"Good for them. Witnesses are Christians."

"Uh-huh, but we go to church and observe holidays. Y'all don't."

"You observing holidays ain't got nothing to do with your faith. You do it because you like having a reason to celebrate and get gifts. That has nothing to do with building up His kingdom."

Rico dropped his fork. "Hol' up. Since when did you get so religious?"

"I think we've gotten away from my point," Candace said trying to keep her attitude in check. She hated it whenever anyone tried to belittle her walk with Jehovah. "Look, I'm telling you we need a spiritual base. I'm telling you that spirituality has to be rooted in a Witness setting. That's what I want for my family. If you're down, great. If not, then we can't get married."

"So I'm supposed to throw away years of what my family traditions have been in order to please you? Where's the compromise in that?"

"There's no compromising in spirituality. And anyway, I'm not knocking having family traditions. I'm just saying the whole materialistic aspect of holidays and stuff isn't of God."

"Okay, Miss Holier-Than-Thou, if you so dead set on not compromising with spirituality and you wanna do everything by the book and shit, then how come it's okay for us to have sex? You always down for a good fuck, and I ain't read my Bible from cover to cover, but I know fornication is a sin."

"I never said I was perfect," Candace stated. "And I stated that I want to be a better person, did I not?"

Rico was all out of comebacks. He couldn't believe the stuff that she was throwing at him, but if he wanted her to agree to marry him he needed to give her what she wanted. "Fine," he said. "Fine. If you go, then I'll go."

"No oppositions?" she asked wanting to make sure that he was truly serious.

"Naw, no oppositions."

Candace smiled and took a sip of her wine. Maybe they stood a chance after all.

"So what's the third stipulation?" he asked her.

"Oh, that one's simple." She pushed the application sitting in the middle of the table closer to his side. "Make sure you fill this out so you can get this job. We need two stable incomes if we gon' do this thing. My girls already clowning me about you not having a job and wanting to rap. I can't show up with an unemployed husband. That ain't gon' work for me at all, point-blank period."

Rico's eyes grew narrow. He looked across the table at the woman he was trying to make a deal with. "What you mean your girls clowning you about me?"

The moment his question resounded through the room Candace wished that she could take her statement back. "Um, it was nothing . . . We were just having a discussion, and they were just concerned is all."

"Concerned about what? Why the fuck you discussing me with your friends?"

"'Cause that's what girls do. We discuss our relationship issues."

"Wasn't aware that I was an issue for you."

Candace held her hands up. "Wait a minute, wait a minute . . . Hold on, Rico. Calm down. I didn't mean it like that, babe. Really. The girls just have my best interest at heart, and they wanted to make sure that I was making a good decision by getting into a relationship with you. I mean, I have my own set of problems, and I need someone by my side that can help me and not hold me back."

"So your girls got you wondering if I'm holding you back?" Rico was upset. "'Cause I'm between jobs?"

"Like I said, they just have my best interest at heart." She realized the words were true and made a mental note to call and patch things up with the girls as soon as possible. "You know Jada's the mama of the group and she just wants to—"

"Check this out, Jada don't know shit about me. She didn't even stick around that day to get to know me in order to even have an opinion about me. Quite frankly, I ain't studying nothing her or ya' other girl got to say. At the end of the day

I'm ya' man, and that's how it's gon' be. Girls be real quick to put another chick down or clown her dude when they jealous and insecure with themselves."

"Um . . . It wasn't really like that. They just—"

"So I'd thank you not to discuss our business with your li'l friends anymore," he said cutting her off again. "They ain't got shit to do with what we do over here. Unless you fuckin' one of them too 'cause you know how you get down."

"Okay, you know what? I'm just about tired of you taking shots at me, Rico." She was close to telling him to go shove his proposal up his ass.

Sensing that she was really pissed Rico tried to calm down. "My bad. I ain't mean it like that. I'm not trying to come for you or nothing, I'm just saying . . . Let's keep our business between us. I'd rather you didn't sit around telling them jealous birds our business and listening to any of their whack-ass advice."

Candace decided to pick and choose her battles wisely. They were trying to make a positive move and arguing over her discussions with her friends wasn't beneficial to what they were trying to do at all. She decided to tell him whatever he needed to hear to get them past this moment so that they could make the final decision that would impact their lives forever. "Okay," she said softly. "I'm sorry. You're right. Our business is our business. So you'll fill out the paper, and I'll turn it in to HR for you. Cool?"

Rico nodded and remained silent for a moment. "Cool," he finally said. "So how about we go 'head and make this thing official sooner rather than later."

"How soon?" Candace asked feeling a little pressured.

"Soon, soon. We can skip that whole wedding fiasco bit and save some money by just going to the courthouse and getting it done."

Candace liked the idea of saving money but knew that her parents would have a fit when she told them she'd eloped. But that was a bridge she was going to have to cross whenever she got to it. "Okay. I'll do some research to see how much the license is and what time they do it and stuff."

"Let's do it next week," Rico said. "I don't wanna wait."

"You don't wanna wait until you start the job?"

"You said the job's as good as mine, right? So why wait? Let's get married next week, baby. I don't wanna wait another minute longer to start my new life with you."

Candace sat back in her chair and eyed him. He appeared to be dead serious. A giddy feeling overcame her. In the midst of all the frustration and drama she was enduring Rico had ridden in on his little white horse and saved the day. They had a lot of logistics to work out, but the prospect of having a complete family excited her. She had a second chance to be a wife and lead a good, healthy life. She looked over at Zoe who was finally asleep as the swing continued to sway back and forth. Her baby deserved to have a complete family instead of a stressed out mom and an absent father. Candace cut her eyes back over to Rico who was waiting for her to respond.

"Okay," she said sweetly. "Let's do it."

Chapter 72

Jada

The room was silent. She'd been floating in and out of consciousness for days now it seemed, and she could have very well been hearing things wrong. The medication they'd given her to stop the contractions had her shaking uncontrollably. At times it was so hard to focus on anything that someone was saying because of the trembling being so aggravating. But while Candace was sitting on the edge of her hospital bed with that stupid grin on her face Jada wanted nothing more than to steady her hand so that she could reach out and slap the girl, assuming that she'd heard her correctly.

It was Jada's last day in the hospital. The doctor had said that they would release her in the morning because the contractions had successfully been stopped. She was being placed on bed rest for the next month so she wasn't exactly out of the woods yet. Right now she just wanted to relax and get her thoughts together while her in-laws were away and Jordan was at work. Candace's visit would have been a little more welcomed if she hadn't come with this crazy shit.

"You don't have nothing to say?" Candace asked her.

Jada lay on her right side and stared out of the window. She couldn't think of any tactful words to share so she decided to remain quiet.

Candace patted her leg. "Come on, girl. Can I get a congratulations or something?"

Is she kidding? Jada wondered. She continued to stare out of the window. She hadn't gotten fresh air in days and was excited about getting out of the hospital room.

Candace was growing impatient with her friend. "You okay, girl?"

Jada nodded.

"Then why you not talking to me, chick? I just told you the most important news of my life. and you laying up here like you mute or something."

"What do you want me to say?" Jada asked.

"Umm, I just told you that congratulations or something like that would be nice."

"Congratulations," Jada said without feeling. She hoped that her girl would just let it go now and move on to something else.

"You all dry with it. I'ma let it slide though because I know that you're going through something right now. But when you get back to you usual upbeat self I expect you to get your party planning skills on and throw me a reception."

I bet you do, Jada thought. The last thing she was in a position to do was throw a party, especially to celebrate a decision that she found completely ridiculous. It perturbed her that Candace continued to make illogical decisions, then expected everyone around her to pretend that she was the luckiest girl in the world. Jada wasn't in the mood to play make believe today.

"Anyway, so I rented a small U-Haul to move Rico's things out of his parents' place," Candace said. "So he's moving into my apartment as we speak. It's been so long since I've lived with a man. I hope he don't do no crazy stuff, like leave the toilet seat up or leave the cap off the toothpaste."

"Did he do any of that anytime that he spent the night?"

"No."

"Then you should be fine, considering how much time that dude was staying over your place," Jada said rolling her eyes.

"It really wasn't that often. And sometimes people switch up on you the second you start living with them."

"It's possible."

"I needa go shopping for a ring. I can't be married without a ring. That's not cool."

Yep, because that ring really makes a difference, Jada thought. "While you moving him in and shopping for a ring, have you told Khalil?"

Candace sucked her teeth. "Told him what? Khalil ain't my man, and I don't owe him any explanations for what I do with my life."

"He's still your daughter's father."

"He don't act like it." Candace didn't want to admit that she'd overlooked Khalil. She knew that he had a habit of dropping by whenever he pleased, and now that she and Rico were getting married it wasn't going to be cool for him to continue doing that. It also wasn't going to be cool for him to be expecting to sex her in the house where her husband now resided. Deep down, Candace knew that Jada was right. She needed to let Khalil know about this change immediately.

"What about your parents?" Jada asked.

Candace shook her head. "They don't know yet. We're going to invite them over for dinner the night after and break the news to them together."

"Good luck on that."

"What you mean by that?" Candace was defensive.

"Just what I said, suga. Good luck." Jada wasn't about to argue with her about this. It was pointless. Over time, Jada had come to realize that no matter what she said to her girls, no matter how pointedly she warned them against something, they were going to do it anyway. Now that she was stressed to the max with her own relationship issues the last thing she needed was to be getting riled up about Candace's or Alex's mess.

"It's going to be good," Candace said. "This time is going to be different. Oh, and I wanted to just apologize for the way things went down at my house when you and Alex came by."

Jada waved it off. "Water under the bridge," she said.

"You guys are important to me, and I value your opinions. But Rico is important to me too. I just want everybody to get along. I don't know what it's going to take for y'all to like him and him to like y'all."

Jada's interest was now piqued. "Excuse me?"

"What? I just want everyone to be cool. Y'all my family."

Jada sat up straight. "No, what you mean you want him to like us? What reason does he have to *not* like us? Hell, he doesn't even know me."

Candace shrugged. "He's a man, girl. I was telling him how y'all were concerned about me being with him, and he just got all upset and started going off, saying stuff about not listening to my jealous friends."

"Jealous friends? We're supposed to be jealous of you now and y'all's thrown-together relationship?"

"Don't attack me, girl. These aren't my words. I'm just telling you what he said."

"And I hope you set his ass straight." Jada could feel her blood pressure rising.

"I told him y'all were my girls and that you just had my best interest at heart. He asked me not to discuss our personal business with y'all anymore, which makes sense, and we just left it at that."

Jada shook her head.

"What?" Candace asked feigning innocence.

"Your boyfriend is a little punk bitch, that's what. How is he over there throwing a tantrum because we don't want our girl being used by some leech?"

Candace laughed. "Why he gotta be all those names though? Remember, he's about to be my husband, girl. Calm down."

Jada wanted to throw her out. Her friend simply didn't have a clue. She wondered how defensive Candace had gotten when Rico was sitting in her face going in on her girlfriends. Jada lay back down. It boiled her blood to think of the things this girl would do just for the sake of having a man smiling in her face. It was really becoming sad and kind of pathetic. Between her girls and Jordan, Jada was going crazy. She needed a vacation from everyone's bullshit before the stress caused something fatal to occur.

Chapter 73

Miranda

Relationships. All it seemed like they ever talked about was relationships. Whether it was your relationship with your parents, your friends, or your significant other, Doctor Dunham wanted to explore the depths of it. Much like all the other things they discussed, this too seemed pointless to Miranda. Sitting in another private session she toyed with the bottom of her T-shirt. It was too big for her. She'd lost weight since being there. She wasn't eating much. It wasn't because the food was nasty; honestly, she didn't know if it was or not because her taste buds seemed to be out of whack. It was just that her appetite was nonexistent. She was probably the smallest she'd ever been in life. One of the staff members had made a comment earlier about her looking as if she was going to waste away to nothing. Miranda hoped that the notion was possible. She figured it would make things so much easier were it so.

"The others are starting to receive visitors now," Doctor Dunham stated. "It's important in your progression that you know you have an outside support system."

"I don't," Miranda said.

"I was thinking you may want to reach out to your girl-friends. At least your friend Jada."

Miranda shook her head.

"What about your parents?"

Her parents. The thought of them made her shutter. She hadn't spoken to them in so long they probably thought she was dead, which was just as well. The less they knew about her and what she'd been going through, the better. If they saw her on the street they probably wouldn't even recognize her as their own flesh and blood. Disappointing them anymore than she already had wasn't something she wanted to do.

"Not calling my parents," she said with finality.

Doctor Dunham nodded. "When people love you, Miranda, they worry about you. I'm sure your parents are quite concerned about you. But I know that when you're ready to face them . . . When you're ready to face that part of your life you will."

You don't know shit, Miranda thought to herself.

"Family is a bond that's unbreakable," Doctor Dunham stated. "Family loves you even when you've strayed. Remember that."

"Family can hurt you more than a complete stranger," Miranda countered, taking the shrink by surprise. "Family can try to break your spirit and your body. Let me tell you about my family. My family landed me in the hospital, raped me, beat the shit out of me, stole from me, and had the nerve to walk out on me when all I ever tried to do was love and support him." Thinking about all the things Norris had done to her made her shiver. "Fuck love. Fuck family. Fuck trust. It's all a bunch of bullshit."

"I'm sorry that all of that happened to you, Miranda. But you can't turn your back on love or your entire family because of one person's ill doings."

Miranda stared at Doctor Dunham's degrees on the wall. "You got your master's from Georgetown," she stated.

"Um-hum." Doctor Dunham followed Miranda's glance.

"And your Ph.D. from Stanford."

"That's right."

"All that education . . . all that training . . . and you *still* don't know shit." She returned her eyes to meet the psychiatrist's. "They didn't teach you to listen to what the hell your patient is saying? How are you going to form a conclusion when you don't even retain the information that's being given to you? What?" She read the shock in Doctor Dunham's face. "You're surprised that I can make sense just because I'm a fuckin' junkie? I haven't always been a J, Doc. I haven't always been depressed and withdrawn. It happened over time, like I said before, or did you miss that too?"

"What is it that you want to say, Miranda?" Doctor Dunham asked without changing her even tone.

"I'm trying to tell you that the whole time I'm walking around with bruised eyes, ribs, and feelings, who the fuck do you think was seeing me? That's right, boo, my family. Maybe I didn't come out and say, 'Hey, I'm getting my ass kicked,' or 'Hey, I'm on crack,' but these were the people that saw or spoke to me often and said nothing. They did nothing."

"What did you want them to say or do?"

"Something!" Miranda snapped. "Anything to show that I wasn't alone . . . that I had somewhere else to turn to. Sure, the girls ambushed me once, but that wasn't in the name of helping me. That was them trying to figure out how stupid I really must've been to stay with a dude that was putting his hands on me. So, yeah, I can turn my back on love and all that other shit because it's been done to me plenty of times."

Doctor Dunham nodded. Miranda wanted to knock her glasses off of her face. What the fuck was she nodding at?

"I told you—" Miranda said wiping her eyes with the back of her left hand, "no one understands, and when they don't understand, they'd rather distance themselves and pretend that there isn't a problem."

"What I'm hearing is that you wanted someone to save you from your husband and from your growing addiction."

Miranda looked down. "No. I needed someone to save me from myself."

Chapter 74

Alex

She'd been in hiding and was tired of it. She hadn't talked to the girls, hadn't returned any of Clay's calls, and hadn't wanted to so much as think about the turmoil that was her life. Candace had texted her to advise about Jada being in the hospital, but she hadn't even been able to pull it together enough to swing by and holler at her girl. Thank goodness her old roommate Kacey hadn't moved out of their old apartment and hadn't gotten a new roommate. She'd been camping out on the floor in her old room, feeling like a squatter. The entire situation was depressing. Alex missed her comfortable bed, she missed having meals she didn't have to prepare for herself, and she missed Clay's presence. But the memory of that hoochie tonguing him down like they were in the privacy of a hotel room was driving her mad. What she really wanted to do was go home and set his car on fire—with him in it.

Tired of sitting at Kacey's home bored and alone, the girl was never ever there, Alex decided to kill two birds with one stone. She needed some advice about her issue, but she also needed to show her support. As she stood at Jada's doorstep she felt a little bad about the fact that she hadn't brought the girl a card, a plant, or something. She'd taken the train and a bus to get to Jada's house. She was tired and exhausted and wished more than ever that she had the luxury of borrowing Clay's car.

Jada opened the door looking sheepish in her lavender pajamas and hair pulled back in a messy ponytail. Alex's visit was unexpected. "What? Your phone not working?"

"I missed you too, friend," Alex said giving her friend a hug.

Jada hugged her back and allowed her to cross the threshold. She closed the door behind her and returned to her place on the sofa where she'd been getting ready to take her medicine before she'd heard the knock at the door. "Where you been hiding?" she asked Alex.

Alex sat on the sofa by her and dropped her purse beside her. She thoughtlessly kicked her feet up on the ottoman in front of them. She was wearing platforms, and her feet were tired from the long trek she'd had to make from the bus stop to Jada's front door. "I've been at Kacey's."

Jada reached for her glass of water. "Why? What's wrong with Kacey?"

"Nothing. I just temporarily moved back in."

Jada placed her medicine in her mouth and swallowed it down with the water. "Why?" she asked weakly. "Where's Clay while you playing sleepover with Kacey?"

"Probably sexing the chick I caught him in the bar with."

Jada's pill hadn't gone all the way down. She began to choke mercilessly upon hearing Alex's statement. She raised her hands in the air to try to help her choking spell. Tears welled up in her eyes as she struggled to get herself together. "What the hell are you talking about?" she asked barely able to breathe.

"Girl, this Negro blew up at me one night . . . that day we went to see Candace and she tripped out."

Jada nodded.

"Yeah, so that evening he blew up at me because we were late to get to his boss's birthday party, and then he just straight walked out on me. He left me at home, friend, and went to the party by himself. I was real pissed for a minute, then I tried to be the bigger person, right? I was ready to apologize and admit that I could have been a little more considerate seeing as though I knew we had plans. So I catch a ride to the lounge where the party was. I walk in and guess what I see? Clay all wrapped around some half-naked hoochie with their lips practically glued to each other."

Jada was in shock. This was not the Clay that she knew. She wondered how much of the story Alex was embellishing. "Oh my God. Please tell me that you didn't go up in there showing your ass."

"Oh, I showed my ass, and then some. How he gon' try to play me like that?" Alex crossed her arms and pouted. "All that trash he talked about T and Mario when he's just bad. All dudes are dogs."

Jada was feeling her on that but didn't feel like now was the time to share her own hardships. "You need to talk to him, girl. Clay's a decent guy. Maybe there was something else going on and it just looked like—"

"Friend!" Alex exclaimed cutting her off. "Really? Do I look stupid to you? I know what a kiss looks like, and they were damn near fuckin' at that bar when I walked in. She was all grabbing his crotch and stuff. Ugh! Whose side are you on?"

"Yours," Jada said weakly while wondering whose side her friends would be on if they knew that Jordan was screwing around on her. "I'm just saying . . . Things aren't always as they seem."

"Well, it seemed like I was ready to whoop that chick's ass when I threw that drink on her and things were just like that! I was ready to go in on that ass."

Jada died laughing. She held her belly as she doubled over in amusement. "No, you did not! Please tell me you didn't turn it out like that."

"Yassssss, girl!" Alex giggled. "They put all our asses out. Ole' girl knew that she was about to be getting the floor mopped with that dingy-ass dish towel of a dress she had on."

Alex was behaving way out of character. It was that moment that Jada realized that her friend had real feelings for Clay. She'd never wanted to fight any chick over a dude ever. This whole possessive thing was new for her. But still, Jada was having a hard time digesting the fact that Clay was out whoring around like that after everything he'd gone through to get with the love of his life. It made Jada chuckle once more because the same could be true for her own trifling husband. It was all a bit much to digest.

"His dog ass," Alex stated pouting again. "But what really sucks is that I miss his ass. What the hell is that about?"

"You're human," Jada replied leaning back and wishing that Alex would move her feet. "And you love him. That doesn't just go away overnight."

"It should. It shoulda went away the moment I caught him."

"Talk to the man," Jada said once more. She figured she probably needed to start taking her own advice.

Alex leaned over and lay her head on the swell of Jada's belly. "Friend, why is this happening to me? Clay was supposed to be it for me. He was supposed to be my Jordan."

"The hell are you talking about?" Jada asked fighting the urge to slap Alex upside her head for lying on her stomach like it was a cushiony pillow.

"Come on, girl. You know you got it easy peasy over here with your boo thing. I just want my happily-ever-after."

"Is that what you think this is over here?" Jada asked astonished. How wrong her friends were to assume that she didn't have hardships just because she wasn't crying about them all the time.

"You're over here all pregnant and barefoot, living the good life."

Jada was over it. She pushed Alex's head away and repositioned herself. "That's your problem right there. Stop striving to be like someone else or have what someone else has, boo-boo. The grass isn't always greener on the other side of the fence." She hoisted herself up from the sofa and began to waddle toward the bathroom. "And the baby's doing just fine, bitch. Thanks for asking," she said sarcastically.

Alex leaned back and considered Jada's advice. Talk to him. It sounded simple enough, but how could she talk to him when all she really wanted to do was run him over with his car? Was she going to be able to hear anything he said over her anger? She didn't want him to take her for some doormat-type of chick and think that he could just treat her however he wanted simply because he'd swept her off of her feet at some point. Wasn't it his responsibility to continue to sweep her off her feet? *Talk to him,* Alex thought. She was going to give it a try. Maybe it was time. Perhaps if they had a civilized discussion they could come to a conclusion about the relationship one way or the other. Either they were going to work it out or let it go. She wasn't sure exactly which way she wanted it to go.

Chapter 75

Clay

Jesus, if you have any mercy please spare me and return my angel, Clay prayed silently as he sat at his kitchen table. *I can't deny that I love this woman, and I know that if we both give it a heartfelt try we can make it work. Please bring her back to me, Jesus. I'd do anything for a second chance.*

It was lonely in the apartment without her. Clay missed feeling her next to him at night, rubbing her feet as they watched television and trying her attempts at cooking dinner. His jones was so bad that he almost even missed tripping over her heels when he walked in his front door each evening. He'd sent her numerous texts and left several voice messages, but she had yet to respond. At some point while he'd been at work he could tell that she'd come in to retrieve some of her things. The gesture pained him. He wasn't ready to throw in the towel on a battle he'd waited so long to be allowed to fight.

In front of him sat a carton of lo mein that he couldn't even stomach. Food had no taste since she'd left. Nothing seemed to feel right. During the ordeal he'd been sure that he was going to be embarrassed as hell upon walking into work the following Monday. But the only thing he'd felt that Monday, and every day since the fight itself, was sadness and heartbreak. He'd never had his heart broken before and felt genuinely sorry if any woman he'd ever dated had felt even an ounce of the pain he was experiencing now.

He heard the lock turn on the front door and thought his ears were playing tricks on him. He stood still for a moment waiting to see what was next. The sound of the door opening and closing made him grasp the Chinese takeout carton tightly. Were things turning around for him? Was his princess actually back? He couldn't move. He didn't know what to expect. He wasn't sure what he was supposed to say after having not seen her for nearly two weeks.

Alex walked into the kitchen and set her purse on the counter. Their eyes locked, and Clay felt his heart melt. Looking at her beautiful chocolate skin, the way she made even some jeans, a long sleeve T-shirt, and platforms look as sexy and glamorous as an evening gown, and the inviting way her lips seemed to pout, made him want to run to her and throw his arms around her. But he remained seated. He didn't want to bum-rush her, not knowing how she was feeling or what her intentions were.

"You look tired," Alex said softly.

Clay shrugged. "Haven't slept very well lately."

She nodded. "Yeah. I know what that's like."

"Where've you been staying?"

"Kacey's."

He'd figured as much but hadn't wanted to just pop up at the old apartment on a whim. He fought the urge to rise up to kiss her and continued to fondle his carton of tepid noodles. "I've missed you."

Alex felt a smile creeping to her lips but fought to keep it at bay. If he thought that a few sweet words were going to work to smooth things over, he had another thought coming to him. "We need to talk," she said.

He lowered his eyes into the food carton. When a woman said those words nothing good could come out of it. "Let me start," he said. If he could lead them off, perhaps things would work out smoothly and he could get his woman back in his arms soon. "What you saw that night was a misunderstanding."

Alex crossed her arms and shifted her weight. Attitude bounced off of her immediately.

Maybe those were not the words to lead off with, Clay thought, taking in his girlfriend's demeanor. "Yes, the woman was kissing me, but that was just it," he said. "She was kissing me. Not the other way around. I didn't invite it. I didn't encourage it. I didn't participate. I wasn't kissing that chick back. I was trying to peel her off of me without creating a huge scene at my man's party."

"Why would some random woman just walk up to you and try to basically ride you on the dance floor?" Alex challenged.

"For one, we weren't on the dance floor," he corrected.

Alex dropped her hands and stomped her foot. "Seriously? You wanna get all technical and semantic with me about this?"

"The truth is the truth, Alex."

"Yeah? And what is the truth, Clay? The honest to goodness truth." She walked over to the table, sat in the chair across from him, and then placed her face in her hands staring him dead in the eyes. "Look me in the face and tell me the truth."

Clay looked into her beautiful round eyes. He reached across the table and touched the softness of her cheek. "The truth is that I love you, and nothing was happening with that woman. She came on to me, I shot her down, and she came harder by trying to force her tongue in my mouth. That's it."

"You're not cheating on me?" Alex asked, leaning her head over to the left, allowing her cheek to be cradled by his palm.

"No, babe. I love you. I've always loved you."

"Then why did you leave me here and go to the party alone?" she whined.

Clay winced. For just a second it seemed like things were about to end well, but now here they were visiting the heart of where their issues really lay. "You were just overwhelming me with your selfishness."

"Selfishness?" Alex repeated the word as if it had been spoken in a foreign language.

"I just felt that you could stand to be a little more considerate of me and a little more of a team player when it comes to our relationship. We need to be on the same page if we're going to work, babe."

Alex sat up straight. "And what page is that? *Your* page? You're not my daddy, Clay. You're my boyfriend."

"I know that, and I never intended to come off like I wanted to be your daddy. Hell, I'm trying to become your husband one day. That ring on your finger symbolizes how I'm in this for the long haul, all the way up to the day that I meet you at the altar, baby."

Alex fingered the diamond solitaire ring Clay had given her for her last birthday. The day she'd opened that box and realized the depths of his feelings for her she'd been sure that she had finally found the man of her dreams. Clay was it. He was everything she'd ever needed and wanted. But even with him she just couldn't seem to get it right. "I want us to work, precious."

Clay grabbed her hands. "Me too. We just have to work together, and baby . . . You have to trust me. I would never ever hurt you."

Alex smiled. "Never?"

He got out of his chair and kneeled down before her. Alex wrapped her arms around his neck and looked him in his pretty brown eyes.

"Never ever ever," he told her before covering her lips with his.

Alex savored his kiss. She hadn't been embraced by him for so long. It was time for them to make up for the time they'd missed. Makeup sex was in order.

Chapter 76

Jordan

"You look nice," Jada said to him from the doorway of the bathroom.

Jordan looked up in the mirror to see his wife looking at him pensively. She hadn't had two words to say to him since the night she'd set their marriage certificate on fire, and she hadn't uttered anything at all to him since coming home from the hospital. He'd been feeling horrible more and more with each day that passed. Being stuck in an environment where you felt like the villain all the time was depressing and exhausting. He was trying his best to take care of her and show her that he was there for her, but Jada was a stubborn one. She hadn't made him feel the least bit at ease with the way she gave him the cold shoulder and continued to make him sleep out on the sofa like a visitor in his own house. Now here she was complimenting him out of the blue. Jordan was leery.

He fiddled with the buttons on his shirt and contemplated what his wife could possibly be thinking. He was preparing to go out for the night. Martin was getting married in a week and wanted to hang out in lieu of having a traditional bachelor party. The two of them and a few friends from college were going to dinner and maybe a club or two afterward. Jordan had mentioned to Jada that he was going to be going out tonight, but she hadn't responded when he did. Now here she was admiring his attire and looking at him as if she was going to try to pull a fast one.

"Thanks," he said trimming the hairs of his mustache.

"Where you going again?" she asked.

"Dinner and chilling with Martin and the guys."

She nodded her head and crossed her arms. "Know when you'll be back?"

"Naw." He put his hygiene bag away and turned around. "It's his night. We just hanging 'til he's ready to call it a night."

"Right." Jada looked skeptical. "We need to talk."

There it was. He knew that she had something up her sleeve. There was no way that he was going to cancel his plans to sit home and argue with her about things that he was ready to put behind them. If she wanted to hash it out it was going to have to wait. "I been trying to talk to you for the longest," he told her as he moved past her to head back into the living room. "Now all of a sudden you wanna have a discussion."

"It's not all of a sudden," she replied. "A lot has been going on, and I was entitled to a time period of sitting with my thoughts."

He rolled his eyes as he sat on the couch to put his shoes on. "Okay, well, I'm entitled to a time period of hanging out and not sitting in here on punishment with you treating me like I'm not shit."

"*Excuse* me?" Jada placed her hands on her hips and stood in front of him. Her belly was in his face. "How am I treating you like shit when *you're* the one running around doing all this dirt?"

"I messed up, Jada. I apologized for that, but instead of forgiving me and working on us, you decided to just shut me out. Well, now, I'm going out so just 'cause you're ready to talk now doesn't mean that I am."

"That's very mature of you," she countered. "How you gonna go out and play with your boys and leave your pregnant wife, who's on bed rest, at home, alone, with all these issues we have looming in the air?"

"Jada, don't do this, okay?"

"You didn't even bother to ask me if I wanted to go. When's the last time I got out of this house and had some fresh air?"

Jordan stood up. "I made these plans while you were busy ignoring me, and I'm not canceling. So, if you're serious about talking things out, we can do that in the morning. I'll make you breakfast, and we can talk all damn day. But tonight I'm going out." He grabbed his jacket from the sofa and stepped close to her. He kissed her forehead. "Good night."

***

The table was filled with his old crew from college . . . Martin, who was throwing drinks back in celebration of his pending nuptials, Curtis and DeAnthony, Jordan's old college roommates, and AJ, their comrade who had spent more time partying than studying in college and subsequently hadn't graduated. They were all good friends and remembered when Martin and Ashley had first started dating. The two were inseparable from the moment they'd met. The crew had been waiting for years to see the two of them get married. Now the time was upon them, and they were celebrating to the fullest. Sitting around the table at a local Applebee's they were as loud and belligerent as ever as they recounted stories and memories from years gone by. The seat next to Jordan was empty. They were expecting yet one more person to complete their crew.

"Aye, man, I thought for sure that Martin and Ashley was gon' be the first to tie the knot," Curtis said. "That shit made my head spin how quick Jordan and Jada just up and got married."

AJ had to cosign. "Hell, yeah! It was like one day he was like 'Aye, y'all, this my girlfriend,' then the next day, 'Aye, by the way, this my wife.'"

Everyone laughed, including Jordan. It had happened rather quickly, but he was convinced two years ago that Jada was the woman he wanted to spend the rest of his life with. Even his mother and sister had been shocked, but despite everyone's warnings he'd gone through with it. He'd never been prouder than the day he'd given Jada his last name. It didn't matter to him that no one else understood why they were doing it. All that mattered was the way that he felt when he was around her. It all seemed so simple back then. Now, with the way things were going, he was having second thoughts way too late.

"That nigga ain't been right ever since," DeAnthony said. "All locked down and shit. He don't hang no more. Nothing."

"Dawg used to be a playa for real," AJ commented. "Chicks left and right. Just sniffing pussy from all directions."

Curtis laughed. "Now he only gets to sniff one pussy forever. How's that been working out for you, playboy?" Curtis asked reaching over to slap Jordan on the back.

Jordan looked over and saw Martin doubled over with laughter. "A'ight, man. Laugh on. That's 'bout to be you too, so join the club."

Martin raised his glass of mint julep and smiled drunkenly. "Damn right, and I'm proud of it. I'll just live vicariously through y'all muthafuckas."

The crew laughed again.

"So, J, you telling us in all this time you ain't tapped nothing else?" AJ asked. "I mean, *nothing?*"

Jordan chuckled and looked down into his own glass. "Come on, man."

"Aye, J, ain't nobody here but us," Curtis said revving him up. "You know you can talk to yo' boys, nigga. You ain't gotta front over here."

"Yeah, this a no front zone 'round this way," DeAnthony said stuffing his mouth with nachos.

"Well," Jordan said slowly. "I didn't *say* I haven't." The way that he placed emphasis on the word *say* made the others go wild as they caught his meaning.

"That's my nigga!" AJ hollered. "That's my nigga. I knew you couldn't stop being you, nigga. You's a pussy chaser. It's just who you are." AJ shrugged and smiled.

A pussy chaser, Jordan thought to himself. *Is that really what I am? Who wants to live their whole life chasing pussy?* It didn't seem like an appealing trait to have. Jordan wasn't sure that he wanted to be labeled the pussy chaser of their clique.

"Uh-huh, that's just who he is," Curtis said, narrowing his eyes and focusing across the restaurant. "And he been chasing around this one pussy for years."

All eyes darted in the direction of Curtis's glance. They watched as LaTanya made her way across the restaurant in her skinny jeans, crop top, and heels. Her jet-black wavy tracks were pulled back into a loose ponytail, and her full lips parted into a large smile as she took her seat beside Jordan.

She put her arms around him and squeezed tightly. "Hey, booskie! Long time!" She looked over at the rest of the crew and smiled. "Hey, y'all! Y'all missed me?"

LaTanya was cool as hell. She was the one female that had attached herself to their clique. The others always assumed that she tagged along because she was really trying to hook up with Jordan. Over time, they came to trust her and didn't bother censoring their discussions in front of her because she knew how to keep her mouth closed. Eventually they saw her as just one of them. None of the others ever tried to get with her. She was cute, but something about her just didn't resonate "wifey material" in their eyes. It also didn't help matters to know that she was breaking something off for Jordan every now and then. Quiet as she thought it was kept, everyone knew what was going on.

"What's good, girl?" AJ asked LaTanya, winking at her knowingly.

"Living life, boo-boo. Living life." LaTanya looked over at Martin. "So I hear you finally getting married."

Martin smiled. "Yup. Marrying my baby."

"That's so sweet."

"When you gon' get married, 'Tanya?" Curtis asked.

She shrugged. "I guess when a dude comes around that can handle all *this*."

DeAnthony laughed. "What you gon' do? Wait for Jordan to get divorced so he can handle it?"

LaTanya nudged Jordan. "J don't want none of this."

The crew started laughing. Everyone knew better than that.

Jordan put his arm around her. "I missed you, baby."

"Really?" She frowned at him. "You don't call nobody."

"You know how it is. Been busy with work and—"

"And Jada would cut his dick off if she found out he was kicking it with you," Curtis cut in.

LaTanya shook her head. "That's crazy. Men have female friends. She trips like that?"

Jordan just shrugged. He'd never once mentioned LaTanya to Jada in all the time that they'd been together. He hadn't seen the point. Honestly, once they got together and got married he didn't really see the point in bringing LaTanya up. The crew rarely hung out anymore anyway. He also didn't think that Jada would be feeling the idea of him having LaTanya as a friend. Jada had a way of reading people that was unreal. She could always tell when something was up, and he knew that she'd see right through his bullshit story of the two of them just being friends.

"Hell, yeah, she trips like that," DeAnthony stated. "Jordan don't go nowhere unless Jada's ass is right there. Shit, I'm surprised she didn't end up coming with him here."

"Naw, I wasn't gon' let that happen," Jordan said. "This was for the homies, and I made sure that was known. I wasn't gon' let her mess that up. And shut up, nigga. She don't go everywhere with me."

The crew laughed.

Jordan leaned over and whispered in LaTanya's ear. "You know I wasn't gon' let nothing keep me from seeing you again."

LaTanya giggled. "I know. I don't know why you married her anyway. She doesn't sound nothing like what you need. What kind of wife is so controlling and possessive that she can't let her man hang out with his friends?"

Jordan didn't intend to start bashing his wife. Deep down he loved Jada, but it felt so good to have people on his side, and to have a pretty girl cozying up to him. "That's why her ass is at home. I need a break from all that for a while."

LaTanya squeezed his leg under the table. "Well, anytime you need a break you needa call me. You ain't gotta put up with that mess. That's not a real woman."

Jordan pulled his camera out of his pocket and handed it to DeAnthony. "Aye, bruh. Take our picture."

"Sentimental-ass nigga," DeAnthony said taking the camera. "Snapping pics and shit."

"Memories, man," Jordan stated. "Never know when we'll all be together again."

Jordan wrapped his arms around LaTanya, and together, they smiled wide at the camera clicking in front of them. After that the camera was passed around and everyone was getting caught in fun poses. The night ensued with lots of laughter, drinks, and stories. Finally AJ decided that it was only right for them to take Martin to a strip club. Everyone was down, even LaTanya who had decided that she would ride over with Jordan.

As he pulled into the parking lot of Strokers, LaTanya leaned over and looked at him. Jordan turned the car off and turned to see her staring him dead in the face. "What?" he asked.

"Are you happy?" she asked him.

"Hell, yeah. I'm here with you. Hanging with my boys. Couldn't be happier."

She shook her head. "No . . . I mean, are you happy with Jada? Because from what I've heard you don't seem very happy to me."

"I wouldn't say that I'm unhappy. Marriage ain't easy, though."

"So why'd you marry her ass in the first place? I mean, really. If you were all that thrilled about being her husband you wouldn't have made it sound like being with me is the thrill of your life."

Jordan wasn't sure what LaTanya's intentions were. He was a little tipsy from the drinks they'd had at the restaurant, and admittedly, he was caught up in the moment of being back in his old routine of hanging with his homies. He didn't want to talk about his marriage or his feelings. He just wanted to have a good time.

"We should go on in," he told her reaching for the door handle.

LaTanya grabbed his face and forced him to look her in the eyes. "You don't really want her, do you?"

"Huh?" He could feel that familiar stirring down below and knew that nothing good could come from it.

"You heard me. You don't really want her, do you?"

"I love her. We just . . ."

LaTanya leaned in closer and licked her lips. "You just what?"

"She ain't you, baby," he found himself saying as he crushed his lips against hers.

LaTanya parted her lips so that their tongues could tackle each other. She reached down and squeezed his thigh, then groped his protruding manhood. She knew exactly what kind of pleasure that part of his anatomy could bring her, and she knew that he would be more than willing to go there with her. It made no difference to her who he was married to. If he didn't care about his vows or the woman he'd made them to, then why should she? LaTanya had always assumed that it was she that was truly the apple of Jordan's eye. Timing just hadn't worked out for them. He thought he was ready to settle down at an early age, but LaTanya knew that that wasn't the move for her. Although he'd never approached her with the proposition of them trying to be a real couple she could feel the chemistry between them and knew that he wanted her. Maybe in another time they could have tried to make it work if he hadn't up and married Jada so soon. But now that he appeared to want out, LaTanya was sure that she could be all the woman his current mistake couldn't be for him.

Jordan didn't protest when LaTanya unzipped his pants and reached inside to pull out his dick. It felt good to feel her stroke it. He assumed that she was going to give him head right quick, but LaTanya had other plans. She reached into her purse and pulled out a three-pack of Lifestyle condoms. Hastily she tore the box open, pulled one out, and tossed the box onto the dashboard. Jordan swallowed hard and let his seat all the way back. He pulled his pants down and took the condom from her so that he could slide it on. LaTanya kicked off her shoes and peeled off her skinny jeans and thongs before climbing over and mounting him in the driver's seat.

His windows were tinted, and it was dark so neither of them were worried much about anyone catching them in the middle of their lustful act. The boys were inside the club already and were probably wondering where the hell they'd gone. But then again, the crew knew Jordan and LaTanya's history and wouldn't have been the least bit surprised to know that they were off somewhere sneaking in a quick fuck.

LaTanya grinded her hips and gripped his dick tightly with the muscles of her pussy. Jordan was in second heaven. The last sexual contact he'd had was head from Mona in his office. He was long overdue for some sexual healing. He grabbed LaTanya's breasts as she moved about rhythmically. The windows were fogging up from the heat that their ecstasy was creating. LaTanya's moaning was driving him insane as he bucked into her tight, wet pussy madly. In moments he was grabbing her ass and coming so hard that he thought he was going to break her small, thin body in half.

LaTanya rubbed his head as he released himself while inside of her. A smile crossed her lips, knowing that she'd just forbiddingly pleasured this man that didn't belong to her. Now she could send him back home to his sorry-ass wife knowing that he'd be thinking of this moment he'd just shared with her. She lifted her hips, and his plastic-wrapped dick slipped from her entrance. She scampered back over to the passenger seat and pulled some baby wipes out of her purse to clean herself up.

"You came prepared, didn't you?" Jordan asked, pulling the wet condom off.

LaTanya handed him a wipe to wrap it up in, and then another to clean himself off. "You just never know," she said smiling.

Silently they both got cleaned up and redressed. LaTanya was feeling a sense of accomplishment. She knew that she had Jordan back in her good graces and that his wife had better watch out for her. Jordan, on the other hand, felt a little guilty. Jada was sitting home on bed rest stewing over the problems that he'd created in their marriage, and here he was getting his freak on with a woman that he'd never really see past her superficial beauty and easily accessible pussy. He had no business being anyone's husband. He wondered how he could ever really be the man that Jada wanted him to be. He looked over at LaTanya, who quickly blew him a kiss. The affection of women just made him feel like something special. Jordan couldn't control himself around a female.

"Come on," LaTanya said. "Let's go see what these fools are doing."

He moved to get out of the car but noticed the box of condoms on the dashboard. Quickly he removed it and tossed it into the glove compartment, making a mental note to get rid of it before going home. Together, he and LaTanya headed toward the door of the popular strip club.

LaTanya grabbed his hand and whispered to him. "When you get ready to get your life together and walk away from that mistake you made, you know I'm here for you."

Jordan remained silent. Had marrying Jada really been a mistake?

Chapter 77

The Girls

Their last impromptu meeting hadn't gone so well so Candace wanted to do something to make it up to her girls. With all of the changes going on in her life she wanted to be able to share her happiness with them versus having any distance between them. She'd talked to Jada already, but she hadn't really been able to catch up with Alex aside from a text here and there. Today they were going to come together and chill the way girls were supposed to.

Zoe was away for the weekend with Candace's parents, who were currently not too pleased with her. Rico was out with his friends at the studio. Candace had the apartment to herself and had gone out of her way to make things comfortable for the ladies. She had her cheese dip on deck already in the center of the coffee table with a bowl of chips surrounding it. For dinner she'd whipped up some homemade Chinese food like only she could do, including veggie egg rolls, chicken fried rice, and sweet and spicy wings. On the dining-room table sat two bottles of wine. She planned for them to drink and talk the night away.

The doorbell resounded, and Candace hurried over to let her girls in. She didn't even stop to check the peephole. "What's up, chicas?" she exclaimed as she threw the door open. Her heart stopped the moment she saw Khalil standing before her in jeans, a solid back shirt, and an expensive-look-ing leather jacket.

"Hello, beautiful." He smiled at her as if there wasn't anything at all wrong with the fact that he'd just popped up at her house unannounced after being ghost for nearly a month. In his mind he was just doing what he always did. No big deal.

Candace wasn't pleased at all. She hadn't been able to get him to answer his phone lately so that she could fill him in on her life changes. The man couldn't return a call, but he had no problem just showing up. It irked her to no end. "What are you doing here?" she whined looking over his shoulder. She wanted him gone before her girls showed up.

"Came to see my girls."

"*Your* girls? What are you talking about?"

"You and Zoe," Khalil replied looking at her questioningly. "You okay? You look a little flustered."

"You think?" she asked. "Look, Zoe's not here, and I'm about to have company."

"A dude?" he asked with attitude.

"No, not a dude but—"

"Then let me in, woman. I'm not scared of your friends." Khalil pushed past her and made his way over to the couch, helping himself to her cheese dip. "You got it smelling good in here, gorgeous. Looks like I showed up right on time."

"No, you did not!" she snapped. "You should have called first, Khalil. You can't just keep popping up on me whenever you get ready."

"Why you trippin'? As long as my daughter lives here I'm coming by. Long as you don't have some dude laying up in here, everything's cool, baby."

"You're so stupid!" she shouted moving away from her open front door. "You pretend to be all perceptive and shit, but you're so stupid. You just don't get it." She held her left hand up so he could see the faux gold diamond ring she'd purchased at Wal-Mart for herself two days ago. "I'm married, Khalil. I have a husband now. You can't just come up in my house whenever you feel like it, and you damn sure can't come at me like you think you're gon' get any booty."

Khalil dropped a chip back onto the plate and rose from his seat. "You're married?" he asked.

She nodded. "And I don't think my husband would appreciate you coming to our house out of the blue like this. I've been trying to call you. You better start learning to communicate better for the sake of our daughter."

Khalil walked over to her and stared down at the short woman. "What the hell's wrong with you, Candace?"

"*Excuse* you?"

"Explain to me how you marry one out-of-touch brother that can't take care of you, cheat on him with me, and act like you love me, have my baby, then run off and marry the very next dude that smiles at you? You *that* hungry for attention? You just gotta have a man up under you? Damn, baby! You needa fuckin' breathe for a minute. Let your pussy breathe for a second before you let another nigga run up in it."

On impulse Candace reached up and slapped him. Her anger was at full capacity. "What you won't do is come in my house and call me a ho. Not when you're the biggest ho of them all, going around making babies everywhere that you can't take care of."

Khalil shook it off and grabbed her into a tight embrace. "What I know is that this pussy belongs to me. Who you think you fooling, baby? You done went and found you a cheap imitation of me. Some nigga that can't even afford to move you out of this one-bedroom apartment. You made a mistake, sweetheart. How you gon' give my good stuff away?"

Candace was appalled. "Get your hands off of me. We're done."

"We're never going to be done." Khalil held her by the shoulders with one arm and reached down to stick his free hand between her legs. "Nobody can get it wet like me. You know that. You know you like the way I make you scream. You want me to fuck you right now, Candace. I can feel the heat from your pussy."

She struggled to push his hands away. "Fucking with you again was a mistake, Khalil. But I'm over it now. I'm married. You're not getting any of this anymore!"

"Anymore?" Alex's voice shocked both Candace and Khalil.

The couple hadn't noticed Alex and Jada approach the apartment taking root at the threshold of the open door. Jada remained silent as she rubbed her belly, and Alex's mouth hung wide open. This was more drama than they could have ever imagined.

"Um . . . hey, y'all," Candace said, pushing Khalil away. "I don't think y'all have ever officially met. This is Khalil, Zoe's dad. Khalil, these are my girlfriends, Alex and Jada."

Khalil smiled, not the least bit fazed that they'd just walked in on him molesting Candace. "Nice to meet you ladies."

"Um, do we need to come back later?" Jada asked, failing to budge from her spot in the doorway.

Alex moved on into the living room carrying a bag of ice per Candace's instructions. "Why should we leave? It looks like there's a lot going on here to keep us entertained."

Candace rolled her eyes at Alex and motioned for Jada to come in. "Girl, no. Come on in. Khalil was just leaving."

Jada entered and shut the door behind her.

Khalil shot Candace a look. "Was I? I don't think our business is done yet."

"Oh, believe me, we're done," Candace retorted. "We're so done you might as well burn the memories you have."

"A lover's quarrel?" Alex joked.

Candace frowned at her. "Ha-ha. We're not lovers. Go put that ice in the kitchen, girl. It's melting. You're dripping water all over the floor."

"Don't blame me because y'all got it so hot and steamy up in here," Alex shot back before walking off to the kitchen.

Jada took a seat on the sofa. She wasn't sure what was going on, but she had to agree with Alex. It was clear that they'd walked in on a very steamy moment between Candace and Khalil.

Candace turned back to Khalil. "As you can see I have plans, and like I said, Zoe isn't here so you can just go."

Khalil popped his knuckles. "Can I have a word with you in private?"

"Ooh, in *private?*" Alex said coming out of the kitchen. "Why y'all gotta go be in private now? You had the door wide open so the whole complex already knows your business. Now what's this about you being married again?"

"Not now, Alex!" Candace snapped, annoyed that her friend was behaving so childishly during such a frustrating moment for her. She pointed toward the hallway. "Bedroom, now," she said to Khalil.

"With pleasure," he stated, leading the way.

"I'll be right back, y'all," Candace told the girls before scurrying off.

They heard the bedroom door slam, and Alex ran over to the sofa laughing. "Oh my God, girl! What is going on with your friend?"

Jada shook her head. "I don't know. This seems like a whole bunch of mess if you ask me." She reached for a chip and scooped some dip out. "But I know one thing. If she's back there fuckin' ol' boy while we're sitting out here waiting I'm leaving."

"Forget her. I'ma go in there and start making those egg rolls she made disappear." Alex laughed again. "Candace and her baby daddy drama. And do you know anything about this marriage business?"

Jada munched on her chip and screwed up her face.

Alex pointed at her. "Jada! You better tell me what's going on, friend."

"It's not my business to tell, but you gon' find out anyway . . . she married Rico."

Alex frowned and clutched her chest. "Oh God, no. Say it isn't so."

Jada reached for another chip. "Would if I could, honey. They went to the courthouse yesterday."

"Then why the hell aren't they having a honeymoon instead of her having us over here for girls' night and having her boyfriend back there arguing?"

Jada chuckled. "'Cause I wasn't about to come off of any money or my time to throw together no reception to celebrate her haphazard nuptials. Plus you know that dude don't have no money for no honeymoon."

Alex shook her head. "This is like déjà vu. How does one person marry two totally wrong-for-them dudes back-to-back?"

Jada shook her head. "I don't know, girl." She couldn't understand herself how she could be married to a man that had seemed perfect a year ago but was now making her completely miserable. Who was she to judge what Candace was doing?

Suddenly the front door swung open and in walked Rico looking just as hood as ever. His pants sagged, displaying his forest-green-colored boxers, and his hat was pulled low over his eyes. He had to tilt his head back to get a good look at them.

"What's up?" he greeted them before throwing his eyes at the table.

"Hey," Alex stated dryly.

Jada remained silent. After what Candace had told her about Rico not caring much for them she wasn't too interested in exchanging pleasantries with him.

"Where Candace?" he asked.

Jada pursed her lips. She wished that she'd followed her gut instinct and never stepped foot inside the apartment. This wasn't the kind of stress that she needed to be engulfed in. Alex shook her head. She too could feel the impending doom lingering over them.

"Umm . . . she had to handle something in the back," Alex said nervously. "Umm . . . oh yeah. Jada, I think we need to go do that favor she asked us to do."

Jada caught the hint and was glad that Alex had given them a way out of this tragic situation. "Yeah . . . Yeah, you're right." She struggled to pull herself up from the couch. "Come on, let's go before the store closes."

"Y'all still doing your ladies' night thing?" Rico asked.

"Um . . . We were," Alex answered. "But um . . ."

"I ain't trying to interrupt y'all party. I just needa get at Candace real quick, then y'all can get back to ya male bashin' and shit."

"Male bashing?" Alex asked.

Just like Jada hadn't told Alex before about Candace marrying Rico she also hadn't told her about Rico not liking them. The moment just seemed to grow darker and darker. Jada pulled on Alex's arm and tried to get her to abandon the discussion so that they could make a break for it.

"Yeah. You know how y'all do," Rico said smirking.

"And what y'all are you referring to?" Alex asked getting offended.

"Alex, come on," Jada said softly.

"I'm talking about you and your homie," Rico said pointing at Jada. "I don't know what kinda stuff you really be saying to my wife, but I'd appreciate it if you left me out of your discussions."

"What makes you think you're important enough to warrant a spot in our discussions?" Alex shot back.

"Candace tells me everything."

"She does, huh?"

Jada could feel the tension rising. She knew that Alex could get real reckless with her mouth when she got angry, and the last thing they needed to do was add any fuel to this fire that was already about to blaze out of control. "Alex!" she hissed.

"Yeah. So you can keep your opinions to yourself. You and your li'l sidekick. I know how misery loves company."

Something clicked within Jada, and her goal to get out was quickly forgotten. "You calling me miserable? You don't know anything about me, sweetie."

"You don't know nothing 'bout me either. All the more reason for you to fall back and stay out of our business."

"Let me tell you something, you short-ass, insignificant, crusty-ass, self-righteous son of a bitch. Don't nobody care about you. We care about Candace. I could give two fucks about you. So when she comes to me with whatever she wants to talk about, I'ma give my two cents whether you like it or not."

"And you can kiss our ass in the process," Alex chimed in.

"Aye, man, you can—" Rico's words fell short as a crashing sound from the back made everyone turn to look up the hall.

Candace's bedroom door flew open, and she stormed out, hollering, "Hope you remember what it tastes like because you'll never taste it again!" she screamed. She turned to walk up the hall and noticed Rico standing in the middle of the living room staring at her. "Oh my God." It was too late for her to do anything.

Khalil exited the room adjusting his pants and hollering behind her. "You don't have to put on a show for your friends, sweetheart. I'm sure you've already told them how good I put it down, so we all know you'll be back."

"What the fuck!" Rico's young voice barked.

Khalil stopped dead in his tracks. Understanding washed over him, and he smiled at Candace. "This must be your new beau." Khalil laughed. "Yeah. Way to marry up, beautiful."

"Shut up," Candace hissed behind her. She hurried over to Rico and placed her hands on his chest. "Baby, I can explain."

He shoved her, and that one act was enough to make everyone else spring into action.

"You punk-ass bitch!" Alex screamed, running over and kicking Rico in the ass with the heel of her shoe.

Khalil stepped forward and literally picked Candace up to spin her around and place her behind him. "You wanna put your hands on somebody, young buck? Put your hands on a man."

"No! No! Don't do this!" Candace cried, trying to pull Khalil away to get him to back down.

Rico looked from Alex to Khalil. He was fuming and the piercing pain from Alex's blow was bothering him. "Get the fuck out of my house, all of y'all."

"Negative," Khalil said. "How you gon' keep a woman when you don't even know how to treat a woman? I'm not leaving. *You* leave."

"You fucking this nigga in *my* house?" Rico yelled at Candace. "You fucking this nigga in the room I sleep in, and now you got him in my face?"

Candace stomped her foot. "I'm trying to tell you it's not what it looks like. He just came over to see Zoe."

"Right. That nigga never comes to see his daughter. That's *my* daughter."

Khalil stepped closer. "The fuck is wrong with you?" He raised his fist to swing, but Candace caught him by the elbow.

"No! Get the hell outta my house." She let go of Khalil's arms. "Please, just go!" she screamed. "You've single-handedly turned my home upside down, you selfish bastard. Get out. Please. I'm begging you to go."

Khalil stared at her as if she was crazy. "I just watched this dude put his hands on you."

"He pushed me . . . That's all." She held her arms out. "I'm fine. Okay? I'm fine, and I can handle myself. Go. Please just go."

Khalil nodded and wolfed up at her. "You're not the woman I thought you were. Don't call me once your husband starts whooping your ass." He took one final look at Rico, then pushed past him to make his way out of the door.

Jada held her stomach and her breath. The shit had certainly hit the fan.

"You told me you was having girls' night," Rico said accusingly to Candace.

She lowered her arms and shook her head. "I didn't know he was coming. He does that all the time. I tried to tell him he can't just disrespect us like that by just popping up. Then he wanted to talk—"

"In the bedroom?" he squealed.

Candace shrugged. "For privacy," she replied weakly.

"Right!" He turned around and looked at Jada and Alex. "Then you got your homies in crime out here listening while you in there getting it on with dude."

"Nothing happened, baby," Candace cried. "Nothing happened."

Rico pointed at Jada. "I bet you practically pulled his dick out and shoved him in there inside of her."

Jada frowned. "You're a demented little fuck. Don't address me please. In fact, Alex, let's go." She turned away to leave.

"Yeah, get the hell on. And *don't* come back." He turned to Candace. "You can't fuck with these grimy bitches anymore. What kind of friend lets you cheat on your husband and don't try to stop you?"

"Grimy bitch?" Alex repeated. "*Grimy bitch?*"

Rico looked at her. "Did I stutter? Fuck out my house, man. Surprised y'all bitches even have a man. Probably why your man didn't even wanna go out with you," he said pointing to Jada. "He probably cheating on yo' stuck-up ass. Told you . . . misery loves company."

"I'm not gon' be too many more bitches and what-not," Alex said balling up her fist.

"Guys, please," Candace begged them to let it go. Her party wasn't turning out the way she'd expected it to.

Jada walked up to Rico. Her belly nearly poked him in his midsection. "You know what? You ain't shit. What kind of man comes for a chick like this? A pussy-ass punk, that's who. I wish you would say one more word to me. Call me out my name one more time and I promise you my husband will squish your ass like the little bug you are." She reached down and picked up Candace's bowl of cheese dip.

Candace's eyes grew wide, and she held up her hands in fright. "No, Jada. Don't, please don't—"

Jada threw the dip on Rico and tossed the bowl at his head. He lunged for her, but Alex stepped forward before he could make a move.

"You gon' hit a pregnant woman?" Alex asked. "That's the day yo' ass is going to jail."

Rico flung cheese dip from his eyes. "Get the fuck out of my house!" he yelled.

"Gladly," Jada said. "Once you get one, ya' broke bitch." She turned away and headed for the door once more. "Let's go, Alex." She walked out without bothering to say good-bye to Candace. She was eager to leave the girl and her drama behind.

Alex smirked at Rico. "You met the right ones today, sweetie." She looked at Candace and shook her head. "You got some real mess to clean up, friend," she said, *not* referring at all to the cheese dip that was ruining her carpet. Alex exited the apartment and slammed the door behind her.

Candace fell to the floor. She was exasperated. Everything had gone totally wrong, and she didn't know what to do now. She vowed to never have a dinner party at her place again. Every time she did, things seemed to go left. Candace feared that this time she'd lost all of the relationships that were most important to her. All she could do was cry.

Chapter 78

Corey

"What you got for me?" Corey asked his boy. He lit up the blunt he'd just rolled and inhaled the herb deeply.

"Man, I'm telling you I know where their stash house is, but I don't know for sure who did what," Antonio said. "I mean, it ain't like I can just go up there and start asking questions. I heard that Man-Man and Justin are running the block. I can only assume that they're the ones that . . . you know. But they keep a gang of niggas around like they know you 'bout to come for them."

"As they should," Corey said passing the blunt over. "So we gotta see how we can get them two dudes alone without they crew. Gotta figure out how to get them alone where they can get to talking."

Antonio pulled hard on the blunt. "You know they say pussy is the greatest weakness known to man."

"So get a chick to do what? Go over there and front like she buying some shit or something?"

"Naw . . . Get a chick to make them think they gon' get some. They not gon' bring their homeboys through for that."

Corey shook his head and snatched his blunt back. "Nigga, you sound crazy. How the hell is that going to work?"

"What else you got?"

Corey thought about it. He really didn't have a better idea. "Fine . . . sounds extra but find a chick and run it."

"You want me to find a chick? I'on know, man."

Corey leaned back and gave it some consideration. He needed someone who wouldn't be scared to strut their stuff and lead these potentially dangerous dudes on. He needed someone who quite possibly owed him a favor and would feel obligated to do him this solid without him having to offer her anything in return. He could only think of one chick that fit the bill. "A'ight. It's going down tomorrow."

Antonio was high already. He had a lot of things on his mind these days. "What's going down?" His heart was racing thinking that Corey was ready to make a move without having figured out how to get Man-Man and Justin alone.

"The chick, dawg. We gon' send the chick 'round that way tomorrow. By this weekend we gon' get some get back."

Antonio wasn't so sure that things would work out that smoothly, but he was hoping that they'd hurry up and get past this whole ordeal.

He checked the time on his cell phone again. Where the hell was she? She hadn't sounded too happy to hear from him after all that had gone down, but he didn't care. He was on a mission and he wasn't about to be deterred by her feelings. He was about to send her a text to see what was up but an unfamiliar car whipped into the parking spot next to his, causing him to pause. He watched as she got out of her car and slammed the door. She opened his passenger door and slid inside.

"I'm here," Candace said, crossing her arms and not looking him in the eyes. "Now what do you want?"

"Why you gotta be so salty?" he asked her.

"You already know the answer to that."

"No, I don't."

"Did you call me down here to harass me about why I'm unhappy about being in your presence?"

Corey sucked his teeth. He wasn't going to be able to jump to the business without putting her in her place. "We're both grown. Say what's on your mind, Ma. Let's get it all out on the table so that we can move on."

"That's my problem," she said finally turning to look at him. She couldn't believe that she'd ever gone there with him. "I don't understand why we have anywhere to move on to. We don't have no business with one another, so why the hell are you bothering me?"

"You feeling some kind of way about me now?"

"I shouldn't? I mean, if I hadn't been fucking around with you I would have never been there arguing with one of my best friends before she died."

"Check this out . . . I didn't make you do shit. You're a grown woman, and you made a decision on your own free will. I didn't rape you, I didn't beg you for the pussy, and I definitely didn't trick your ass into opening your legs. So don't blame me for how you got ya' self caught up. It is what it is. On another note, don't be making light of this shit and regarding me like it was my fault. Stephanie didn't die, Candace. She was killed. There's a fuckin' difference."

Candace opened her mouth to speak, then closed it. There was no point in arguing with him. Corey was right, to a degree. She'd made a decision and had suffered the consequences rightly so. He saw the change in her demeanor and the anger in her face turn to hurt. He had her roped in emotionally.

"And that's what I called you for, Candace. I'm 'bout to fix the niggas that shot Stephanie," he told her.

Candace frowned. "Why are you telling me this?" she asked softly.

"Because I need your help. I need to get these niggas alone, and I need a chick to do that."

"Why me?"

"Because I know you wanna do something to help avenge your girl's death considering how y'all fell out."

Candace shook her head. "You trying to guilt me into being an accessory to some shit? I have a kid, Corey. I can't be putting myself in no dangerous situations with you. And I damn sho' shouldn't be sitting here with you with the damn feds hounding me to give them more information about them niggas and you and your associates."

"My associates?" His interest was piqued.

"Yes. This agent is gunning for you and wants to know about whoever the hell you hang out with or whatever. I don't like being tied to none of this criminal shit."

It was clear that the feds were trying their best to build up a case against Tommy and BDM. That had to be who the agent was questioning Candace about. Lucky for him no one but Antonio truly knew about his connection to the crime mob.

"I need you in on this, Candace," Corey said. "Help me do this. Help me get revenge for what they did to her."

Candace shook her head. She'd made a lot of bad decisions up to this point. Everything she touched fell apart, even her friendship with Stephanie. If she could take it all back she would, but she couldn't. She also didn't know how to fix any of it ongoing. How could she make any of it right? "What do I have to do?" she asked as a tear trickled down her left cheek.

They'd been sitting down the street from their rival's trap waiting for the dudes to bust a move. The front door opened and two young guys walked out with three other dudes following close behind them.

"That one right there with the hat on is Man-Man," Antonio said. "My cousin fucks with his sister."

Corey nodded. "A'ight, so I'm assuming the nigga beside him is Justin."

"Most likely."

The crew hopped into a black Suburban and drove down the street. Corey tailed them, being sure to stay far enough behind to not raise any red flags. They drove to the BP gas station and parked at a pump. Corey kept going and parked on the side of the convenience store. They watched from the window as the duo got out of the ride and walked inside with only one of their crew members trailing them.

Corey turned around to look at Candace who looked a little nervous. "You know what to do," he told her. "Keep it short, simple, and to the point. Make sure you sell it. A'ight?"

Candace nodded. She slowly exited the car and hurried to the front of the store. Wearing skintight jeans and a low-cut shirt accenting her breasts Candace knew she'd have no problem getting their attention. She could see them on the snack aisle and made her way around to come up the other end of the same aisle. Keeping her eyes low she walked toward them.

"What's up, Ma?" the guy Antonio said as Man-Man eyeballed her like he wanted to rip her clothes off.

She smiled at him. "What's up, Pa?"

Feeling himself, Man-Man sauntered over to her and touched her arm lightly. "Baby, you what's up, for real. What's yo' name?"

"Candy."

"Candy? Mmm, I bet you sweet like candy too, ain't you?"

"You already know."

"How 'bout you show me?"

Candace smiled coyly. "On one condition."

He raised an eyebrow. "And what's that?"

She looked over at the other guy Justin who wasn't paying them any attention. "Bring yo' boy with you."

Man-Man's eyes extended. "Word?"

Candace nodded.

At eighteen, Man-Man hadn't had a threesome yet and was ready to get it popping now if she was down to do it. "Stay right here." He stepped back and slapped Justin on the arm. "Aye, nigga, that girl wanna do a train."

Justin looked at Man-Man like he was crazy. "What you talkin' 'bout, stupid?"

"Ole girl wanna give us some of that good good. She told me herself she wanna fuck with us."

Justin looked over at Candace. She smiled at him seductively. Justin shook his head. "Get out of here. That girl ain't say that."

"I'm dead ass. Come on. What, you don't want no pussy?"

"I ain't desperate for no trim, nigga. And don't you got a bitch?"

Man-Man shrugged. "Ain't no pussy like new pussy."

Justin waved him off. "Man, I'm 'bout to get my shit and go to the car. You trippin'."

Candace approached them. The bigger brother standing behind Justin stepped forward. "Can we help you?" he asked her.

Man-Man gave the big guy the side-eye. "Aye, she cool, bruh."

Candace focused her attention on Justin. "Y'all gonna come holla at me or nah?"

Justin's facial expression was serious. "You just going 'round jumping niggas off?"

"Naw. But I fucks with bosses. You a boss, ain't you?"

Justin nodded. She had a point there. He nodded his head toward Man-Man. "Text my man ya' address and shit. We'll roll through."

Man-Man eagerly gave her his number, and she sent him a text with her address.

"Make sure you come by yourself," she told Man-Man. "Just you and ya' boy. Leave ya' homeboy over there at the house," she said eyeing the dude that tried to step to her.

Man-Man nodded. "We got you, Ma. We gon' roll through around eight. That cool?"

"Yep. That's cool." She reached out and touched his manhood for good measure. "I'ma see you then."

Candace grabbed a Little Debbie cake, went to the counter to pay for it to make her visit to the store seem legit, then hurried out of the store and to the car. She slid into the backseat and leaned back. Her heart was pounding. Corey pulled out of the parking spot and rode off in the opposite direction.

"We good?" Corey asked her looking in his rearview mirror.

She nodded. "Eight o'clock. This ain't gon' be messy, is it?"

Corey shook his head. "Not at all. Get 'em there, we gon' come in and snatch they ass out, then it's over. Simple as that."

"I don't need this shit coming back to me, Corey," she said cautiously.

"I'm on it, Candace. I got this."

She turned away and stared out of the window. Corey knew she was nervous but the hard part of her role was over and done. He was gonna take care of it from here on out. He looked over at Antonio. "Make sure you got two good runners ready."

Antonio nodded. He'd already had two of their men ready for action. The plan was simple. While Corey was handling Man-Man and Justin, the runners would knock off the two dudes they assumed would be left at the stash house, assuming one of their crew members drove them over to Candace's. While Corey was getting his revenge his men would be knocking over the stash house and getting his money back.

What could possibly go wrong?

Chapter 79

Miranda

Six Months Prior

"It all makes sense to me now," Stephanie said, brushing back her friend's hair.

"Don't judge me," Miranda said curtly. "Like you're perfect or something. Don't judge me. You don't know what my life is like, what I'm going through, or how I feel."

Miranda stated. "You're really just glad to know that Corey isn't fucking around on you . . . Well, at least not with me."

Current Day

She could remember it as if it was yesterday. It was the day Stephanie had caught her outside of the traphouse. The way Stephanie had looked at her; the feeling of embarrassment that came over her. The annoyance she felt knowing that Stephanie would run right back to the others and paint her out to be a monster. It was the moment she'd decided that Stephanie wasn't shit. It was one of the memories that had fueled her desire to get even with Stephanie and her dope boyfriend. And she'd done it. But in the end, she didn't feel any better because of it. Thinking about all the lies she'd told and all the mischievous things she'd done while not in her right mind made her shutter. She wanted to not care. None of them cared much about her. They'd all been so much more concerned with the irrelevant drama going on in their own lives to give a damn about her.

"Do you think it's fair?" Doctor Dunham asked her.

Miranda stared at her. "Do I think what's fair?"

She was sitting in her first group session since the time she'd assaulted Missy. Consequently they'd made sure not to seat her next to the girl who was still itching to get even with Miranda.

"We were talking about blaming others for the decisions that we've made. Do you think that's fair?"

She thought back to her previous admittance of having wanted someone to save her from herself. Since no one had done it she felt trapped within her own madness and was upset with the world. She blamed the girls and her family for not being the support system they claimed to be, but she certainly didn't blame them for the decisions she'd made.

"No. It's not fair," she said. "We're all grown. We're responsible for our own actions."

"Hmmm. So do you think it's fair for us to turn our backs on others when they fall short of what we think they should do or how we think they should be?"

Miranda blinked hard. Was it a trick question? "That's called disappointment. People shut down when they've been disappointed so many times."

"So at what point do we start to forgive?"

Miranda shrugged. "I don't know."

"If you hold the anguish in forever you're gon' always need some substance to take you away from it," Stacey, a heroin addict, commented. "Something to numb the pain."

"That breeds addiction," Doctor Dunham said.

"So you're saying we should start forgiving folk that have hurt us so we can kick our habits?" Miranda asked, trying to connect the dots.

Doctor Dunham nodded. "Forgiveness is for you. Not for the other person. It frees you up emotionally and mentally."

Miranda crossed her arms. She was going to have to think about that one. Perhaps it was time to forgive everyone for being absent when she'd needed them present the most. If Doctor Dunham was right she needed that freedom that came with forgiveness.

"The most important thing that you must do is forgive yourself," Doctor Dunham added. "First and foremost, you need to forgive yourself."

Forgive myself, Miranda thought. She needed to figure out how to do that.

Chapter 80

Candace

She was nervous. It was 8:10 p.m., and they still weren't there. It was just as well because Khalil hadn't shown up to pick up Zoe at 6:00 like he'd promised. Candace really wanted to pull out her cell and call Rico to see if they could talk about things. Ever since the fiasco with him and Khalil and her girls she hadn't been able to get a word in with him. He'd packed a bag and walked out of the house without any explanation of where he was going. Candace had been distraught. As she sat there now watching the seconds tick away on the clock above her television in the living room she wondered how she'd gotten herself to this point. Nothing was right, and she had a sense of unrest rooted inside of her that made it almost impossible for her to smile or feel any amount of joy.

Zoe was playing with her rattle in the swing that she loved so much. Candace shook her head. If Khalil was going to choose now to pull a disappearing act she was going to have to put the baby in the bedroom until this whole ordeal was over. She knew that Corey was parked outside somewhere in the parking lot near her building waiting for the dudes to arrive. With the way everyone else was not doing what they were supposed to be doing Candace prayed that Corey was keeping watch and that he'd show up immediately after the dudes knocked on her door because the last thing she was going to do was whore herself out in the name of exacting revenge against Stephanie's killers. That's where she drew the line.

It frightened her to think that the men that had gunned down her friend were going to be standing in her living room. Looking at them up close in the middle of the day earlier nothing about them had struck her as familiar. She wondered just how sure Corey was that he had the right guys. She didn't believe in Corey's method of revenge and tinkered with the idea of calling that GBI agent to come pick up the hoodlums. She dismissed the idea the moment she realized that she'd be questioned about just how they'd come to be in her apartment. She didn't want to implicate Corey in anything, not that she owed him that courtesy. Truth was she didn't want to face any charges of her own for her involvement in this dangerously stupid stunt.

Candace's phone rang, and she jumped. Nervously she picked it up and looked at the caller ID. Great, she thought. He would be calling back at the most inconvenient time. She answered the phone and tried to keep her tone light. "Hey, Rico."

"What's up?" he asked nonchalantly.

"I'm glad you called," she told him. Never mind the fact that she wished he'd waited just a little later to do so. "I miss you, baby."

"You sure 'bout that?"

"Why wouldn't I be? You're my husband." She figured it was a good selling point, even though they'd been married for a very short amount of time.

"So you trying to tell me you ain't been fucking that dude since we've been together?" he asked. "Not just since we been married. Since we've been together. Period."

"No!" she exclaimed, hoping that he believed her. "Absolutely not. It's just been me and you, Rico. You know that."

"No, I don't know that. I know that I saw dude coming out yo' bedroom fixing his pants like he'd just pulled them joints up . . . like he'd just been knee-deep in some shit that belongs to me."

"You have to trust me, Rico," she said watching Zoe swing back and forth in amazement. "Nothing's going on with me and Khalil. It was all just one big ugly misunderstanding. Please . . . come home."

Rico paused. "A'ight. I'ma come."

She smiled, but before she could comment there was a knock at the door. She'd almost forgotten about the plan that was about to go down. She needed to hurry up and get these

fools out of her house before her husband came home. She
didn't need to have a repeat performance from the last time
he'd been there. "So you gon' catch a ride over here?" she
asked opening her door and holding up her finger to silence
the thugs.

Justin gave her a funny look and hesitated in the doorway.
Man-Man, on the other hand, waltzed right in and took a seat
on the sofa. He had a box of condoms burning a hole in his
pocket.

"Yeah. When I leave the studio with my homeboy I'll be
there," Rico said over the phone.

"Okay. See you then," Candace said, avoiding the cold hard
stare that Justin was giving her as she disconnected the call
and set her phone on her dining-room table.

Justin closed the door and moved to stand by the sofa.
He saw the baby amusing herself in the swing and shook his
head. "You usually get down with your kid in the room?"

Candace shook her head and tried to relax. "Naw. Her dad
was supposed to come get her, but the jerk didn't come."

"So you just gon' leave her there?"

Candace shrugged. "I mean, I planned to just put her in her
bed."

"You should do that."

Candace could sense that something wasn't right with
Justin. "You okay?" she asked him. "You seem all on edge and
shit." She prayed that he wasn't on to her somehow.

"Who's ya' baby's daddy?"

"Why? He's nobody that you know or wanna know. Trust
me."

"Aye, man, chill," Man-Man interjected. "We supposed to
be having fun with ole' girl. You in here grilling her like you
the DA or some shit."

Justin shook his head. "Naw, something just don't feel
right."

Candace looked away from him and walked over to Zoe's
swing. Where the hell was Corey already? She didn't want
this experience or conversation to go any further. Justin
hurried over to her and started patting her down everywhere
abrasively.

"Hey!" Candace yelled feeling violated and scared. "What the fuck?"

"Just checking," he said eyeing her. "Relax. This what you wanted, right? For us to come fuck the shit out of you."

Candace cleared her throat. "Yeah," she said uncertainly. "I just figured you'd be a li'l more gentle about it and shit."

Man-Man walked over to them and grabbed her ass. "You ripe as hell, Ma," he said. He reached around, placed his hand under her tank top and squeezed her breasts.

Candace worked hard to fight back the tears of fear and frustration that threatened to fall. She didn't want them to sense that she was scared. "Let me . . . uh . . . let me take the baby to the back."

"Naw, you don't needa go back there," Justin said. "What's back there?"

"Nothing. I just don't want my baby exposed to this."

"You a good mother like that, huh?" Justin asked. "Well, your daughter's gon' learn that her mom's a ho sooner or later, so what difference does it make?" He pulled his gun from behind his back out of the band of his jeans. "Get on your knees."

"Aye, man, why the piece?" Man-Man asked his partner.

"'Cause I don't trust this bitch just yet."

Candace was biding her time now. "If you weren't down, then why'd you come?" she asked trying to sound completely legit with her freakiness.

"Curiosity," Justin told her pointing the gun at her forehead. "Now get your ass on your knees. You for real, then show me." With his free hand he unbuckled his jeans and slightly unzipped his pants.

Candace was afraid for her life and Zoe's. She fell to her knees. She was surprised that she hadn't started boo-hooing.

"You should be nicer to the ho," Man-Man stated whipping his dick out quickly and reaching down for her hand. He forced her to stroke him.

Candace wanted to throw up as she slowly unzipped the remainder of Justin's fly while slowly jerking Man-Man's penis. Just as she'd reached into Justin's musty-smelling drawers to pull out his dick, her front door flew open. Corey and Antonio stood in the doorway with their guns drawn and fixated on Justin and Man-Man.

"How 'bout you let the barrel of my bitch right here suck your dick off," Corey said.

"What the fuck?" Man-Man asked, reaching for his piece out of his sock.

"If you move I'm going to shoot your dick off," Antonio stated.

Immediately, Man-Man placed his hands in the air.

Justin smiled at Corey, pushed Candace away, and rezipped his fly. "I knew some shit wasn't right. So what now, nigga? What you gon' do now?"

Corey walked up to the trio and surveyed Candace quickly. "Get up and get the baby," he told her.

Shaking, Candace rose from the floor and fumbled to undo the snaps that held her baby securely in the swing. As she tried to move quickly Antonio walked over to Man-Man and motioned for him to walk toward the door. He did as instructed.

Justin laughed. "Shoulda known y'all niggas would use some pussy to try to come for us. Don't you know if you fuck with me, then Martinez just gon' send some dudes to fuck up the rest of yo' crew and knock off BDM?"

Candace didn't know what he was talking about, and she didn't care to hear any more of their street talk. She freed a fussy Zoe from the swing and moved to walk toward her bedroom.

Antonio was standing at the door aiming his gun at Man-Man's head and looking back at Corey. "Come on, man. Let's go."

"You shot my girl, didn't you?" Corey asked Justin. Everything inside of him told him that this was the exact heartless thug that had taken Stephanie's life.

"I see you got the message," Justin said ruthlessly. "You don't fuck with Martinez's crew. You gon' shoot me, nigga? Shoot me then. I ain't afraid to die. I'm 'bout this life." He then spat in Corey's face.

The sound of his voice as he mentioned Corey getting the message and the way he spat in Corey's face brought back a sudden painful memory. It was like Candace was watching Stephanie being assaulted all over again. The way the man had jumped out of the car and issued the warning to her already dead body, and then spat on her like she was a pile of dirt. She turned to look at Justin in fright. She knew without a doubt that that bastard had been one of the men hurling bullets into her friend that unforgettable night. "Oh my God," she said without realizing that she was speaking at all.

Justin looked over at her and squinted hard. He could see the recognition in her eyes. Before anyone could say a word a bullet flew out of nowhere. Man-Man now had his piece in hand after the two seconds Antonio had slacked in his alertness caused by Candace's exclamation. The baby began to wail loudly, and before Candace could run to her bedroom more gunshots erupted, and she felt a jolt that caused her to drop to the floor with Zoe in hand. The feeling of déjà vu had Candace on the brink of going crazy.

Before Man-Man could bust another shot Antonio put a bullet through his chest. Man-Man dropped to the ground in the doorway and was immediately gone. Antonio then hollered at Corey to come the hell on. His urges were drowned out by Candace's screams and the two more rounds that Corey left off as he placed bullets, one behind the other, between Justin's eyes as the man lay lifeless on the floor. Things moved in slow motion for a moment as a sense of relief washed over him. *This was for you, Steph*, he thought as he closed his eyes briefly.

Candace was distraught. There was blood all over her arm, and Zoe was shaking and screaming uncontrollably. Corey turned around to view the scene. He raced into the kitchen, grabbed a dish towel, and then returned to throw it at Candace.

"My baby!" Candace cried out. "My baby! My baby! You mutherfuckers shot my baby."

"Corey!" Antonio was shaking. He knew the police would soon be coming following all the gunfire.

Corey couldn't afford the repercussions if he was to get caught. He knew he had to bounce. It tore at his heart to watch Candace sitting in the middle of the floor cradling her daughter who had apparently got caught in the crossfire. He touched her head lightly, turned, and ran from the apartment, leaving Candace alone.

"Corey!" she screamed. "Corey! You mutherfucker! Help!" No pain in the world could compare to what she was feeling now. Out of all the things she'd done, agreeing to this scheme had to have been the worst. It was definitely the most costly because here she was sitting with her dying toddler in her arms and no one around at all to help her.

"Jehovah, help me," she pleaded lying down on the floor cradling her daughter as shock began to set in. "Help me. Please don't take my child. Take me instead."

Chapter 81

Clay

Clay was preparing to go home after a long day at the office. As he shut down his computer his office door swung open and his boss, Anthony, walked in with a wide smile. Clay shook his head. If the man was about to ask for a favor he could forget it. All Clay wanted to do was go home, have dinner, and wrap his arms around his girlfriend.

"No can do," Clay said making his position on the matter known. "I'm out of here, Anthony."

Anthony chuckled. "Relax, Clay. I have excellent news for you."

"What is it?" Clay asked grabbing his keys out of his desk drawer.

"That opportunity I told you about in Cali . . . they wanna interview you," Anthony said with his arms opened wide. "This is your opportunity, Clay. They've been going over your portfolio and are very interested in you."

Clay was shocked. Since the Monday after the mishap at Clay's birthday party Clay hadn't heard anything else about this golden opportunity. Since he'd been trying to patch things up with Alex he hadn't had a chance to give it any thought at all. Now Anthony was telling him that the prestigious entertainment agency was considering him for the job of a lifetime. "When?" Clay asked barely able to articulate the word. "When's the interview?"

"In the morning."

Clay stared at his supervisor. He couldn't have been serious. "In the morning? How long have you known this? When were they going to call and actually extend the interview to me?"

"My buddy there called me this afternoon to advise."

Clay shook his head and felt his temperature rise. How could this be slipping from his hands when he hadn't even had a second to revel in the fact that they wanted him? "There's no way I can get a flight out of here on such short notice, Ant. I can't just—"

Anthony reached over and punched Clay's arm playfully. "Trust your mentor, Clay. Harold Remington is flying out here to visit one of their Atlanta clients. He's the one hiring for the position. While he's here placating the outta control rapper he's going to swing by to meet you here at the office. Around one." Anthony leaned back against the desk, crossed his arms, and smiled at Clay. "Relax, brotha. This job is yours. Don't say I never did anything for you."

Clay looked down at the floor, popped the collar of his shirt, and nodded. Anthony had definitely come through for him. "What can I say, man?"

"Don't say anything. Just make sure you're on top of ya' game tomorrow. Don't do anything to piss the man off and get ready to get your stuff out of this office. Trust me. You got this in the bag. Meeting you in person tomorrow is a mere formality. With the research they'd done on you and the reference I've provided, the only thing that can mess this up is if he hates you. So you better be likeable, damn it!"

Clay laughed nervously. "Yes, sir."

Anthony held his hand out. "Good luck, Clay. I'll see you tomorrow."

Clay shook the man's hand. "Thanks, Anthony. I appreciate it."

He walked into the apartment with a bottle of wine ready to celebrate what could quite possibly be the beginning of something wonderful. He wasn't really sure how Alex was going to take the news, but this was monumental for his career. During the ride home he'd mentally gone over ways to make sure that their relationship didn't falter because of his pending location change. He wanted Alex with him, but he knew that she had to finish fashion school. Well, she at least needed to finish out the term. Surely they could find a school for her to transfer to out in Cali.

"Alex!" he called out as he stepped over her heels at the door and ignored the bags she'd dropped on the floor earlier. He hurried to the kitchen where he set down the wine bottle and grabbed two wineglasses from the cabinet. "Alex, baby! What you doing?" He filled the glasses to the top and carried them off to their bedroom.

Alex was sitting on the left side of the bed lacing up her shoes while staring over at the television positioned across from the bed. The sound was muted and the news was on. Clay didn't bother to ask her why she was watching the news in silence. He walked around to her and held out a glass of wine for her to take. Alex's eyes didn't venture over to him. She was too busy staring at the television screen.

"Baby, take the glass," Clay told her. "We need to drink tonight."

Alex nodded. "You're so right." She took the glass and guzzled it down.

Clay's eyes widened. "Um, you could've waited for the toast. And wine wasn't meant to be chugged. It's meant to be sipped, baby. You should know that."

Alex set the glass on the nightstand and ignored her boyfriend's remarks. She was in no mood to be berated by him for her lack of couth today. She tied her other shoe and glanced back over at the television.

Clay was feeling annoyed. "So you don't even want to know why we're drinking? Something big happened to me today. Well, not actually today. It's going to happen tomorrow. Well, tomorrow's the start of it." He was rambling, but he was excited, and he desperately needed the love of his life to be excited with him.

Alex stood up and looked him in the eyes. "I can't right now, Clay."

"You can't what?" he asked feeling deflated. "I'm just asking you to listen to me. You can't listen?"

Alex walked away from him. She walked around the bed and got a ponytail holder from the dresser.

Clay was annoyed. He'd been ecstatic the whole ride home; now he gets here and Alex was acting like he was bothering her. He walked around the bed and flipped the light switch on. Whether she wanted to or not they were about to get to the heart of whatever was causing her to rain on his parade. "I need you to tell me what's up with you! I'm in here trying to share a moment with you and . . ."

Alex turned to look at him and his words trailed off. For the first time he noticed the dark circles under her eyes, the redness taking over the whites of her eyes, and the sullen expression on her face. He set his glass down on the dresser and stepped forward to survey her closer. "What happened?" he asked softly.

Alex's eyes drifted away from his and back to the television. Quickly she walked to the bed, grabbed the remote, and then turned the sound up. Clay turned to see what was so important on the news that his girlfriend was in tears.

"It's a tragic day in DeKalb County for this mother of one, John," stated a reporter standing outside with a grim expression on her face. "Candace Lawson Perry of Doraville is facing a life-changing experience that no mother ever wants to face. We're here at the Children's Hospital of Atlanta in DeKalb County where Lawson's daughter, just shy of turning six months old, was admitted after being shot during an apartment break-in. Perry says she and her daughter were alone in their home when two men burst into their home. Per Perry, one of the robbers fired shots the moment she tried to race off to the back of the apartment with her daughter. Perry was found in her home several moments later by her husband. Lawson Perry's daughter, Zoe, is not the biological daughter of her husband. Little Zoe was shot in the head and has undergone two surgeries since the horrific event this past weekend. She's here in critical condition in ICU at Children's Hospital. Officials haven't given us any further information about the child's health. Police have questioned the mother about the shooting, noting that nothing was stolen or removed from the apartment. We currently have no information on whether police have a lead on the suspects. Candace Lawson Perry suffered a traumatic labor and delivery earlier this year when she was an eyewitness to the murder of her best friend Stephanie Johnson, the girlfriend of known drug lord Corey Polk, who was recently

exonerated for the murder of Montae Stokes. As a result, baby Zoe was born prematurely and is now fighting for her life following this incident. We'll bring you more information once the hospital staff releases an official statement."

The male news anchor shook his head solemnly. "Tragic life this child has had, indeed, Carla. Stay tuned to Fox Five News. This is one story I'm sure many will want to keep up with."

The feeling of déjà vu washed over Clay as he turned from the television and looked at Alex. There always seemed to be some devastating events going on in her circle. It was draining and taxing. The evidence was written all over Alex's face. Clay wished that he could remove her from this toxic circle she was involved in but knew that it was pointless to try to extract her from her friends. But deep down he honestly felt like a change of pace was exactly what they both needed. The possibility of him getting this job in California now sounded even more appealing to him.

He placed his arms around her. He kissed her forehead, then held her tightly. "I'm sorry for your friend," he said softly.

She leaned into his embrace, placed her arms around him, and closed her eyes. "It's so horrible, precious. Nothing's been the same since Stephanie got killed. Really, nothing's been the same since the whole drama with Miranda started popping off. I just can't . . ."

"Some things you just have to pray about and step away from," he said. "When you don't know what else to do, you just gotta pray."

"What is happening? If we pray it isn't going to change what's happened."

"It gives you strength and helps you to deal."

"Poor Candace."

Clay took a breath. The whole story had sounded kind of fishy to him as the news anchor relayed it. He wondered what had really happened in that apartment that night. What kind of mess had Candace been involved in now to cause her daughter's life to be placed in harm's way yet again? He didn't want to bring up his concerns with Alex right now, knowing that she was in turmoil. Instead, he wanted to lift her spirits.

"What if I told you that I have a way to change some things? Brighten the mood and take you away from all of the stuff going on around here?"

Alex pulled away. "I can't do vacation now, Clay. Candace needs us now more than ever. I gotta go. I need the car to go down to the hospital. I'll be back later." She walked out of the room without so much as giving him a peck on the cheek.

Clay sat on the edge of the bed and stared at the doorway as if willing her to walk back through it. He heard the front door open and close and knew that she wasn't coming back any time soon. This should have been a joyous night for him, but instead, he was brooding over the fact that his girl was upset and he couldn't pull her away from the destructive magnet that kept pulling at her. Clay wondered if his feelings were selfish, but then decided that he'd been there for her more times than not. This time he wanted her to be there for him in his moment of accomplishment. *Her girlfriends need her*, he thought. Clay fell back onto the bed frustrated with the course of their relationship. *What about what I need?*

Chapter 82

Jada

The stress was mounting. After the big fight at Candace's place with her husband and with dealing with her own issues with Jordan, Jada just couldn't find any peace. She knew that it was affecting her pregnancy so she was trying with everything within her to remain positive. They hadn't really worked things out, but they were at least being cordial to each other. Jada considered it a start. She noticed that Jordan was spending more and more time on his phone but she tried not to let it bother her. He wasn't the one carrying this baby, she was. For the sake of their son she needed to keep her feelings and blood pressure in check. For that reason she was also avoiding her girls. All of the unnecessary drama was driving her crazy and causing her physical issues. She knew all too well how the others couldn't care less about what she had going on or how she felt. It was time for her to start taking better care of herself and looking out for Jada above all else.

She'd returned to work and was trying to get back in the swing of things. Coming home one Monday she realized that she was extremely exhausted. She stopped to get the mail, then walked on slowly back to her unit as she looked through the envelopes. Seeing that their new insurance cards had arrived Jada decided to be nice and place Jordan's card inside of his glove compartment. She used her spare key and unlocked his car door. She slid into the driver's seat and leaned over to open up the little gray door. To her surprise, a green box fell out of the stuffed compartment and onto the seat. Quickly she picked it up. She went to toss it back inside, but her hand stopped in midair the moment she realized that it was a condom box.

Jada looked at it closely and noticed that it was open. She read the front of the box and discovered that it was supposed to be a three pack. Peering inside she saw that there were only two condoms in the box. All of her suspicions had been confirmed within those few moments. She tossed the insurance card into the glove compartment, exited the car, and made her way to her cozy little cottage-style apartment. Jordan was in the kitchen cooking dinner; no doubt he was trying to redeem himself from all the trouble he'd caused. Jada placed her purse on the sofa and waddled into their kitchen.

"Hey, babe," Jordan greeted her as if they were the happily in love couple they'd been just a few short months prior.

"Hello," she answered dryly as she took a seat at their tiny kitchen table. She set the box of condoms on the table in front of her.

"I made some Chicken Alfredo that I think you're going to love."

"Is that right?"

"Once the garlic bread is done it'll be time to eat." He went to the refrigerator and poured her a glass of pink lemonade. Then he walked over and set the glass in front of her. She saw his eyes bulge the moment he took in the box of condoms.

"What's the matter?" she asked him, picking up her lemonade glass. "Cat got your tongue?"

Jordan just looked at her. Once again he found himself trying to figure out a believable story to dish out to her as she stared him down.

"No," she said. "Cat doesn't have your tongue. Your dick got some cat. That's what happened, right?" She gave him a scary smile.

"Baby, that's not mine."

She held her hand up. "Save it. I don't want to hear any more of your tired excuses, your weak-ass lies, or your stupid fabrications. You're a liar, Jordan. You're a cheater and a liar. At least you had the decency to use protection," she said fingering the box. "But it doesn't matter because it'll be a cold day in hell before I let you touch me again." She rose from the table.

Jordan reached out to her. "Baby—"

"Baby *what?*" she snapped. "What can you possibly say to me, Jordan, that you think is going to fix this? Here I am trying to give you a baby, and you're going around making every bitch in the world *but* me feel like they're something special. I really wish I'd never married you." She walked out of the kitchen.

The smell of burning garlic bread pulled Jordan out of his daze. He hurried to remove the pan from the stove and tossed the bread into the garbage. How could he have been so stupid as to forget about the box of condoms LaTanya had left in his car? Since that night he'd talked to her every day, and every day she'd tried to encourage him to divorce Jada saying that he was better off without her. Some days he felt maybe LaTanya was right. Maybe he needed someone a little different from Jada to keep him satisfied. But as he watched his pregnant wife's eyes as she told him she wished they'd never gotten married he knew that all he wanted was his family. He'd fucked up royally, but he just didn't know how to stay away from temptresses like LaTanya that were helping make it so easy for him to ruin his marriage.

Jada's cell phone rang. She looked at the caller ID and saw that it was Alex calling. She didn't have time for whatever theatrics her friend had going on today. She sent the call to voice mail. Finally back at work and off of bed rest, she was finding it hard to focus on anything aside from the fact that her marriage was one big epic failure. She tried to review all the things that she'd said or done that could have possibly made her husband feel that she wasn't worth his love, energy, devotion, or affection. Like everyone else, she thought that they had a stellar relationship. Once she'd finally gotten pregnant all of that seemed to change. At this point, she wasn't sure there was a way to get them back on track.

"Jada, I need that McKenzie file when you get a minute," her supervisor said poking her head into Jada's office.

Jada turned to look at her and offered a fake smile. "Sure thing."

As she pressed the keys on her keyboard to finish the memorandum she was working on she saw the incoming mail indicator for her Yahoo! account at the bottom of her screen. She clicked on her Yahoo! window and saw that she had an e-mail from Jordan. Curious about what he had to say she began to read it. It didn't take long for her to realize that this definitely was not a message from Jordan.

Dearest Jada,

I know you must be excited to be getting mail from your dear Jordan. I hate to break the news to you, but this isn't Jordan. This is your friendly computer hacker doing his good deed for the day. It seems your true love Jordan has been a naughty boy! Not only has he tried to hack into your e-mail, but he has also saved some interesting mail from other women on his Yahoo! e-mail account . . .

Given this, I don't feel that it is a bad thing that you have our dear Jordan's password so that you may see for yourself.

The password for this and probably all of his e-mail accounts is "only me."

Have fun and go easy on him. He is only a lying, cheating scum who has zero respect for a lovely woman like yourself!

Love,

Your friend

Jada's eyes couldn't believe the words she'd just read on her screen. What the hell was happening? Apparently someone had hacked into Jordan's account, and now they'd felt inclined to further ruin her faith in her marriage by sharing Jordan's dirty little secrets. Her fingers trembled as she tried to type a reply back to let whomever her informant was know that they could come on with whatever other information they had. Jordan didn't know it but his ass was about to be put out of their home for good.

Before she could hit the send button on the message she was attempting to compose she noticed that she'd received another incoming message. She clicked off of her e-mail and clicked into her inbox. There was another message from

Jordan's account, but this time it was a copy of an ongoing chat conversation he'd obviously been having.

> Jordan_Pluv: She wouldn't want us to be friends. She'd think that you have a hidden agenda . . . This bitch is crazy.
>
> SexyTJ83: I'm not tripping off her. I don't trip that you have a wife . . . So if you wanna still kick it, it's cool with me . . . It's your call.
>
> Jordan_Pluv: I'm not letting you go, LaTanya . . . You was right, tho. I was better off just being without her . . . I want you!
>
> SexyTJ83: I know it's not right . . . but that makes me feel better . . . I want you too. Some bitches were meant to be wifed up.
>
> Jordan_Pluv: At least thanks to you my dick ain't dry no mo'.

Jada was shaking. She couldn't believe the things that she was reading. Jordan had clearly lost his mind. She quickly printed the two e-mails she'd just received, shut down her computer, grabbed her purse, and then walked out of her office. She stopped by her supervisor's office on the way out the door. "Hey, I have an emergency. Doctor called me. I needa go by the office for some lab work."

Her supervisor nodded. Jada had just come back to work from being on bed rest, now this. But what could she say? "Okay. See you tomorrow."

Jada didn't feel bad lying to get out of work. She just needed a quick excuse so that she could go handle her business. The drive from her office to the downtown building where the radio station was located took a little under twenty minutes. During that time Jada had shed some tears, cursed a thousand times, and prayed to God that she didn't go to jail today. Her anger had reached critical mass, and Jordan was about to be in for a very rude awakening.

She parked her car, found the elevator, and headed up to the floor where the station was located. She knew that he was still on air with about an hour and a half left of broadcasting time. She walked in and went straight past Michelle, the receptionist.

"Hey, Jada. Jada!" Michelle called after her.

Jada didn't give a damn. If the girl called security, then, oh well. It was going down today whether they wanted it to or not. Jordan was in the studio with his sound producer, intern, and other people that Jada didn't know nor understood their purpose. Jordan's eyes lit up when he saw his wife enter the room.

"Hey, look at this," he said into his mic. "We've been pleasantly surprised by the one and only Mrs. Jada Presley."

"Or not so pleasantly," Jada said as she reached over to grab the cup of coffee that he had sitting in front of him. She threw the contents into his lap, and he quickly hopped out of his seat.

"What the fuck!" he screamed in a panic from the sensation of the scalding hot liquid.

"Shoot to a commercial now!" Raven, the producer instructed.

"What the fuck is wrong with you?" Jordan yelled at Jada. "Why you bring your crazy ass down here showing your ass at my job?"

Jada threw the copies she'd made at him.

Jordan grabbed the paper and glanced down at it. "What the hell is this that it couldn't have waited 'til we were home?" He got his answer as soon as he recognized the message strand between himself and LaTanya. He looked up at Jada nervously.

"Because yo' ass don't have a home to go to. Let me be very clear about this, Jordan, so there's no fuckin' misunderstanding. You can have this bitch you talking to in that message and any of your other skanks you been fucking with. I'm done with you. I can raise my baby without you 'cause ain't nothing your lying, pathetic ass can teach him about being a real man. I hope your dick falls off in one of these bitches and you both die from AIDS."

A crowd gathered outside the window of the studio watching the scene play out. Mona sat quietly in the corner on the computer praying that Jada didn't start hurling insults her way. She hoped that her name had never come up in any of their previous arguments. Secretly, Mona was pleased to see Jordan getting his ass handed to him, especially since he hadn't been giving her the time of day since she'd given him head in his office awhile back.

"Baby, let me explain," Jordan said weakly. He still hadn't recovered from the stinging in his crotch.

"Fuck you. It's over." Jada turned to leave the studio but ran into the station manager just as he entered the door.

"You wanna tell me why you're having a Jerry Springer moment in my goddamn studio?" Raymond belted.

"I'm sorry, Ray," Jordan said. "We're done. We'll take it outside."

"You still have a show to finish. I suggest you handle your family issues on your own time. You're on *my* time right now." Raymond looked at the swell of Jada's belly, and then up at her swollen eyes. "I'm sorry, Jada, but we gotta keep some order around here."

"It's okay, Raymond," Jada said. "I'm done with his ass. He's all yours." She exited the studio and prepared to go home. She had some serious packing to do.

Chapter 83

Candace

Her head was spinning. Way too much was going on for her to handle. People were constantly in and out, and everyone had questions. Doctors, police, her parents, reporters, and even Rico. The one person who had yet to put in an appearance was Khalil. It was just like him to be hiding out somewhere when his daughter needed him the most. With all of the questioning she was enduring, the most frightening interrogation had come from the social worker from the Department of Family and Children Services. She hadn't expected to be paid a visit by DFCS, but it certainly made sense, especially since Candace knew that the story she'd woven together for everyone was a complete lie.

She sat in the small family room at the end of the ICU floor with Rico holding her hand. Her parents were down in the room with Zoe. The social worker sat at the table with her tan suit and professional demeanor. It was all just another case to her, but for Candace, it felt like the end of her life as she knew it.

"I don't want you to feel like we're trying to make your life more complicated," Ms. Campbell, the social worker stated, without looking up from her notes. "This is just a precaution we're taking. We're working in the best interests of Zoe, therefore, the county needs to be able to assess whether your daughter is safe in your home environment."

"Why wouldn't she be?" Rico asked defensively.

Ms. Campbell looked up from her papers. "The child was shot in the head. She's sitting in a hospital room on life support right now, Mr. Perry."

"Shit happens. It was a break-in."

"You see, that's the thing. Your wife states it was a break-in but the police found no evidence of forced entry and nothing was taken from your home. That doesn't sound like a break-in." Sensing the tension from Rico she hurriedly dressed up her bluntness. "Now, I'm not saying that it didn't happen the way your wife says, I'm saying that the police called us in to make an assessment about your family's environment and background to see if this child is safe based on their speculations about the incident."

Candace raised her tear-swollen eyes to meet the social worker's. "The police called you in?"

Ms. Campbell nodded. "Yes. So I want you to know how this process will work. After I'm done talking to you I'll be interviewing others close to you. The grandparents, any friends you have that are frequently around, the child's biological father—"

"Good luck on that," Candace said sarcastically.

"Once we get a good feel for Zoe's home life I'll turn my assessment over to the police."

"If you don't like what you find out about us, then what?" Rico asked.

"If I find some things questionable or unsafe about your lifestyle, I'll have to give a recommendation to the agency to remove Zoe from the home," Ms. Campbell answered matter-of-factly.

Candace began to tremble as the tears ran rampant once more. That was exactly what she feared, that her child would be taken away from her. She wanted so badly to go back to that moment in the living room when Rico had found her on the floor cradling Zoe's limp, bleeding body. She'd been so scared, and all of the horrible possibilities were attacking her mind at once. She was afraid that she'd be arrested. She was afraid that Zoe was dead on the spot. She was scared that the bodyguard for Man-Man and Justin would come back and kill her once he realized that something had happened to his boys as a result of her con.

Once Rico had walked in and saw the dead men on the floor he was perplexed. She'd quickly spun a web of lies explaining that the assailant that was with them had shot their two comrades and left. It was the same story she repeated for the police after Rico called them. She wondered why her neighbors hadn't called the police before. Surely someone had heard her cries and the gunshots.

Here she was facing having her child taken away and lying to everyone in sight while Corey was roaming the streets free. It was because of him that she was in this mess. She'd lied for him, but the lie was protecting her too. But while she was so busy protecting Corey and herself who was protecting her daughter? She looked up at the social worker and tried to take a deep breath. The police and the county were trying to protect Zoe. They were trying to protect her from her mother who was constantly putting her in these dangerous situations.

"I've run a background check on both of you," Ms. Campbell stated. "So while I'm waiting for that information to come back I'll be conducting my personal interviews. Do you have any questions for me at this time?"

"How long will all this take?" Rico asked. "'Cause if you haven't noticed we're trying to take care of our daughter and you're kind of making this difficult for us."

Ms. Campbell gave him a cold smile. "Of course, Mr. Perry. I'll try to wrap my visit up as quickly as possible."

There was a knock on the door before Mrs. Lewis stuck her head in. Her eyes were also red and puffy. "Candace, honey, the doctor needs to speak with you."

Candace nodded and looked over at Ms. Campbell. "I have to go. Do what you need to do, but please . . . don't disturb me again." She rose from the table and headed out of the door followed by Rico.

Rico had wanted to ask the woman more questions about the background check she'd requested. He was feeling apprehensive about a few things and didn't want any more stress to be added to Candace's plate right now. He also understood why the police and everyone were giving Candace the side-eye. Her story made no sense, but it was all any of them had to go by. The only other surviving person that had been found in that living room was baby Zoe, and she was too young to say anything to either cosign or negate Candace's story.

The couple entered the room, and Candace almost fainted seeing her tiny baby girl bandaged up and attached to so many machines. She'd seen her like this for the last day or so but the sight never got easier to bear, especially with the massive amount of guilt she was holding on to. Candace was distraught. She immediately walked over to stand next to the tiny baby bed that housed her daughter's suffering body.

"I wanted to get the whole family together to explain what's going on," Doctor Gordon stated. He was a world-class neonatal neurosurgeon, and Candace was grateful to have him caring for her daughter.

Candace's parents, Mr. and Ms. Lewis, stood near the door holding hands. Rico stood next to Candace by Zoe's bedside.

"Your Zoe has really tried to be a trooper," Doctor Gordon stated. "When she came in she'd lost a considerable amount of blood and there was hemorrhaging in the brain. We were able to go in and remove the bullet, but she has since gone into hypovolemic shock."

"What . . . What does that mean?" Candace asked.

"It means that she's not getting adequate oxygen to her other organs." He pointed to a nearby machine. "This machine is basically breathing for her, attempting to give her the oxygen she's not producing on her own. A bullet wound to the head can be very traumatic for an adult so you can imagine the effects it's having on a premature baby. Mr. and Mrs. Perry, you should prepare yourselves . . ."

Rico placed his arm around Candace for support the moment her body began to stagger. Her spirit was telling her that she wasn't going to be able to withstand what was said next.

"Jehovah be with us," Mrs. Lewis prayed from the back of the room.

"Even with the machine providing her the maximum amounts of oxygen we can pump into her, Zoe's organs are already starting to fail." He pointed to another machine. "This monitor is telling us that despite our greatest efforts there is little to no brain activity."

Candace shook her head.

"But she's still here," Rico said. "I mean, you got her hooked up to stuff. None of this stuff can fix the brain activity?"

Doctor Gordon shook his head no. "Unfortunately, there is no way for us to revive her brain. Medically speaking, Zoe is brain dead. Her body is only still here, as you said, because of this first machine. But like I said, her organs are very weak and are already starting to fail despite the machine. Zoe's not going to come back from this. But keeping her on life support is your family's right and decision to make. However, in my professional opinion, no matter if you opt to keep the life support going she's not going to make it to the end of the week. I'm sorry."

Candace was silent. The room went dark, and she felt her body swaying. She could hear the others firing questions to the doctor, but her brain wasn't able to process anything that was being said. She was lost in the memory of hearing the doctor basically tell her that her daughter's life was over. This was the end. She'd never wanted to be a mother, but the moment she'd laid eyes on Zoe she was completely in love. She adored the little girl, and now she'd successfully lost the one person who probably loved her unconditionally. She might as well have pulled the trigger herself because Candace felt that this was all her fault. Her body hit the floor and everyone lunged forward to retrieve her.

"Candace! Baby! Get up," Mrs. Lewis called out as her knees hit the floor.

Doctor Gordon pressed a button on the wall and a nurse ran in. "Get me a full-length gurney!" he shouted to the nurse.

The nurse ran right back out, and Doctor Gordon towered over Candace. He lifted her eyelids one at a time and examined them with his retinoscope. "Candace, can you hear me?"

Rico was stroking her hair. He'd never been so scared in his life. "Come on, baby. Come on."

The door opened. Everyone expected to see the nurse, but it was Alex. She stood in the doorway with her mouth gaping open at the sight of her friend laid out on the floor. "What happened?"

"She passed out," Mr. Lewis said, turning away from the girl he remembered to be one of his daughter's stuck-up friends.

He was in no mood to fill any of her wayward comrades in about what was currently going on in their family. "You should wait outside."

"But I—"

"Ma'am, I think it's best if you wait out in the waiting room," Doctor Gordon stated.

Alex nodded and stepped back just as the nurse returned with a tech to help assist the doctor.

Chapter 84

Alex

"Jada, it's Alex. You need to get down to the hospital imme-diately. I think the baby's in really bad shape and Candace was out cold on the floor when I walked in. Call me back, girl. This is serious." Alex ended her message and took a deep breath. Things were out of control. She had no idea what she should do next.

"Excuse me," a female's voice interrupted Alex's thoughts.

Alex turned around to see who would dare bother her while she was in a moment of despair. The last thing she wanted to do was have casual conversation with someone while her friend's world was being turned upside down. It was as if their circle just couldn't get any peace.

"I'm sorry, I overheard you on your phone," the thin woman with the wrinkled suit stated. "You're friends with Candace Perry?"

Alex nodded. "Yes. Why?"

"Well, I'm Ms. Campbell, and I'm an intake worker from DFCS."

"Intake? What . . . What are you talking about?"

"I'm from the Child Protective Services division."

Alex understood completely. "Uh-huh. And what can I do for you?"

"I'm conducing personal interviews with people that know Ms. Perry and Zoe. We need to be able to get a look at what their home life is like given what has recently happened to the baby."

Alex stared at the woman hard. "You want me to tell you stuff about my girl to help you build a case against her? Are you serious right now?"

Ms. Campbell shook her head. "No no no. This isn't about building a case against anyone. This is about making sure that Zoe is safe when she leaves this hospital."

Alex turned away from the woman and took a seat. She was filled with so many emotions that it was becoming a little unbearable. She wished that Clay had been considerate enough to come down to the hospital with her. She fought the urge to call and ask him to take the MARTA to come be with her. She could really use his shoulder to lean on right now since Jada had yet to put in an appearance.

The social worker quickly took a seat next to Alex. "Look, you care about your friend, I can see that. I'm sure you care about that baby too. So if you just allow me to ask you a few questions, then you can possibly help make sure that your friend doesn't lose custody of her daughter."

Alex thought about it. It was the least she could do. "Fine."

"Great." Ms. Campbell pulled out her notepad. "Okay, so how long have you known the mother?"

"For years. We've been friends for several years."

"And would you say that she's a responsible individual?"

"Yeah, for the most part. She's real big on making a name for herself. Candace always wants to make sure her star is shining bright so she does what she has to do to achieve that. She's been working and taking care of herself for a minute. After she had Zoe she was busting her butt to balance her life."

"What about her decision making? Do you think she makes good decisions as they affect her life and the baby's?"

It wasn't an easy question for Alex to answer, especially given some of the recent events. She didn't agree with Candace's decision to marry Rico on a whim. She hadn't agreed with her decision to marry Quincy either or to sleep with Khalil knowing that he was married. Alex had been dismayed by Candace's gall to be creeping around with Corey before, but for the sake of burying the hatchet, it was a thing that none of the girls harped on any longer. It was funny how everything they were trying to move past had a way of floating right back to the surface.

"Um . . . I don't know how . . . I guess I'd say . . ." Alex didn't want her opinion about the way Candace conducted her personal affairs to have a negative impact on her daughter's future. She now wished that she'd never consented to answering any of the woman's questions.

"It's really a simple question," Ms. Campbell said growing annoyed with the young woman's hesitance. She took it to mean that the mother was obviously not a good decision maker since her own friend couldn't readily answer yes to the question.

Before Alex could say anything Zoe's room door opened and Rico appeared as he ushered Candace out. She had recovered quickly but was still a little shaky. The doctor appeared behind them. Sensing that her interview with the friend was stalled, Ms. Campbell called out to the parents. "Mr. and Mrs. Perry?"

They stopped in front of her. Candace was staring at the woman but her head was continuously spinning. All she wanted was to lie down and wake up when the whole ordeal was over. Rico had a scowl on his face. He'd just about had enough of the social worker.

"I wanted to advise you that your background checks were back," Ms. Campbell said.

"Um, perhaps now's not the time, miss," Doctor Gordon advised.

Candace's eyes drifted over to Alex who was sitting on the edge of her chair with her eyes wide as a shocked doe's. Candace looked back at the social worker. "What's going on? What are you doing?" she asked in a slurred tone. "What are you doing with her?"

Ms. Campbell looked over to Alex and shrugged off the question. "Personal interview," she stated matter-of-factly. "Which you consented to earlier. Anyway, several things alarm me considering your background check, Mr. Perry, and I thought you two might want to discuss it before I leave for the day."

"If you want to handle this I'll meet you down in my office," Doctor Gordon stated before briskly walking away. He'd never cared much for how the county workers swooped down on the parents of his patients when they were in the midst of dealing with the most tragic experiences of their lives.

"This ain't the time for this," Rico told the woman. "I need to get my wife down to the doc's office."

"I think your wife would like to know about your criminal record, Mr. Perry. That is, of course, unless she already knew that you were previously charged with marijuana possession, obstruction of an officer, and child coercion."

Alex gasped. This day was simply not getting any better. Candace jumped to life and pushed Rico's arm away from her. She was appalled by what she was hearing. All this time she'd been sleeping with this man and had even allowed him to talk her into getting married and she knew absolutely nothing about him. She wanted to kick herself for not having the foresight to have his ass checked out before she'd ever signed a marriage license. She was losing everything today. She needed Jehovah now more than ever.

"You bastard!" she spat out at Rico. "You shady-ass bastard. I knew that you and those drugs were never a good thing. Talking about how you was 'gon' stop.' You never once told me that you had a drug charge against you. And child coercion? Child coercion! You sick mutherfucker! I have a kid. I let you in my home around my daughter, and you're out messing with children?"

"Candace, I can explain all that," Rico said, reaching out for her.

"Don't touch me you sick fuck. Don't you ever, ever, ever touch me again. You're a criminal." She shook her head, and the tears fell hard.

Alex ran to her side and placed her arms around her in a tight hug. Candace looked over her shoulder and stared at her husband through her tears. "I hate you. You're no better than the rest of them. You're a lying, conniving son of a bitch. That's why you couldn't ever get a job, you bum! You obviously have a rap sheet a mile long." She sobbed loudly. "I hate you! I hate you!" Her words turned into screams.

Alex continued to hold her friend but looked up to see two well-dressed men heading their way. Something about them told her that they were official, and she just knew that more trouble was headed Candace's way. "Shhhh," she whispered into her ear. "Calm down, friend. Calm down. Not here, okay?"

"Ms. Lawson, or Mrs. Lawson Perry?" one of the men called out as they stopped in front of the group.

Candace broke Alex's embrace and turned around just as her parents walked out of Zoe's room in tears. "Yes?" Candace asked confusedly.

"I'm Agent Wilbur," the man said.

Candace wiped her eyes and nodded. She recognized him. "What now?" she asked, feeling like the weight of the world was upon her.

"We'd like to ask you a few questions about the incident at your home. The murder of Michael Banks and Justin McClinton."

"Hasn't she answered enough questions about that break-in?" Mr. Lewis spoke up as he moved closer to his daughter.

"I'm afraid not, sir. You see, this series of murders, which your daughter has had a front-row seat for, are more than likely connected. Our sources tell us that Banks and McClinton were the individuals that gunned down Stephanie Johnson. The streets are talking. In fact, all of these incidents have Mafia ties, and your daughter here is the key to getting the answers that will help end the madness."

"Mafia?" Alex asked. What in the hell was going on?

"What are you talking about?" Mr. Lewis asked.

"Damn, shawty," Rico exclaimed, feeling as if anything he'd ever done was miniscule next to whatever it was that Candace was involved in.

Ms. Campbell silently jotted down notes as Mrs. Lewis clasped her hands together and prayed for them all to be delivered from this hell.

"If you don't mind coming with us, Mrs. Lawson Perry," Agent Wilbur stated.

Candace was shaking. It was all making sense to her now. Apparently Corey was in some shit with whatever Mafia the agent had referred to and now that she'd allowed him to use her she was caught up. There was no way she could tell the truth now. Not only did she fear the legal ramifications, but she also feared that whoever these Mafia people were they might be somewhere lurking and waiting to pounce on her if she said the wrong thing. She didn't know exactly what Corey had going on, so there wasn't much she could say, but she figured it was best for her to keep his name out of it. The moment she let it be known that she had any connection to Corey it would be over for her.

"I do mind," Candace stated. "My daughter is in there practically dead. I'm about to go sign papers to terminate her life support and finally end what's left of her sickly little life. I can't help any of you right now because I need to take care of my daughter. Please . . . Let me grieve in peace and handle this before you try to hit me with anything else because I can barely handle this as it is."

Alex was crying now. The pain Candace was harboring was rubbing off on her.

Candace looked back at Alex. "Walk me to the doctor's office," she said through her tears.

Alex nodded. She held Candace's hand and looked up at Agent Wilbur questioningly. She wasn't sure they were going to allow Candace to just walk away, but no one made a move as they inched their way down the hall. She could hear Candace's heavy breathing as the girl fought to hold it together. The moment they turned the corner Candace's legs gave way and she wavered.

Alex was right there to catch her. *Where the hell is Jada?* she thought as she leaned against the wall holding Candace in her arms. *I can't do this without her.*

Chapter 85

Jordan

"How's Jada?" Mrs. Hood, Martin's mom, asked Jordan.

They were all enjoying the reception at the Othello Event Hall which Ashley's parents had rented out for the nuptials. The wedding party was small and consisted of only the bride and groom and Martin's nephew as the ring bearer and Ashley's niece as the flower girl. The reception was taking place in the venue's green room. The walls were painted a mint green that made an interesting contrast to the baby blue and white wedding colors that Ashley had chosen.

Jordan forced a smile as he placed his cup under the fountain to get another drink of peach punch. He was growing weary from answering the same question over and over again. "She's fine."

"Why isn't she with you today?" Mrs. Hood probed deeper. "Martin mentioned something about complications with the pregnancy, but I thought she was out of the woods with that."

"The baby's fine. Jada just decided it was best for her to stay home and rest." It was a lie, but he couldn't very well tell his homeboy's mother that his wife had actually thought it best to stay away from him because he was constantly making her life miserable in every way that he could.

"Hmmm. Well, we're wishing you both all the best." She pecked Jordan's cheek. "It's good to see you again. Don't be a stranger."

"Yes, ma'am." Jordan took a sip of his drink and scanned the room for the guys. He'd made it to the wedding late and had ended up sitting in the back while the others sat together up front. Part of him hadn't even wanted to show up. How could he sit there and watch his boy start his happily-ever-after knowing how he'd recently messed up his own?

"Looking for anyone in particular?"

The voice behind him made Jordan close his eyes tightly and wince. The one person he did not wish to see today while he was mourning the death of his marriage was LaTanya. But, of course, she would be there to torment him further about his relationship with Jada. He turned around and gave her a polite smile thinking he'd just be cordial, and then get the hell on. "What's up, 'Tanya?"

"You and your disappearing act," she responded, smiling wickedly. "You haven't hit me up lately. What's going on?"

"Just been busy." He stared down into his cup and wished that there was some alcohol in it. Damn Martin and Ashley for having a dry wedding.

"I see you didn't bring your wife. Calculated move or nah?"

"She didn't want to come."

"I bet. I bet her ass never wants to do anything."

Jordan shrugged. "I'ma go find DeAnthony and them."

LaTanya placed her hand on his arm and gripped his bicep. "I'm sure wherever those fools are they are just fine. I know you not running away from me."

"Naw, it's just that I probably shouldn't be over here looking like I'm booed up with you."

She frowned. "What? You think somebody gon' go back and tell Jane . . . June . . . Judas . . . whatever her name is that you were talking to me?"

"Really, 'Tanya?"

"Really what? You're the one that said she'd never want us to be friends, which I think is stupid. Anyone that's that insecure with herself needs to have several seats."

"I'm not trying to make things worse than they are."

"What are you talking about? It ain't like she knows anything."

Jordan's eyebrows rose, and then fell. He remained silent.

LaTanya studied his facial features. "She knows? About us?"

"She knows."

"How the hell did that happen?"

He shrugged. "I'd rather not talk about it."

"So now what? You just gon' pretend like I don't exist? Fuck her, Jordan."

"Shh!" He held his index finger up to his lips and took a look around the room to make sure that no one had overheard her outburst. "You need to watch your mouth. If Ms. Hood hears you showing out you know she's gon' hand you back your feelings."

LaTanya was disinterested in who was listening to what. "Jordan, I hope you aren't trying to tell me that you're gon' kick me to the curb over your silly little wife's insecurities."

Jordan looked at LaTanya as if she'd lost her mind. The girl was speaking as if she hadn't been present the night they'd screwed in his car. "I have to do what's best for me and my family right now."

"Really? Well, you and I both know that you might be faithful to her for all of two minutes before you come calling me again. And if not me, I'm sure it'll be somebody else."

Jordan set his cup down on the table. "Thanks for the vote of confidence." He turned to walk away.

LaTanya followed him. "Am I lying? You don't wanna be married to that bitch. You said it yourself. Why don't you do yourself a favor and divorce her ass before you spend the next ten years of your life in a miserable situation?"

They reached the outside and Jordan quickly turned around to face her. "Are you trying to embarrass me?"

She shook her head. "No, I'm trying to save you." She calmed down and moved a step closer to him. "Look, I'm your friend, and I care about you. Despite any of the other stuff, I'm your friend, and as your friend, I'm telling you that being married to this woman is going to ruin your life. If you wanted her you would have never sniffed around my way."

Jordan didn't have a response. He felt like he wanted Jada, but LaTanya was saying some things that were logic. If he loved his wife why did he feel the need to seek pleasure anywhere else? It wasn't a question that he readily had an answer to. Before he could speak Curtis walked over and patted him on the back.

"What's up, man?" Curtis asked. He winked at LaTanya knowingly. "'Tanya. You over here hogging ya' boy?"

LaTanya shook her head and smiled. "Nope. He knows he's free to go whenever he wants 'cause he knows exactly where to find me when he's ready to come back." She looked at Jordan and dared him to break the stare she initiated. "Call me," she told him before walking away.

Curtis chuckled. "What the hell was that about?"

Jordan shook it off. "Nothing."

"Uh-huh. I know a lovers' quarrel when I see one, homie. You ain't slick. You ain't bring Jada either 'cause you knew ya' girl was gon' be here. But you know what? I woulda gave you mo' props if you had been able to handle both of 'em in the same place. That woulda been some real playa shit."

Jordan sucked his teeth. "Man, fuck being a player. That shit's getting old."

"Like hell," Curtis responded. "Everybody knows ain't no pussy better than new pussy. Ya' boy right here gon' be a player for life."

"Yeah, until you find the woman that locks yo' ass down."

"Ha! They ain't built a pussy yet that can put my ass on lock." Curtis laughed at his own joke. "Come on, man. Martin and them waiting in the back to take a shot together."

"A shot? Where they get alcohol from?"

Curtis shot him a look. "You know AJ ain't going nowhere without some shit in his trunk. Let's go."

Jordan followed Curtis back into the event hall in search of the fellas. He considered telling them all how he'd fucked up and how Jada had put him out, but the moment he saw the extra cheesy grin on Martin's face he decided against it. It was his boy's day, and he was thrilled about the possibility of everlasting love. Jordan didn't want to ruin Martin's high and his positive feelings about marriage by imparting news of his failure. Now wasn't the time. As they took their shots Jordan's eyes met LaTayna's across the room. She was cute, but she wasn't the type of chick that he could see himself spending a lifetime with. She lacked the qualities he wanted in a wife. It was funny because the one woman he'd found that had those qualities was the one woman he was giving the least respect to. He just couldn't understand how things had gone so wrong.

***

He didn't want to be disrespectful by using his key to let himself in. A part of him was sure that she'd changed the locks by now anyway. Jordan rang the doorbell and waited with his hands behind his back for his now estranged wife to let him in. His stomach felt knotted, and he was nervous about how she would receive him.

Jada opened the door slowly and shot him a "what the hell" look. "Is there something you need?" she asked.

He looked at her and felt as if he would cry. She was beautiful. She didn't have on any makeup and her hair was pulled back and partially covered by her scarf. She was wearing an oversized T-shirt that read "too blessed to be stressed" with leopard print lounging pants. She was completely tacky, but her skin glowed so angelically and her eyes were bright and radiant. The swell of her belly made him want to reach out and touch it, but he restrained himself. He didn't want to upset her, but he was so taken aback by the wonderment of his pregnant wife. It was as if he was seeing her for the first time.

"Um . . . I wanted to get some of my things . . . and talk," he told her. "Well, I mostly wanted to talk."

"You couldn't have just called?" she asked.

He shrugged. "I figured you wouldn't have answered the phone anyway so what would be the point."

"You figured right." She took a deep breath before stepping back and opening the door wider.

Jordan stepped in, then handed her the flowers he'd been hiding behind his back as she closed the door. Jada slowly took the flowers and eyed him suspiciously.

"You didn't think that you could bring me some roses that are just going to die in three days and that everything would magically be okay, did you?" she asked. Her tone was harsh and her look was deadly.

"No, but I was hoping it would be a start," he answered honestly as he moved to sit on the couch. "Can you sit with me?"

Jada laid the flowers on the coffee table and took a seat on the sofa, making sure to leave some space between them. "So what now, Jordan? You wanna convince me that I misunderstood everything that's been going on? You wanna tell me that it's all in my head and I'm tripping?"

"No."

"You wanna tell me that I might as well take you back because who is going to want a ready-made family?"

"Of course not. I know that you're a good woman and any man would be lucky to have you. But the thing is, I want to still be your man. I want to be the one to have you by my side."

"No, you don't. You specifically told that chick that you don't want me. If you said it to her, then I'm sure you've said it to others, including your boys. So why the hell should I want to be with someone who thinks so little of me and trash-talks me every chance they get?"

Jordan finally reached out to place the palm of his hand on her lump of life. "Because we're a family. I made some mistakes, Jada. I can admit that. But I love you, and I want our family to work. I want *us* to work."

Jada wasn't convinced. "If you wanted us to work you should have worked on us instead of going outside doing all this other extracurricular shit."

"You're right. And there's nothing I can say to that. But I'm here now, and I want to try now."

"Why?"

"Because I love you, Jada." His eyes grew misty, and he didn't care about looking like a punk. "I don't want to be without you, baby. I know I messed up, but I'm begging you . . . Please give me a chance to make it right. Please give me the chance to fix it."

Jada was tired. With the stress of going back to work and trying to figure out how she was going to make it as a single mother, the hurt she'd been feeling over Jordan's betrayal, and the horrible ordeal that Candace was going through, she felt completely overwhelmed. So much was happening at once, and it seemed that everyone's lives were being rocked in one way or another. She loved Jordan, but she didn't want to deal with a lifetime of drama. For the longest she'd been the one everyone turned to and looked up to; the responsible one who could show them all how to love and how to carry themselves. Jada was sick of being the responsible one. She was sick of being taken for granted. She wanted the others to know what it was like to feel half of the things that she'd experienced over the years so that maybe they could appreciate the kind of friend and wife she'd been to them all.

"Baby, please, let's try to make this right," Jordan begged as he fell to his knees, threw his arms around her, and buried his face in her belly. "I need you."

Jada rolled her eyes to the ceiling wondering which of them would regret the decision first. "One chance," she said softly. "One chance, Jordan. I swear to God if it wasn't for this baby and the fact that deep down I really do love you I'd spit in your face."

He held her tighter. "It's going to be better," he told her. "I'm going to be better. You'll see. I'm going to be a better man for you."

She touched the top of his head and closed her eyes. She knew that some things would never be the same and wondered if they were fooling themselves to ever think otherwise.

Jordan lifted his head and looked into his wife's face. "You're beautiful, woman. For every day that I failed to tell you and every moment that I caused you any pain, I'm sorry. All I wanna do is love you, Jada. That's all I really wanna do."

Jada remained silent. It was time to show and prove. The time for talk was well over and done with for her.

Jordan rose from the floor and cleared his throat. "I'm gonna go take a piss, and then if you're hungry I'll go out and grab something to eat."

"Krystal's," Jada said. "I'm in the mood for some Krystal's."

Jordan laughed. "That's random. You gon' have bubble guts messing with that stuff."

Jada rubbed her belly. "The baby's craving it so . . ." She shrugged. "Besides, I just cleaned myself out real good before you got here so you might wanna spray when you go in there."

"Ewww," Jordan laughed as he walked to the bathroom. He closed the door and said a quick prayer of thanks before relieving himself. As he pissed a vibrating sound caught his attention. Jada's phone was lying on the vanity counter near the sink and was constantly buzzing. Jordan flushed the toilet, and then washed his hands. The phone buzzed again. Someone was really trying to get ahold of Jada.

Jordan picked the phone up mindlessly to take it to her. Reaching for the doorknob he looked down at the screen as the phone buzzed again. The name caused him to stop. Amir. Who the hell was Amir? Insecurity and curiosity caused him to click on the text to see what was being said. The conversation strand made him put down the toilet lid and take a seat. He scrolled up to the top and held his breath as he read.

Amir: Hey, sexy. What you doing?

Jada: Watching TV and enjoying the quiet.

Amir: You ain't let that man come home yet?

Jada: No.

Amir: You got room over there for me to lay down too?

Jada: Next to me and my big belly?

Amir: I'll rub it for you . . . and your feet . . . and that clit.

Jada: Really?

Amir: You think I won't?

Jada: It kinda scares me to know that you will.

Amir: Don't be scared, sexy. Just be ready. I'm glad you found me on Facebook. I been looking for you for years.

Jada: You ain't look too hard.

Amir: Water under the bridge. I found you and I don't intend to let you go.

Jada: You do know I'm still married.

Amir: You do know what he don't know won't hurt him . . . but I'ma hurt that pussy again as soon as I get back to the A.

Jada: LOL. You just know you gon' get this, right?

Amir: I'm your first love, boo. I'ma always be able to get that.

Amir: Where you go, girl?

Amir: You done fell asleep on me over there?

Amir: A'ight, hit me when you wake up. I love you, sexy.

Jordan couldn't breathe. It was clear that in the short time he'd been gone Jada had wasted no time in moving on. Here she was having a nigga tell her what he was going to do to her and she was still carrying his baby. His blood was boiling. Jordan didn't know whether to call the dude and curse him out or run out of the bathroom and shake Jada to death. He was livid. How could she want him to be faithful and true to her when it only took the slightest bit of turbulence for her to run off and start messing with someone else? He rose from the toilet and gripped the phone tightly. He guessed that the saying was true. Once a good girl's gone, she's gone forever. He only had himself to thank for that.

Chapter 86

Miranda

Miranda slowly walked to the private visitation room. Who in the world would show up out of the blue like this was beyond her. She'd purposely distanced herself from everyone and hadn't asked anyone to come out. She walked into the room and was confused. The only man present was a heavyset balding guy in a cheap suit. She turned to leave the room.

"Miranda," he said. "Surely you aren't going to just turn your back on me again."

Again? She turned around to look at him. She didn't recognize him at all.

"Please, take a seat," he encouraged her.

Miranda didn't budge. "Who are you and what do you want?"

"It took us a long time to find you. Somehow we weren't able to find any identifying information about you from the myriads of databases available to us. No information about your birth. No vehicle registration or voter registration info. Nothing. I wonder how that came to be when we were able to trace your name and phone number the day that you called me."

She was nervous. It was clear to her now. She hadn't given them any more thought since the night that she'd tried to end it all. She pressed her hands together and tried to think clearly. Time wasn't on her side now, that much she knew. She wasn't afraid of the thick guy full of his own self-importance. It was the man that was surely trailing him that she was concerned about.

"Why'd you run?" he asked her.

"Huh?"

"We had a deal. You were supposed to come to the office, sit down with me to get your statement out, and then we were going to throw the book at Polk and ultimately get the real bad guys."

"The real bad guys," she repeated, shaking her head. She was the addict, but she seriously wondered what the hell he'd been smoking.

"Why'd you run?"

"Who said I ran?"

"You didn't show up. I pulled strings to get Polk taken in, and you didn't show up."

"Who told you to get ahead of yourself? I didn't tell you to run out and arrest the man without any concrete evidence, asshole."

He banged the table with his fist. "I had a good feeling about you."

"You were a little too overly optimistic, huh? Bet you won't do that again."

Agent Wilbur looked into the short woman's eyes. Her hair was plaited in unruly cornrows, and she looked as if she could stand to eat a couple of more meals. Her eyes were cold and unfeeling. Even her tone was harsher than he'd remembered. It had taken forever for his team to track her through her ER visit which had ultimately landed her at the treatment facility. He had been completely surprised to find out that his eyewitness was nothing more than a stoned out crackhead. Still, it didn't mean that her testimony wouldn't be able to help them.

"It's not too late," Wilbur told her in a calmer voice. "We can still get your statement. Maybe you saw something, anything, that'll help us pin a conviction against the others."

"The others?" She wanted to hear him say it. She wanted to force him to say that which the media continued to gloss over every time they ever mentioned Stephanie's death and even recently the unfortunate demise of baby Zoe. She wanted him to say that which she'd found out the hard way.

Agent Wilbur leaned back in his chair and cracked his knuckles. "This is a big deal. Your friends have suffered a great deal. Anything you know . . . Anything would be helpful, Miranda. Just tell me about the execution of Stokes."

She shook her head. "I can't," she said giving a throaty gulp at the end of the statement.

"Can't or won't?"

"I can't," she repeated backing up until her back was completely against the wall with the exit just to her right.

Agent Wilbur leaned forward and placed his elbows on the table with the fingertips of both hands pointed at Miranda. "Do you have any idea how important this is? How many more have to die, Miranda?"

She shook her head again feeling tormented and helpless. "I can't." They were the truest words she'd spoken in ages.

He rose from the table and walked around to the front of it. Several feet stood between him and the fragile woman. "Do they have you that scared? You're safe here, Miranda. Tell me what I need to know, whatever you know. My original promise still stands. I'll make sure no one bothers you. I will personally make certain that you are safe."

She covered her face with her hands. She just wanted him to go. The more he spoke the more she realized how useless and detrimental her existence was. He brought back memories that she was now forced to act upon sooner than she'd wanted to. She just wanted him to leave her alone with her thoughts.

"Say something!" he yelled. "You can't continue to say nothing! You just may have the power to stop this."

She didn't have the power to do anything. He was giving her far too much credit. Miranda slid to the floor and buried her face in her hands, feeling herself about to lose it.

"This is ridiculous," Agent Wilbur stated. "Citizens complain about us not keeping our communities safe, but people like you allow the villains to scare them into silence. Silence kills, Miranda. Zoe is dead! Stephanie is dead! Montae Stokes is dead! Justin McClinton is dead! Michael Banks is dead! That's five bodies attributed to this drug war. *Five* murders, Miranda. If you don't want there to be another you better start talking! Tell me something."

"I can't!" Miranda screamed looking up at him with hazy eyes and tears escaping rapidly. "I can't tell you anything because I don't know anything. I . . . lied! I lied. I didn't see anything! I was never there! I lied!"

Agent Wilbur stared at her in shock. He hadn't considered the possibility that she had played him to this extent. He'd been sure that Tommy Castello's crew had silenced her. He had been a little surprised that they hadn't killed her. Now here she was telling him that she'd been yanking his chain the entire time. He massaged his forehead. "What do you mean you lied? Why would you call the GBI to make a statement if you had no statement to make?"

She leaned her head back against the brick wall and closed her eyes. "I'm a crackhead, Agent Wilbur. I'm an addict. I'm liable to do or say anything. Corey was my dealer. He pissed me off. I wanted to piss him off. Mission accomplished."

Agent Wilbur was disgusted. People were dropping like flies around them, and she thought that it was funny to call and make a false report. She knew that they had bought every word she'd fed him over the phone that day. He could just imagine the sound of desperation she'd picked up on in his voice as he'd continuously begged for her assurance that she'd come in the next day. He was going to be the laughingstock of the bureau for sure once word got back that he'd made a pointless arrest of Polk to begin with; that he'd had no merit at all behind his arrest. Then another thought occurred to him. "But you knew about the wallet."

"Luck," she told him. "I'd honestly just happened to be following Stephanie that night and saw her toss something. I'm telling you I didn't see the murder." Telling the truth felt like a burden had been lifted. Even her breathing felt different.

None of it made sense to him. He'd been certain that Tommy's crew had been on to the girl and had eliminated her. But here she was overcoming addiction and admitting to him that she was simply full of shit. There were no other words to say. Without so much as a good-bye the agent exited the door, allowing it to slam loudly behind him.

Miranda bit her bottom lip. She had moves to make. She rose from the floor and left the room, intent on heading to the shrink to make a request. But as she passed the nurse's station a thought occurred to her. She stopped at the desk and smiled nervously at the receptionist. "Um . . . May I have a sheet of paper, please?"

Kenni York

The receptionist looked at her inquisitively.

"I want to write a letter to my folks," Miranda explained.

It seemed like a healthy gesture considering everyone there knew that Miranda was distancing herself from everyone she knew on the outside, even after being encouraged to reach out. The receptionist handed her a sheet of stationary and a pen with a smile. "Here you go. Good for you."

Miranda gave her a half smile in return. She knew the receptionist was thinking positively. If she only knew the truth about the words that were about to be penned she would have prayed instead of smiled warmly.

Chapter 87

The Girls

Alex was the first to arrive. She'd borrowed the car and left while Clay was still in the shower. It was easier that way. Lately it had just been too difficult to have a conversation with him. Nothing she seemed to say or do was ever right, and he didn't seem as interested in her life as he used to be. Something was missing for them, but Alex didn't have the time to stop to figure out what it was. Between school, work, and staying most days with Candace she just didn't have much time to nurture their relationship.

She sat in a meeting room looking around at all the sofas and chairs wondering where the hell everyone else was. She'd been surprised to get a call from the rehab facility. Miranda had been very clear early on that she didn't want any of them around while she tried to get herself together. Alex wondered if this meeting was Miranda's way of showing them that she was in a better place now.

"Hey, you," Jada said entering the room. Her stomach kind of led her, and the rest of her body followed.

"Hey, yourself," Alex responded.

They hugged and Jada joined Alex on the couch.

"Miranda hasn't come in yet?" Jada asked.

"Nope. Not yet."

"I hope she's good. I can't wait to see her. It's been too long."

The door opened, and they both turned around to see Candace stagger in with a thin white woman behind her. Candace wore dark shades and didn't move with her usual diva strides. She gave her girls limp hugs and sat next to Jada on the couch.

"You okay, girl?" Alex asked, looking over at her.

"How okay is one supposed to be after burying their six-month-old daughter?" Candace asked.

It was a sad time in Candace's life. The family had wasted no time in funeral arrangements for Zoe. The only thing Candace had left of her were her baby pictures and clothes. Every night she was tormented by the memories of the deaths of her only child and one of her closest friends. The images that ran through her mind made her want to die and never again have to feel the pain that was ripping her heart apart. She wanted out.

Jada grabbed Candace's hand. She could feel the tremble running through the girl's body. No parent ever wanted to succeed their child in life. Jada couldn't imagine the hurt Candace was feeling.

Doctor Dunham cleared her throat. "Um, ladies, I'm really glad that you could make it out. This is very important to Miranda, and I know that she's kind of a bundle of nerves over seeing you all again."

"Who are you?" Alex asked bluntly.

"I'm the center's therapist, and I've been working with Miranda to come to terms with certain things . . . so this is a very huge step for her. I'd like to ask you all to bear with her and have an open mind. I'm not sure what will be said. Miranda's kind of a live wire."

"She is?" Alex asked thinking about the meek, timid woman that had once sulked on Candace's living-room floor and softly admitted that she just needed to feel loved even if it was a lie.

The door opened and the three girls were speechless as a different version of Miranda entered. She took her time walking across the floor and taking a seat in the chair across from them. She was so thin that they could see the bones of her skeleton. Her eyes were dark, and her face looked sadder than they had ever seen. It was a heartbreaking sight, and no one said a word. They didn't have to. Miranda knew exactly what they were all thinking.

"I'm a little skinnier than usual," Miranda voiced. "But this is nothing compared to my coked-out look. So you can stop staring at me like I'm the ghost of Miranda."

"Your friends came out to support you, Miranda," Doctor Dunham stated to deter Miranda from going into defense mode off the bat. She took a seat in a chair beside the girl. She looked at her to see if she was calm. Sensing that she was okay Doctor Dunham looked over to the girls on the couch. They all appeared stunned. "Okay, to kick-start things I want to say this. Miranda once made a very striking statement in group. She said that no one understands. She feels no one understands her or what she's been through. There are a lot of things on her heart and mind that she just never shared with you for fear that you didn't care or wouldn't understand."

"When did we ever give you the impression that we didn't care?" Alex asked. "We've always been tight. What couldn't you say to us?"

Doctor Dunham was a little nervous about the way Alex snapped at Miranda, but Miranda responded before she could intervene.

"There are just some truths that you're not ready for . . . that I knew you wouldn't have been able to handle," Miranda answered. "That's also why I didn't tell you about Norris hitting me. You proved your inability to understand by badgering me about how I could stay with him that night we had girls' night after he'd put me in the hospital."

"Is that not a logical question?"

"Someone who's being domestically abused doesn't really wanna hear, 'Girl, why you staying?' They want to be loved on."

"You needed help," Candace said dryly. "We were telling you what you needed to hear not what you wanted to hear. Tough love."

"Tough love? Hmmm . . . Maybe I could have used someone going to my meetings with me. Maybe I could have used someone calling me to see how I was and if I was still alive while stuck in my situation."

"You weren't stuck," Candace countered. "You chose to stay. There was nothing holding you there. Not even the man. Didn't he leave you?"

Jada squeezed Candace's hand that she was still holding. She was stunned by how snarky Candace was being. Candace responded by snatching her hand away.

"Why don't we go about this a different way," Doctor Dunham stated. "Miranda, why don't you tell the girls what you want to say."

Miranda bit her lip. She was having second thoughts about this. She just wanted it to be over with. She'd already sent out copies of her letter, and they would each have them by morning. This meeting was just a way for her to lay eyes on her circle one more time. "Alex . . . I love you, girl. But your whole life you've just been so absorbed with Alex's world that you really never had a moment to open your eyes and see anything or anyone else. Kinda explains why you never realized Clay was in love with you."

"I saw you," Alex argued.

"You judged me."

"I stood up for you when Stephanie sat at Jada's table that night downing you. I've been your friend from the jump. Don't try to paint it any other way."

"You've been my friend . . . when it was convenient for you. When it didn't interrupt the Alexandria Mason story."

Alex crossed her arms. "I resent that. What did you want from me?"

"You. You act like you were so concerned, but you never once came knocking on my door to see if I was still alive—did you?"

Alex wanted to snap back and tell her that she probably would've been too stoned out to know if she had but realized that it would have been catty. Miranda was clearly purging. If this was a part of her treatment process she would just take it. She didn't have the energy to go back and forth, not when she had to figure out what was going on between her and Clay.

"So this meeting was designed for you to hand us back our feelings?" Candace asked. "Because I'm fresh out of those, and I don't want to waste your time."

"You have this air about you, Candace . . . this air like you're so perfect when we all know that is not the case. I don't have to remind you of your shiftiness. I think that you've strived so hard to be the perfect image of yourself that you created and see in your head that you just destroy everything in your path. I think . . . I think you've been trying for the longest to be Jada."

Candace pulled her glasses from her face and slid to the edge of her seat. She looked at Miranda through the stingy redness of her eyes. "Are you high right now? The only thing I strive to be is the best me that I can be. I don't want to be like any of you. Have I made some mistakes? More than I care to mention, and trust me, I'm paying for them all day, every day. The memories that I have . . . The pain that I'm suffering is killing me. But I own it all, Miranda. Don't sit here and try to point blame at any of us because of what you've done or been through. We've all made choices that we just gotta deal with."

"Exactly," Miranda agreed. "We've made choices that we have to deal with and not play the victim because of them. You got that victim thing down pat, don't you? Wanting folks to feel sorry for you because you got knocked up by your married boyfriend. You shouldn't have slept with him. Wanting folks to feel sorry for you because Stephanie died hating you. Again, your doing."

Candace rose from the sofa. "I don't need this."

Jada stood up and grabbed her. "Wait, don't go. Come on. We're all friends. What are we doing here?"

"Stop it," Miranda said.

Jada looked at her. "Huh?"

"Stop it! Stop pacifying folks. Stop trying to hold it all together. Shit falls apart sometimes, Jada. Let it and just pick up the pieces later and move on but don't put a fuckin' Band-Aid on it and pretend like everything's coming up roses."

Jada was shocked. "What are you talking about?"

"You're so busy fixing it all that you're really fixing nothing. We don't even know you. Candace is trying to compete with the perfect front you show us, but nobody's perfect. She's competing with a phantom Jada. A Jada that doesn't exist."

"I never said I didn't have issues," Jada responded. "I just never had time to address them because of you heifers and all of your drama. It is tiring being everything to everyone. I am tired."

Miranda nodded. "As much as you tried did any of it work?"

Jada looked around at her friends and considered their lives. So much was wrong. So much was beyond her grasp.

Nothing she'd said or done along the way had stopped them from ending up at this moment of total despair. No one was okay. She took a seat on the sofa and looked at Miranda. "We all could have been a little better to one another . . . a lot more real with each other."

Candace returned to her seat as well. "So you've told us all how you feel about us. What about you?" she asked Miranda. "How do you feel about yourself?"

Miranda's right brow rose. "I'm not my favorite person. We've all been harboring secrets and behaving horribly to some degree. I'm not exempt."

"Your secret's been out," Alex stated.

"Not all of them."

The others looked at her expectantly.

"I was mad at Corey for refusing to sell to me," Miranda said slowly. "I was mad at Stephanie for looking down on me. She was so mean and judgmental. I wanted to get back at them. Both of them. I was following Stephanie one night and I saw her throw away Montae Stokes's wallet. I was the one that tipped off the GBI. I told them where to find the wallet, and I told them that I'd seen Corey kill the Stokes dude."

"What?" Alex exclaimed. "You never . . . You never told us that."

"Because it was a lie," Miranda said flatly. "That's why Corey was picked up. After it happened . . . after the call and after they got Corey I called Stephanie and left a message for her to watch the news. I was gloating about how I got her boyfriend caught up. But that was the night she was killed."

"She was at Corey's getting his things," Candace stated. "Corey must have sent her there to clean the place out after you dropped the dime on him. If you hadn't done that . . ." Her thoughts trailed off.

Miranda had considered the possibilities herself many times. "If I hadn't done any of it she would have never been there, and those men would have never gunned her down. But then again, who knows? They could've picked her off at any time."

Jada was in shock. The secrets kept among them all were outrageous. Anyone on the outside looking in would surely wonder how the hell they could call themselves friends.

"I just wanted to tell the truth," Miranda stated. "I've been lying and stooping to all kind of lows for the longest. I just wanted the opportunity to come clean."

Candace considered sharing her truth but she looked up at the therapist and realized that it was best for her to keep quiet. None of it mattered anyway. None of it was going to bring her daughter back. "So you've let it all out . . . Now what?"

"Now I pray that you'll all see yourselves and each other differently," Miranda stated. "Really be there for each other, not just Jada trying to be the glue, and not just falling together after the shit has hit the fan."

"We needa be better friends," Jada stated. "Point-blank."

"And be better to yourselves," Miranda added.

"Why are you talking like you don't need to do these things too?" Alex asked. Something didn't sit well with her.

"I do. I just wanted to make sure that I give you guys something to think about. I did a lot to create the problems in our relationships. I just wanted to do something to work on fixing it." As the words left her lips Miranda realized that she honestly wanted to leave them with something good to repair their friendship. It was the least she could do considering all the trouble she'd caused.

Chapter 88

Alex

Feeling completely drained and wanting only to sink into a hot lavender-scented bubble bath Alex slowly made her way inside of the apartment. She could hear the low lull of the television coming from the bedroom. Kicking off her shoes she took a deep breath and headed toward the back. She hoped that Clay was awake. She could really use some comforting. As she entered the room the wind was knocked out of her and she gasped. Clay was not only awake but he was packing a suitcase.

"What are you doing?" she asked nervously, trying to recalculate everything that had happened between them in order to figure out how they'd gotten to this moment. "Where are you going?"

Clay didn't look at her as he placed a suit into the garment bag that was lying on the bed. "Business trip."

Alex clutched her chest and sighed. With the year she was having her emotions were all over the place and she was apparently paranoid. "Oh my God. You scared me," she said walking over to the dresser and taking off her jewelry. "For a minute I thought you were leaving me."

"I am leaving," he said slowly and almost inaudibly.

"Excuse me?" His tone wasn't low enough because Alex heard him loud and clear. She stared at the back of him holding and toying with the promise ring he'd given her.

"I've been trying to tell you this for a minute. Everything has been moving so fast and you've been so caught up in other stuff."

"Tell me what?" she demanded. "Precious, what have you been trying to tell me?"

He finally turned to face her. "I had an interview with an entertainment agency in Cali."

That was news to Alex. "You did?"

"Yeah, I did. And they offered me the job. I'm going there for two weeks for some training, fill out some paperwork, and handle some other business."

"And then?"

He sighed as he turned to zip up his suitcase. "And then I'll come back for the rest of my things."

Immediately she felt as if she couldn't breathe. Alex clutched her shirt with her right hand while her left hand lingered by her side as her thumb nervously fondled the solitaire diamond resting on her ring finger. "What about me?" she asked softly and innocently. "What about me?"

Clay turned and sat on the edge of the bed. He looked at her with gentle eyes. "What about you, Alex?"

"You're just going to leave me here? Is this job a permanent thing? I mean, can't I come with you? How are we going to maintain a long-distance relationship? That's not what you had in mind, was it?" She was rambling, and she knew it, but she needed him to put to rest her greatest fear.

"I'm not asking for us to have a long-distance relationship," he told her.

She nodded and held her hands out. "Good . . . good. Then I can start looking for schools out there so I can transfer next term. And I can put in my notice at the boutique. Shoot, I'll have to let the girls know ASAP. They're probably gonna go crazy."

"Alex . . ."

"I really should be going with you now because don't we need to find a place? Surely you don't wanna find a place that I end up hating. Not that you have bad taste or anything but—"

"Alex."

Alex turned around and rummaged through her drawer for a notepad. "I need to make a list. There's so much to do, and I don't want to miss anything."

"Alex!" Clay raised his voice.

Alex stopped talking, but she was too afraid to turn around to face him. She knew in her heart what was coming next but didn't want to see it in his face as the words escaped his lips.

"I'm not asking for us to have a long-distance relationship," he repeated. "And I'm not asking for us to have a relationship anymore. Period." He rose from the bed and started to walk over to her but stopped midway. "I love you, Alex. I've loved you for a long time. I don't think that's going to ever change but . . . I need someone that can love me the same way that I love her, and I just don't think you're ready."

Alex set down her notepad, took a breath, and then slowly turned around. "How can you say that? I'm here with you. After everything that's happened I'm here with you."

"You're here physically, Alex . . . at times anyway. But you're not here with me," he said motioning his hand between the two of them. "You're caught up in Alex-world, baby, and I don't think there's any room for me."

"That's crazy," she said choking back tears. "I love you, precious. There's always room for you."

"I think you need some time to figure out what you want out of life. I think I need to go on and pursue this dream, and you need to figure out what you want; see if you can tear yourself away from being the center of attention, if you can make a move without being glued to your girls."

Alex shook her head and reached out for him. Clay pulled her toward him, held her tightly, and kissed her forehead. She closed her eyes and cried into his chest.

"Please don't leave me," she begged. "If you leave me I don't know what I'll do."

He took a deep breath. "If it was meant for us to be together we'll find our way back to each other, Alex. But right now I feel like we're forcing this, and you're just not ready for the type of relationship I need."

She looked up at him. "But I can try harder. I promise, precious. I can do better."

He kissed her lips, and her tears dripped onto his mouth. He ignored the saltiness and relished in the moment of their final embrace. "We need time," he told her as he pulled away. "We need time."

Alex buried her face back into his chest and cried. He was right. She hadn't been the attentive girlfriend he needed. She didn't even know what was going on in his life. But she wanted him so badly that losing him was tearing her apart. Maybe Miranda had been right. She was just a little too self-absorbed, and now it was costing her the love of her life. Her only hope was in his statement that if they were meant to be they'd find their way back to each other. Alex prayed that it would all work out for them.

Chapter 89

Corey

"You killed a baby," Knuckles said. "How could you have been so stupid?"

Corey took a deep breath and tossed the trash bag of bills into the trunk of the car Knuckles was driving. While he was busy shooting it out with Man-Man and Justin, his boys had taken over their rivals' stash house. They'd only been able to secure one bag of money, which was only half of what Corey owed Tommy, but some money was better than none. They didn't dare touch the product that was in the house, knowing full well that Martinez's product was of no use to their hustle.

Corey was worried about what would happen to him next. He'd gotten even with the fucks that killed his girl, and he'd gotten lucky that Candace hadn't fingered him in the shoot-out at her house. He didn't understand why she wasn't snitching. He knew that she'd been interviewed half a dozen times by the county police and the GBI. They wanted badly to pin Martinez's boys' murders on him. The only thing keeping them from it was Candace's testimony. He owed her his freedom. It hurt him that she'd lost her daughter in the process.

Although he was free now he didn't know for how long. Surely Martinez wasn't going to take too lightly the fact that he'd wiped out the strongest members of his Atlanta street force. The war between Tommy and Martinez was sure to escalate now, and Corey was right there in the line of fire. If Martinez didn't get to him Corey feared that Tommy might retaliate for the money he still owed him. But even if neither of them came gunning for him he still had to face the drug charges that the state was pinning against him. There was always something.

Knuckles took a look at the kid and shook his head. He'd shown so much promise. To Corey's left stood Antonio, quiet and watching. He was a good kid. He did whatever Corey told him to do, and he kept up that front of loyalty. It was too bad that his esteemed leader wasn't as on top of his shit as he thought he was.

Knuckles nodded in their direction. "You know what needs to be done now," he said before getting into his car and pulling off.

Corey sighed and nodded toward Antonio's whip. "Let's ride." He knew what needed to be done, he just didn't want to do it. He was sure that the night Montae was killed there had been no one in sight, but the fact that Miranda had contacted the GBI claiming to be an eyewitness disturbed him. How was it possible? It simply wasn't. But no matter what he thought he was sure of, he knew that Tommy didn't want to risk the chance of him being wrong. With all the blood that had been shed already Corey knew that this wouldn't be the end of it. He just wondered when his turn was coming.

Chapter 90

Miranda

It was time. She clutched her hands by her side as she made her way down the hall to her room following the center's final roll call. Her roommate, Alicia, had left the program a week ago. She'd decided that it wasn't for her and checked herself out. Miranda was going to check out as well but in a different way. The plan was simple. She would wait until the final room checks, then unscrew the lightbulb from the lamp in her room. After breaking it she would then use the shards to cut herself in various places. By the time the nurses rounded in the morning she would have bled out and all the pain would have evaporated from her body.

The plan was very simple indeed, but as she entered her room she knew that things were not going to go accordingly. She closed the door slowly and quietly. Honestly, she had to admit that she was surprised he'd waited so long. She'd been fooling herself to think that she could kill herself before he showed up. She faced him with his stone-cold expression and waited for him to speak. The last time they'd seen each other he'd given her enough coke to kill two people. But as luck would have it, Jada had to come and save the day, thus sending her to the hospital which ultimately landed her right here in this dorm room at the rehab center.

"I see you're still with us," he said.

She shrugged. "Not my fault."

"You said you wanted it to be over. I thought we had a deal."

"Again, it wasn't my fault," she said sounding agitated. "But maybe you can help me with something."

He crossed his legs. They had very little time, but he didn't mind entertaining her thoughts for a bit.

"I've told you that I was lying . . . only trying to get even because I was caught up in my feelings. I didn't go through with my story, and even after the GBI found me here I still didn't say anything because I have nothing to say . . . because I know nothing."

He nodded his understanding.

"Okay, so then why is it that you still feel inclined to do away with me?" She was genuinely curious about their interest in her.

"Because we can't leave anything to chance," he told her in an even tone. "Maybe you were lying, maybe you weren't. Maybe you know something, maybe you don't. But the easiest way to make sure that the possibility of you knowing something is no longer a factor is to do away with you altogether."

"And that's just it? No loose ends, huh?"

He smiled, pleased to know that she understood. "That's right, Miranda. No loose ends." He opened his jacket slightly to reveal the pistol covered with a silencer.

Two swift pulls of the lever and her chest was burning with bullet holes. He watched as her body fell to the floor and her eyes stared at the ceiling as she took her last breaths. It reminded him of the day he'd paid her a visit at her modest apartment following the tip they'd gotten from Royce. Tommy watched her take hit after hit until her body had convulsed and she began to spasm on the floor of her bathroom. He'd been sure that there was no coming back from the damage she'd done to her body and had left her to die alone on the cold tiles. He should have followed through. Leaving her as a potential loose end had been just as much his fault now as he had been Corey's. The difference between them though was that he had no problem effectively correcting his mistakes—all of them, including bringing Corey on as well.

Chapter 91

Candace

It was quiet in the house. The silence forced her to be alone with her thoughts, and that was killing her. She'd been packing up the remainder of Zoe's things and just couldn't do it any longer. Throwing down a plastic bag she lifted herself from her Indian-style position on the floor and started to head out of her bedroom. Her cell phone rang from its place on her dresser. She turned around and picked it up, being careful to read the caller ID before answering. If it was Rico she was going to send his ass straight to voice mail. She didn't have time or the energy to deal with him. As soon as she was able to think clearly she was going to file for an annulment. Staying married to his criminal behind was not an option. But it wasn't Rico calling. It was Khalil, which wasn't much better.

"What do you want?" she asked him. Now that they no longer shared a child together she figured they really didn't have any further business with each other.

"I just wanted to check on you, beautiful," he said. "How you holding up?"

"I wish people would stop asking me how I am. They should already know how I am. What do you want?" she asked again, in hopes of moving the conversation along.

"You need anything? I can come over."

Candace walked out of the room, through the living room, and out into the hall of her apartment building to go to her mailbox. Khalil's request was insane, and she didn't feel like entertaining it. "No. You have no reason to be here."

"We lost our daughter, Candace. We're both grieving."

Candace thought about the way Khalil had showed up just before the memorial service for Zoe had started. He hadn't paid for anything, and he certainly hadn't been there to hold her hand through the process of getting everything together. Now that their baby was returned to the earth she certainly had no use for his "help" or his false sense of unity. She returned to her apartment and sifted through the mail. "Khalil, I'm only going to tell you this once. I have no need or desire for you in my life. We're done with each other. Done."

"You don't mean that. I know you're hurting right now, and you don't need to be alone. We're in this together, gorgeous."

Candace's eyes fell upon a letter addressed to her from Miranda. They'd just had their little powwow the day before and now she was looking at an envelope that Miranda had sent to her. The meeting had been tense and cutting at best. Candace wondered what could be in that letter that would be any different from the tone of their meeting. Khalil was still rambling on in her ear about how they needed to lean on each other as Candace ripped open the letter. She sank down onto her couch cradling the phone with her shoulder as she read the first few lines.

Dear Chicks,

You're not going to believe this. I don't even believe that I'm writing it so I know you're not going to believe it . . . or maybe you will. But I don't love myself. I look in the mirror every day and want to just shatter the glass. I smile, I say the right things, I make the right moves, and I play the game. And I think I've done it all this time so that you all, everyone around me really, could be more at ease. At first, I thought that being honest with you would help free myself of some of the anguish that's been built up inside of me for so long. This letter is proof of what I thought . . . but with each word I write I realize more and more how empty I am, whether you know the truth or not. And that's all about me. So I've made a decision that I'm sure you're not going to like or agree with, but for once, I am not hiding what I think, feel, or do.

Candace gasped as her spirit picked up on the sadness and despair laced in the words written on the page. By the time she got to the end and realized what Miranda had planned to do she'd dropped the phone and her tears were smearing the ink of the letter. It was too much. Death was all around her, and sorrow consumed her. Quickly she grabbed the phone, hung up on Khalil without a word, and dialed Jada's number. They had to do something before it was too late.

Chapter 92

Antonio

They sat in the car in silence for a moment. Corey was ready to go, but Antonio had other things on his mind. He looked over at his buddy and shook his head. Some careless decisions had been made, and it simply wasn't going to fly any longer.

"Aye, come on. Let's go, man," Corey snapped. "We needa handle this ASAP before Tommy has another reason to be pissed with me."

"Naw, he ain't gon' be pissed with you no more," Antonio said reaching under the seat.

"Yeah? You think this shit gon' smooth over in my favor?" Corey asked hopefully as he lit a blunt.

Antonio sat upright and turned to face him. "I think it's over for you."

Corey looked over to ask him what he was talking about and could only process the silencer pointing in his face as his joint dangled from his lips. Antonio didn't give him a moment to speak. They didn't have any more time to waste. He shot him once in the head and once in the chest. There was no way he was going to survive that. The joint fell into Corey's lap as his blood splattered the window and his body slumped over in death.

On cue, a car rolled up beside the old Mustang. Quickly, Antonio wiped the steering wheel, driver's seat, and the door down before getting out and hopping into the ride that awaited him. His breathing was heavy but not as weighed down as his heart. He'd been rocking with Corey for a minute, but he knew that the man was going to be his downfall with all the careless moves he was making.

Antonio had helped Tommy clean up the mess surrounding Montae's death. Everyone was gone. The niggas that retaliated and now the dude that had pulled the trigger and was going around acting on impulse. Antonio looked over at Knuckles wondering if he had confirmation on the last piece of the puzzle.

"Boss handled it himself," Knuckles said, noticing Antonio's pensive look. "Ain't nobody left to talk about nothing, and if Martinez wants to run up again, he better watch his back. But I have a feelin' he's got the message that Atlanta belongs to BDM."

Antonio nodded. Things were about to change. He was about to fill Corey's shoes and run the streets of the A as BDM took over. He didn't have a girlfriend getting in his business and clouding his judgment like Corey did. He knew that he was better suited for this life than Corey was. He wasn't flashy, and he was loyal to the game, no emotions involved whatsoever. Antonio felt bad that so many lives had been destroyed surrounding Corey's dealings, but so be it. What's done was done. Everyone's dirty little secrets had to catch up with them at some point. Now he needed to focus on making sure his never did.

Epilogue

The Girls

Jada sat on the front pew massaging her protruding belly and staring forward. It took everything in her to regulate her breathing and avoid having a panic attack right there in the small viewing room of the funeral home. She couldn't believe that they were doing it again; burying another friend.

"Here you go, girl," Alex said, handing her a small plastic cup of ice-cold water. "The director said they may have some crackers they can give you."

Jada took the water and shook her head. "I'm fine. Thank you." It was a lie. She was anything but fine. From the moment she'd read the letter sent to her from Miranda she hadn't been okay. Truth be told, since all the drama began to pop off over a year ago none of them were okay.

Alex took a seat next to her friend on the pew and looked up at the casket that held the lifeless body of their previously troubled homegirl. It was surreal. Alex reached over and grabbed Jada's hand. "You did good," she commented in regards to the outfit that Jada had chosen for Miranda's funeral.

Jada simply nodded. Miranda's parents had been shocked to learn about their daughter's original suicide attempt which had landed her in rehab to begin with. It appeared that they hadn't been in contact with her for quite some time and had no idea about the physical abuse the girl had suffered at the hands of her husband or the drug abuse she'd turned to as a defense mechanism. The fact that Miranda had been killed while presumably in a safe haven while trying to overcome

her issues was even more shocking. The center had contacted
Jada immediately with the news and promised the family that
a full investigation would take place. Jada had kept Miranda's
letter a secret from her parents. Knowing that their daughter
would have ended up dead anyway, only by her hand, would
have only made matters worse. To help the family, Jada had
chosen Miranda's pale pink casket, the black slacks, and
pretty pink blouse she was being buried in, and the flowers
that would cover her casket the next morning as they laid her
body to rest. Yes, Jada had done well. She always seemed to
be able to come through for everyone else, but how on earth
had she managed to find herself in an unhappy life situation
with no clear plan as to how to turn things around?

The duo heard the sound of footsteps behind them. Alex
turned to witness Candace approaching them. Jada didn't
budge. Candace wore dark shades and failed to remove them
as she took a seat on the pew directly behind her girls.

Alex let go of Jada's hand and shifted her body to address
Candace. "You know there's no sun in here, right?"

Candace sighed. "I can't deal with you today, Alex."

"I'm just saying."

Candace reached into her pocket and pulled out the letter
she'd received from Miranda. On the day she'd first read it,
she'd called the girls after getting herself together and learned
that they'd each received a copy of the exact same text. With
everything that was going on in Candace's life, she felt as if
the wind had been knocked out of her. She couldn't breathe
the majority of the time. Given the incident with Zoe and not
being completely over the loss of Stephanie, Candace just
couldn't cope with the death of yet another person close to
her.

"I keep going over and over this," Candace said, looking
down at the letter in her hand. The paper was crumpled
badly from the many times she'd read it and refolded it. "I
keep going over it and I just . . . I just don't get it. I don't
understand how she could just . . . how life could be that bad
that she'd just kill herself. Like, why not call us? Why not
come to us? Wasn't that the point of the whole group meeting
thing we had? And who would have any reason to sneak into

the center and just . . . just bore holes into her like some . . . target dummy?"

The others remained silent.

Candace reread the letter for what felt like the hundredth time and felt her eyes tear up. Sighing deeply, she refolded the paper and stuck it back into her pocket. "I don't get it."

"I get it," Jada whispered after taking a sip of water.

"Well, please clue me in."

"We keep parading around here like we're some solid sorority sisters or something, and that couldn't be any further from the truth."

"Jada," Alex said in an astonished tone.

Jada turned her head to the right to meet Alex's eyes. "You deny it? I mean, really . . . How much do we know about the other these days? Friends are honest with one another. Friends look out for one another. Friends notice when something's not right with the other. Hell, friends care enough to check in to see what's up with the other. Honestly, we haven't been that close-knit in a long while, especially since . . ." Her words trailed off, but the others knew where her thoughts were heading.

"Stephanie's death shook us up a little bit, but we're still here," Alex stated. "We're still friends."

"Are we?" Jada countered. "The relationships in your life are supposed to help build you up. It seems like our relationships only help to tear us down."

Candace felt as if the last statement was mostly targeted at her. "Why don't you just say what it is that's on your mind, Jada."

Jada looked at Miranda's casket and didn't bother to wipe away the tears that freely flowed down her cheeks. "We're horrible friends. We're not people that Miranda felt she could turn to. She was filled with so much turmoil and found absolutely no security in coming to any of us. What does that tell you? Some of the shit that's been done is deplorable. I can't breathe," she said, placing her right hand over her chest. "I can't breathe from being suffocated by all of the lies and secrets that linger between us all. Hell, even I don't feel comfortable coming to you guys about the things in my life . . . keeping it all bottled up.

From the panic disorder that none of you knew about until all the drama before Steph died, to the fact that my husband had been cheating on me and my marriage is practically a joke."

Alex gasped and reached over to grab her friend's hand. "Oh my God, Jada. I'm so sorry. I didn't—"

"You didn't realize," Jada interrupted and finished the girl's sentence. "Exactly."

Alex's bottom lip trembled. "I'm so sorry," she repeated. "If anyone deserves to be happy it's you. You two seemed so perfect together. I guess no relationship is perfect." She paused for a moment. "Not even mine. Clay left me. That's why he wasn't at Zoe's funeral," she said looking back at Candace. "He took a job in Cali and left me."

"I was helping Corey." The confession came out of nowhere. She hadn't planned to ever tell anyone the complete truth, but it was eating her alive. "He wanted to get back at the dudes that killed Stephanie and guilted me into helping him. Things got out of control at my place, and that's how Zoe got shot."

Alex stared at her in disbelief. "Are you crazy? What the hell would possess you to get involved in that? And with your kid around. Have you lost it?"

"Don't judge me." Candace's voice quivered as she used her index finger to push her shades up on the bridge of her nose. "Trust me, I constantly beat myself up about it so I don't need to hear it from anyone else."

"I can't understand how it is that you're always finding yourself in these damning situations where someone ends up dead. Damn!"

Candace finally removed her shades from her face to reveal her red, swollen eyes. "You think I'm happy about any of this? You think I *wanted* to help Corey? You think I *wanted* Steph to die? You think I *wanted* my child, my own flesh and blood, to be killed over some foolishness? You think I wanted *any* of this?" she asked, spreading her arms wide. "I'm dying on the inside." She looked over Jada's shoulder to gaze at Miranda's casket. "It should be me being buried tomorrow. I should be the one dead."

"So what?" Jada broke in. "You going to go home tonight and kill yourself now?" It was a crass response, but Jada didn't care. She was over the bullshit. "This is over."

"What are you talking about?" Alex asked, feeling a little nervous about what was to come.

"Tomorrow we're saying good-bye to Miranda. I'm done burying people, keeping secrets, being lied to, being hurt, and being caught in the middle of an emotional wreckage that just can't be fixed. This friendship, this whatever it is we're supposed to be to each other, can't be fixed. It's over." She rose from the pew and turned to walk away from the girls.

Candace quickly stood up and grabbed Jada's hand before she could bypass her. "Wait, wait! Don't do this, Jada. We need each other." Her eyes grew big and pleading as she spoke. "This isn't the time to turn our backs on one another."

"You really don't get it. We've already done that, Candace! Because of this friendship and the crap between us all, two of us have died. Enough is enough. I'm getting off of the roller-coaster ride. I have enough of my own issues to sort through. I can't carry the burden of all the extra drama any-more."

"But I need you. You can't walk away from me when I need you the most," Candace cried. "Please! Please don't do this."

Jada was unmoved. She was convinced in her belief that they all needed to go their separate ways and work on them-selves. How could they be good friends to one another when they had so much personal stuff of their own to deal with? It seemed that nothing but hurt and heartbreak surrounded their friendship, and Jada no longer felt it was a healthy situation.

Jada snatched her arm away from Candace who looked as if she was about to crumble to the floor at any moment. "Sometimes friendships end, Candace. Sometimes the end is merely the beginning." Without another word she walked away, failing to so much as throw them a final glance over her shoulder.

Candace fell to her knees and screamed. Her heart was broken into a million pieces. Everything she'd ever had was gone—love, friends, family. It was all destroyed. "Help me, Jehovah," she prayed aloud. "Help me. Please help me." Feeling completely lost, she turned to the only source she felt could give her an ounce of strength to carry on. Perhaps it was time for her to rekindle her relationship with her Savior.

Alex stared into space as Candace continued to cry and pray on the ground. The shift in her life had happened so quickly that she was unsure of what to do or say next. She could have gone after Jada and tried to smooth things over, but a part of her felt that Jada was right. Perhaps they'd all gone as far as they could in their relationships with one another. Just like her relationship with Clay, sometimes it just wasn't meant to last forever. Everything in life happened for a reason or a season. Maybe the season of their bond had expired, and it was time to move on. Together they'd learned a lot, lost a lot, and grown a lot. Alex wasn't sure what the future held, or if they would ever be able to repair their friendships later in life. But today, she was grateful for the time she'd had with the girls, and she knew that she'd never forget any of the lessons learned during their era.

THE END